NEVER LAY DOWN

By:

Eyone Williams

Fast Lane Entertainment
#245 4401-A Connecticut Ave NW
Washington, DC 20008
www.eyonewilliams.com

ISBN: 9780983627920
LCCN:

Chapter 1

    A light snow fell on the streets of Northwest Washington, D.C.—Uptown—on a cold October night in 1993. The streets were messy and wet; not a soul seemed to be outside. An old, black Nissan 280 ZX with dark tints flew through the back streets and alleys, taking a lone police car on a dangerous, high-speed chase. The driver, a young, nineteen-year-old, black male by the name of Redds looked into his rear view mirror as he flew through another dark alley. The blaring sirens and flashing lights weren't far behind. Redds was riding dirty. He had five bricks of powder cocaine and a 9mm Ruger in the car. There was no way he was going to get caught with any of the above.

    Skidding out of the alley, Redds almost lost control of the car. He did all in his power to avoid slamming into a light pole. As he straightened the car, he stomped the gas and rocketed down 9th Street, flying across Kennedy Street. Hitting another alley, fishtailing into the brick wall of an apartment building, Redds kept it moving as if his life depended on it. Right on his back, the police car fishtailed into the brick wall as well and continued the chase. Redds was already bending the corner at the end of the alley. Flying into another alley, Redds drove like a stunt car driver and made a quick right at the end of the alley. His heart was pounding as thoughts of fighting a federal case crossed his mind. His father always told him that whatever he did he should do all in his power never to get caught with a gun and drugs together.

    Coming back out onto 7th Street, Redds busted a left on Jefferson Street and flew toward 5th Street. He could only hear the sirens at this point. He'd lost the police for the time. Close call.

A short time later, inside his girlfriend's house on 2nd and Longfellow Street, Northwest, Redds lay on the bed in her bedroom. Thinking about the event that had taken place a little over an hour ago, Redds knew he'd come close to a federal case. The streets were mean and had no mercy at all. Nevertheless, he had to do what he had to do to get paid. Simple as that.

Necci, Redds' girl, walked into the bedroom wearing nothing but a black bra and panties. He looked at her sexy brown body and cracked a smile. She was phat to death by all means and put most females to shame without trying. Short, just over five feet five with a head full of individual plaits and an attitude to match that of a female pit bull, Necci was a bad bitch. She was from First and Kennedy Street and was proud of it. Street smart and rough around the edges, Necci didn't take no shit. Before Redds, she used niggaz like tampons, killers and cowards alike. Redds changed all of that. He was a different kind of nigga by all means. Necci always told him that he was one of a kind. He was from 5th and Kennedy Street, a few blocks from where she was from. Yet and still, he was cool with all the First Street niggaz; he'd gone to school and played sports with most of them. In fact, in the process of coming through First Street to holla at the twins—Kobi and Karim— Redds started digging Necci. She began digging him as well and the rest was history.

"Want some Chinese food, boo?" Necci asked as she sat on the bed with Redds. She was calling the carry out on the cordless phone.

"Yeah," Redds said, rubbing Necci's back, loving the feel of her smooth skin. Changing the subject, he said, "You got some more Backwoods in here?"

"Yeah, they in my coat pocket." Necci pointed at her huge, blue Eddie Bauer Bear that hung on the outside of her closet door.

Redds got up and got the pack of Backwoods from her coat to roll some weed. He and Necci sat on the bed talking and smoking tree as they waited for their carry out to be delivered. Redds' beeper went off, vibrating in the pocket of his Versace jeans. It was his man, Mike. Redds was supposed to serve Mike a half of brick, but hadn't been able to do it because of the police chase. Once he made it to Necci's house safely, he really didn't want to go back out again. Nevertheless, he called Mike.

"What's up, joe?" Mike answered. "Can I see you tonight?" He needed some work bad. The strip was pumpin', even as snow fell.

Redds thought about the money, but decided against going back out. "It don't look good on my end right now. I'm gon' have to see you in the mornin'."

"Damn, joe. For real?" Mike was missing all kinds of money due to the fact that he was out of coke.

"Yeah, shit hot right now. Them peoples got on my back a while ago. I ain't comin' back out tonight," Redds said.

"What's up wit' Dontae. He straight?" Mike asked.

Dontae was Redds' right hand man.

"I don't know what's up wit' young, beep 'em and see what he talkin' 'bout." Redds said.

"Okay, holla at me tomorrow."

"Got you." Redds hung up and turned his attention to his Necci, who was smiling at him. "What you smilin' at, boo?"

"I'm glad you ain't leave back out cause we woulda' been beefin' like shit," Necci said.

Redds laughed.

Days later, Redds jumped into his cocaine white Lexus coupe and took a trip down I-95 to Lorton, Virginia where his father, Amir, was doing time for murder. Even though Amir was serving hard time, he and his son were very close. Amir was behind The Wall—Maximum Security. The D.C. Department of Corrections considered him dangerous because of the influence he had in the prison system. He'd been locked up for ten years; three of those years had been spent behind The Wall.

Amir and Toya, Redds' mother, weren't together, but it wasn't always like that. When Amir first went to prison Toya was his ride or die chick, down for whatever. She made sure all of his business in the streets was taken care of. She was down Lorton every visiting day with Redds right beside her. From 1983 to 1988, Toya stood by her man, then crack hit the hood with the force of an F4 tornado.

Toya fell victim and began a battle with addiction. The relationship between Toya and Amir went to the dogs. Around the same time, Redds began running the streets, hustling, carrying guns, and catching cases. He was growing into a man without his father in a world where there was no love for the weak. With all of the above, Toya was always and forever Amir's first love and there was nothing he wouldn't do for her. At this point in time, Toya was back on track and clean. Drug use was the last thing on her mind. She ended up meeting a guy by the name of John in rehab and a new relationship began to bloom. Yet and still, Amir maintained a special place in Toya's heart.

Inside the 2-Block visiting trailer, Redds sat in the back waiting for his father to walk out. The visiting trailer was packed like a Baptist church on a Sunday morning. Redds looked around at the shackled convicts with their visitors and wondered if he would ever have to sit in a visiting hall somewhere. He knew it was all a part of the game when a nigga was deep in the streets.

Aside from the things he had done in the streets, Redds didn't look like the kind of dude that would be sitting in a prison cell. He was smart and smooth. Necci called him a pretty boy—he never liked that. He had light skin with a stocky frame like a running back. His boyish looks could make a person take him the wrong way, but they would soon learn that he was all business. Redds made it his business to always stand his ground as a man. One thing that was imbedded in his heart was the fact that a man should always stand on his feet and never live on his knees for any reason at all.

Amir stepped into the visiting trailer like a proud man, despite the fact that he was a convict. He was hand cuffed and shackled like the rest of the convicts. He stood at the front of the trailer and looked around for his son. Spotting Redds in the back of the trailer in a black leather Hugo Boss jacket, Amir began to make his way toward his one and only son. Redds reminded Amir so much of himself. So much so, that Amir feared what the future would hold for his son. Redds was nine-years-old when his father was sent to prison; at this point, he was a grown man, no matter what age he was.

At 38, Amir was a bigger, thicker version of Redds. Age and a thick beard were the only things that separated them from looking like twins. Amir often looked at old pictures of himself and was amazed at how much Redds looked just like him at different ages.

Redds stood up with a smile on his face as his father approached. "What's up, Pops?" He hugged his father firmly, paying no attention to the restraints. Visits with his father was a very important part of Redds' life, he made it his business to get down Lorton at least two or three times a month.

"Al-hamdu'lillah," Amir said in Arabic, giving all praise to Allah.

They sat down and began to kick it. As always, Amir spoke to Redds like a man and not like a child. His son had been taking care of himself for the longest, taking care of Toya as well. Amir desperately wanted his son to leave the streets alone. As far as he was concerned, the streets only led to one of two places, dead or in prison. It was a known fact that Redds had a few dollars put up. Being as though that was the case, Amir wanted Redds to start thinking about doing something legit with his paper like starting a business of some sort. He knew his son was smart enough to do something positive with his life. Redds took automotive repair classes three nights a week and was almost most done. Redds' man, Dickey, already had an auto repair shop. Once Redds was done with his classes he planned to open his own spot with the help of Dickey.

Amir looked Redds in the eyes and said, "You know how I feel about you playin' with them streets. You need to go ahead and put your plan into action as far as that auto shop. That's the move there. Messin' around in them streets is like being in a crap game, the longer you shoot the dice the higher your chances are to crap out. You already know that, Redds."

Redds nodded. "I'm hip." He knew his father spoke the truth. "I'm puttin' everything in motion. I just need a little bit of time."

Amir nodded. He didn't want to ride Redds too hard. He knew his son had a lot on his shoulders. "So, how's Necci doin'?"

"She's good."

Amir had taken a liking to Necci. Redds seemed to always have her with him. Aside from that, Amir had known of her since she was little girl being as though he used to do business with her uncles, Sam and John-John, who were known gangsters in the D.C. streets.

Amir said, "I'm surprised that girl hasn't slowed you down some. I know she loves you to death."

Redds laughed. "She stays on my back, trust and believe. That's my baby there. I don't think I ever loved a girl like I love her. She's one of a kind."

"I can't tell, I don't have no grandchildren yet," Amir joked.

"We gon' take care of that soon, don't worry yourself, Pops."

Redds and his father enjoyed the hour-long visit and before they knew it time was up. Father and son hugged and then went separate ways.

Uptown, the corner of 14th and Spring Road, Northwest, was jamming. Open-air drug market was the best way to describe the scenery. Young dudes in oversized Eddie Bauer coats, black skullcaps, and tan Timberland boots were posted up serving coke hand-to-hand like a scene out of New Jack City. Most people were avoiding the cold weather, but the young dudes were paper chasing, and the cold weather and snow did not deter them. Two young dudes broke away from the crowd when they saw the black 280 ZX bend the corner and pull over by the bus stop. Redds rolled down the window on the driver's side and Top and Lil' Man walked over to his car. "What's up wit' y'all niggaz?" Redds said as they approached the car.

Lil' Man said, "Ain't shit, young. Same ole' shit out here. Niggaz tryin' to get paid. We tryin' to come up." He then handed Redds a handful of cash with a rubber band around it.

"You know how we livin', Redds. Shit real out here," Top said.

"I see you niggaz on top of business. I hope y'all stack that paper and not blowin' it. Shit 'bout to get real good for me and when shit get good for me, it's gon' get good for you niggaz, too," Redds said as he pulled a brown paper bag from under his seat. He handed the paper bag to Lil' Man, who wasted no time stuffing it inside his coat.

Lil' Man was Necci's little brother, they looked just alike. They shared the same father, but different mothers. He was dark skinned and stood about six feet tall with a slim frame like his father. The young nigga was well before his time as far as his thinking and his outlook on life in the streets. He understood how things worked and played by the rules no matter what. The code of the streets had been instilled in him since birth. At sixteen-years-old, death before dishonor was a way of life for him.

Top was Lil' Man's right-hand man, they had been partners since they were old enough to walk. If you saw one you saw the other, and if you had beef with one you had beef with the other. It was understood that they did everything together. Even in the drug game, they put their money together to cop coke from Redds. Short and dark skinned as well, some people thought that Top and Lil' Man were real brothers. They were not to be played with. The two sixteen-year-olds were cold killers and there was no secret about it. Their names rang in the streets from Uptown to the south side. Young and old, niggaz knew without a doubt that if they had problems with Lil' Man and Top, that it there was going to be work call and guns would blaze.

However, Redds had no issues when it came to dealing with the two teenagers. They respected him and he respected them. Necci was the one that sparked the relationship between Redds and her brother. She begged Redds to put Lil' Man and Top on their feet in the coke game so they would stop robbing everything moving. At first Redds was skeptical about dealing with the young dudes because he knew what they were about, but after Necci pressed a little more he came around and gave them a chance. After a while, they were his "little men" and he had nothing but love for them. On the other hand, they had nothing but love for Redds and would do anything for him. No one could say anything bad about Redds as far as they were concerned. He was the big brother that neither of them had ever had and they loved him to death.

Redds said, "Ay, look, I'm dirty. I can't sit here too long. Y'all straight wit' what I just hit you wit', so handle your business and holla at me later. I might hit the mall. We can all go together. I know how y'all lil' niggaz love Tyson's. Let's go out there and grab some Hugo shit or something."

"I'm wit' it," Lil Man said.

"Me, too. Say no more," Top added.

"Cool." Redds pulled off and headed back up Kennedy Street.

A group of dudes stood around outside in the cold on Kennedy Street. The whole crew was in front of Redds' mother's apartment building, the first building from the alley. Redds, Dontae, Heavy, Mookie, Mike, and Dickey were the main dudes that controlled the block. Nothing went down without their hands in it. They were known as The Kennedy Street Crew. Smoking weed and talking shit, the six of them were involved in crap game where hundreds of dollars exchanged hands with every shake of the dice. A few younger dudes from 5th and Kennedy stood around watching the crap game, but knew they didn't have long enough money to fuck with the big boys. Other young dudes served pipeheads in the alley. It was just another day at the office on Kennedy Street.

Redds noticed a blue Ford Taurus wagon with tinted windows pull up. Everybody seemed to be on point, a few young dudes even pulled out their pistols.

"Redds!" a female voice called out as the driver's side window rolled down. Redds and his comrades took notice of the attractive female that was driving the car.

Dontae said, "Redds, Necci gon' kill your red ass if she find out you got broads comin' up here lookin' for you." The homies laughed, knowing Necci didn't play no games when it came to her man and other women.

Redds recognized the girl. "What's up, Tia?" He and Tia had gone to Roosevelt High School together. He walked over to the car and got inside to see what she wanted.

Once the crew saw that everything was cool they went back to what they were doing. After losing a few dollars, Dontae stepped off to get some more money out of his car. He stood a little over six feet tall and carried one hundred and sixty five pounds of muscle from his time spent in the boxing gym. He had light brown skin and curly hair that he wore in a temple taper. The ladies loved him. Out of the whole 5th and Kennedy crew, Dontae was known to be the most violent, by far. When Redds first moved Uptown from Southeast, D.C., Dontae was the first dude he met.

Dontae lived across the hall from Redds and his mother, and they used to spend hours in the alley behind their apartment building playing basketball. The two childhood buddies were both nine-years-old at the time. Dontae had Redds' number in basketball back then, he was taller and stronger, but in time Redds learned that his speed and jump shot were the tools needed to beat Dontae. Once Redds began to win their games of one on one, Dontae wanted fight. Redds and Dontae fought almost every day, so much so that Toya and Dontae's father would have to pull the boys apart. Nevertheless, love and respect grew between Redds and Dontae, and formed a bond that was like blood.

By 7th grade, Redds was selling coke. He started getting a little bit of money and needed a pistol, so he bought a little .32 automatic that Dontae always carried. Donate was the first to use the pistol as well. Redds was on his way home from school wearing a brand new velour Fila sweat suit when two older dudes tried to strong arm rob him. Redds wasn't going for it, he rumbled the two older dudes. However, he didn't stand a chance against his attackers. Out of nowhere, Dontae came flying down the street in a car he'd rented from a pipehead. He was strapped with the .32 automatic. When he saw Redds being attacked, Dontae jumped out and fired the pistol into the air. The two dudes that were jumping Redds backed off of him and look at Dontae with surprised looks on their faces. Once Redds was out of harm's way and Dontae had a good shot, Dontae began firing at the two older dudes.

Dontae hit both attackers, but didn't kill either of them. At a later time, Dontae and Redds found out the whereabouts of the two older dudes. Needless to say, the two dudes turned up dead. After that, it was all about gunplay for Dontae and Redds.

Coming back from his car with more money for the crap game, Dontae saw Redds getting out of Tia's car. Redds had a wild look on his face, like he'd been given some bad news. Dontae immediately became concerned.

"What's up, joe?" Dontae asked.

Redds shook his head in disbelief. "Let me holla at you real quick, Tae." Redds and Dontae walked back to Dontae's car.

"What's up, Redds?" Dontae asked, very concerned about what was on Redds' mind.

Redds got right to the point and explained to Dontae what was up. Tia was Lil' Sam's girl. He was a dude they were cool with from Morton Street. Lil' Sam was down Lorton doing thirty six-to-life on a murder beef for killing a dude in front of the Black Hole, a go-go spot on Georgia Avenue, Northwest. Mike from 5th and Kennedy saw the murder and later, after catching a gun case of his own, made a statement to police about it. The information

Mike gave police led to Lil' Sam's arrest and Mike later testified against him in trial. In an effort to appeal his case, Lil' Sam sent his girl up Kennedy Street to holla at Redds, and see if he could get Mike to recant his statement and help him get a new trial. Redds couldn't believe it at first. Mike was his man, they were homies and everybody around the way had love for Mike. Redds, Dontae, and Mike had put in work together and done all kinds of things. If he had testified against Lil' Sam he would surely testify against them if it came down to it. A rat had no loyalty to anyone except himself.

Dontae shook his head in disgust and looked over at the group of dudes that were shooting dice. Mike was the one shooting the dice at the time. "That nigga hot? For real? Get the fuck outta' here." Dontae was blown away. Mike and Dontae, on a number of occasions, discussed hot niggaz and how they should be dealt with. Death before dishonor was supposed to be the code for life.

Shaking his head, Redds said, "Yeah, shit look fucked up. Look at this shit here." He handed Dontae some paperwork that contained Mike's testimony from the witness stand.

Dontae read the paperwork on the spot and shook his head as he thought about Mike sitting on the witness stand going into detail about how Lil' Sam had smoked a nigga. "This nigga ain't right, Redds, he gots to go. He know too much shit about us and all that." In the back of his mind, Dontae was already plotting Mike's murder. The fact that they'd know each other all of their lives meant nothing to Dontae at this point. Once a nigga worked with the government, there was no more love for the nigga in Dontae's heart, even if the person was his own flesh and blood. That was how serious he was about the code.

"Lil' Sam want me get the nigga to take his statement back, so we can't just bring the nigga a move. Let me holla at him," Redds said.

"I feel you on all that, but I don't think he gon' help Lil' Sam get his case overturned. Once he find out that we know he done told, he gon' be on some other shit, believe that. We should trick that nigga to take a ride wit' us and leave his ass somewhere. I'm tellin' you some good shit. Don't forget how much shit he know about around here, Redds."

Redds thought about what Dontae said and understood where he was coming from, but something inside him told him that if he spoke to Mike and made him believe that no one knew about his cooperation with the government, then he just might do what was right and recant his testimony. Redds looked at Dontae, and said, "I gotta' try to holla at the nigga and make him feel like it's the right thing to do. I'm gon' act like I'm gon' keep the shit under my hat as long as he gets in touch with Lil' Sam's lawyer. After that, we can smoke the nigga."

Dontae took a second to think about what Redds had said. "Cool, I'm wit' it. Do it your way." He shook his head in disgust once again. He still couldn't believe Mike was a rat and had broken the code.

After Redds and Dontae finished talking, they walked back over to the crap game. Redds looked at Mike, and said, "Ay, Mike, let me holla at you." Redds spoke in such a calm tone that no one would have ever thought something was up, especially Mike.

"What's up, Redds?" Mike said.

"Let me put a bug in your ear about something real quick," Redds said as he put his arm around Mike's shoulder, and led him down the street so they could speak in private.

Once they were down the street, Mike said, "What's up, young?"

"Read this for me." Redds handed Mike the paperwork and paid close attention to his reaction. Inside, Redds still couldn't believe that Mike had gotten on the witness stand. Never in his wildest dreams could he envision Mike working with the prosecution.

Mike frowned. "What the fuck is this, joe?"

"Just read it, young." Redds folded his arms as he glanced back up the street. Dontae watched the whole situation very carefully.

Mike's whole facial expression changed in seconds. He looked like he was about to shit on himself. Despite the cold weather, he began to sweat instantly. Redds noticed everything and his stomach began to turn. He couldn't stand a rat. However, he covered his emotions with a blank facial expression. Mike broke the awkward silence with a sigh, and said, "Who else know about this?" Mike folded the paperwork with an ashamed look on his face. It was killing him to know that Redds knew what he'd done.

Redds looked Mike in the eyes for a second. His feelings were a mixture of anger and pain. He really had love for Mike and hated the fact that his homie had done some slimy, rat shit. With a slow and measured tone, Redds said, "It don't even matter who knows for real, but to answer your question, I'm the only one around here that knows about this situation." In the pocket of his coat, Redds had his finger on the trigger of his pistol.

Mike had a strong feeling that Redds was lying. Nevertheless, he rolled with the punches. "So, what's up? What you got to do wit' this shit here?"

Redds slightly shook his head. "It's like this, Mike, you know how this shit go out here in the streets. You know what you did was some hot-ass shit. You need to do whatever you can to fix this shit. Lil' Sam ain't never done nothing to you. He tryin' to get back in court, and all he need for you to do is contact his lawyer and take back your statement. Simple as that. That's the right thing to do. You know that, joe."

Mike nodded in shame. "You right, I'm gon' get in touch wit' his lawyer."

"Don't just tell me anything, this is some important shit, homes."

"I got it. I'ma get on top of it," Mike said as he tried to hand Redds the paperwork back.

"Keep that, it's yours."

Chapter 2

Scarface's Money and the Power was thumping inside the Lexus coupe as Redds pulled up in front of Mike's grandmother's house. Jumping out into the cold morning air, Redds jogged up to the door and rang the bell. He had beeped Mike first thing in the morning but Mike didn't hit back so Redds decided to go to his house and take him downtown to holla at Lil' Sam's lawyer himself. He didn't want to hear any excuses.

Mike's grandmother answered the door. She'd known Redds since he was a little boy. Back in the day, he used to spend the night over her house playing Nintendo all night with Mike. She always thought Redds was such a nice kid. "Little Reggie, how are you doing, baby?" the sweet old lady said.

"I'm okay, going to school and staying out of trouble. That's all," Redds said with a smile.

"That's all you can do, sweetheart. Stay out of those white folks way. They don't want to do nothing but all of our children in those prison they building everywhere. It's all a plan to erase the youth. Don't you forget that."

"I know that's right," Redds said. "Is Mike home?"

The sweet old lady rolled her eyes. "I don't know where that boy is, I ain't seen him in two days."

"Okay. Tell him I came by when you do see him."

"I'll tell him, baby."

"Thank you. See you later."

"Okay, you take care of yourself out here," she said as she shut the door.

Redds jumped back in his car and pulled off. He made his way up Georgia Avenue and grabbed something to eat. The situation with Mike was all he could think about. In his heart, he felt terrible after talking to Mike's grandmother when he knew what kind of plans he and Dontae had for Mike. However, there were rules to the game and everyone knew them. If they broke the rules, there had to be consequences. After grabbing something to eat, Redds rode through the hood looking for Mike. He hit a few of Mike's hangouts. He floated through First and Kennedy, 7th and Kennedy, and then headed downtown and slid through 7th and O. Mike was nowhere to be found. Redds tried one last spot and check Mike's girl's house. He wasn't there. After spending his whole morning looking for Mike, Redds decided to give it a break for the meantime. He had other things to do. Mike would pop up in due time.

Redds headed back up Georgia Avenue and made his way to Chevy Chase, MD, to find his mother something for her birthday. He hit Miller's Furs on Wisconsin Avenue. A top-notch fur coat would surely put a smile on her face. Inside the store, Redds spotted a pretty white mink and knew his mother would love it. He had it gift wrapped and paid with cash. With that done, he headed back home.

Toya decided to take the day off from work for her birthday. She needed some down time, anyway, as far as she was concerned. She and John had plans to go down Georgetown to get her something for her birthday and then go out to eat at Ruth's Chris Steak House. She looked forward to every minute of it.

Sitting on the sofa in her living room watching the news with John, Toya was waited for Necci to come over and do her hair. At 36, Toya looked good for her age, despite all that she'd been through with drug addiction. She had light skin with short, silky hair. Her slim frame had a few curves here and there.

Redds walked into the apartment carrying a white box with a red ribbon on it. Necci was right behind him.

Redds and Necci gave Toya a hug, and wished her a happy birthday. Toya's eyes lit up when she saw the box Redds was carrying. She was dying to find out what was inside.

"What's in the box?" she asked with a smile on her face.

"None of your business," Redds joked.

Toya laughed and tried to snatch the box out of Redds' hands. He faked like he wasn't trying to let it go.

"Reggie, you betta' stop playin' with me," Toya said as she yanked the box away from him and opened it. "Oh my God!" She covered her mouth in surprise and excitement. "How much did you pay for this, boy?"

"Something small, don't even worry about it. You deserve it, Ma." Redds walked over to the living room window and looked out onto Kennedy Street. He saw Dontae and a few other homies were leaning against the fence in front of the apartment building. Redds turned around and gave his mother a kiss. "I'll be right back. I need to talk to Dontae real quick." He walked out the door.

Pulling his skullcap down over his ears as he stepped out into the cold, Redds looked up and down the street. He walked over to his homies and spoke. They all showed love back. Dontae walked over to a red '92 Nissan 300 ZX and leaned in the passenger window to talk to a bad ass broad. While Dontae got his rap on, Redds asked a few of the other homies if they'd seen Mike. None of them had seen the hot nigga all day. Redds began to wonder if Mike had left town or something.

"What's up, joe?" Dontae said as he walked over to Redds, and gave him some dap.

"I'm good. Same ole shit. You seen Mike?" Redds asked as he watched traffic fly up and down Kennedy Street.

Dontae frowned. "I ain't seen that nigga."

"I been looking for that nigga all morning. I don't know if he done skipped town or what, but he ain't nowhere to be found. His grandmother said she ain't seen him in like two days."

Dontae shook his head and sighed. "I told you we should'a just smoked that nigga. For all we know, he could be workin' wit' the feds against us right now. That nigga might be wearin' a wire when he around us and all kinds of shit. You know how them peoples play, joe. We need to find that nigga and put him in the dirt."

"I feel the same way. We need to find out where he at and just lay on his ass so don't nobody know we hit him."

"You know he always be over that bitch LaShell house. Did you check that joint?"

Redds rubbed his chin. He'd forgot that Mike was fucking LaShell. "We can lay on that joint tonight and see if he come through there."

"Say no more. I'm down for it," Dontae said.

Days later, no one had seen Mike. It was like he'd fallen off the face of the earth. Word had gotten out that he was hot and that he'd told on Lil' Sam. Redds really didn't want everybody talking about the fact that Mike was a government witness. He felt like that would make things hotter once he and Dontae caught up with him. However things went down, nothing was going to change the plans that they had for Mike.

Sitting in the back seat of Lil' Man's metallic blue 1988 Toyota 4Runner, Redds blew weed smoke into the air as Lil' Man told him how some niggaz had come through 14th and Spring Road firing assault rifles from an old Park Avenue. When the shooting began, Top, Lil' Man, and their comrades fired back, leaving countless shells all over the place. While in the shoot out, Top's Tec-9 jammed. He wasn't feeling that. He needed something more reliable as soon as possible and he hoped that Redds could help him and Lil' Man out with some new heat.

"I got a man wit' some fresh shit still in the box. Whatever you want." Redds passed Top the burning Backwood. "In the meantime, take me up my apartment. I got something for you." Lil' Man started the truck and pulled off.

Inside Redds' apartment, Lil' Man and Top sat on the black leather sofa in the living room. They loved the fact that Redds always looked out for them. He walked out of the bedroom with a black AR-15 assault rifle in one hand and a Colt .45 with an extended clip in the other. Top and Lil' Man looked like kids at Christmas.

"Damn, joe." Top jumped to his feet and grabbed the assault rifle from Redds' hand. He aimed it at the wall like he was at a gun range. "This what the fuck I'm talkin' 'bout. I'ma tear some shit up wit' this muthafucka."

Redds smiled and shook his head. "Don't do no dumb shit, lil' homie." He then handed the Colt to Lil' Man.

Still sitting on the sofa, Lil' Man examined the pistol. It felt heavy and powerful, it was just right to down any nigga that dared get in his way. "This joint here ain't nothin' to be played wit'."

Redds' beeper vibrated. He pulled it out and checked the number. "Let me make a call real quick." He stepped off. Walking back into the living room with a Nike box, Redds opened it and showed the two younger dudes boxes of bullets. "This will hold you down."

Top gave Redds five. "Thanks, my nigga. You make sure we always straight and I respect that about you."

"Same here," Lil' Man said, giving Redds five.

"It ain't nothing. I fucks wit' you lil' niggaz. I got you."

Behind the Wall, 2-Block was live. The 24-cell tiers housed convicts of all walks of life, most of which were convicted of violent crimes. 2-Block was a block where only the strong survived. Weak dudes didn't stand a chance. Amir had no problems in 2-Block or any other block, for that matter. On this day he and a comrade of his by the name of Gator were standing on the long, narrow tier kicking it for a moment. They were talking about Amir's co-defendant, Croc. Amir had just received a letter from Croc stating that he was in the hole over Occoquan, a high-medium security facility that was a part of the Lorton complex. Croc was a gangster through and through. Where Amir was now laid back and deep into his religion, his co-defendant was the exact opposite. Croc was into everything, and had racked up several stabbings and other charges while in prison.

"What Croc locked down for now?" Gator asked, smoking a Newport.

"You know how slim go. He done hit a nigga. Burned 'em, too."

"Who was the nigga?"

"Some dude that just came back from the feds, I really ain't hip to the joker," Amir said.

Amir and Gator spoke for a little while longer, and then parted ways. Gator went down the tier to holla at his man Chico, who was locked in his cell working out. Amir went down on the bottom tier and got on the phone, stopping at a few cells along the way. He called Redds to see what was up with his son.

"Hello," Redds answered with N.W.A's Real Niggaz Don't Die playing in the background. Seconds later, he accepted the collect call from his father. "What's up, Pops?"

"I'm holdin' on. You know what's up with me," Amir said. The noise of prison filled the background. "How are you?"

"Just came in the house from class. I'm tryin' to go over these lessons real quick before I go pick Necci up."

Amir laughed. "How can you study with all that kill-a-nigga music blastin' like that?"

Redds laughed as he turned the music down. "It stimulates my mind," he joked.

Amir got a good laugh off of that one. "You trippin', but I feel you, youngster."

"Ay, on another tip, Croc's girl called me. She said he need some money. What's up with that?"

"Croc done got caught up. He on his way back here wit' me. I think he like it behind the Wall or something. They might take him to court for this one here, you know how them peoples play, they be wanting to prosecute a brother for any little thing."

"I feel you," Redds said, looking down at his vibrating beeper. It was a weight sell for some hard white. "I'ma send him some money in the morning."

"That's big. You got a good heart, just like me. That's gon' take you places in life, Redds, it ain't a petty bone in your body."

"Thanks, you taught me well. It's in my blood, Pops."

Amir smiled. "For sure. Oh yeah, Whitey sends his love, him, Garnett, and Black Face still working on their case."

"Tell them I send my love. I just got at them last week, so they should be straight for a second."

"Okay, I got that for you. Other than that, just stay focused out there. Don't let them streets trick you, Redds. Use your mind, it's chess, not checkers. Always remember that," Amir said as he watched a C.O. enter the tier.

"I'm focused, Pops. Trust that."

"Okay. Well ... I'm 'bout to get off this phone. Talk to you later, insha Allah."

"Bet," Redds said as the call came to an end.

Inside Necci's house, her mother was fussing about her daughter messing with Redds. Necci wasn't trying to hear the shit. She grabbed her coat and rushed outside when she heard the car horn. Necci's mother couldn't stand Redds and wanted her daughter to have nothing to do with the young thug, as she called him. In a way, her feelings weren't wrong. Redds' name had been in The Washington Post once for his alleged involvement in a murder. Necci's mother felt that her daughter could find a better young man to fall in love with.

With her mother still fussing, Necci slam the front door behind her as she stepped outside. She jumped in the car with an attitude and slammed the car door.

"Damn, baby, what's wrong?" Redds asked.

"That bitch be gettin' on my fuckin' nerves some-times." She frowned and shook her head. "I swear to God, I'm movin' out."

"What I tell you about that shit?" Redds checked her about calling her mother a bitch. "That's your mother, no matter what y'all go through. Don't forget that. You only get one mother."

Necci sighed. "I know, I know ... I'm just sayin', she be getting' on my damn nerves sometimes. She always got some shit to say about me and you fuckin' wit' each other. That shit be blowin' me. I'm sick of that shit!" Her frustration was off the charts.

Redds thought about the situation. He understood where Necci's mother was coming from and he respected it. At the same time, he loved Necci and would do anything for her. The only move to make was to get Necci to move in with him. It would be the perfect resolution to the problem. "Pack your shit, Necci. You movin' in wit' me, that's how we'll deal wit' that."

Necci looked at Redds and smiled. "I love you, nig-ga!"

With that out of the way, Redds took Necci to the Cheesecake Factory in White Flint Mall. That made her day, she loved the Cheesecake Factory. After they ate, they did a little shopping and then headed back to Redds' apartment on 16th and Rittenhouse Street, Northwest. While Redds took care of some business, Necci took a quick shower. Redds had to weigh out a few packages that he had sells for, so he hit the kitchen and knocked that out. When he was done, he beeped his man Heavy and left a code on his beeper letting him know that the work that he needed was ready. Redds then went into his bedroom and began counting money that he'd made the night before. Wrapping a thick brown rubber band around a stack of money, Redds threw it into his safe. Going through the same motion a few more times, he was at the $10,000 mark just like that.

Necci walked out of the bathroom wrapped in a towel, looking sexy as shit. She glanced at Redds, and said, "Damn, boy, you such an Uptown nigga." She laughed.

Redds smiled. "What's that supposed to mean, baby?"

"It means that you always about your money."

"For sure." Redds nodded.

Necci sat on the bed and grabbed the remote. She turned the TV to HBO. Amityville Horror was on.

"What's up wit' you and all these horror movies?" Redds said as he untied his shoes.

Necci took her towel off and rubbed her hair with it. "I just like these joints, I don't know what it is about them. Lil' Man used to beg me to take him to see these joints when he was little, fuckin' wit' shorty I started feelin' these joints. I been in love wit' horror flicks since I was a little girl."

Redds shook his head with a smile on his face. "You ain't right, something wrong wit' you," he joked.

Necci playfully punched him. "Shut up, nigga!"

Redds laughed as he rolled a Backwood. "You tryin'
to smoke?"

"Yeah, go 'head and put that in the air," Necci said.

Redds finished rolling the Backwood, took a few
hits, and then passed it to Necci. She hit it a few times and
let the weed smoke set in. Feeling the effects, Necci put
the Backwood in the ashtray and wrapped her arms around
Redds. She rubbed him, kissed him, and loved being close
to him. Turned on, Redds stopped her for a moment so he
could undress. After taking off his clothes, he took her in
his arms and kissed her deeply, as if it was a last kiss. He
laid her on her back and planted kisses from her lips to her
neck, from nipple to nipple, all over her flat stomach. He
took pride in making love to her. Moving back up, Redds
licked her nipples as he grew between the legs. With her
eyes closed, Necci rubbed his wide back as she moaned
softly. Enjoying the satisfying feeling of Redds sliding inside
of her, Necci whispered, "I love you so much, baby. Fuck
me ..." Desire to feel Redds inside of her continued to
grow.

Redds knew what time it was. He went back down
south and used his tongue to drive Necci crazy. "Ssssssssss-
shit ..." she moaned, inching away from him, but there was
nowhere to go. With her legs wide open, Redds continued
to please. By the sounds she made, he knew she loved every minute of it. Licking around her clit slowly and softly,
Redds took pleasure in what he did. Biting on her clit softly,
she tried to move away but he held her in place. He then
slid a finger inside of her and made her cum in seconds.
Rubbing the top of his head, Necci said, "Come on, baby ...
fuck this pussy ... fuck this pussy for me." She shook as she
came. Finally, with cream all over his face, Redds came up
for air and slid inside her with one deep stroke that made
her gasp for air. "Oh shit ... sssssssss ... yeah, just like that,

baby. Fuck me harder ... uhhh ... uhhhh ... uhhh. Yeah, damn ... ooooooooo ... shit! Fuck me! Fuck me! Fuck me!" Necci wrapped her legs around Redds and clawed at his back while he stroked her into a state of bliss. In and out of her he stroked slow, then hard, then side-to-side, then slow, then hard again. It drove her crazy. "Oh, my God, I'm 'bout to cum again ... ahhhhhhh ... shit!" With an explosion of deep pleasure, Necci came again. She held Redds as tight as she could and enjoyed the intoxicating feeling. Squeezing him tight while holding him inside of her was exactly where she wanted to be. If it were up to her, she would never let him go, ever. He was her everything.

Pulling up in a dark alley behind Toya's building, Redds slid his 9mm inside his coat pocket and hopped out of his car into the cold air of nightfall. Looking around carefully, he paid close attention to his surroundings. Everything was the same. Niggaz served pipeheads in the alley alongside the building. A few niggaz were stood on the sidewalk smoking weed and watching out for the police or the stick boys. It was business as usual on the strip. Stepping out of the alley onto Kennedy Street, Redds saw Dontae's white BMW. Crossing the street, he spoke to a few of his homies along the way. Dontae stood on the other side of his car talking to their homie, Dickey.

Dontae was talking about Redds when he popped up. He gave Redds some dap, and said, "You seen that nigga Mike yet?"

Redds shook his head as he gave Dickey some dap, and said, "I don't know what's up wit' that nigga, joe. I can't find his ass nowhere. He might've left town."

Dickey shook his head. "That nigga hot for real, huh, man?" He couldn't believe what he'd heard about Mike. He'd known the nigga for years and had done all kinds of dirt with him as well.

Dontae stamped it. "I read the paper work myself, joe. The nigga fucked up, for real for real."

Everybody in their circle was now aware of what Mike had done. For years, they all had love for him. That all went out the window when word of his action hit the streets.

On the other side of the street, Toya opened the front door to her building and yelled across the street for Redds to get her some chicken wings from the carry out. Redds laughed, and yelled, "I got you." He then stepped off and headed to the carry out.

Dontae and Dickey continued talking and ended up lighting a blunt. As they smoked, a stranger in a Redskins jacket walked up and asked if either of them knew where he could buy some coke. Dontae and Dickey looked at each with confused looks on their faces and then looked back at the stranger like he was crazy. There was no way in the world they were going to serve a stranger some coke. Dontae shouted, "Get the fuck outta' here, ain't nobody sellin' no drugs out here! I should smack the shit out your dumb ass!" The stranger made his way across the street and into the dark alley. Looking back at Dickey, Dontae said, "They got undercovers out on late night tryin' to box a nigga up."

"It's not a game, joe. Believe that," Dickey said, looking around for any sign of the police. He felt like it was time to go.

Moments later, Redds stepped out of the carry out with his mother's food in a brown paper bag. Just as he was about to cross the street gunshots rang out. Boom! Boom! Boom! It sounded like a cannon was going off, and it kept going off. Redds took a knee with the quickness and tried to see where the gunshots were coming from. They sounded close. Dontae and Dickey ducked behind Dontae's car and pulled out pistols. Gunshots continued to go off.

Dontae and Dickey didn't know where the shots were coming from, but they still aimed their pistols over the car and fired in the direction of the sound. It seemed like the shots were coming from the alley. Redds saw Dontae and Dickey firing toward the alley and figured that whoever was shooting was shooting at them from that direction. Redds dropped the food he was carrying and whipped out his pistol. Wasting no time he bagan firing. With every pop of his pistol, shells flew in the air as fire spit from the barrel. Police sirens hit the air almost instantly, with cars coming from all directions. Dontae and Dickey took off running. Redds wasted no time doing the same, except he ran in the opposite direction. Gunshots continued to crackle through the air.

Chapter 3

Forty minutes after the shooting, Redds walked into his apartment out of breath. He was in great shape, but the run from 5th and Kennedy Street to 16th and Rittenhouse Street was a vicious feat for even the best athlete. Wiping sweat from his forehead, Redds flopped down on the sofa with his mind racing as he tried to catch his breath. His beeper was going crazy in his pocket. It was his mother blowing up his beeper. After taking a few minutes to get himself together, Redds got on the phone and called his mother back. He knew she was worried to death about him.

"Hello!" Toya answered the phone loud and excited. At the same time, she was very relieved to hear her son's voice.

"Ma, what's up?" Redds asked, still out of breath.

"Are you okay, boy? I was worried to death about you."

"Ma, I'm good. I'm okay. I'm in the house right now."

"Boy, the police are all over the place, like the fuckin' president got shot or something."

Redds knew it was going to be hot as shit around the way now that there had been another big shooting. It had been two other shootings the week before when the younger dudes got into a beef with some other young dudes from Taylor Street.

"Baby, whatever you do, just stay in the house. I don't want you out in the streets while this stuff is goin' on, okay?"

"Ma, I feel you. I ain't goin' nowhere. Let me get myself together and take a shower real quick. I love you.

I'm fine. I'll call you back in a little while." Redds hung up and then took off his wet and muddy clothes. After that, he jumped in the shower and let the hot water soothe him for a second. The street life was stressing him out.

Necci was in the bedroom sleep when Redds walked in the house. She was sleeping so good that the sound of him moving around the apartment didn't wake her. However, the sound of the telephone in the bedroom did. Whoever it was called back to back as if it was very important. Slowly, Necci woke and answered the phone. It was Toya, she needed to speak to Redds immediately. Necci went in the bathroom and called Redds' name.

"What's up, baby?" he asked, peeping from behind the shower certain.

"Toya on the phone. She said you need to cut the TV on right now," Necci said.

Redds got a terrible feeling in his gut. He knew that wasn't good news. It could never be good news in the hood when someone told him to turn on the news after a neighborhood shooting. Dripping wet, Redds jumped out of the shower and wrapped a towel around his waist. He walked into the bedroom and locked eyes on the TV once Necci turned it on.

"... there has been a deadly gunfight in Northwest, Washington about an hour ago, according to D.C. police. Police officers from the Fourth District Police Department allegedly engaged in a deadly gunfight with members of the notorious Kennedy Street Crew—a drug gang that D.C. police say controls the 400 block of Kennedy Street, Northwest. We now take you to the scene." The anchorwoman's reporting of the events had Redds' heart pounding overtime.

Redds sat on the foot of the bed with Necci, who passed him the phone as they both watched the breaking news in shock. Redds put the phone to his ear and heard

Toya's voice. She asked a thousand questions. Redds gave her very short answers as he paid close attention to the TV.

"... I'm here on Kennedy Street, Northwest, as you can see, the scene is quite chaotic. Law enforcement is calling this the act of senseless murder where one of their own has been killed in the line of duty ..."

Redds swallowed hard when he heard that a police officer had been murdered. He knew that was going to take things to another level. It was never good when a cop got killed on the block.

"... about an hour or so ago, police were performing a drug sting undercover, when something went very wrong and members of the Kennedy Street Crew opened fire on undercover officers, killing one. One of the suspected shooters has been taken to the hospital where he is in critical condition and under heavy police guard. Another suspected shooter was fatally wounded in the gun battle, a police spokesman said."

The next day, Amir was in a state of panic internally. The news of what happened around Kennedy Street had him feeling sick inside as he worried about his son. Trying to get Redds on the phone was an impossible mission. That only added to his stress. The news was all over the TV, on every channel. Niggaz down Lorton were talking about it in every direction that he turned. Every newspaper in the area had the shooting on the front page. The front page of The Washington Post had a story with pictures to go along with it. What Amir read in the paper kept flashing through his mind. ... Mr. Dickerson, A.K.A Dickey, was shot and killed by police. Three other members of the crew—Dontae Davis, Henry Jones, A.K.A Heavy, and Mike Barns—were arrested a short time after the shoot out ... Two other members of the crew are still at large, their names are James Green, A.K.A. Mookie, and Reggie Williams Jr., A.K.A. Redds ...

After getting no answer on every number he called for Redds, Amir called Toya.

"Hello!" she answered the phone and accepted the call. "Reggie!" she shouted, calling Amir by his government name. "Oh, my God! I know you have seen the news! I don't know what to do!" She was hysterical, talking a hundred miles per hour.

"Hold on, hold on, calm down. I can't hear you," Amir said.

"They got Reggie's face all over the news."

"Do you know where he is?"

"He called me earlier saying that he had to lay low. He didn't know what he was going to do. He said he would get in touch with me later." Toya took a deep breath. "I don't know what to do. I don't want them to kill my baby."

"Listen," Amir said. "Reggie knows how to take care of himself, he's grown. Let him think everything over. He will make the best move, I trust that. He can think very well. Once he thinks everything over, he will figure things out. In the meantime, he is going to need a lawyer. A real good lawyer. I want you to contact the dude Smith that I used to deal with. He will know exactly what to do to begin putting a defense together."

"Okay," Toya said.

Redds was on the run and that changed everything for him. Life as he knew it changed overnight. Once he saw the news, he wasted no time leaving his apartment and checking into a hotel under a fake name with Necci in Gaithersburg, MD. The next morning, he turned the news on and saw the chief of police on TV vowing to bring the Kennedy Street Crew to justice. The walls were closing in on Redds. The stakes had never been so high for him. He thought about it so much that he gave himself headaches. One thing that he knew for sure was that he was going to need all of his money out of the streets that dudes owed him to stay run and to pay for a lawyer at the same time.

Not being able to collect it himself, he called on Lil' Man and Top to put them on a mission. He was still mapping out what he wanted to do, but he was sure that he had to get far away from D.C. At the same time, he knew he had to start thinking about fighting the charges against him if he was ever going to clear his name. He had no idea there were police on the scene when he participated in the shooting. He thought some niggaz were shooting at his homies and he fired back. The last thing he intended to participate in was killing a police officer.

Looking out the hotel window like Malcolm X, Redds wondered what the fuck had really gone wrong when the shooting kicked off. He was there. He knew for a fact that Dontae and the others didn't shoot first. He shook his head in frustration. A sick feeling in his gut wouldn't let him rest. Thoughts of his man Dickey saddened him. They had been friends for as long as he could remember, and now his man was dead and gone in the blink of an eye. There one minute and gone the next. Dontae and Heavy were locked up, facing murder charges. Mookie was on the run. Shit was out of control. Mike was locked up, too. Redds didn't understand that part. Nobody had seen the nigga in a while. How and why was he locked up with everyone else? It weighed heavy on his mind.

"Baby, try to get some rest," Necci said as she walked up behind Redds and rubbed his back. She was worried about the situation, but she was riding with her man no matter what. "You not gon' be able to think straight unless you get some rest. I will stay up and make sure nothing looks out of place. Please, baby, just try to get some rest."

"I can't. I got too much on my mind. I gotta' try to think this shit out."

"Okay." Necci nodded. "Well, whatever you do, I got your back."

Redds looked Necci in the eyes and kissed her lips. "I love you, girl. You are one of a kind."

"You, too."

"I don't want you caught up in this shit here. You can't go wit' me. I gotta' run as long as I can in order to give myself a fighting chance."

"Fuck all that shit." Necci frowned. "I'm riding it out wit' you. I ain't tryin' to hear nothin' else. You can cancel that shit there. It's me and you, nigga."

Redds gave her a long, firm look in the eyes. He could tell that she meant every word. "Okay, I won't fight you on that, baby."

On the third floor of the Washington Hospital Center, Mike laid in an elevated bed in a white gown with IVs coming out of his arms. He was handcuffed to the bed, being as though he was under arrest. The morning news was on the TV that hung from the wall. He knew he was fucked. His name was nothing in the streets anymore. He was now charged with killing a police officer, which meant that he was on his way to prison for sure. Life in prison would be hell on wheels once word got out that he was a rat that had testified on a good man. Options were few in his world. As he tried to weigh them, he thought about the events from previous night. Out of everyone that was involved in the shootout, Mike was the only one with all of the answers and could fill in all the blanks.

Being known as a rat was killing Mike inside. He couldn't show his face in the hood. Everybody he went around wanted nothing to do with him. With everyday that passed, more people learned of what he'd done. He blamed Redds and Dontae for putting the word out about him, and the hot shit he'd done. As he thought about them, he thought about murdering them. If he could get away with it, he thought then maybe he could put an end to what people heard about him. With his mind made up, Mike loaded up his AK-47 and went around the way to kill anyone that knew his secret. As he crept up the alley, Mike encountered the undercover officer in the Redskins jacket.

The undercover spotted the AK-47 in Mike's hand, identified himself as a police officer, and pulled his Glock. Mike had the ups and wasted no time opening fire with the assault rifle. In seconds, the officer was cut down in a quick burst of gunfire. The officer never got a shot off. After killing the undercover, Mike ran toward the mouth of the alley, and sprayed across the street at Dontae and Dickey. Shots were returned and the gunfight heated up. In seconds, police came from everywhere. Mike was eventually shot seven times as he tried to flee the scene.

Mike was snapped out of his thoughts when two FBI agents entered his hospital room. The two white men were a part of the Violent Gang Task Force; they were also the agents that were behind a secret 18-month investigation into the drug activities and murders connected to the 5th and Kennedy Street Crew. Agent Bulger, a tall, slightly overweight agent with blond hair and blue eyes, stood over Mike with a brown folder in his hand. The look on his face was a smug look that said, We got your bad ass, nigger!

Agent Schoenberg, an ex-marine, was short with the looks of a young boxer. He was no nonsense all the way around the board. His mindset was to do whatever he had to do to make the case against the Kennedy Street Crew. Schoenberg folded his arms and stood on the other side of the bed as Bulger questioned Mike.

"Mr. Barns, I understand you have —" Bulger began.

"Look here, I ain't got shit to say to you muthafuckas," Mike snapped.

Schoenberg let out a little laugh and leaned over to look Mike in the eyes. The smell of cigarettes was all over his breath as he said, "You look here, tough ass. You don't have a leg to stand on here. You are fucked. Your life is over. You need us in a big way. We know you have already testified for the government before, so you can cut the tough guy act. That's not you. We got the AK with your fingerprints all over it. That's the same weapon the under-cover was killed with, so you better start talking or your black ass is going to fry for this one."

Bulger cut in. "Mr. Barnes, we got you and your homeboys by the balls here. As we speak, the FBI and D.C. police are kicking in doors. Your whole crew will be in jail shortly."

Mookie's grandmother's house was one of the houses that had been raided. His 59-year-old grandmother was arrested for 150 grams of coke that was found in the basement of the home where Mookie slept. The cold-hearted agents that found the coke in the basement knew it belonged to Mookie and still arrested the old lady. Don-tae's father's apartment was raided, and he was arrested for a MAC-11, an AR-15, a .45 automatic, and two bullet-proof vests, all belonging to Dontae. Toya's apartment was raided and a Glock .40 and $13,000 that Redds reluctantly left in the apartment was found. She was arrested. Redds' apartment was raided, but nothing was found and his Lexus was confiscated. All together, twenty people were arrested and jailed in connection with the case.

Mike looked up at Bulger, and said, "What do you want to know?"

"Everything, and you need to start talking fast cause my time is limited." Bulger took out his pen and pad.

Schoenberg smiled. "You're making the right move."

Mike began talking and when he started, he didn't stop for hours. He gave up so much information that the agents knew they had to give him a sweet deal. They were sure they could secure life sentence for the other defendants and the D.A. would be very pleased.

Just after 7 p.m., Dontae and Heavy sat side by side on the crowded court bus heading to D.C. Jail. They were blown away by what had gone down. It all happened so fast. After appearing in court and talking to their court appointed lawyers, they had figured out that Mike had to be the person who started the shooting. The charges of murder were the least of their worries. They knew that conspiracy charges were to follow and that would mean the federal government would step in. The matter they were dealing with was nothing little. Their lives were on the line.

Bruised, battered, scared, and chained like slaves, Dontae and Heavy discussed their situation. They threw all kinds of ideas around. Neither one of them were certain how things would play out. In fact, they wouldn't know much of anything until they got real lawyers.

"Y'all was supposed to kill that nigga Mike," Heavy said.

Dontae sighed. "I know. I told Redds that shit, but he was tryin' to help out his man so I rolled wit' the shit. I knew the nigga Mike knew too much about all of us and shit we've done in the past." He shook his head in regret as he turned and looked out the caged window of the bus.

"Shit is fucked up, joe. We got our hands full, believe that."

Heavy shook his head as well. The charges they were facing were serious shit and they didn't know anybody that had beat such charges in court. "Whatever we do, we gotta' get the best lawyers money can buy."

"You ain't said nothin' but a word," Dontae said. "I ain't gon' let these people just fuck me around. That ain't happening at all."

News of the raids had Redds kicking himself in the ass. He knew damn well he wasn't supposed to have left anything in his mother's apartment. Now she was locked up and he had no one to blame but himself. The thought alone was killing him inside. Not being able to run to her aid only added to his pain and regrets.

Sitting on the bed in the hotel room counting money, Redds explained his plans to Lil' Man and Top. With $80,000 that they had collected for him, Redds was ready to make his move out of town somewhere. "Check this out." Redds looked at the young niggaz. "In the morning, I need y'all to go down to the court building and make sure my mother is okay. It's very important." Redds handed Lil' Man three stacks of cash. "That's thirty Gs right there. That should be enough to see what's up. Also, holla at Pinky, and check on Dontae and Heavy. She should know somethin'. Cool?"

"I got you," Lil' Man said. "Whatever you need, I got you."

"Good lookin', my nigga," Redds said.

"So, when we gon' hear from you?" Top asked.

"As soon as shit cool off," Redds said. "I can't let these people snatch me up right now. I gotta get some shit in order."

"I feel you," Top said.

Redds got up and grabbed a duffel bag off of the nightstand. He opened it and pulled out three bricks of coke. Handing the bricks to Lil' Man, he said, "That right there should put you two on your feet."

Lil' Man looked at the bricks. He knew for sure there would be no looking back for him and Top. "Thanks, Redds."

"Don't worry about it." Redds walked to the window and looked outside. Everything was normal. "It's 'bout time for me and Necci to get out of here."

"I got you," Lil' Man said.

Moments later, they were all inside Lil' Man's truck heading to the bus station.

Chapter 4

Outside of Cleveland, Ohio in a small town called Elyria, Redds and Necci, under another fake name, checked into the Econo Lodge. Redds knew Ohio was nowhere far, but it was far enough away from D.C. to give him a chance to think and map some things out. He had cousins in Ohio, and one that he was close to was in the drug game. His name was Shell. Redds hadn't seen Shell in a long time, but they were family and that was all that mattered. Shell would understand what was going on in Redds' life and assist him while he was in Elyria. He was sure of that.

"Redds," Necci said, lying beside her man. They both needed some rest, the bus ride had them tired. "I'm hungry. I think I'm gon' walk down the street and get us somethin' to eat. Okay?"

Redds thought about it for a second. "Nah, don't worry about it. It cold as shit outside. I got you. What you want?"

"It don't matter for real, anything will do. But, I really don't even want you out outside. Your face been all on the news and shit."

Redds thought about what she said. It made a lot of sense. Even though they were in a small town, he still needed to lay low. "You got a point. Be careful."

"I got it, boo. I'm a big girl." Necci threw on her coat and walked out of the door. As she made her way down the street, she took the time to reflect on what was going on in her life. She didn't know how things would turn out for real and the future was so uncertain that it had her worried, although, she tried her best to hide it from Redds. She knew he had enough on his mind. Whatever the future held, she planned to hold him down no matter what. He was her everything and the love they shared knew no limits.

After Necci left the room, Redds went to the window and watched her walk down the street. He questioned himself about pulling her into his situation. He loved her more than he had ever loved a female before and wanted only the best for her. Never in a million years would he do anything to allow harm to come her way. At the same time, he knew for sure that she would never have agreed to let him go on the run without her. That was the kind of girl she was. Letting out a sigh of frustration, Redds sent up a little prayer to the Creator and asked Him for help.

A week later, Toya was down Lorton visiting Amir. She filled him in on all she knew about the case against Redds and his homies. With a case herself, she put him on point about what she was facing. Lil' Man and Top made sure she was straight; they picked her up from the court building the day after she was arrested. She had been released on personal recognizance. When she got out, Lil' Man gave her the $30,000 Redds had given him; he figured she would need it, being as though Redds was gone. By all means, she was pissed the fuck off about going to jail, but she was more concerned about her son and what was in store for him. After getting her affairs together, Toya went over the jail to check on Dontae and see what he needed.

While on the visit, Dontae told her everything he could to put her on point about what he'd learned from his lawyer. Things were not looking good.

Rubbing his chin and thinking about every different angle of the situation, Amir let out a sigh, and said, "This whole thing is way bigger than I first thought. This is a federal case. That changes the whole ball game. The federal government plays by its own rules. We have to make sure we get Reggie the best defense we can get him. Them people are tryin' to wash those young brothers up."

Toya scratched her head, and said, "I know, this shit is driving me crazy. The FBI been sitting in front of my apartment every single day. They watching me like I'm really some kind of criminal or something. Everywhere I go I see those bastards."

"That's how it goes when you are dealing with the feds. It's going to get on your nerves. In fact, the longer Reggie is on the run the worse it's going to get, so prepare yourself for what's to come. They are going to get more aggressive as time goes on. It's all a part of the games they play. They figure if they press you enough and make your life a living hell, you will talk Reggie into turning himself in or you will turn him in."

Toya shrugged. "I'd never turn my son in, that's out of the question."

"I know that, I'm just telling you how those people play." He rubbed her hand trying to comfort her. He could see the stress in her eyes and all over her face. Redds was her one and only son. The whole situation was killing her inside. The fear of losing her son to the system was like looking death in the eyes; it shook her to her core.

"I contacted the lawyer you told me to get in touch with," Toya said as she looked around the visiting hall wondering if or when she would visit her son in a visiting hall somewhere. The mere thought gave her chills.

"What did he say?" Amir asked.

"He said that he would check into the case for me and would check into things about Reggie as well. I told him not to worry about me. I'm not concerned about my case. They don't really want me, we all know they really want Reggie. Anyway, I gave him a retainer and asked him to begin functioning as Reggie's attorney."

"That's good. I'll keep you in my prayers and we'll just have to see what happens. I'm going to check on some things on my end. This situation is not going to go away overnight."

"I know." Toya shook her head. That thought frightened her.

As nightfall fell upon the D.C. streets, Lil' Man and Top were hard at work putting their plans into effect. They were in the kitchen of a crack house on 14th Street cooking powder into crack. With the work that Redds had left them with, they were determined to get their pockets right once and for all. Lil' Man watched as Top put his whip game down. The young nigga cooked coke like he'd been doing it for years. He was a pro at it; it was a skill he learned from his mother.

Looking back at Lil' Man, Top said, "We gon' be straight for real for real after this shit here. We the only ones that's cookin' up our own shit now. Everybody else buyin' they shit hard."

Lil Man smiled. "I'm hip. We should have been goin' like this."

"We ain't have nobody givin' us the shit on this level before, joe. It ain't what you know, it's who you know, feel me?"

"No bullshit."

When they were done cooking their coke, they weighed it out and packaged it. It was game time. Lil' Man hit the pipehead off with a little coke for letting them use his house and they were out the door.
Inside Lil' Man's truck riding down 14th Street, the partners discussed their plans to get paid.

"I say we pump this shit hand to hand, fuck it. Let's get all the money, you know what I'm talkin' 'bout?" Top said as he popped in the Spice 1 CD. "We can kill the game if we lock down the block wit' the biggest and best shit. Who could fuck wit' us, joe?"

"I feel you, but we need to think about movin' weight, too. That's where the money at. We can hit a few niggaz here and there, and still put work out on the block. It's like the best of both worlds."

"I like the way you think, young. That makes all the sense in the world," Top said as he rolled a Backwood full of weed.

"So who you wanna' fuck wit' as far as coppin'? Redds is out of the picture. We gon' need a connect. I was thinking about the New York nigga Apple. What you think?"

Apple was a 25-year-old Dominican from Harlem that was getting money in D.C. He was flashy and real slick with his words. Money was his MO and most dudes that were trying to get some real money got along with him for the sake of paper. His coke was good and the prices were always the lowest.

Top frowned his face. He didn't like Apple. "I don't fuck wit' that bamma-ass nigga, joe." Top had had a few run-ins with Apple's man, Jay. Jay was from D.C., but he fucked with Apple like they were blood brothers. It was a known fact that if you fucked with Apple you had to go through Jay to do it. Jay was not to be played with; he didn't do much talking, he was all about action. Nevertheless, Top felt like he was all about action as well and didn't give a fuck about how tough a nigga was supposed to be. If anybody got out of line, Top was trying to let the guns blaze off the top.

"Well, if we don't fuck wit' Apple, who we gon' cop from?" Lil' Man asked.

"I say we fuck wit' Rome. We don't need that nigga Apple. I can't stand bitch niggaz anyway."

"Cool, let's see what kind of numbers Rome talkin' and we move from there."

"Cool," Top said.

The next day inside the U.S. Attorney's Office, the powers that be were putting their offensive together. It was time for them to make their move. Behind a thick wooden desk covered with papers and files of all kinds, Assistant U.S. Attorney James Burling discussed the status of the Kennedy Street case with FBI agents Bulger and Schoenberg, who sat in a chair in front of the desk. Burling was eager to prosecute the Kennedy Street case in federal court. It would be just what he needed to further his career. He had dreams of one day being a federal judge.

Aside from that, he'd also invested close to two years of his life into the investigation that was supposed to net a RICO conspiracy case and bring down one of Washington's most notorious street crews.

Burling was short, very light skinned—almost white looking—and very aggressive when it came to his methods of prosecution. He did any and everything to get a conviction in court. When his name came up in court, most defendants asked their lawyer what kind of plea bargains they could get because they knew that nine times out of ten, Burling was going to barbecue their ass quick, fast, and in a hurry if they went to trial. In big cases, he didn't lose. The Washington Post dubbed him The Prosecutor of the Century due to his high conviction rate.

Opening a Kennedy Street file and pulling out pictures of Redds and Mookie, Burling addressed the agents on the case. "Do you have any leads on these two guys?"

"Not right now, but we're working on it," Schoenberg spoke up. He was working hard on bringing Redds and Mookie to justice.

Burling nodded his approval. "I'm sure the FBI is doing all it can do to make sure these two individuals don't make fools of us."

"Yes, sir," Bulger said. "They won't run for long, they don't have what it takes."

Burling smiled. "What makes you think that?"

"They don't have the connections," Bulger said.

"Most individuals that go on the run and succeed for any amount of time usually have connections all over. These guys don't have connections outside of the D.C. area."

Burling rubbed his chin for a second. He wasn't sure he believed that story, but time would tell. He moved on to the next order of business. "Do we have all we need for the racketeering indictment? Is that part solid? I know the event with the murder of the police officer threw a premature monkey wrench into the investigation."

Bulger said, "In cases like these, as you know, Mr. Burling, we could always use more evidence, but I'm sure we have more than enough to get an indictment. If we look at it like the law states, racketeering is the act of operating an illegal business or scheme in order to make a profit. That is exactly how these guys operated. They had a solid structure from the top to the bottom in their crew. The bulk of the drugs came in from the top of the food chain and made its way all the way down to the street workers.

There are countless documentations of a broad category of criminal acts that range from drug dealing, gun-running, armed robbery, assaults, and murders, even some murders for hire. I have a number of witnesses. I feel very good about this case. The killing of the police officer only sealed the deal, for lack of better words."

Schoenberg added, "We have enough to lay their asses down for good. I feel strongly about this case, sir."

"Okay," Burling said as he studied the pictures of Redds and Mookie. "I want these two guys off the streets before we really start moving forward with the case. Judging by the things they have already done, I don't want them out in society trying to find ways to fuck our case up, if you know what I mean."

"Trust me, Mr. Burling, we are on top of it. I really don't think we have to worry about Mr. Green. He should be easy to locate. Mr. Williams is the one with all of the brains, so we are focused on him right now. We will have them both very soon."

"Do whatever you have to do, Bulger. After all, you're the FBI!"

Back in Elyria, Redds had hooked up with his cousin Shell. Shell was a brown skinned dude that stood around 5'9" and carried a little over 200 pounds. He wore his hair in long plaits that he kept freshly done. He had just turned 19-years-old, but he was still somewhat the man in his small town. He was getting plenty of cash in his hood, the Wilkes Villa Projects. He also had some things jumping off in South Park. It was money over everything for him. Cocaine was his game and he was good at it.

Sitting on the sofa smoking weed and watching football on TV—the Browns vs. the Jets—Redds and Shell caught up on some old times. Shell told Redds how things were going for him, and Redds put Shell on point about the trouble he was in back home.

"I got fifteen-hundred dollars on the Browns," Shell said, blowing smoke in the air.

"It look like they gon' get your money right," Redds said.

"My nigga, Big Iz hit my pockets for a G last week on that Cowboys game. I figure I'd get my money back, plus five hundred on this game, you feel me, Redds?"

"Yeah, I feel you," Redds said.

Necci and Shell's girl, Angie, had been in the bedroom where Necci had done Angie's hair. They walked into the living room and smelled the strong weed smoke in the air. Angie was thick and sexy like a Luke dancer. She had smooth brown skin, sexy lips, pretty green eyes, and a walk that was out of this world. "Y'all out here smoking without us?" she said.

"What's mine is yours, baby. You know that." He passed her the blunt. "I like your hair, too. Necci did a good job."

"Thanks, boo," Angie said as she hit the blunt.

"I thought she would look good her hair to the side like that." Necci said as she took a seat in the chair next to Redds. She looked at Redds, and said, "Hey, boo, Angie want me to go out with her. You cool with that?"

"Yeah," Redds said. "Ain't nothing wrong with that, she family. Just don't get in no trouble." He smiled. Angie didn't know Redds was on the run and Redds wanted it kept that way. Shell was to keep it to himself. If anybody was to ask any questions about Redds, the story was that he was Shell's cousin from down south and he was in town visiting.

Angie and Necci left the guys in the apartment alone. As soon as the door shut behind the girls, Shell looked at Redds, and asked, "You got a game plan?"

"Right now, I'm just trying to get my thoughts together. You know what I mean? I haven't thought things all the way out."

"Well, whatever you wanna do, just know I'm here for you. I know what you going through. Anything you need, I got you. I know you gon' need some money and some fake IDs. I got you on that, too."

"Thanks, cuz. I got a few dollars with me, but I could sure use some fake IDs for me and Necci. I want to get rid of the IDs we have already used, feel me?"

"Say no more. I will get on top of it ASAP. I got you. Just lay low and get your thoughts together. You in good hands wit' me. You can put your life on it," Shell assured   Redds.

Hundreds of miles away from Elyria, Ohio, the scene was much different.

"How are you doing this morning?" asked a young, white, female teller inside the Bank of America in North-west, D.C.

"I'm doing okay," said the young, handsome, black male in the slick, black Armani leather. He then slid a note to the teller that read: Slide all the money over slowly or I'm going to blow your brains all over the wall. Please, take me serious.

The tellers bright smile died quickly as fear took over. Instantly, she understood what was going on. Mookie's heart pounded as he eased his coat open to show her his .45. In a whisper, he added, "If you scream or act dumb, everybody dies." Quickly, he glanced around the bank.

There were two other tellers at their stations. An old, armed guard and two other customers were to his left. He could see them out of the corner of his eye. The petrified teller got with the program with the quickness. Inconspicuously, she slid him all of the money in her drawer, a little over $15,000. Mookie slid the money inside his coat where there was a slit in the lining.

"That's it, sir. That's all the money," the teller submissively whispered. Her facial expression was, Please don't kill me. Shaking and sweating, feeling weak in the knees, the teller could almost taste death in the air. Mookie winked at her and slowly walked out of the door like there was nothing to it. Everything went according to plan. It was like he'd done it before. With his back against the wall, Mookie had to do whatever he had to do to survive.

Chapter 5

Geto Boys' Mind Playing Trick on Me pumped through the powerful speakers that surrounded Shell's living room as the men smoked weed and discussed business. Redds had been in town for just over two weeks and things were smooth. He laid low and checked things out. D.C. seemed so far away at the time, even though Redds thought about going back home every day. Being the type of dude Redds was, he always paid close attention to what went on around him. When it came to getting money, the wheels in mind turned instantly. He could spot an angle or a lick from miles away. Shell was buying bricks of cocaine for $28,000 in Cleveland, Ohio; every now and then he would take the trip to Detroit where he would get the bricks for $25,000. Once Shell got his work, he returned to Elyria and the coke disappeared overnight. He had clientele lined up and waiting as soon as it came out of the pot.

Needing cash to live on the run and make it out of the country, Redds saw a way to stack money and he wanted in. He could help Shell step his game up and he could get paid like never before himself. Seeing all of the opportunity that was in Elyria, Redds was sick that he'd never tried to get any of the small town money before. If he would have made a trip to Elyria earlier, he was sure he would have been rich in months.

"I can get you bricks for eighteen or nineteen from my man," Redds said, plucking ashes in the ashtray. "We can put our bread together and get the number even lower than that. You got a goldmine up here. I wish I would have known you was getting' like this. I would have been left D.C. and came up here."

Shell laughed. "I kept tryin' to tell you to come get some of this change. It's sweet. You still got niggaz up here that don't even cook it up they self. At least in my town, anyway. Niggaz just catching on to the cook game. You talkin' my kind of talk. Let's do it. How can we put the shit together?"

"That ain't nothin'. All I have to do is get word to my man and we can put the shit in motion like that." Redds nodded his head as he thought about how he would map the plan out. He was a thinker by nature and when he put his mind to it, he came up with great ideas and plans that he saw through to the end every time.

"Sounds like a plan to me." Shell got up and looked at his watch. He had a move to make. "Well, look here, cuz, you think the move out and we will put the shit into effect. I got run to South Park real quick to pick up some money. I'll be back in a few."

"Cool." Redds gave his cousin five. "We 'bout to get paid like never before. Watch what I tell you."
Shell left the apartment.

Redds' mind raced as he thought about the best way to put his plans into effect. It would only be a matter of time before he and Shell took Elyria to another level. Walking into the bedroom where Necci was under the covers watching New Jack City on VHS, he said, "You done watched this joint three or four times, ain't you?" Redds took a seat on the bed and rubbed her leg.

"Ain't shit else to do up this boring ass joint, besides, I like how Keisha be going hard as shit in this joint." Redds laughed. "I feel you. We won't be here that long. Soon as I figure out what the next move is, we getting' out of here. I won't last long in a small town. I'm gon' start standin' out real soon, plus, I got family here so the feds gon' eventually get on my trail."

"So, where do we go from here?" Necci raised up to look Redds in the eyes. Whatever move he made, she trusted that he knew what he was doing.

"When you got money in this world, real money, you can go wherever you want to, believe that there, baby." He kissed her on the lips. "Things are going to work out. They always do."

"Okay. I'm here for you no matter how it goes. Always know that, Reggie. You are my everything." Her words came from the heart. She'd never met a dude like him. In a perfect world, she would spend the rest of her life with him. The love that she felt for him was one that she couldn't explain. The only thing she could explain was that she loved Redds and she would go to the ends of earth with him and for him.

Rubbing her chin softly, Redds looked into her eyes, and said, "Listen to me, nobody ever knows what the future holds, but I can promise you this, whatever happens, I will always find a way to make it right in the end. You are my everything and I will do anything for you. Always remember that, baby."

Necci melted inside. She was speechless. "I love you, Reggie. I will always love you."

Northwest D.C. continued to be about money and power. Everybody wanted a piece of the pie, young and old. Sursum Corda Cooperative Complex was one of the roughest spots in town and it was a place where there was plenty of money to make. On this night it was alive with nightlife and drug traffic. Top hung out in the Cordas from time to time; he had a cousin by the name of Jelani who lived there. Top, Jelani, and another dude they fucked with by the name of Rome stood in front of the market talking about Apple. Lil' Man and Top began buying coke from Ap-

ple; it was the best move after they'd weighed their options. Before they started copping from Apple, they'd tried
to cop from Rome but he was experiencing a slight dry
patch. Apple gave them five bricks for $90,000; the deal
was the best deal they could find in the streets at the time.

Rome understood why they copped from Apple, it
was a business move in his eyes. "Y'all made the right
move fuckin' wit' Apple. Get your money right. It's not like
it's a friendship, it's business. You know the nigga is a
snake and he ain't to be trusted, so don't trust. If ever y'all
have a fall out with the nigga, you know you gotta kill his
ass. Simple as that." Rome pulled no punches.

"I feel you," Top said.

"Stay focused on what you gotta do," Rome said as
his beeper went off. He checked the number. It was business. "I got some shit to do, I'ma catch you in a little
while." Rome gave Top five and stepped off.
Jelani thought about what Rome had said. He looked at
Top, and said, "Rome is right, be careful dealing with that
nigga Apple. The nigga is a snake. Keep your eyes on him."

"I feel you. I don't even fuck wit' the nigga for real.
I let Lil' Man deal wit' the nigga. If it was up to me, that
nigga would be handcuffed and left for dead somewhere.
You know how I go," Top said.

Jelani laughed. "I know, young. If ever you wanna
bring the nigga a move, I'm wit' it. The only thing about
that is we gotta make sure we hit the nigga for something
nice, so you gotta cop from him for a minute and get him
comfortable."

Top nodded. "I know."

"After you get the nigga comfortable, then we get
his ass. We hit 'em where it hurts, kill 'em, and never talk
about it. Simple as that."

"I'm down. Just give me some time. I will figure
something, joe."

"Bet." Jelani gave Top five.

Inside the FBI building in downtown D.C., Bulger and Schoenberg sat in their office watching an enhanced version of the police murder on one of the many surveillance tapes they had on the Kennedy Street Crew. The footage was taken from cameras that were placed on top of light poles, and on the roofs of apartments and stores along Kennedy Street. The videotapes would be a vital part of the evidence.

"We still can't see much in the shadows of the alley." Bulger pointed at the TV. "We are going to need more than this."

Schoenberg smiled. "You gotta be kidding me. We have more than we need. We have informants that are going to put the case where we need it. I'm not worried about any weaknesses in this case. So many of these guys are trying to save their own asses that we can ride this one all the way to the bank. Trust me. We don't have anything to worry about. These guys are going away for a very long time."

"I understand that, but I really want someone to fry about the murder of this cop. We can't allow anyone to get away with these types of things. I want to make sure the cop killing is a part of the RICO conspiracy," Bulger said as the phone rang. "Hold on one second." He held is finger up at Schoenberg as he answered the phone. Bulger had a quick conversation and then got off the phone with a concerned look on his face.

"What's that all about?" Schoenberg asked.
Bulger sighed. "That was Dick from robbery. Our guy, Green, just hit another bank. This one was in Silver Spring."

"Was anyone hurt?"

"No. He slid a note to the teller, and walked out with the cash nice and smooth."

Schoenberg laughed. "That kid has balls. I give him that. So, what's that, three banks in ten days or something like that?"

"Yes, sir, that's exactly what it is. The guy is really making the Bureau look like an ass. How in the fuck can he be wanted by the FBI and still be in the D.C. area robbing banks? The shit doesn't make sense!" Bulger was clearly pissed off and took Mookie's action personally. "We have to catch this guy as soon as possible. I don't care what we have to do. We have to turn up the pressure."

"We will get his ass. Trust me, he will slip and we will be there to bag his ass."

D.C. Jail's visiting hall was packed with relatives of men housed there. Dontae sat behind the glass talking to Lil' Man, who'd come to see what was going on with the case. Lil' Man really didn't want to be the one to bring Dontae bad news, but he had asked him to check on his girl, Pinky, for him. She'd been playing games with Dontae's money and lying about different things. All of her actions were out of the ordinary as far as Dontae was concerned.

The shit bothered him and had all kinds of thoughts going through his head. After all, he hadn't been locked up a month yet. Something had to give.

After Dontae asked Lil' Man to check on Pinky, he and Top went by her house a few times. The third time they went by there, they saw a black Benz parked out front. Lil' Man decided to go knock on the door. Pinky answered acting like she had an attitude because he'd knocked on her door. She wanted to know what the hell he wanted. Lil' Man told her that he was just checking up on her as Dontae had asked, and they ended up getting into a heated argument. Lil' Man ended up leaving before he had to smack the taste out of her mouth.

Filling Dontae in on what went down at Pinky's house, Lil' Man said, "I don't know what was up wit' her, young."

Dontae sighed. "Man, fuck that bitch. I want you to go back over there, and get money and everything else. I don't care what you have to do to get it. Cool?"

Lil' Man nodded. "I got you. That's shit ain't nothin'. What you want me to do wit' the money?"

"Give the money to Redds' mother, Toya will hold it for me. She'll make sure I'm good. You can keep the coke."

"Say no more, big homie."

Apple sat in Jay's dark blue 1992 Nissan 300 ZX twin turbo reading the USA Today. Jay sat behind the wheel rolling a Backwood and watching everything moving on Georgia Avenue. Apple was deep into an article about Mookie that had made the newspapers. His bank robberies were headline news. However, Apple had other things on his mind: a nigga had smacked his girl and he wanted the nigga dead.

"I want that nigga put to sleep, no question asked," Apple said.

Jay nodded. "Ain't shit to it, slim. I'ma holla at Lil' Moon. Shorty 'bout his business, believe me. I seen his work. Young nigga's a cold killer." He lit the Backwood and turned up Dr. Dre's The Chronic.

At nineteen-years-old, Jay was before his time. He was truly an old soul in a young body. When Apple first arrived in town, he messed with Jay's aunt. Back then, Jay was a fifteen-year-old killer that was all about armed robbery. Apple saw something in Jay and took him under his wing. He made sure Jay was always taken care of and for that, Jay was loyal to him with no limits.

Rubbing his chin as he thought about Lil' Moon, Apple said,

"Put youngin' on the job. I got a few Gs for him."

Apple always used money to get what he wanted. It

worked for him. For the right price, he felt that he could get a nigga to do anything he wanted. He'd paid niggaz to kill their own family members. Jay himself had killed a childhood friend for Apple after being paid $5,000.

"Lil' Moon will put his ass to sleep in less than twenty four hours. Don't even sweat it."

"Cool." Apple nodded. "That'll teach his ass a lesson."

Just after nine thirty a.m. Friday morning, Mookie was on another mission as he walked into First National Bank of Fairfax, Virginia. Adrenaline pumped through veins as he scanned the small bank. As he sized up the situation, he felt that it would be an easy take. There was an armed guard, an old white man with gray hair making a deposit, and two white female tellers. The guard stood by the coffee watching everything closely. It seemed like all eyes were on Mookie, the male that wore the black Armani leather. An awkward tension filled the bank as things seemed to go into slow motion.

"How may I help you, sir?" a woman asked Mookie, looking at him like he was out of place.
Mookie smiled. "I'd like to open an account." He maintained the smile, but he had a bad feeling in his gut. For a second, he thought about pulling the .45 from his waistband and going hard for the money, but he thought against it quickly. Shit would get out of hand too fast and he wasn't looking forward to that. He'd prefer to try to make it a smooth move again.

The bank manager, an older white man, walked from the back and addressed Mookie nicely. "Good morning, sir. I'm the manager, I can get you squared away in no time. All I need to see is your ID..."

Mookie didn't let the manager finish his statement. He pulled his pistol, reached across the counter, and grabbed the manager by the collar. Looking over his shoulder, he pointed his pistol at the guard, and hissed, "Don't move, muthafucka! I will put bullets in your ass!" The female tellers screamed for help. Looking back at the manager, Mookie said, "Do as I say and you will make it back home tonight."

The guard dropped his hands to his side and for a split second, he thought about going for his weapon. Mookie saw the guard and it was like he could read his mind. "Don't do it, pops. You gon' get everybody in the bitch smoked. It ain't gotta' go down like that."

"Do what he says!" the manager yelled.

The guard reached for his weapon. It was the wrong move. Mookie let him have it and the .45 went off like a cannon. Slugs hit the guard in the head, killing him instantly. The women screamed louder, fell to their knees, and covered their heads in fear of losing their lives. Mookie shoved the manager to the floor and jumped clear over the counter. "Stupid muthfucka!" he hissed. At gunpoint, Mookie made the manager fill a mailbag with cash from the drawers of all of the tellers.

After the mailbag was filled, Mookie burst out of the front door with his pistol still in hand. The mailbag was flung over his shoulder. Gunshot rang out. Bullets flew past Mookie's head and crashed into the wall behind him. Mookie ducked, continued to run, and returned fire. A Fairfax police officer was on his way into the bank when he saw Mookie running out of the front door. It was clear to all what was going on. The officer and Mookie traded more shots in the parking lot as he made a run for his ride. The officer fired more shots at him, barely missing him. Ducking behind a parked car, Mookie fired back at the officer, making him take cover. Running out of bullets, Mookie popped in another clip and fired more shots at the officer as bystanders ran for their lives. The officer called for backup as bullets flew in his direction.

Mookie jumped into Nissan Maxima and tried to start the car. Bullets crashed through the side window. There was an AK-47 on the back seat under a Polo jacket.

He grabbed the assault rifle and jumped back out of the car on a death wish. All he could think about was the fact that he was not going to be taken alive. He sprayed the chopper from left to right with bullets flying in all directions as fire spit from the barrel. Shells spit from the rifle in a high arch, littering the ground. The officer tried to step from cover and was taken off of his feet by the assault rifle. Jumping back in the Maxima, Mookie tried to flea the scene as backup arrived. Two police cars tried to box him in and Mookie knew it was over. There was no way he was getting out of the parking lot. Officers popped up from all directions and they fired at the Maxima. Mookie sprayed the AK-47 from the window, dropping another officer right before taking bullets in the chest. His body jumped as the bullets slammed into him.

Still, he used every bit of fight he had left in him to spray the AK-47 out of the other side of the car, hitting two more officers. The scene looked like something out of a movie. More sirens hit the air as gunfire continued to rip through the air as two more police skidded onto the scene. Officers jumped out firing. Mookie sprayed the last of the bullets in his chopper as bullets tore through his body. Shots hit him in the head and he slumped over into the passenger seat lifeless. It was over. Slowly, officers approached the car.

"He's dead! He's dead!" an officer called out.

Later the same night, Lil' Man and Top were in ski masks lying in the grass beside Pinky's house waiting for her to step outside. They were on a mission and she was in for a rude awakening. Fucking over Dontae while he was in jail was the worst mistake she could've made in her life. It really made no sense because of all people, she should have known how he would act once she crossed him. He had no more love for her.

Dressed from head to toe in Dolce & Gabbana, Pinky stepped out the front door on her way out to eat. Lil' Man and Top sprung into action. Top grabbed her from behind and put her in a deadly chokehold as she tried to scream. Lil' Man put a gun her face, and said, "If you scream, I'ma kill you right her on the front porch." They forced their way into the house where Top slammed her on the floor. Lil' Man then closed the door behind them. Looking up at the masked gunmen that pointed pistols at her, Pinky yelled, "What the fuck do you want from me?"

"Shut up, bitch!" Top snapped and smacked her in the face with his .357 magnum. "Don't say a fuckin' word." Pinky shut her mouth and cried. She wanted to beg for her life, but the sight of the huge revolver in her face made her keep her thoughts to herself.

Lil' Man dashed upstairs and searched the house. Like clockwork, he found $65,000 and three bricks of cocaine. He threw the goods inside a pillowcase and returned to the living room. Looking at Top, he said, "Let's go."

Top looked down at Pinky, who was balled up in a protective knot out of fear, and said, "What about her?" Lil' Man gave her a short glance, then looked back at Top, and said, "Man ... fuck her. Let her live, she don't know who we are."

Without another word, the teenagers dashed out of the house.

Two days later, Necci and Shell checked into a hotel in Silver Spring, MD. They were on a mission. Redds had gotten in touch with his man, Donnavan, and set up a move to cop bricks of coke at a great price and take the coke back to Elyria. Donnavan and Redds had done business for a number of years and there was a strong trust between the two of them. So, when Redds called on him, it was a given that he would look out.

Lil' Man and Top would be needed to make sure everything went smooth while Necci was in town. After all, the feds knew she was Redds' girl and they were looking for her as well. She called her little brother and told him to meet her at the hotel. Lil' Man and Top were there in less than an hour, and she introduced them to Shell. They wasted no time filling Necci in on all that happened in the city while she'd been out of town with Redds.

"... shit been wild as shit," Lil' Man said. "Mookie's shit was all on the news. He went hard as shit. Killed like three or four police and some more shit."

Necci thought about what her brother told her. She wondered what Redds' fate would be when it all said and done. She got a sick feeling in her stomach and hoped it wouldn't be anything like Mookie's.

Lil' Man went on to tell her about everything that was going on with him and Top. She warned him to be careful when dealing with Apple, and the whole situation with Pinky had her blown. Necci couldn't believe that Pinky would play games with Dontae. Everybody that knew him knew for sure he wasn't to be played with.

Necci looked from Lil' Man to Top, and said, "Y'all sure she ain't know it was y'all that went up in the house?"

"We was masked up," Top said.

Necci shook her head and sighed. Times were changing fast. Pushing her thoughts to the side, she got down to business, and said, "Well, let's go handle this business."

They got in Lil' Man's truck and headed into the city. They rode down Georgia Avenue for a while, and then pulled into a dark alley and parked. Top looked around from his position in the back seat and gripped his .357 magnum. "This where the nigga wanna meet?" Top asked.

He wasn't feeling the location. The alley had four entrances and ran behind a group of apartment buildings. It was the perfect spot for a robbery or a murder.

"This where he told me to meet him. He said for me to be here at eight," Necci said.

"Well, we here," Lil' Man said.

Shell looked around carefully. He was strapped, so he really wasn't tripping. He knew that Lil' Man and Top were both young killers, so they would make sure all went well. Nevertheless, Shell paid close attention to all that went on. After all, his money was involved.

Looking over her shoulder, Necci saw the huge revolver that Top had on his lap, and said, "Put that joint up. We good. This Redds' man. Ain't nothin' gon' happen."

Top sucked his teeth and slid the pistol back in his waistband. He never went against Necci. She was the big sister that didn't play.

Moments later, Donnavan tapped on the passenger side window. Necci jumped a little. Lil' Man and Top didn't flinch, they were ready for whatever. "What's up?" Necci said as she lowered the window.

"I'm okay," Donnavan said as he took a look inside the truck. "Let's talk."

"Okay," Necci said as she got out the truck. Lil' Man got out with her and grabbed the gym bag that had the money in it. Donnavan give Lil' Man a funny look. Necci caught the look, and said, "That's my little brother. He got the money, he's good. Don't trip."

"No problem," Donnavan said. He had no worries. He had two of his men close by with Uzis watching everything. "It's all good. Redds already put me on point."

"Cool," Necci said. She then nodded at Lil' Man, who handed Donnavan the gym bag.

Once the gym bag was handed to Donnavan, a young dude wearing a gray hoodie appeared from the back of one of the apartments carrying two book bags. The dude in the hoodie handed Donnavan the book bags and returned from where he'd come. Donnavan handed them to Lil' Man. He then looked at Necci, and said, "Tell Redds I send my love. Let him know I'm here for him if he needs me for anything. I have been in his situation before. It can get stressful. However, all he has to do is stay two steps ahead of the game and think twice before he makes any move."

"I'll make sure I tell him what you said," Necci said.

"Also, tell him that next time he wants to do business, we can work the old move and I will have the work shipped to him wherever he wants me to send it. I trust him."

Necci nodded. "Cool. He'll be glad to hear that."

Chapter 6

Back in Elyria, Ohio, inside the Wilkes Villa Projects, Redds and Shell had just finished cooking coke. They'd turned five bricks of powder into ten bricks of crack and were breaking some of the coke down into smaller weight.

Eights, sixty-twos, ounces, halves, and quarters were packaged in plastic on Angie's kitchen table. N.W.A.'s Niggaz 4 Life played in the background. While taking care of business, Redds and Shell discussed their game plan to get paid. Redds saw something real big in the opportunity to get money in Ohio. He'd like to start in Elyria and then move out into other areas. Cleveland, Columbus, Toledo, Cincinnati, they were all areas Redds felt they could move in on, being as though Shell already dealt with dudes in those cities that were getting money.

Looking down at all the coke they had on the table, Shell said, "We gon' take shit to another level real fast once I put the word out. It ain't gon' be no turnin' back, cuz."

Thinking about ways to stack his paper and get out of the country, Redds said, "That's the idea. In a minute, if all goes well, you gon' have to move away from here. You gon' get too big for a small town. You know that, right?"

"Hell yeah. If we get shit movin' like you say, that shit gon' bring the feds to town."

"And, that's when you gotta' stick and move," Redds said.

"You right about that." Shell looked at his Rolex. It was time for him to make a run. "I'll be right back. Gotta' drop some of this work off."

"Cool."

When Shell left, Redds took a seat in the living room and thought about some of the things Necci had put him on point about, and felt somewhat lucky to have made it out of town. He thought about Mookie and shook his head. So many of his niggaz were dead and gone or in prison. The thought made him wonder about his own future.

The game was mean and had no love for anybody. When Redds heard of how Mookie went out, it was no surprise to him. Mookie was always a little over the top. He'd fell in love with George and Jonathan Jackson while in prison; revolutionaries were the people he looked up to. However, Redds felt like Mookie was better off dead than in prison for the rest of his life. In a cage for life was no way for a man to live out his last days, Redds believed that with all of his heart.

Necci also told Redds that his mother had gotten a lawyer for him. Even though Redds had no immediate plans of turning himself in, it was still a good thing to have a lawyer already on standby for whatever was to come. Who was to say the lawyer couldn't clear his name while he was still on the run? Nothing was certain. As far as Pinky, he couldn't believe she played games with Dontae like she had. He'd known her since they were kids and would have never thought she'd do anything like that. She deserved everything she got in Redds' mind. The thought of Lil' Man and Top buying coke for Apple didn't sit well with him, but he knew the young niggaz had to survive so there was nothing much he could really say about it. At the end of the day, he knew they could take care of themselves by all means. Wanting to clear his mind for a second, Redds turned on the TV and dazed off into relaxation.

Just after nightfall a few days later back in D.C., Sursum Cordas was live in front of the market. A rack of niggaz was outside in the cold going hand-to-hand, chasing that all mighty dollar. It was all they knew. Jelani was on the front line right in the mix. Off to the side, a few dudes smoking P.C.P.—Love Boat. After serving a pipehead, Jelani stuffed a balled up fifty-dollar bill into his pocket and turned his attention to the dudes that were smoking Boat. Jelani had bet a nigga that he couldn't take a shotgun of Boat, and the nigga did it and now Jelani was waiting for the P.C.P. to take effect. Sure enough, the dude started lunchin' real good. In no time, he took his clothes off in the freezing cold, dancing to a go-go song that only he could hear. Next, he started yelling at the top of his lungs as he jumped up and down like he was jumping rope. "I got a heavyweight fight coming up!" he yelled. "I'm gon' fight for the belt against Mike Tyson. I'ma show you niggaz how it's done."

Everybody outside laughed. Even pipeheads got a good laugh off of what was going on. On the real it was a sad situation, but it was the affects that P.C.P had on a nigga.

Boom! Boom! Boom! Gunshots rang out from a Glock .40, sending the crowd scattering in different directions. Boom! Boom! Boom! The Glock continued to rock. It popped at least another ten or fifteen times. In seconds, the crowd was gone and it was like a ghost town outside. Jelani was stretched out in a pool of blood with his brains hanging out the side of his head. The masked gunman was a little guy. He ran up on Jelani's body, stood over it, and let loose again, emptying the clip without a blink of the eye. Feathers from Jelani's coat flew in the air and mixed in with the gun smoke. Looking around for any witnesses, the gunman took off running with the smoking Glock in hand.

An hour later, the gunman was in the passenger seat of Jay's twin turbo telling him how he had smoked Jelani in front of everybody. The gunman was a 14-year-old killer by the name of Lil' Moon. His baby-faced looks would throw off anybody. He had the look of a little boy, somewhat like Emmanuel Lewis, but he was nothing sweet. He looked up to Jay like a father figure. Anything he saw Jay do, he wanted to do. He wanted to be just like Jay. Growing up without a father in his life and a mother that was on drugs made it easy for Lil' Moon to look up to him.

With a smile on his face, Lil' Moon looked at Jay, and said, "They never saw it comin', young."

Jay smiled. "That's 'cause you know what you doin', shorty. It's called the element of surprise. Remember that." Jay handed Lil' Moon $2,000, and two and a half ounces of coke that he had in a brown paper bag. The money he gave Lil' Moon was only a fraction of what Apple gave him to have Jelani murdered for smacking his girlfriend. Truth be told, Apple gave Jay $10,000 to kill Jelani.

However, in Jay's mind, he wasn't doing Lil' Moon wrong because he knew that the young nigga would have done the killing for free just to because Jay said the nigga had to be killed. Cutting his eyes at Lil' Moon, Jay said,

"Keep that shit to yourself, don't let nobody know what you did. Niggaz always go to jail for running they fuckin' mouth after they kill somebody. Always remember that, too. No witness, no crime. The only one that knows you killed that nigga is me and you know I won't ever tell a soul. It's death before dishonor wit' me, all the way to the grave."

"It's death before dishonor wit' me, too. You know that, big homie."

"That's right, young nigga." Jay patted shorty on the top of the head.

In life, there's a reaction for every action, always. In the streets, the reactions can be swift, violent, and, sometimes, premature. Top was, and had always been, a young nigga that was quick to react. Many times he would react without a lot of thought, and although that may have kept him alive, it didn't make his actions the smartest ones. He went off as soon as he got news of Jelani's murder. He didn't want to hear anything from anybody; all he wanted to do was kill shit. As soon as he got word of the murder, he and Lil' Man went down the Cordas to holla at Jelani's man, Mike P. Mike P gave them all the facts as he knew them to be. Those facts were unclear and inconsistent. Word on the streets was that another group of Sursun Corda niggaz had killed Jelani. After all, the niggaz from the circle were beefin' with the niggaz from the market. Jaleni was from the market. That was all Top needed to hear. His attention was turned to the niggaz from the circle and he was out for blood.

Top, Lil' Man, and Mike P strapped up over Mike P's apartment. They loaded and checked their assault rifles, an AK-47, a MAC-90, and a Mini-14, before jumping in an old, beat up Chevy Impala. Lil' Man was the best driver, so he got behind the wheel and headed for the circle. They pulled up not too far from the circle, and then got out on foot wearing ski masks. Their weapons were clear for everyone to see. It was dark outside, but it really would have made no difference to them if it was broad daylight. They had no intentions of leaving any witnesses. As soon as they laid eyes on a group of young niggaz they opened fire, spraying bullets from about fifteen to twenty yards away.

The young niggaz scattered and returned fire as best as they could, considering they had been caught off guard. An intense gunfight ensued for what seemed like a half an hour, but in reality it was only a minute or two. When the gunfire died, those that were still alive took off running. Two dead bodies were left on the ground like litter along with close to three hundred shell casings. It looked like a small war had taken place.

As fate would have it, shit really hit the fan after the gunfight. The very next day, the niggaz from the circle struck back with a vengeance and hit the market niggaz hard, opening fire with assault rifles, killing three market niggaz. Sursum Corda was now beefin' with Sursum Corda—the market niggaz against the circle niggaz. 14th Street niggaz that fucked with Top and Lil' Man rolled with the circle niggaz. Vicious shootings began to spring up like wild fires. Anywhere, anytime, on sight. The police were all over the Cordas for days raiding homes, locking niggaz up, and doing all in their power to put a stop to the shootings. Eight murders were recorded in connection with Jelani's murder. Nevertheless, Top and those who backed him still didn't really know who actually killed Jelani

A gold 1992 Nissan 300 ZX twin turbo turned onto a dark side street just minutes away from Takoma Station. The Nissan pulled up beside Lil' Man's 4Runner. He hopped out the truck carrying a gym bag and got in the Nissan.

Apple smiled and gave Lil' Man five. "What's up, gangsta?" Apple looked like new money as always. He was dressed in a black, silk Versace shirt with a gold chain hanging from his neck with a diamond flooded charm that was shaped like a stop sign with a dollar sing in the middle. A black Desert Eagle sat nice and snug in a brown leather shoulder holster like Apple had a permit for the firearm. "I see you lookin' good, look like a young nigga that's getting money."

Lil' Man smiled. "That's what it's all about, ain't it?"

"For sure. You know that. You remind me of myself when I was your age. I was all about my paper, nothin' else mattered."

Lil' Man dropped the gym bag on the floor of the car. There was another gym bag on the floor. Lil Man grabbed the other bag, knowing that it contained the bricks of coke. "It's money over everything wit' me, Apple."

Apple smiled. "That's what I like about you. A lot of young niggaz your age are all about reputation, you about that paper. That's gon' take you far in this game. Mark my words, son."

"I feel you." Lil' Man looked around, making sure everything was cool. He really didn't like doing a lot of talking when he was taking care of business. He liked to stick and move.

"Look here, you wanna get some real money?" Apple raised his eyebrows.

"What you mean by real money? I'm gettin' money. I'm movin' this yay as fast as possible."

"Don't get me wrong, you movin' like shit. I see that. That's why I'm asking you if you wanna' get some real money."

Lil' Man looked confused. "What you gettin' at, young?"

"Money makes money, you know that, right?" Apple asked.

"I feel you on that," Lil' Man said, wanting Apple to get to the point.

"I want to see you get some real money. If you gettin' real money, then we gettin' real money together." Apple went on to tell Lil' Man that he should be buying more than five bricks by now. He'd copped from Apple a few times already, so he knew that money was passing through his hands. Apple wanted him to know that the more money he spent with him, the lower the prices would be. "I know you saving your money and all that shit, but five bricks ain't shit for real, not when you dealing wit' a nigga like me. Fuckin' wit' me, you could be gettin' twenty-five or fifty bricks. Who knows?"

Lil' Man thought about moving twenty-five or fifty bricks. That was more than he'd ever thought about. In fact, he wasn't even sure if he could move that many kilos.

Apple thumbed his nose, pulled another gym bag from between his legs, and handed it to Lil' Man. "That's five more bricks for you. I'm frontin' you them joints there.

Now you got ten. Next go round, you should be grabbing twenty birds, then forty, and so on. You get it?"

Lil Man looked down at the second gym bag and thought about what was going on. Apple was moving fast. Lil' Man wasn't sure if he really wanted to move that fast with him. However, he wasn't going to give the coke back or tell Apple that he didn't want the work. "All I have is one question, joe."

"What's that, son?"

"What happens if I fuck the money up? What if I can't pay you?"

"We not gon' even worry about that. You know what you're doing. Don't worry about not being able to come up wit' the money. Focus on what you gon' do wit' all the money you gon' make now that you sittin' on bricks."

Lil' Man smiled and gave Apple five. A deal with the devil had been made.

Inside their lavish hotel suite in Atlantic City, Redds and Necci lay in the huge bed watching TV. Shell and Angie were next door in the connected suite. The couples decided to hit Atlantic City for a little rest and relaxation. They deserved it. They'd been focused on nothing but moving bricks for a while.

Rolling over and resting her head on Redds' chest, Necci said, "So, how much money you gon' give me to gamble wit', boo?"

Redds laughed. "You not gon' lose all our money at these crap tables up here. That ain't what we came here for. We came here to chill."

With a playful frown, Necci said, "How we gon' be in Atlantic City and not roll the dice? That don't make no sense, man!" Necci knew how to shoot dice well. She'd learned watching Lil' Man with his homies. However, Atlantic City was another ball game.

Redds smiled, and said, "Here's what I'm gon' do, I'm gon' give you a thousand dollars. If you lose the bread, don't ask me for no more. Cool?"

Necci rolled her eyes. "Okay, cool. I'm gon' show what I can do on one of them tables. Watch."

Redds got up and grabbed $1,000 from his luggage bag. "Here you go."

"Thank you, baby." Necci was excited. She couldn't wait to hit the casino floor and roll the dice. "Are you goin' wit' me?"

Redds shook his head. "Nah, I'm gon' stay up here and relax. I don't want to be walkin' around this joint like I ain't wanted by the FBI. Shit ain't that sweet. Ain't no tellin' who might see me and know who I am. Go have fun. I'll be here when you get back." He smacked her on the ass, and added, "Go get us some money."

"Okay." Necci went in the bathroom to check her hair and then left the room to hit the casino for a little while.

Down on the casino floor, Necci made her way through the thick crowd of gamblers as she headed to the $25 table. She felt safe there. The table was surrounded with gamblers betting all kinds of chips. One Arab dude had all $100 chips and bet nothing less than ten of them at a time. Necci watched for a second as the huge dice went back and forth from one shooter to another. A short while later, it was her turn. Like magic, her first few rolls were winners. It was like she had brought luck with her from some magical place. As she rolled winner after winner, the crowd yelled in her favor and began to bet with her. Her lucky strike caught the eye of a smooth looking young, black dude in a blue Polo sweat suit. He bet big on Necci's rolls. In three rolls he won close to $2,500 off of Necci. She saw him watching her, but didn't pay it too much attention.

Shaking the big dice, Necci said, "Come on! Give me a seven right here!" She rolled the dice and hit a twelve.

"Awwwww!" the crowd deflated. Her luck had worn off for the moment.

"You did good, honey!" a Spanish lady said, collecting her winnings.

"I'm still up a few hundred dollars," Necci said as she placed her bet for the next person on the dice.

"Excuse me." The guy in the Polo sweat suit tapped her on the shoulder.

Necci gave him a funny look. "What's up?"

"Why the attitude, sweetheart? I just wanted to speak."

"My man is here." She looked him up and down.

"Oh, okay. My bad," the dude said. "My bad, no disrespect. I saw a beautiful girl by herself and just wanted to say hello. That's all."

"It's no problem. I just wanted to let you know," Necci said as she turned her attention back to the dice that rolled across the big, green table.

"Take it easy, sweetheart." The guy in the Polo sweat suit went back to his spot, and continued betting big and winning on the dice. Necci kept a careful eye on him. He had to be somebody, it was written all over his face as well as in the way he bet large amounts of money. Nevertheless, none of that mattered. Redds was her everything and that was all that mattered to her.

As time passed, Necci's luck died off. She was still up $600 when she left the crap table. That was a good thing for her because she did not want to hear Redds' mouth about her losing her little bit of change. She wanted to return to the suite with more than she'd left with. She decided to take her chances at the black jack table. Like magic, she had some luck there. In just a few hands, she was up a few more Benjamin Franklins. Things looked good.

Wanting to make sure that she didn't lose any of the money she'd won, Necci decided to trade some of her chips in. On her way to the cashier, she spotted Shell and the dude that had on the Polo sweat suit. They were in a deep conversation like they'd known each other for some years. Necci watched them for a second and then brushed it off. After trading in some of her chips, she returned to the table where she won a little more money. It was her lucky night. Knowing how fast her luck could go bad, she decided to head back up to the suite.

Redds was staring out the window at the ocean in deep thought when she walked back in the room. Staring out at the ocean helped him clear his mind and get his thoughts in order. He turned his attention to Necci, and said, "So, how did things go?"

A huge smile crossed her face. "I came off."

"For real?"

"I won like two thousand dollars."

Redds smiled. "That's good, and you must've known when to quit."

"Hell yeah!" She laughed.

A few seconds later, there was a knock at the door. Redds and Necci looked at the door. "Who is it?" Redds said.

"Shell!"

Redds opened the door. "Why you ain't come it from your room?"

"I don't know, fuck all that! Guess what!" Shell was excited, like he'd just hit the Powerball.

Redds gave him a confused look. "What's up, joe?"

"Man, I just met a nigga that got bricks out the ass! For the low, too!" Shell said. He went on to tell Redds how he'd met the dude in the blue Polo sweat suit. His name was Calvin, people called him Cali Cal. He was a Crip with a direct connect to Mexican cocaine dealers. He was on the east coast looking for some dealers that were interested in doing business on a major level. Shell had the look of the type of dude he was looking for. Shell's 'get money' look, flashiness, and big betting at the crap tables grabbed Calvin's attention off the top. Calvin overheard Shell talking to a dude he knew from Cleveland that was at the crap table. When Shell was done talking to his homie, Calvin cut into him and told him that they had some things in common.

The first thing that caught Shell's attention was the fact that Calvin told him that he could get him bricks for as low as ten-thousand a brick, depending on how many bricks he could buy at one time. Shell was a little skeptical at first. It wasn't everyday that a stranger cut into him talking about cocaine on a major level. Any other time, Shell would have told a nigga to get the fuck out of his face talking about drug business like that. However, for some reason, Shell got a good vibe from Calvin and decided to hear him out. In Shell's mind, some things were just too good to pass up.

Redds shook his head and smiled. "What are the chances of running into a connect like that?"

"That's what I'm sayin'!"

"So, what you gotta do now?"

"The nigga said all I gotta do is catch a flight out there and we can go from there. He said for starters, he will send something to any address I give him. He said the work can be there overnight."

Redds thought about it for a second. He was concerned about Shell bumping into a stranger that was supposed to be a big deal connect, but he knew that shit like that could happen from time to time. "Well, I say let's see what the nigga can do."

"You wanna holla at him?" Shell asked.

"Sure, let's put this shit in motion." Redds looked back at Necci, and said, "I'll be right back."

"Okay." After Redds and Shell left the room, she thought about how the dude in the red Polo sweat suit watched her. She wondered if he was really who he said he was.

Back on the casino floor, Shell introduced Redds to Calvin. Just like Shell, Redds got a got vibe from Calvin. However, Redds made sure not to let Calvin know too much about him. At the same time, he couldn't be scared to make something shake. If he was going to be scared, there was no reason in meeting Calvin. After talking a little business, Redds got down to talking numbers. Calvin could give them bricks of quality cocaine at $10,000 a brick if they could cop a hundred at a time. That had Donnavan beat by more than $7,000. The only problem was that Redds and Shell couldn't come up with the money to buy a hundred bricks at the time. It would take them a minute and Redds had no problem telling Calvin, who understood.

"Look here," Calvin said, sipping his drink as they stood off to the side a few feet away from the crap table. "I can tell you cats are into getting money. It's written all over you. Here's what I'll do. I'll catch a flight to Cleveland, hang out with you cats there for a few days. Y'all get your money together. I'll have the bricks sent in and we can go from there. We can get together in, let's say, two weeks or so. That'll give me enough time to check you cats out and it'll give you cats enough time to check me out."

"Sounds good to me," Redds said.

"Me too."

"So, you think you guys can have five-hundred grand ready by then?" Calvin asked.

"Yeah, we'll have the money, trust me."

"Cool." Calvin shook hands with Redds and Shell, and sealed the deal.

Two weeks later, snow fell in Cleveland as Redds and Shell pulled up on the east side in a black Jeep Chero-kee and parked behind a blue Chevy Suburban with Okla-homa tags. The truck was clearly a rental. Redds and Shell got out of their ride and got in the Suburban with Calvin.

"Man, it's cold as shit up here," Calvin said. "Next time we meet, it's gon' be in Cali."

Redds and Shell laughed. "Cali sure would be the place to be right about now," Redds said. He could use the sunshine and nice weather. Not to mention, a change of scenery.

"I'd love to come out Cali myself," Shell said. He'd never been on the west coast. "I know it's like heaven out there with all them beaches and shit, movie stars, and fast cars. That's where I need to be."

"And, it's tons of money to be made. It's no place like it. Why don't you guys come out there and kick it with me? I'll fly you out, show you how I do it at home."

"Maybe we will, but let's get down to business right now," Redds said. "We got the money straight."

Calvin smiled. "Okay, I like that. I see you cats held up your end. I held up my end as well. How 'bout you two follow me to my hotel room and we take care of everything like that?"

"No problem," Redds said.

Redds and Shell followed Calvin a short distance to his hotel. When they pulled up and parked, Shell grabbed the duffle bag with the money in it and Redds grabbed the pistol. Although they got a good a good vibe from Calvin, they were on their toes.

Inside the hotel room, there was a beautiful Mexi-can girl lying across the bed with an Uzi beside her when Redds and Shell walked through the door. Calvin smiled when he saw the way they looked at the girl. "Don't mind her," Calvin said. "She's my bodyguard, so to speak."

"She's on her job by all means," Redds said as he glanced at the Uzi.

"Yes, she is," Shell said, looking around the room. There were suitcases beside the bed.

Calvin nodded toward the suitcase, and said, "The coke is right there, you can test it if you want, but I assure you it's the best you will find here on the east coast. I give you my word. May I see the money?" Shell handed him the duffle bag.

Calvin checked the bag and felt safe that it was what it was supposed to be. Redds checked the coke and felt it was what it was supposed to be. Everything was on the up and up.

Calvin looked at Redds, and said, "Very good. Next time, the shipment will be coming to the address you gave me. It will come overnight and all you have to do is have somebody sign for it. If ever there's a problem, all you have to do is call and I will make sure it is taken care of. We will get a lot of money together. I promise you that."

Redds shook Calvin's hand, and said, "Let's make it happen."

Chapter 7

Time passed quickly. By March of 1994, Redds and Shell had stepped it up in the drug game. They brought in one hundred bricks a month between the two of them. They sold weight all over Ohio and the money came in faster than they could count it. They bought homes in Lorain, Ohio, nothing too flashy, but homes nevertheless. Redds never intended to stay in Ohio for months, but time had moved so fast that he got caught up in what was going. He actually thought about moving to L.A. with Necci under an assumed name. On the other hand, Ohio treated him good.

He got money under the radar and never knew it could be done in such a way. In D.C. there was always some bullshit in the mix. However, in Ohio, for some reason, he and Shell had no problems whatsoever and the prices they paid for the coke was far less than the prices they charged for it. They sent money to California and, in return, bricks of cocaine flew into Cleveland. Their operation cranked like a well oiled machine. Redds and Shell had also taken a few trips to L.A. to secure further business deals with Calvin. Their relationship with him turned out to be the best move they'd ever made. Yet and still, aside from how great things went, Redds was still on the run and had the FBI on his back.

Sitting between Necci's legs on the floor in Shell's living room, Redds enjoyed the feeling of her twisting his dreads while they watched TV and smoked weed. He'd began growing them in an attempt to change his appearance. Redds' Sky Pager went off. He checked it and saw that it was a Maryland number followed by his mother's special code as well as 911. A sense of urgency became very present.

Necci saw the look on Redds' face, and said, "What's wrong, who is that?"

"My mother." Redds got up and grabbed his coat. "Take me to a pay phone."

"Okay," Necci said as she grabbed her jacket.

Redds and Necci jumped into the little white Honda Civic that Redds had bought for Necci to get around. They drove thirty minutes out to a pay phone and Redds called the number that Toya hit him from. His mind raced as he wondered what was going on. The only time she paged him was if something was wrong. On top of that, she never used code 911.

"Hello," Toya answered. Redds could tell that she was out in public somewhere from the background sounds.

"Ma, what's up? You okay?" Redds zipped up his Nautica coat to protect himself from the cold wind.

"I just spoke to your lawyer. They indicted y'all to-day. Everybody. I think it was like eleven or twelve people. It's all in the paper and on the news." She spoke fast and frantically.

"Calm down, Ma. We already knew that was going to happen, right?"

"Boy, listen!" Toya snapped. "I know that, too, but that's not what I'm worried about now. The fucking prose-cutor on the damn case is talking about seeking the death penalty. The indictment has over one hundred counts. The murder of the police officer is what has them seeking the death penalty."

Redds started sweating, even though it was cold outside. He got a sick feeling in his stomach just thinking about what she said. The RICO case was one thing, but the death penalty was another monster, it changed the game. Getting out of the country shot back to the top of Redds' priority list. There was no way he could see himself facing the death penalty in anybody's courtroom. "Ma," Redds said, taking a deep breath. "Don't worry. I'll figure this out. Be strong." Redds ended the conversation with his mother and headed back to the car with his mind racing. The world was closing in on him and he could feel it.

On the way back to the house, Redds told Necci the news. She couldn't believe her ears. To her knowledge, D.C. didn't have the death penalty. Redds had to explain to her that the case he was caught up in was a federal joint and the feds could pursue the death penalty.

"So, what do we do now, baby?" Necci asked. It really didn't matter what Redds wanted to do because she was down with it.

Rubbing his chin, Redds said, "I gotta' get all the money I can together and find a way to get us out of the country. I know I been saying that for a while, but these people tryin' to kill us now. I can't go for no shit like that. As long as I got money, I can make us disappear somewhere."

"Whatever you think is best is what we will do. We've been in Ohio for a while. Things have been smooth here, but it may be time for us to keep it movin'."

"You're right, baby." Redds sighed. "I'll figure it out."

The Ibex was a club right off of Georgia Avenue in Northwest D.C., and it was packed with young people from all over the city. The sound of go-go music had the whole club turned up. Back Yard Band did their thing. The females were deep and looked good. A contest had just been won by a bad ass broad that looked like she was out of a Miami strip club. She won five hundred dollars by "poppin' that coochie" and taking off her clothes before sitting on a Moet bottle. The sight was vicious. Dudes threw money on stage, going crazy at the sight.

"Okay, baby girl," Big G said on the mic. "You stealin' the show." Back Yard got back down to business performing a go-go version of Slick Rick's 1988 hit Teenage Love. The club was all the way live. Big G called out hoods. "14th and uh … 14th and uh … 14th and Clifton!" Niggaz from 14th and Clifton raised their hands, putting up the one-four sign. Big G went on to call out other hoods. "35-double-O … 35-double-Oooooo! 640, hey 640! LeDroit Park, LeDroit Park, yeah!"

Ivy, Apple's girl, made her way out of the club and walked down the street to her red BMW 325i. She pulled her hair back into a ponytail as walked. Once she reached her car, she pulled her keys out and unlocked the door. Slowly, a grey Buick .225 with tinted windows pulled up beside her. Ivy looked at the Buick with contempt. *I know these niggaz ain't trying to holla at me at,* she thought.

Suddenly, the passenger side door of the Buick flew open. "Come here, bitch!" a masked gunman hissed as he grabbed her by the hair. Ivy screamed and tried to yank away while clawing at his arms. Playing no games, the gunman bashed her in the face with the butt of his gun and dragged her in the car. She continued to scream and struggle for her life as fear set in.

Inside the car, the gunman pointed the pistol in her face, and said, "Stop making all that fuckin' noise or I'ma put a bullet in your head right now!"

Ivy looked into his eyes and felt that he was not playing with her. She whispered, "What do you want? What did I do? Please, don't hurt me."

"Shut the fuck up, bitch!" the gunman snapped as he eased off his ski mask.

"Top!" Ivy screamed as the fear of God set in. He was the last person she wanted to see. "I swear to God I ain't know they was gon' kill him. I swear … I swear I ain't want that to happen!"

Top had gotten word that Ivy was running around town bragging about getting Jelani killed. As soon as word got to him, he wasted no time making a move. By all means, as far as he was concerned, everybody that had something to do with his cousin's murder was going to pay dearly.

Top punched Ivy in the mouth viciously. "You muthafuckas thought you could kill my fuckin' cousin and I wasn't gon' find out about it!"

Ivy sobbed, knowing that she was in the hands of death. "I'm sorry ... I'm so sorry! I didn't want them to do that. I told them not to do that ..." She broke down and had a sobbing fit. "I swear to God ... I didn't want that to happen."

Placing the barrel of his gun to her forehead, Top said, "Who all was wit' it? Who knew something about it?"

"Apple and Jay, it was Apple and Jay!" she sobbed. "I swear I didn't know they were going to kill him. I really—"

"Stupid-ass bitch!" He smacked her with the pistol again.

"Ahhhh!" she screamed out in pain. "Please, don't kill me ... please ... please!" She sobbed and covered her bloody face.

Top wasn't moved by her tears or cries for mercy. All he could think about was how his cousin had been murdered and left on the sidewalk with his brains blown out. The mere thought of Jelani being shot in the head, and then filled with slugs while lying on the cold ground, enraged Top and he wanted everybody that had something to do with it to pay dearly.

Lil' Man was behind the wheel trying to make sure he drove carefully so as not to attract any police attention. He was down with his man one hundred percent and agreed that everybody that was a part of Jelani's murder should pay dearly, however, the sounds of Ivy in the back of the car pleading for her life got to him. He started to question himself about the whole move to kidnap her and kill her. Nevertheless, he pulled up in a dark parking lot in the woods of Rock Creek Park and parked the car in an isolated corner. Turning off the car and killing the lights, he looked back at Top, and said, "Hurry up, joe. You know them fuckin' park police be out this bitch at night."

Sensing what was about to happen, Ivy screamed and kicked. She knew she had to fight for her life. Top wasn't fazed one bit. He dragged her out of the car by her hair with all of her screaming and kicking. Lil' Man felt sorry for the girl, but knew that she had made her bed and had to lie in it. Top dragged the screaming girl into the darkness of the woods and a second later, two loud gunshots went off. Top jogged out of the woods and jumped back into the car.

Down Lorton, Amir and Croc were back together again. Croc was a tall man that stood six feet three and weighed one hundred and ninety pounds. His dark skin and almost constant scowl made him look dangerous. A number of dudes that were supposed to be tough guys were nothing more than prey for him. He was an official tough guy that put the G in gangster. In prison, he was the kind of guy that strong-armed niggaz and that kept him in maximum security most of his bid. As always, he was back in maximum security for a stabbing that occurred while he pressed a dude for a package of heroin that the dude had gotten while on a visit. The dude wasn't a push over and refused to hand over the drugs. Croc ended up stabbing him close to twenty times, almost killing him. In the end, Croc got away with the stabbing, but an informant told on him, and he was sent to maximum security and faced at least another 18-months behind the Wall.

Locked in his cell rolling a jay of weed, Croc sat on his bunk watching his five inch color TV. At 35-years-old, he smoked weed like a young nigga and had to have it. It made his time go by faster. Amir walked up to his cell reading an article in The Washington Post about Redds and the Kennedy Street Crew. The look on Amir's face was a stressful one. He was really worried about what was in store for his son. Folding the paper and putting it under his arm, Amir looked in Croc's cell, and said, "What's up, slim?"

"Layin' back, you know me, partner. How you doin'?" Croc sat the jay down and walked up to the bars to talk to Amir. Leaning against the bars, he used his small plastic mirror to look up and down the long tier.

Amir sighed. "They talkin' 'bout seekin' the death penalty against Reggie and his men. The feds ain't playin'."

Croc shook his head and sighed. He could feel Amir's pain. "Shit way different nowadays. "When we was comin' up in the streets, the feds wasn't comin' at us wit' all this new shit. They takin' things to a whole new level wit' this RICO shit."

The two had, in fact, done things in the 70s and 80s that would have had them doing life in the feds if they would have fallen into a federal investigation like the one Redds and his men were the targets of.

Amir sighed and rubbed his chin. "These young dudes today are wilder than we were. They don't know how to stay under the radar. For what we used to get ten or fifteen years for, they gettin' life sentences. It's crazy. In a minute they are going to have so many of our young brothers locked up that it's going to be no men on the streets to reproduce. It's really sad. This RICO act thing wasn't even meant to be used against street crews for real. It was meant to be used on mob dudes and whatnot, but since it's an easy way to send our youth to prison, they using it clean the inner cities. It's amazing."

"They railroading the young brothers wit' all that bullshit," Croc said. "I fucks wit' the young dude, Antone and them. You know they got one of them RICO joints. Tone was tellin' me how they work that shit there on a nigga. They be bringing up old street beefs. They even be bringing up old murders and shit that a nigga done beat in court before. That's some wild shit when you can beat a murder in court and still get life for it in federal court if they bring it back up on a RICO indictment. It's a no win situation."

Amir rubbed his thick beard and sighed again. All he could do was call on Allah and ask for the Creator to protect Redds. His son was going to need all the help he could get.

Over D.C. Jail, Dontae and Heavy, along with a few other niggaz from Kennedy Street that were also under indictment on the RICO conspiracy, held it down by all means. Most of the Kennedy Street Crew defendants were locked down in segregation units because the administration didn't want them in general population. The Kennedy Street Crew defendants had a number of outstanding beefs from the streets that boiled over inside the jail. Most of the beefs were due murders that had been committed over the years that were just coming to light because of the indictments coming down. In the months spent over the jail, Dontae had to stab three different niggaz behind beefs that came from things that went down on the streets. D.C. was far too small for enemies to coincide. When someone was murdered in D.C., the victim always had peoples somewhere. With all that said, Dontae didn't give a fuck about who was supposed to be somebody. His attitude was that he wasn't ducking anything that came his way. He was a man on the streets and he planned to be the same way on the inside, no matter what. One thing his father told him that always stuck with him was that a man had to always stand on his feet no matter what he faced in life. In Dontae's eyes, only cowards lived on their knees.

Heavy was housed on the same tier as Dontae. They were both in North-1, which was a cellblock that housed the worst of the worst. Heavy was in the block for beating the shit out of a nigga that had tried to stab him as he got out of the shower. He not only beat the shit out of the joker, but took his knife as well. For the most part, Heavy took the whole case harder than everybody else. It was stressing him out. On top of all of that, his baby's mother, Erica, was acting up on him. She wanted him to make a deal with the government and cooperate against his homies. Heavy wasn't trying to hear anything like that. He would never go against his men. It was death before dishonor with him. His baby's mother accused him of picking his men over his son. She told him that if his men were more important than being in his son's life, then he didn't need to ever see his son again.

Heavy couldn't believe that Erica had no understanding of honor and loyalty. "Fuck them niggaz!" she said over the phone. "Tell on they ass and come home. They don't give a fuck about you. They don't give a fuck about your son. You really want to face the death penalty for them niggaz when your son is out here and needs you?

You's a dumb mothafucka if you let some code take you away from us." Those words from his baby's mother played over and over in Heavy's head. He lost all respect for her and if it wasn't for his son, he would have cut her off completely.

Some of the other Kennedy Street Crew defendants didn't hold it down like men. In fact, they caught hell all over the jail. Some of them got caught in blocks were their enemies outnumbered them; at those times it was open season and they seemed to get the short end of the stick in the worst ways. Some of them even checked in on P.C. Dontae was fucked up about that and he disowned every nigga from his neighborhood that checked in on P.C. He called them cowards and lost all respect for them.

Locked in his cell thinking about Erica, Heavy paced back and forth steaming mad. He didn't know what to do. He felt helpless.

Dontae walked up to his cell wearing a blue jail jumper, and said, "What's up, big boy? You alright?"

"My baby mother got me fucked up, young." Heavy went on to tell Dontae how Erica made him hate her. He never thought he could hate her. After all, he loved her with all of his heart before he got locked up.

Disgusted with what Heavy was telling him about Erica, Dontae said, "Look, slim, I know that's your baby's mother, but she ain't cut from the same cloth we cut from. If she was my baby's mother, I would cut her ass off ASAP if she tried to get me to tell on my men. I ain't feelin' that shit at all. She don't understand our struggle. She wasn't talkin' all that hot shit when you was on the bricks gettin' money and makin' sure she was good, and them fuckin' bills was bein' paid. I don't honor that shit at all."

"I know, slim!" Heavy shook his head. "She tryin' to use my son against me, she tryin' to get me to cooperate wit' them peoples by using my son against me. I can't believe that shit."

Moving closer to the bars of Heavy's cell, Dontae said, "Big homie, we over here fighting for our lives. You gotta' put that shit out of your mind. It's going to drive you crazy of you don't. I know it's hard, I know it's hurting you, but if you don't focus on what we facin', you gon' lose everything, maybe even your life. The most important thing at the time is this case we fightin'. Nothing else can come between the fight at hand. We can never lay down, no matter what!"

Across town, inside the U.S. Attorney's Office, Assistant U.S. Attorney James Burling sat behind his desk looking over the Kennedy Street Crew's RICO indictment. He was pleased with the work that had been done during the investigation. He was sure that he would get numerous convictions once the trial was over. The Justice Department had picked the right man for the job as far as he was concerned. Burling's entire life was all about the Kennedy Street case at this point. He bet his career on it, so to speak. It would make him the top prosecutor in the town if he was able to get the convictions to stick. For the past few months, he only got three or four hours of sleep at night.

He was up at all hours of the night going over every little detail of the case, making sure he had all of his ducks in a row. He studied case law from the top to the bottom, making sure there was no way any defense attorney could back door him in court. He had his shit together and was ready for war. He made all kinds of deals with informants to make sure the story the jury got was the one that he needed them to get. He made deals with witnesses under the table in return for their testimony. There was nothing that would stand in his way.

The phone in his office rang and snapped him out of his thoughts. It was the call he'd been waiting for. He smiled as he answered. It was good news and it made his day. When the call was over, he spun around in his office chair and looked out of the window. It was a nice clear day outside. "Today is a great day," he said out loud. "Things are moving along very well." The Attorney General's office had just given the okay for the death penalty against three defendants in the Kennedy Street Crew case. Redds, Dontae, and Heavy would face death when they had their day in court. If Burling had anything to do with it, they were surely going to pay for their crimes with their lives.

Lil' Man and Top had fucked up. Fucked up bad. They tried to hit Apple and missed, and he wasn't to be played with. If somebody was going to kill him, they needed to be on their A game and they needed to be swift and deadly, somewhat like grabbing a snake by its head. Now, Lil' Man and Top had prices on their heads.

When Lil' Man and Top plotted Apple's murder, they wanted to do it in a way that Apple wouldn't see it coming, therefore, Lil' Man hit Apple with a story about how he and Top were no longer friends, and that he needed to make a move with him that didn't include Top. Apple agreed to meet Lil' Man. When he showed up, Lil' Man and Top were supposed to ambush Apple on sight. However, Apple had been on high alert ever since Ivy had been murdered and found in Rock Creek Park. He didn't go anywhere without Jay and a few of his young killers on deck.

As fate would have it, when the move was supposed to go down, Apple had turned onto a dark, tree lined side street behind Tokoma Rec. on 4th Street Northwest. He spotted Lil' Man's truck and pulled up in his gold twin turbo with Jay and Lil' Moon behind him in a black Nissan Pathfinder. Apple had a sixth sense and seemed to be able to smell a move coming. His gut feeling told him something was wrong. Lil' Man got out of his truck to holla at Apple, but Apple told him not to get in the car with him. Instead, he told him to holla at Jay about business. Lil' Man felt like the tables were about to turn. He wasted no time pulling his Glock with the 35 shot clip and opened fire on Apple's car, hitting him a few times. Apple slammed the car in gear and took off flying down the street damn near out of control. Lil' Man continued to pop at the back of the car.

Lil' Moon jumped out of the passenger side of the Pathfinder and started firing. Lil' Man and Lil' Moon traded shots at close range as Lil' Man tried to take cover behind his truck. As Jay jumped out of the driver side of the Pathfinder, Top sprang from the bushes across the street and began spraying his AR-15. Jay got low and fired back. Bullets were flying in all directions. Outgunned, Jay and Lil' Moon managed to get back in the Pathfinder and take off, taking heavy fire from Lil' Man and Top. From that point on, the beef was on sight.

Focused on what needed to be done now that they'd fucked up on the hit on Apple, Lil' Man and Top were riding along the beltway in a big, green Mercury Grand Marquis with a comrade of theirs by the name of Lil' Reel. They were heading back to D.C. after buying some bullet-proof vests in Charles County, MD. Lil' Reel was telling Lil' Man and Top how the word in the streets was that Apple had money out for anybody that could kill them.

Smoking a thick blunt, Lil' Reel said, "My man, Face, fuck wit' a bitch that be fuckin' wit' that nigga Jay. She heard the nigga tellin' another nigga that Apple had forty-thousand for either one of y'all."

Top shrugged. "I don't even give a fuck for real. I'm gon' hunt all them niggaz down before I let anybody do anything to me or Lil' Man. I'm 'bout to start hittin' moth-ers and baby mothers, and all that wild shit. They gon' wish they never fucked wit' me. Watch what I tell you, young."

Top's words were harsh and from the heart. Every-one in the car knew that he meant what he said and that he would put them into action.

Lil' Reel said, "Y'all gotta' find out where that nigga Apple layin' his head. You not gon' run him down out in the streets."

"Yeah, I know," Top said. "We gon' find that nigga, but until we do, we gon' fuck shit up all around his bitch-ass."

Lil' Man cut in, and said, "Jay gon' be easier to run down than Apple. You know he think he can't be touched, so he gon' still be out in the open. If we burn his ass up, that's gon' be half the battle."

Top nodded. "That's what we gon' do."

Redds and Necci were cuddled up, naked in the bed with the TV on 60 Minutes. Redds really wasn't paying much attention to the TV, he was thinking about the fake IDs he'd managed to get for them. They were Ohio IDs and they were state issued. They could pass any inspection in the U.S., and that was exactly what Redds needed to pull off what he had planned.

Reaching over and grabbing his ID off of the nightstand, Redds took a good look at it. It was official and it gave him a sense of security. He was sure he could survive a traffic stop with it. He could board a plane with it. The next move was to get passports. That would allow them to flee the country. Sitting his ID down, Redds picked up Necci's, and said, "These IDs really help out a lot."

Necci looked up, and said, "Yeah, they really do. I'm glad you were able to get them. That takes a lot of stress off."

"No bullshit." Redds kissed her on the forehead. He looked her in the eyes and was thankful to have soldier by his side. Necci kept him on point, kept him on his toes, and never allowed him to forget what was most important. "I don't know what I would do without you, baby. You know that?"

Necci kissed his lips. "I feel the same way. I don't know what I'd do without you. You mean the world to me. That's on everything I love, baby. Never forget that. I got your back. Always."

Redds smiled and sat the ID back on the nightstand. Turning his attention back to Necci, he gave her a tight hug and held her close to him. "I love you, girl. I will always love you. Don't you ever forget that."

"How could I?" she asked as she rolled on top of him.

Redds smiled as his hands rubbed her back all the way down to her smooth behind. He kissed her again, sliding his tongue inside her mouth passionately. Light moans escaped Necci's mouth. Making love to Redds was all she wanted at the time. Feeling him grow hard between her legs, Necci eased onto his erection and slowly slid down on him. "Ahhhhh ... yeah," she gasped. The satisfying feeling of her man being inside her made her wet. Redds pulled her down on him gently as he slid in and out of her wetness. Her moans grew louder as she rode him. "Oh, yes, baby ... I love you ... I love you so much ..." Necci bit her bottom lip and moaned louder, loving the feeling of Redds sliding in and out of her.

"Ssssss ... damn, baby." Redds pulled her down toward his thrusting. "Damn, you so tight, baby." Redds continued to thrust up inside her as she fucked him back.

"Oh, my God, I'm 'bout to cum, baby. Uh, uh, uh, uh, uhhhhhh ... shit!" she called out, feeling her climax coming on strong.

Redds began to thrust up inside of her faster and deeper as he felt her begin to shake tremendously. He could tell she was about to cum. The mere thought took him closer to his climax. "Aaarrrrgggghhh ..." he grunted, fucking her harder.

"I'm cummin', oh, my God, I'm cummin' so fuckin' hard, baby!" Necci slammed her body down on Redds over and over. As she rode him faster and harder, it made him explode.

"Damn!" Redds shouted as he came inside of her.

"Damn, I love you, baby. I love you so much," Necci said as she rested her head on Redds' chest. Out of breath, she sighed, and said, "Damn, that was so good. So, so, so good ..." She laughed a little bit, enjoying the feeling of Redds' dying erection still inside of her.

Redds smiled and shook his head. Sex with Necci was always out of this world. "You somethin' else, baby."

Tired and satisfied, they laid side by side in the bed enjoying the moment and exploring their own thoughts. Despite the moment, things were very serious and uncertain for them both. As much as Redds tried his best to maintain control of his situation, he was not in control. He played a game of cat and mouse with the feds, and that game was stressing him out tremendously.

Thinking about his plans for the future, Redds knew what he had to do to stay ahead of the FBI. He'd wasted no time putting certain things into motion to get out of the country. There were two people that he knew could help him and they were Calvin and Donnavan. They both had connections outside of the U.S. and they both could get Redds support and assistance. Being as though Redds was now under indictment for a death penalty case, Calvin and Donnavan understood that Redds had his back against the wall and they were willing to help him out as best as they could. Calvin fronted Redds one-hundred extra bricks in order for him to be able to put his hands his on some real cash. Redds did just that.

Necci could almost read Redds' mind and knew what he was thinking about. Rubbing his chest, she said, "So, once we get to Panama, we gon' already have a place to stay and all that, huh?"

Redds smiled. "You must be reading my mind." Necci laughed. "Yeah, we gon' be straight once we get there."

"You seemed worried about it a little bit."

"I'm somewhat worried about the whole situation. You already know how serious all this shit is. Anyway, once we get them passports, things will feel a little bit better. You know?"

"Yeah, it is what it is. Try not to worry yourself. You on top of your business."

Redds nodded in agreement. "You right, baby." He kissed her again.

Chapter 8

The distinct fanning sound of a money counting machine filled the living room of one of the stash houses that Redds and Shell had on the east side of Elyria. They had been hard at work for days, moving and grooving. Now, they were taking turns feeding stacks of cash into the machine as they sat on an old sofa.

Wrapping a thick brown rubber band around another ten-thousand-dollar stack of money, Redds rubbed his forehead, and said, "I'm lookin' at four-hundred so far." He stuffed another stack of money of cash into the machine. "What you lookin' at over there?"

"Uh ... four ... four-twenty-five right now." Shell pointed at stacks of money on the floor.

Quickly calculating numbers in his head like a gifted accountant, Redds added up the money lying around at the time. Within the last few days, they had counted just over a million dollars in drug money. Neither of them had ever seen anything close to that amount. The plug they had with Calvin was a plug like never before. When he told them that he could make them rich overnight, he wasn't bullshitting. He really could produce whatever kind of shipment they could handle. One-hundred bricks, a thousand bricks, whatever they could move, he could get and in turn, they could control the prices.

Redds looked at Shell, and said, "We killin' the game right now. I wish we would have had this lick a long time ago. We would've been retired somewhere by now."

"No bullshit!" Shell laughed. "It's all good 'cause the way things are going right now, we still gon' be able to retire in no time."

"I feel you. How much work we got left?"

Shell got and went into the back room. He returned, and said, "We sittin' on forty-four joints right now, cuz. We lookin' good. Once I take this ride to Cleveland, we gon' be down to 'bout twenty-four. It's gon' be time to hit Calvin again."

Redds nodded. "We been on top of shit, so that's a good thing."

They finished counting the money as they talked about their game plan. Later the same night, Redds and Shell cruised up West Avenue in Shell's candy-apple red '72 Chevy Chevelle SS with Nas coming through the speakers. They were on their way to Akron to make a move. They'd been on the grind all day and had moved fifteen bricks so far. Some good men that Shell dealt with from Columbus had taken the trip to Elyria to cop the bricks at $25,000.

As Nas rapped about keeping it real with his homies that were locked up, Redds thought about Dontae and Heavy. He wondered how they were doing. He knew they could take care of themselves, but he still thought about them every day and hoped they'd make it out okay. Thinking about what life would be like for him and Necci in another country, Redds felt bad for leaving his men to face death alone. However, there was nothing he could really do about it. If it was him in jail and they were free and on the run, he would want them to get the fuck out of the country as well.

While Redds was in deep thought, Shell was busy talking to him about money. Noticing Redds wasn't paying attention, Shell said, "Man, you ain't hear a damn word I just said, cuz."

Redds smiled. "Damn, my bad, what you say? I was somewhere else."

"What's on your mind, cuz?"

"All this shit I got hangin' over my head." Redds rubbed his temple, trying to ease the tension. "I'm not tryin' to let the FBI get their hands on me. I got to get out of the country. If I go to jail, shit ain't gon' be pretty. I know they wanna hang me."

"Cuz, I feel you on that. We gon' get this dough and you gon' be able to disappear like Frank Matthews, never to be heard from again. You hear me?"

Redds nodded, wishing things would be as easy as Frank Matthews, the legendary gangster that disappeared in the 1970s with a lady friend and $20 million in cash. "Shell, if I could disappear with twenty-million in cash, I would never look back. Believe that, cuz."

"I don't know about twenty-million, but I'm sure you can get out the country wit' a million or two the way shit is goin' right now."

"Let's hope so."

Back in D.C. at a stop light on 14th Street two nights prior, Top was sitting in his red '94 Taurus station wagon watching his back when he spotted an old bucket with tinted windows turn onto to 14th Street coming off of Harvard Street. Something didn't feel right. Top listened to the feeling in his gut. He tried to pass the car in front of him while gripping the MAC-10 on his lap. Gunfire erupted as flames spit out the side of the old bucket. Top fired out of the window of his car as he took off flying up 14th Street.

The bucket gave chase as Top fired out the window behind him. A gunman in the passenger side of the bucket continued to fire at Top's car. It was a high-speed shootout that continued for blocks. With every turn he made, the bucket kept up with him. The person that was driving the bucket was a good driver and kept up with Top every step of the way. Making his way to First and Kennedy Street with the bucket still hot on his tail, Top flew into a dark alley where his men, Ben and Karim, were posted. Top jumped out of his car, leaving it blocking the entrance to the alley, and told his men that niggaz were chasing him, trying to kill him, and that he was out of bullets. Ben and Karim had an AK-47 stashed behind the dumpster and directed Top to it. Top grabbed the chopper and as soon as the bucket bent the corner to enter the alley, Top sprayed it, sending bullets through the windshield. The driver of the old bucket slammed it in reverse and tried to make a run for it. Top ran behind the car, still spraying it with bullets and caused it to crash into a light pole at the end of the block on 2nd Street. With the car crashed into a light pole, Top ran down on it and waved the chopper side to side, spraying the two occupants with the rest of the bullets in the banana clip. When the AK-47 would fire no more, Top took off running, leaving two bodies behind.

Top's brush with death changed the way he looked at things. It made him pay attention to the fact that nobody was untouchable. With the attempt on his life fresh on his mind as he rode up Georgia Avenue in an old, brown box Chevy Caprice Classic with Lil' Man, Top was focused on murder. He planned to make everybody close to Apple pay for the attempt on his life. Nothing would stand in his way. A broad had beeped Lil' Man and told him that Jay's black Jaguar was parked outside of Crisfield's seafood restaurant.

It was like a dream come true for Top to get such information. The plan was to kill Jay right inside the restaurant, right in front of everybody. Murdering Jay in such a way would send a strong message to everybody that wanted to side with Apple that shit was very real. Top was at a point where he didn't give a fuck anymore. On top of that, he was sure that Jay wouldn't expect a nigga to come inside the restaurant and kill him in front a bunch of people. Jay was used to doing all the killing. Never would he think that someone would bring it to his door step in such a way.

As Top and Lil' Man got close to Crisfield's, they pulled on their ski masks and checked their assault rifles behind the tinted windows. Shit was about to go down. Lil'

Man parked the car in front of the restaurant and turned off the car. Top spotted Jay sitting close to the front door.

"There he go right there," Top said. If he wanted, he could have shot Jay through the window.

"It look like they on their way out right now," Lil' Man said, ready to make his move. "You wanna' get they ass comin' out the door?"

Top thought about it for a second. "Let's get they ass right now."

"Let's work."

A daylight killing across the D.C. line in Maryland was no cakewalk. It had to be done quick, fast, and in hurry or Montgomery County police would be all over the place in seconds. With that in mind, Lil' Man and Top wasted no time. They hopped out of the car just as Jay and his crew walked out of the front door. Fully automatic weapons went off, sounding like an Independence Day celebration.

Jay and his crew never had a chance, they were cut down in seconds in broad daylight like a mob hit out of the 1920s. Horrified customers inside the restaurant looked on in disbelief as they got a firsthand view of what an inner city slaying was all about. After spraying the bodies one last time, Lil' Man and Top jumped back in their car and went flying back across the D.C. line. Their work was done, and Jay and his two men were left dead on the sidewalk, riddled with bullets.

Early the next morning, Lil' Man stepped out of the hotel where he'd spent the night and found his tire flat.

"Shit!" he snapped, looking around the parking lot.

He'd checked into a hotel in Columbia, Maryland to get away from the city for a second after the triple murder outside of Crisfield's. The murder was all over the news and had the streets talking. No one could believe that Jay and his men were gunned down without even getting a shot off. It was a perfect hit.

In a rush to get back to the city, Lil' Man began changing the flat on the old white Mercury Cougar he was driving. Apple crossed his mind as he changed the tire. He knew for sure that he and Top had to find him and put an end to the beef before someone caught up with them and bucked their number. It was a kill or be killed game they were in, and the streets took no prisoners at all.

Death was always near. Live by the gun, die by the gun. Lil' Man didn't see the figure with the bandanna wrapped around his face creeping up behind him with a Tec-9 at his side. The D.C. area was so small that someone always knew someone somewhere. Just like a girl spotted Jay's car at Crisfield's, a girl spotted Lil' Man at the hotel and sent word back to Apple. Hearing something behind him, Lil' Man spun around with the crowbar in his hand and swung it at the gunman. In a flash and a burst of gunfire, 9mm slugs hit Lil' Man in the face and chest, killing him instantly. His body fell to the ground lifelessly. The killer stood over him, and hit him close to fifteen more times in the face and chest. The sound of gunfire alerted hotel security. Two guards ran in their direction. The gunman wasted no time turning in their direction and firing shots, making the guards take cover. After firing shots at security, the gunman ran to the end on the parking lot and jumped in a waiting Corvette. As soon as he was inside, the car took off flying.

The driver looked at the gunman, and said, "You dogged his ass?"

"Crushed his ass," Lil' Moon said as he pulled the bandanna off of his face. "He good as gone, that's closed casket shit there ,my nigga. Top gon' get his next."

South Park basketball court was packed. It was a beautiful day outside, warm, not hot at all, and there wasn't a cloud in the sky. It was one of those days that brought everybody outside. Redds was no exception. He had to get out of the house and get some fresh air. Running a few games of basketball was the order of the day. Redds, Shell, and some dudes from Wilkes Villa got in some good rec. No bullshit or egos interfered with the games. After close to an hour, they'd ran two games of whole court. Redds did his thing, shakin' and bakin'. Some of the Ohio dudes called him Allen Iverson due to his killer crossover and wicked jump shot.

After their third game, the dudes took a break. Redds walked to Shell's Chevelle, wiping sweat from his face with his sweat-soaked T-shirt. Grabbing an ice-cold bottle of water from the cooler, Redds took a sip. He then reached in the passenger seat and grabbed his beeper.

Necci was supposed to beep him when she returned from Cleveland with Angie, the girls had gone shopping. When he looked at it, he saw that his mother had beeped him over and over with code #911 behind it. Again, she called from a Maryland number. For some reason, Redds got a terrible feeling in his gut. It felt like something was wrong back home. Wasting no time, he got Shell to take him to a pay phone.

"Hello!" Toya answered. The sound of thick traffic was in the background. It sounded like she was close to the highway.

"What's up, Ma? You okay?" Redds asked as he rubbed his hands through his dreads. He braced himself for the bad news.

"Baby, look, I can't really talk long," Toya said as she nervously looked around to make sure she hadn't been followed. The FBI had been on her back like she was under investigation. They had been sitting in front of her house all day and night in a white cable van like she didn't know who they were. In order to shake the tail they had on her, she had to enter the mall, go in and out of stores, and then sneak out of the back. All that to have a quick conversation with her son.

"Ma, what's wrong?" Redds asked, impatiently. He had no idea what he was to hear next, but he knew it was going to be bad news. Only bad news came from D.C. at this point in his life.

In a low tone, Toya said, "Lil' Man got killed this morning. It's all over the news. They say he was involved in some big drug war."

Redds sighed and shook his head in disbelief. The news of Lil' Man's death hit hard like a mule kick to the gut. Aside from the pain that he felt upon hearing the news, Redds knew that Necci was going to be distraught. "What happened, Ma?"

"I'm not sure. You are going to have to talk to Top. I'm sure he knows what's going on out there in the streets. Them boys are caught up in some very serious stuff. I don't even see them anymore. Anyway, you need to find a way to get Necci back home. Her family needs her."

With another sigh, Redds said, "Okay, I got that. I will deal wit' that. I'll have her back in town by tomorrow—"

"Reggie!" Toya snapped, cutting him off. "You can't risk coming back here, under no circumstances. You hear me? Don't be a fool. Them peoples are looking for you around every corner. You won't last fifteen minutes in this area. You are one of the most wanted people in this city."

"Ma, I know that."

"Ma shit! Make no mistake, if you try to come back here with Necci, you are going to jail. The FBI is all over the place. Anywhere that you know somebody, they have men watching the place. They are not playing, they want you bad. They know what's going on out here in these streets. They know Necci is on the run with you. They know her little brother was just murdered and they are expecting

Necci to come back to town for the funeral. Don't do anything stupid."

"Ma, don't worry. I'm on top of my situation. I'm
not dumb. I got this. Aside from that, let's get off the
phone. You will hear from me real soon." Redds looked
over his shoulder and noticed a police car coming down the
street. He turned his back. "Ma, I gotta go. Be safe."
Redds hung up.

Shell was on point and watched the police car as
well. He was pleased to see Redds on his way back to the
car. They had no time for any slip-ups. Redds got in with a
concerned look on his face. Shell could tell that something
was very wrong. "What's wrong, cuz?"

Redds shook his head in disbelief. He was at a loss
for words. "They killed my little man back home."

"Damn, folk. I'm sorry to hear that."

"It's Necci's little brother, Lil' Man. She's gon' be
crushed when I tell her." Redds sighed again. "I don't know
how to tell her what happened. She's going to have a fit
about this shit. Lil' Man was more than a little brother to
her." Redds shook his head again and slammed his fist
against the dashboard. "Fuck!" he shouted.

Shell could feel Redds' pain.

"Take me back to the house. I gotta' tell Necci
what happened," Redds said as his eyes began to water. He
wished there was some kind of way he could have protect-
ed Lil' Man from his fate.

Shell started the car and headed back to the house.
"I know Necci is gon' have to go back home, you want me
to take her back to D.C.?"

Redds shrugged. He was uncertain about what he
wanted to do. "I'm not sure how I want to deal wit' it for
real. I'll figure it out after I talk to her."

"Whatever you do, I hope you not thinkin' about going back to D.C. wit' her. You do know that you can't do no shit like that."

"I know that, but you don't know Necci. Ain't nobody gon' be able to comfort her or deal wit' her when she find out what happened to her brother. She's going to need me and no matter what, I'm going to have to be there for her."

Shell shook his head. "I don't want nothin' to happen to you, cuz. You got a lot on the line and Necci knows that."

"I'll figure it out," Redds said. He turned and looked out of the window, trying to collect his thoughts.

Necci walked into the house with her arms filled with shopping bags. Redds sat on the sofa smoking weed, deep in thought. Something wasn't right and Necci picked up on it as soon as she walked in the door. Redds was in the house with no lights on, no TV on, no radio on, or anything. That wasn't like him. "What's wrong?" Necci asked.

Redds took a deep breath and got straight to the point. "Lil' Man got killed this mornin', Necci. My mother just told me a little while ago."

Necci's eyes got wide as her body went numb. She couldn't believe what she'd just heard. It wasn't making sense to her. She fell to her knees and began to cry. "Noooooooooo!" she screamed. "Oh, my God, nooooooooooo! Tell me it ain't true!" she sobbed.

Redds got up and held her in his arms. "I'm so sorry, baby." He tried to comfort her, but she continued to sob uncontrollably. He held her tightly as she cried in his arms.

"Who did it?" she shouted. "Who the fuck did it?"

"I'm not sure yet," Redds said.

"Noooooooooo, not my baby! Noooooooooooo!" she shouted. "You gotta find out who killed my brother. You gotta find out for me!"

"I will, trust me, you know I will find out," Redds assured her.

"They can't get away wit' it. They gotta pay, Redds. Them muthafuckas gotta pay for what they did to my brother."

"Let me worry about that, Necci. Don't worry about it."

"I gotta' go back home, Redds."

"I know, I know, I got you."

Redds sat on the floor holding her in his arms until her sobs died down.

The next day, rubbing his finger on the trigger of the smoke-grey MAC-10 on his lap as he drove along the Beltway, all Top could think about was Lil' Man. He felt like he had let his man down. He felt like if he'd been with him watching his back, nobody would have been able to sneak up on him and shoot him in the face and chest. Top kept telling Lil' Man that they shouldn't split up, but Lil' Man kept talking about how he had some things to take care of. Top never heard from his partner again. It had been years since Top had cried tears, according to his memory. However, Lil' Man's murder caused Top to shed tears. The pain was deep. He'd lost a brother from another mother. Top's only mission in life, at the time, was to find Apple and put a bullet right between his eyes.

Adjusting the heavy bulletproof vest that he was wearing, Top pulled into a busy gas station in Fort Washington, MD. He parked on the side by the air pump and looked around for any signs of foul play. With all that was going on, he was on high alert. Nobody could catch him slipping at the time.

Across the street in the shadows, Redds slid the sleeve of his black leather jacket back and checked his watch. It was 8:41 p.m. For a few moments, Redds studied the gas station, making sure everything was cool. He didn't think Top would cross him and set him up for the feds, but he still had to be sure that the feds weren't following Top without his knowledge. With no signs of the feds, Redds pulled his black L.A. Kings baseball cap down snug over his dreads, pulled his hoodie over his head, and crossed the street against traffic. Walking up on Top's station wagon, Redds tapped on the window. Top unlocked the door and let Redds in.

"What's up, young?" Redds said as he shut the door and glanced at the MAC-10 on Top's lap. He could tell that Top had aged a lot since he'd last laid eyes on him. The teenager looked like he hadn't slept in days. He also looked like a man at war. His face told a story of a young man that faced death every day.

Shaking his head with a sigh, Top didn't want to look at Redds. He was dealing with tons of guilt behind Lil' Man's murder. Deep inside, Top blamed himself. They were each other's keeper. Looking over at Redds, Top said, "Shit fucked up on this, big homie. I don't know no other way to put it to you." Top pulled off as he spoke.

"Youngin', why y'all ain't tell me what the fuck y'all was goin' through down here? You know how wicked Apple is. I would have extended my hand. Y'all know that."

"On the real, we felt like you had your own problem, plus we were tryin' to handle the shit on our own. We was crushin' shit. I don't know how Lil' Man let them catch him slippin' like that," Top said as he drove. "We had them niggaz, young. We was crushin' they ass every chance we got, but we missed when we tried to hit Apple. He put money on our heads and niggaz was trying to kill us every time we turned around. Them niggaz started hiding out and we couldn't find them. Meanwhile, nigga was still trying to kill us. We had to start hittin' they men and niggaz they fuck wit'."

"I feel you. I'm not going to hit you with one of them I told you so talks. It is what it is now. All we can do is deal wit' it," Redds said.

They pulled up in front of a townhouse that Donnavan was in the process of selling. Redds and Top entered the house where Necci was in the living room watching TV. Her eyes were still red and puffy from crying. Her anger and pain was written all over her face. At first, Top didn't want to face her, but he knew he had to. He had to man up and tell her what had gone down.

Looking at Top, Necci said, "Who did it, Top? Who killed my brother?"

Top took a deep breath, and said, "I'm not sure who pulled the trigger, but we had a beef with the nigga Apple. He had money on our heads. He called the shot, but I'm sure who really did the killing. It ain't no telling. However it go, he's responsible. That's who I'm looking for. At the same time, the streets talk, you know that, somebody gon' talk about who pulled the trigger on Lil' Man and I'm gon' put they ass in the dirt."

Necci nodded. Top went on to tell her and Redds everything that had gone on since they'd been in Ohio. When he finished telling them all the details, all Necci could do was shed tears as she thought about her brother.

Rubbing her back, Redds said, "Don't worry about who killed your brother. Me and Top gon' take care of that. All you gotta' do is worry about layin' your brother to rest while you are here. Okay, baby?"

Shaking her head as tears rolled down her face, Necci said, "Make them bitches pay, make them pay wit' their life. I don't care what has to be done. I want them bitch niggaz dead!"

"They gon' die!" Top said. "Don't worry about that. They livin' in they last days."

For the next two days, Redds and Top were on a mission. Redds had checked with a few of his people and found out through Donnavan where Apple laid his head. Donnavan and Apple had been cool at one time, but being as though Apple was Donnavan's only competition in town, it would help his cause if Apple was taken out of the picture. Foul shit, but it was how some niggaz played the game. Redds and Top drove along the beltway in a dark blue Pontiac Firebird. Sitting in the passenger seat, Redds was focused. His mind was made up that he would never be taken alive by law enforcement. Top was in agreement. The plan was to shoot on sight if the police got on their back for anything.

Cutting his eyes at Redds, Top said, "You think this nigga gon' be here?"

"We gon' see. Donnavan said this should be a sure thing, so we gon' see what's up." Redds looked down at the Browning 9mm in his lap and wondered how it would sound when it went off with the silencer on it.

"This nigga is like a ghost, young. Me and Lil' Man used to look for this nigga all night sometimes. We would know all the bitches he was fuckin' and still couldn't find him. Even when we smoked his girl, we still couldn't get to his ass."

Redds nodded. "You gotta' really be up on shit to get niggaz like Apple. You not gon' just run into niggaz like him at 7-Eleven, you know what I'm sayin'?"

"I feel you," Top said, paying close attention to the rear view mirror.

A short while later, Top pulled into a complex of townhomes and parked in the back of the dark parking lot. He and Redds pulled on their ski masks and black leather gloves. It was game time. "We gon' cut through the woods," Redds said as they got out of the car.

"I'm wit' you," Top said as he looked around to see if anyone was paying attention to them and what they were doing. The coast was clear.

They cut through woods, guns out, and came out behind a group of nice homes with huge backyards. The homes looked like something worthy of MTV Cribs. Creeping like burglars, Top and Redds hopped the fence of the house they were looking for. Just as Donnavan said, two pit bulls attacked; they charged out of the darkness like trained killers. Their vocal cords were cut so they didn't bark. That was how Apple wanted them. He wanted them to attack anyone that entered the yard without warning. Quickly, Redds and Top let off shots from their silenced weapons, killing the dogs instantly. The first line of defense was breached with no problem. They continued toward the back of the house. There were bars on all ground level windows. Walking around to the side of the house, they went down the steps that led to a sliding door that didn't have bars on it. Stuffing his pistol in his waistband, Redds pulled out a knife and cut the glass out of the window frame. He knew what he was doing. He and Dontae used to break into stores and houses down Georgetown when they were young. Making sure he didn't set off any alarms, Redds carefully finished the job. Without a sound, Redds and Top sat the large plate of glass on the ground and made their way inside.

Being extremely careful, they made their through the dark basement, and up to the first floor with their guns out and ready to fire. One wrong move and they would dead men. One the first floor, the light was on in the kitchen. They checked it and saw that the kitchen was clear with the exception of two unfinished meals. The further they explored the house, the more tense they became.

As they made their way upstairs they heard moans. It was a woman being pleasured. Passing one room after the other, Redds and Top headed toward the sound of the fucking. The main bedroom's door was cracked. A slight glow from the moonlight lit up the room just enough for Redds and Top to make out what was going on. With Top on his heels, Redds stopped at the door to get a better look. Top wondered what the fuck Redds was waiting for. It was time to slaughter shit as far as Top was concerned. Redds squinted his eyes in disbelief. He took a long look at the female that was riding Apple like porn star. Her ass bounced up and down like a stripper getting paid to make it clap. Redds focused his eyes on the tattoo across her left ass cheek. In red letters across her ass cheek was Dontae's name. This dirty bitch, Redds thought. Pinky was fucking Apple's brains out. Normally, Redds remained calm when he was on a mission, but seeing Pinky fucking Apple while

Dontae was over D.C. Jail fighting for his life en-raged Redds. On top of that, Apple was behind Lil' Man's murder. If Redds was going to have any second thought about killing Pinky, they were gone after what he'd just witnessed.

He kicked the door open and rushed into the bed-room, followed by Top. Redds grabbed Pinky by her hair, smacked her with his pistol, and slung her to the floor as she screamed for her life out of fear. Redds kicked her in the face as he trained his pistol on Apple. "Don't move, bitch!" he said to Apple.

Top walked around to the other side of the bed with his pistol pointed at Apple's head.

"Apple!" Pinky screamed. "What's going on?"

Apple was frozen in fear, caught off guard. "What do y'all want, man?" he asked in a shaky voice as he put his hands up in the air in defeat.

Pinky continued to scream.

"Shut the fuck up bitch!" Top hissed. He then pumped two slugs into her head, silencing her for eternity.

He body slumped to the ground with her brains hanging out the side of her head. Blood and brains oozed out onto the white carpet.

Apple screamed when he saw Pinky murdered in cold blood. "Oh, my God! What the fuck is up? What y'all want? I got money! I got coke! I got whatever you want, just ... please, don't kill me!"

Redds cut his eyes at the sight of Pinky and got a sick feeling in his stomach. Top played no games with her. Redds made a mental note of how vicious Top had become. Turning his attention back to Apple, Redds said, "You thought you was gon' get away wit' killin' my little man?"

"Your little man! Who is your little man?" Apple said. He was almost in tears at this time.

Top pulled off his ski mask. "You know who the fuck he talkin' 'bout, bitch-ass nigga!" He smacked Apple with the butt of his pistol.

Apple screamed like a bitch. "I'm sorry, I swear it wasn't me that called the shots on that one. It was Jay's people. It was Jay's people. His cousin and Lil' Moon. It wasn't me."

Top wasn't in the mood for lies. "Fuck you, nigga!" He fired his pistol into Apple's face, blowing his brains against the wall. In a rage, he emptied his clip into Apples face. Redds didn't have to fire a shot. He watched Top clean house like some type of paid assassin. The young nigga was not to be played with at all.

Redds nodded his approval. "Let's get the fuck out-ta here."

"Cool," Top said. He then turned and spit on Ap-ple's body. "Bitch-ass nigga!"

Lil' Man's funeral was packed. Not only did he have a huge family, he was a hood star uptown. Everybody had love for the young nigga. On top of that, the FBI was on the scene. They were on the lookout for Necci, knowing she wouldn't miss her brother's funeral. If they could get their hands on her, they were hoping she would lead them to Redds. Lil' Moon and his crew were lurking around the funeral in hopes of catching Top. When they saw no signs of Top they decided to shoot up the funeral, but noticed the FBI on the scene and decided against it. Redds was the one that told Top not to attend the funeral. He felt like there was going to be too much heat on the funeral and he was right. Three young dudes were arrested for carrying guns right outside of the funeral home.

After the funeral, as mourners began to exit, Necci finally broke down. She couldn't hold it back any more. She tried so hard to hold in her feelings and that only made her emotions explode with greater force. Seeing her brother lowered into the ground for what would be his final resting place was just too much for her. Her family tried to comfort her.

The FBI stepped to her just as she began to sob.

"Ms. Wilson," Agent Schoenberg said, flanked by two other agents. "You need to come with us."

Her family tried to protest, but the agents threatened to make arrests if anyone was to stand in their way.

Hours later, inside their downtown building, the FBI was still questioning Necci about Redds' whereabouts.

"I told y'all bitches I don't know shit and I ain't got shit to say. I ain't committed no crimes, so I don't know what the fuck y'all got me down her for. Y'all gon' come to my brother's funeral with this bullshit when you know what me and my family going through, and you think I'm gon' help you! Please! You muthafuckas must be out your fuckin' mind. Kiss my black ass!"

Schoenberg smiled at the way Necci went off. He took pleasure in getting under her skin. Walking around the table, he said, "Well, Ms. Wilson, you say you haven't committed any crimes, but where have you been since Mr.

Williams has been on the run? You disappeared around the same time he disappeared and we have information that you have been with him. What do you have to say about that?"

"Once again, I don't have shit to say about anything. I'm not charged with anything, so I don't have to answer any muthafuckin' questions. I want to leave and if I can't leave, I want to speak to a lawyer. I'm tired of tellin' you bitches the same damn thing."

Schoenberg gave her a long look, and then shook his head. "You want to play rough, so we are going to play rough. If I find out that you know anything about Mr. Williams' whereabouts and you are helping him, we are going to lock you up right along with him. I hope you understand that we are the FBI and we can make your life a living hell. Trust that."

Necci rolled her eyes, and said, "Are we done yet?"

The FBI had to let Necci go because they had nothing to hold her on. However, they put a tail on her and watched her closely. They already had her mother's phone tapped as well as other members of her family. Redds was many steps ahead of the FBI. He had planned for everything they'd done. He schooled Necci well and informed her of what to expect when they came to get her. It was chess not checkers and Redds was playing to win. For his age, he was far smarter than the FBI gave him credit for.

Necci stilled held a slight grudge with her mother and for that reason, she stayed with Lil' Man's mother for two days. She did as Redds told her and stayed in house, not using the phone. Early Monday morning, she left the house and headed to Union Station dressed in a grey sweatshirt and a pair of blue jeans. Her hair was in long plaits that hung down her back. She carried a blue Polo book bag with her. There was no doubt that the feds were

on her back. She knew it, but didn't care. Redds had everything thought out well.

Once she arrived at Union Station, she walked
around for a good twenty minutes, stopping in different
stores and getting something to eat from the food court.
Mixing in with the huge crowds of people helped her lose
the FBI tail on her. Finally, she went into the ladies room
and walked out in a different outfit. Her new outfit was a
black Polo hoodie, black jeans, a black baseball cap, and no
book bag. The baseball cap hid her long plaits. She could
almost pass for a young male. As she mixed back in with
the crowd, she pulled out a pair of black Versace glasses
and slid them on. In minutes, she boarded a train to Philly.

During the ride to Philly, all Necci could think about
was the death of her little brother. Even though she knew
that Apple had been murdered, that didn't make her feel
any better. She would never be the same. With the death
of Lil' Man, a piece of Necci died. Life began to look dark
for Necci. She didn't know what to expect next. After her
encounter with the FBI, Necci began to worry about Redds.
Losing him would be too much; she wouldn't be able to go
on without him as far as she was concerned. After stressing
herself out with all of her thoughts, Necci dozed off and
took a nap.

When she woke up, she was in Philly. Carefully, she
exited the train and made her way to the street. There
were no signs of anyone following her. She caught a cab to
North Philly and got out on Girard Avenue where she saw
Top's car on 26th Street. Pulling out a piece of paper that
had the address on she was looking for, Necci walked up to
the front door and rang the bell. Redds answered the door
with a slight smile and hugged Necci. His hug made her feel
safe. She looked up at him, and said, "I missed you. I never
want to lose you, baby."

Holding her as tight as he could, Redds said, "I never want you to lose me. You are my everything, baby. I'm always here for you, no matter what." Redds walked Necci into the living room where Top sat at the table smoking weed.

Top looked up, and said, "Necci, what's up? You okay?"

Necci nodded sadly. "I'm holdin' on, could be better, but you know how it goes."

"I feel you," Top said as he got up and hugged Necci. He held her tight, wishing there was something he could do to take away her pain. Only time would heal it.

Redds pulled out a chair for her. "Have a seat, baby."

Necci looked at Redds, and said, "So, what's the game plan?"

Redds sighed. "We gon' hit the road and get shit in order to get out of the country."

Necci nodded.

Chapter 9

Redds wanted Top to get away from D.C. for a while. He didn't feel safe leaving him behind at the time, so he took him to Ohio with him. Top and Shell clicked overnight. Top was Shell's kind of nigga—young, wild, and didn't give a fuck. Shell kept Top with him all the time, showing him around, taking him out to clubs, and serving weight. Top loved the Ohio girls and they loved him back. His style was so different. Overall, the small town was not what he was used to, but it was what he needed, considering what was going on back home.

Once back in Ohio, Redds was focused on one thing only and that was stacking his money. Laying in the bed with Necci, Redds looked at her, and said, "Shit should be in order for us to get out of the country in a week or so. You ready?"

"Ready as ever. I just want you to be safe and far away from here. I can't lose you. I can't say it enough, baby."

Redds kissed her and rubbed his hand through her hair. "I'm gon' be okay. As long as I have you by my side, I'm good."

Necci smiled. "So, what about Top? You think he should stay up here wit' Shell?"

"At least for a little while. It's safer up here for him right now. It will give him a chance to cool off. He gon' end up going back to the city. Shit up here too slow for him, for real."

"What if he start gettin' some real money up here wit' Shell? You think he gonna still wanna' go back home?"

Redds smiled. "Top is one of them young niggaz that has to be where it's goin' down. If it ain't goin' down, he'll get bored or get in trouble. Even if youngin' was rich, he would still wanna be in the hood. It's in his blood and he gon' be like that for a while."

Necci shook her head. "I hope he grows up before it's too late. I really love him like a brother and wit' Lil' Man gone, it's like he's my only surviving little brother. You feel me?"

"Yeah, I feel you. Top is a soldier, he'll be okay. Trust me on that one. Shell likes him. You see they be to-gether all the time. Shell gon' show him what gettin' mon-ey is all about. On top of that, when we are gone, I feel safe wit' Top here to watch Shell's back. Shell's gettin' a lot of money up here now. Niggaz gon' start tryin' him in a mi-nute. With Top around, I know Shell will have some back-ing when I'm gon'."

"I feel you on that," Necci said as she rested her head on his chest.

Wilkes Villa projects was live just after nightfall. Top felt at home in the projects. It reminded him of when he was growing up in Clifton Terrace. Top shot dice with the niggaz from the projects, played ball with them, and fuck bitches from the projects. He fit in overnight. Once everybody knew he was supposed to be Shell's cousin, he had a pass to do as he pleased. On top of that, Top was already as ghetto as it could get, so nothing rubbed him the wrong way about being in the projects. As long as he wasn't disrespected, Top was easy to get along with.

Sitting on the front steps of Angie's unit, Top and Shell's man, Ice, smoked weed and talked about how the drug game was different in D.C. and Elyria. Top liked Ice. He was a cool as nigga and he was about getting paid. Top respected that. At the same time, Top had heard stories about how Ice would down a nigga if he got out of line. Top respected niggaz like that even more than he respected niggaz that were getting paid.

Ice passed Top the blunt, and said, "How the fuck y'all get money in D.C. if y'all killin' all the time? That shit don't mix, for real."

Top took a deep pull on the blunt. "Shit be fucked up sometimes, but when me and man wasn't beefin', we was gettin' paid like shit, young. It's plenty of money to be made in D.C., but you gotta be on point for the snakes. That's anywhere, though. You ain't gon' let a nigga play wit' your life or your money."

"You got that right. I'm gon' put a nigga on ice real quick if he playin' wit' my bread."

A car pulled up while Top and Ice were talking. The driver, an older dude, called Ice over to the car.

Ice looked at Top, and said, "That's business. I'll be back in a few."

"Cool, take care of your business." Top gave Ice five.

A sexy little broad from the projects by the name of Ida had been checking Top out for a few days. She was digging his style. Seeing him sitting alone, she decided to walk over and see what was up with him. "Can I smoke wit' you?" she asked as she took a seat next to him.

"Ain't no thing." Top passed her the blunt. He was hip to Ida. He'd met her brother, Big Iz, through Shell. Ice had also told him that Ida was hot in the drawers and was fucking any nigga she thought was supposed to be somebody. Top took a good look at her and felt like he wanted to try his hand. She wasn't bad looking at all. Her face was cute and her body was in perfect shape. She was right down his alley.

They talked a little while they smoked. After a little small talk, Top smiled, and said, "What's good wit' you tonight?"

With a sexy smile, Ida rubbed Top's leg, and said, "Whatever, I'm down for a good time any day of the week. What you got in mind?"

"I'm thinkin' we hit the hotel and disappear for a second. What that sound like to you?"

"Sounds good to me. Like, make it happen, big boy," she said as she rubbed his leg.

Top stood up, and said, "Wait right here, I'll be right back." He left and returned with Shell's brand new white Lexus coupe. Rolling down the tinted driver's side window, Top called out, "Ay, get in." Ida smiled like she'd just hit the lotto as she ran around the car and jumped in the passenger side. "Why you smiling like that, boo?" Top asked as he pulled off.

Ida blushed. "I don't know. I like your style. You cool as shit, Top. You make me wanna go to D.C. and see how it is down there."

Top smiled as he headed to the hotel.

They checked into a little motel right outside of town. Top and Ida sat on the bed for a second while Top rolled some weed. They smoked another blunt and before it was gone, Ida was giving him some of the best head Elyria had to offer. Top's eyes rolled back in his head as he held the back of her head as she bobbed up and down on his dick. Looking down at her doing her thing, Top locked eyes with her. She enjoyed what she was doing to him, her eyes said so. Her eyes said that she wanted to please him like he'd never been pleased before. At the time, she was doing a good job of it. "Damn, girl," Top whispered. "You suckin' the shit out of this dick."

Ida came up for a little air, holding his dick in her soft little hand, and said, "You like the way I suck your dick, Top?"

"Hell yeah," he said, pulling her head forward as he shoved his dick back in her mouth.

"Mmmmmm ... mmmm ... mmmmmm ..." She deep throated him like a pro and in minutes, he was cumming inside her mouth. She kept sucking him off until he was dry. Swallowing his babies, she slid her mouth off of him and licked all over his dick while looking him in the eyes like she loved him. "You taste good, so good I had to swallow." She giggled seductively.

Top looked down at her and shook his head. "You mean, girl. Got damn!" he laid back on the bed and put his arms behind his head. "Lord, have mercy, girl. You gon' get a nigga in trouble."

Ida laughed as she climbed in the bed beside him. "I like how you move your body when I got your dick in my mouth. You move like you fucking my mouth."

Top smiled. "You are too much, girl. You say I move like I'm fuckin' your mouth?"

"Yeah, in and out, in and out, like you fucking me in the mouth. I like that."

Top laughed. "I like that, too, baby girl."

Ida smiled as she rubbed his dick. "You gotta fuck me from the back now. That's how I like it. I like it from the back. How do you like it?"

"I like it from the back, too," Top said.

Ida began sucking on his dick, trying to bring it back to life. Moments later, Top was rock-hard again. He wasted no time bending Ida over the bed and sliding inside her tight pussy from the back. Grabbing her by the hips, Top pounded her from the back like he was trying to make her tap out. However, she fucked him back with the same intensity. She loved the hard pounding from the back. She was so wet as he slid in and out of her. "Deeper! Deeper! Fuck me deeper!" she yelled at the top of her lungs. Top did just that. He fucked her harder and faster, pulling her to his thrusts. The wetness began to coat his dick with a thick, wet cream. An idea popped into his head. In one quick motion, Top slid out of her pussy and slid right inside her ass with no problem.

"Oh, shit! Ohhhh, shit!" she shouted as soon as his dick slipped in her ass. She felt explosions of pleasure shoot throughout her body and came instantly. The orgasm was strong. She looked over her shoulder, gritting her teeth as she fucked him back. "Oh, my God, you fuckin' the shit out this ass … sssssssssshit … don't stop, don't stop. Fuck me, fuck me, fuck this ass, Top. Fuck me like a whore, fuck the shit out of me. I love it. I never had it in the ass before … ow, ow, ow, ow, ow, owwwwww …" She gripped the sheets on the bed like that was going to help her take the dick. She slid her hand between her legs and rubbed her pussy while he fucked the shit out of her asshole. He turned her on like nothing she'd ever experienced before. "Oh, my God, shit, I'm cummin'! I'm cummin'! Don't stop, don't you stop, keep diggin' in my asshole just like that."

Minutes later, Top came all over her back and her ass cheeks. "Aaarrrhhgggg," he grunted. "Damn, that asshole is so good."

Out of breath, Ida said, "You so nasty. You fucked the shit out of my ass. I never let nobody fuck me in the ass before."

Top laughed. "So, I'm the first nigga to fuck that little asshole, huh?"

"For real, I'm not lying. You the first nigga to fuck me in the ass."

"I can't wait to fuck you in the ass again."

"We got all night to do this. I ain't got nowhere to go." Ida smiled.

Top smiled. Ida was going to be very interesting while he was in Elyria.

The next night, Shell and Top hopped on the highway and shot up to Cleveland to serve some niggaz Shell dealt with. After they took care of business, they decided to hit a club or two. Inside Club Flex, one of Shell's favorites when he was in Cleveland, they popped bottles and partied with the baddest broads. They also made a few new connections with a few dudes that were getting money on Cleveland's east side. Shell had cousins on the east side of town so he knew who was supposed to be somebody. Being as though he and Redds had a real live Cali connect, they could beat just about anybody's prices, so that put Shell in a nice position in the game.

Making his way to the bathroom, Top was stopped by almost every female that he passed. His swag was different and they were drawn to it. A few dudes that had never seen him before mean mugged, but he didn't give a fuck. If they got out of line, he was sure to give them more than they bargained for. Nevertheless, Top made it to the bathroom and back to the VIP section where he continued to party.

Around two in the morning, Shell and Top decided to leave the club and head back to Lorain. A group of bad ass broads walked in front of them. Top had his eyes on them. He thought about trying to holla at one of them but felt a little tired, so he decided not. Shell could almost tell what Top was thinking. "You ain't tryin' to get one of them young bitches?" Shell asked.

Top smiled. "I'm tired, for real. I'm ready to go in."

Shell laughed. "You scared of pussy now?"

"Never that. I'm just ready to get some sleep," Top said as they walked up on Shell's Q45.

They jumped in the car as they continued to watch the girls walk further down the block. They piled up into a big body Benz and pulled off. Shell started the Q45, and said, "Let me find out that little broad Ida got you sprung. I see you feelin' her like shit, young nigga."

Top burst out laughing. "She cool, but never can I be sprung. I don't let my feelings get caught up in these

hoes out here. It ain't in my blood. I fuck 'em and duck
'em. But, Ida cool as shit. She down for whatever and I like
that about her. That ain't no secret."

Shell nodded in agreement as he drove down the
street. "Yeah, she cool peoples. The feds ran up in her
house before looking for her brother and found some work.
She was the only one home at the time, so the feds locked
her up for the coke. She took the beef and ain't say shit. I
fucks wit' her for that alone. Most of these bitches would
have ratted a nigga out off the rip. You know?"

"Hell yeah, most of these weak-ass niggaz would
have ratted a nigga out off the rip."

Shell laughed. "You right about that."

Top dropped his seat way back in order to get some
rest on the ride back. "Shell, who's coke was in the house?"

"It was her brother's shit, I think. I can't remember,
but whoever had the shit in there, she didn't tell on they
ass."

"I feel you."

While they were talking, Shell noticed a dark blue
BMW 735i coming down the street. After getting a good
look at the driver, Shell blew his horn and jumped out of
the car. Top raised up quickly and pulled out his pistol, trying to figure out what was going on.

Shell ran up on the driver side of the BMW and
questioned the driver, a dude by the name of Fat Mike,
about $25,000 that he had owed Shell for over a month.
Shell wasn't really tripping off the fact that Fat Mike owed
him the money, he was more concerned with the fact that
Fat Mike seemed to be ducking him. That was disrespect in
Shell's eyes and he had to address it.

Looking up at Shell from behind the wheel of his
BMW, Fat Mike said, "Family, I got you. Why you steppin'
to me like I'm not gon' pay you? I always pay you."

Shell took a good look in the car and saw that Fat Mike was in the car alone. He leaned down a little in order to look Fat Mike in the eyes. "Fuck all that shit you talkin' 'bout you gon' pay me. You ain't returned none of my fuckin' calls and when I beep you, you don't even hit back. Who you think you playin' wit'? I ain't one of these small time niggaz." Shell was not himself. He was usually calm and smooth when dealing with matters about money or disagreements. However, he'd been drinking and that added to his anger.

Fat Mike opened the car door and stepped out with a 9mm Ruger in his hand. "Who the fuck you think you talkin' to like that, Shell? I'll down your ass out here, nigga. You got me mixed up wit' one of these pussy niggaz that's scared of you. You better check yourself!"

Shell took a step back and saw the pistol in Fat Mike's hand. His eyes went from the pistol back to Fat Mike's eyes. The alcohol mixed with foolish pride influenced Shell to challenge him. "Nigga, I don't know what you got out the car wit' your heat for. You better use it ma' fucka'!"

Top was on point. He'd been watching everything and as soon as the situation seemed like it was getting heated, he grabbed Shell's .45 automatic from under the seat. With no questions asked, Top hopped out of the car and started shooting. Loud booms from the .45 ripped through the early morning tranquility. People that were exiting the club screamed and ran for their lives. Bullets slammed into Fat Mike's chest, knocking him against his car. He was hit five times in seconds. Lifelessly, Fat Mike slid to the ground with his pistol in hand. Shell was shocked. He spun around and saw Top stilling walking forward; the young nigga was trying to make sure he'd killed Fat Mike. Top didn't believe in leaving enemies alive. Seeing Fat Mike still moving, Top stood over him and shot him in the head two more times at close range.

Shell looked at Top in disbelief. Everything that Redds had said about the young nigga was true and Shell had seen it with his own eyes. Hearing police sirens in the air, Shell grabbed Top by the shoulder, and shouted, "We gotta get the fuck outta here!"

They dashed back to the car and took off flying toward the highway. Being on the run had Redds' senses on high alert at all times. He heard a car pull up in back of the house and got up to see who it was. When he looked out of the window, he saw Shell and Top walking up to the back door. Redds opened the door for them and noticed that something was wrong. It was written all over their faces.

"What's up? What's wrong?" Redds asked.

Shell looked at Top and back to Redds, and said, "We got into some shit in Cleveland."

"Some shit like what?" Redds raised his eyebrows.

Top said, "I had to smoke some bamma-ass nigga." Top said it like it was nothing to it.

Redds sighed and shook his head. He couldn't believe his ears. "Are you serious?"

Shell cut in. "It was some wild shit." He went on to tell Redds what had gone down, blow for blow. Top let Shell do all the talking. For some reason, he felt like Redds was going to blame him for what happened. The last thing Top wanted to do was bring heat to Ohio where Redds was laying low. Redds shook his head as Shell told him the facts. He wasn't mad at Top. In fact, he felt like Top may have saved Shell's life. What was to come next was what Redds was more concerned with. Murder changed the outcome of everything. With a murder, there was sure to be an investigation, and investigations were never a good thing.

When Shell was done putting Redds on point about what had gone down, Redds gave him a serious look, and said, "You mean to tell me that you really risked your life for twenty-five thousand dollars? That ain't like you, cuz."

"I feel you, but that nigga was actin' like he wasn't tryin' to pay me. I had to say somethin' to that nigga. It ain't that kind of party wit' me, cuz. On top of all of that, he jumped out of the car acting like he was gon' really do somethin' to me."

"I hear all that, but now we got a murder on our hands. We gettin' too much money for that kind of heat. Did anybody see y'all?" Redds asked, looking at Top and Shell for an honest response.

Top spoke up. "It ain't look like nobody got a good look at us when we was leavin'. They might've saw the car, but I'm damn near sure they didn't see our faces and the nigga was in the car alone."

Shell said, "I already got rid of my car and got Angie to call it in stolen, so that's covered for right now. It was in her name."

Redds rubbed his chin. "That's still a connection to you at the end of the day." He let out a long sigh. He had too much on his mind to be dealing with any extra stress. "So, where's the nigga from?"

Shell said, "He from Lorain. He got a little crew and shit, but they ain't nothin' to be concerned wit'. One of the little niggaz is a killer, but he locked up right now in Cleveland for a murder from last summer."

"So, it's gon' be a beef now?" Redds asked. He was already planning to get far away from Ohio. The last thing he needed was to be connected to another murder.

Shell lit a Newport, and said, "It's not gon' be no beef. Ain't nobody see us, cuz."

"That's what you think. Somebody always sees what happens. I learned that the hard way."

"Cuz, trust me. Nobody saw us. I promise you that. It ain't gon' be no kind of beef. The nigga Fat Mike is dead, so it ain't nobody alive to talk about what went down."

Redds shook his head and walked off. "I'm gettin' the fuck outta' here. I'm 'bout to get hotel room and think about where I'm goin' next. My nerves too bad for all this shit. I can't take no chances."

Walking back into the bedroom, Redds shook Necci softly, and said, "Get up, boo. We 'bout to get up outta' here."

Rolling over, struggling to open her eyes, Necci said, "Why, what's wrong?" She glanced at the alarm clock on the nightstand. It was 4:05 a.m.

Redds shook his head. "Shell and Top got into some shit in Cleveland leaving the club. Top ended up smokin' a nigga. I don't wanna' stay here no more. That's a sign that my time here is up. We 'bout to go check into a hotel."

Necci sucked her teeth as she snatched the covers off of her. "Top ain't even been here a week yet! Damn!" she snapped.

Redds shook his head. "Don't be fucked up at Top. He really ain't do nothin' wrong. On the real, he saved Shell's life as far as I can see."

Necci sat on the side of the bed and just shook her head. "When will it all end?"

The next day, Redds and Necci were in a Columbus hotel chilling. They needed to put some space between themselves, and Top and Shell. Redds had made a few calls to make sure that his move to Panama was in order. Donnavan assured Redds that everything was a go. All Redds had to do was make it to Canada safely, and then he would be able to board a plane to Panama. It was time to get out of the country before it was too late.

As far as Top and Shell were concerned, Redds had given them good instruction on how to lay low for a second until things cooled off. After that, they were to get back to business. He needed them to stay under the radar. He was sure he would need them as time moved on. In a way, he was leaving Top in Shell's care and wanted Shell to make sure Top was well taken care of. Shell assured Redds that nothing would happen to Top and whenever Top decided to go back to D.C. he would be able to do so with a nice stash of cash and a serious cocaine connect. He would be straight, if nothing else.

Thinking about Top, Necci said, "Redds, you think Top gon' be okay up without us?"

Redds smiled. "At the end of the day, Top is a soldier. He can take care of himself. I'd hate to see him get caught up and get himself a life sentence. But, I think what he'll do is lay low wit' Shell for a second and make his way back to D.C. He won't be able to stay away from the city for too long."

"That young nigga is something else. He damn near average a body every week." Necci shook her head as she thought about how Top was living.

Redds nodded in agreement. "No bullshit. Youngin' is a perfect example of the old sayin' that you can take a nigga outta the hood, but you can't take the hood outta of the nigga."

"Not a nigga like Top, anyway." Necci giggled. "I hope he's okay when we leave. I really do love him like a little brother."

"Me too." Redds said. "He gon' find his way. We ain't gotta worry about him."

Necci kissed him. "Let's focus on getting where we need to go. I'll be glad when we can put all this shit behind us."

"Me too, baby," Redds said as he thought about what was in store for him and Necci in the near future.

A few days later, Redds and Necci had their bags packed and ready to go. Inside their luggage was close to a million dollars. That was more than enough to start their journey. They really didn't know what to expect, all they knew for sure was that they were getting far away from law enforcement that wanted to lock Redds up and try to give him the death penalty. Panama was only the beginning. Running was what they would do for a long time. They had to leave their whole lives and their families behind.

Hugging Necci, Redds looked into her eyes, and said, "You ready, baby?"

"For sure."

They left the hotel set out on their mission.

Redds and Necci drove for a few hours until they reached Detroit. Once there, they made their way to a house that Donnavan directed them to. They parked and walked up to the door of the ran-down house. Redds looked around and saw no one on the streets. He knocked on the door and a young, Jamaican lady answered. "I'm here for Donnavan," Redds said.

"You must be Redds," the lady said with her Jamaican accent.

Redds smiled. "Yes."

"Come in. I have been waiting for ya." She directed them to the living room, where Redds and Necci took a seat on the sofa. "Your ride should be here shortly. Like I said, we were waitin' on ya." The lady disappeared into the kitchen where the smell of some kind of curry dish was in the making.

Necci whispered to Redds, "That food smells good."

Redds smiled. "Who you tellin'?"

The lady stuck her head out of the kitchen, and said, "Would you two like something to eat while you wait?"

Redds looked at Necci and smiled. "Sure, we would like that."

"Okay, give me one minute."

Boom! Boom! Boom! A loud banging on the front door startled Redds and Necci, making them both jump to their feet.

"ATF! ATF! Open the door!" The front door came crashing down. Countless ATF agents in riot gear carrying assault weapons, rushed through the front door. Redds couldn't believe what he was seeing. It was like a bad dream, better yet, a nightmare. Necci was frozen with fear. She didn't know what to do. Her heart pounded out of control. Agents slammed her to the floor. Redds reacted quickly. He took off running at full speed and dived through the window, breaking the glass. He hit the concrete sidewalk like a sack of bricks. Agents were all over the place, they had the house surrounded. Before Redds even had a chance to get up, they were right on top of him, choking him, punching him, kicking him, and all around fucking him up as he lay face down in the broken glass. In no time they had him cuffed, searched, and thrown into the back of a police car. His whole life flashed before his eyes. All he could think about was the fact that he was a wanted man and now the ATF had their hands on him.

An overweight, redneck agent walked to the police car and looked Redds in the eyes with the look of intimidation. He chewed on a gob of chewing tobacco that had stained his teeth in the worst over the many years that he'd been chewing. Spitting gob of brown waste onto the sidewalk, the agent said, "What's ya' name, boy?"

Knowing his fake ID stated he was Frank Jones, Redds said, "Frank Jones. You got my ID. You know who I am."

Necci and the Jamaican lady were being walked out in handcuffs as Redds was being questioned.

The agent looked over his shoulder at Necci and the Jamaican lady as they were being placed in the back of another police car. Redds felt helpless. He wished there was something he could do to get Necci out of whatever he'd gotten her caught up in. In his mind, he was the blame for all of her problems. It made him feel like shit inside. Guilt crept up on him in such a way that he damn near forgot what he was facing if the ATF found out exactly who he really was. Looking back at Redds, the agent said, "Boy, I didn't ask you what was on your ID, I asked you what was your name. You hard of hearing or something like that?"

"You arresting me for something?" Redds asked. He wasn't sure if the agent knew who he was or not at this point, but he damn sure wasn't going to tell him his real name. That was out of the question.

"I don't know. Should I be arresting you? We came here for a marijuana warrant and you jump out of a window. It's not every day that a person with good sense jumps out of a window unless they have good reason to. That makes me wonder what's your reason. You sell marijuana or something? You know something about all the marijuana in that house?"

Redds looked at the house and saw agents walking out of the front door with black trash bags of what he assumed was marijuana. He couldn't believe that Donnavan had sent him and Necci to a house that was loaded with drugs. Not only was the house loaded with drugs, but it was on some kind of hot list. Looking back at the ATF agent, Redds knew that things were only going to get worse. "I don't have shit to say about no drugs. I don't know anything about that."

"See, that's where you're wrong, son. You know something about them drugs 'cause you was in that house when we politely came inside. Anyhow, I'm gon' give you some time to think about your answer while we search the rest of the house." The agent slammed the car door and walked off.

Redds took a deep breath and tried to mentally prepare himself for what was next.

Chapter 10

Days later, the FBI had their man. Bulger and
Schoenberg had Redds inside a small interrogation room in
the FBI building in downtown D.C. They tried to question
Redds, but he didn't feed into any of their mind games. He
knew the game well and he wasn't in the mood for any of
their bullshit. Redds asked to speak to his lawyer off the
top. After he asked for his lawyer they were supposed to
leave him alone according to his rights, but they didn't give
a fuck about any of his rights.

After spending three days in a Michigan jail, Redds'
fingerprints came back and identified him. The FBI was
called, and Bulger and Schoenberg took a trip to get Redds
themselves. During the car ride back to D.C., all Redds
could think about was the death penalty and everything
else he was facing once he went to court. Redds didn't
know much about the law, but he knew that the RICO act
was one of the federal government's big guns. The thought
of what he would have to face had his stomach in sick
knots. Aside from all of that, not knowing what had happened to Necci tore his heart out. He didn't know if she'd
been charged with something in Detroit or if the feds had
snatched her up in connection with his shit. Nothing was
clear except for the fact that he was now in federal custody.

Once they arrived in D.C., Redds took in as many
memories as he could. He had no idea if he'd ever see his
hometown again. He had no idea if he'd ever be a free man
again. As he gazed out the back window of the unmarked
fed car, Redds thought about the game and how things
were in the streets. When he first got in the game, he had
no idea that all the heat from the feds was going to be a
part of it later on down the road. All he wanted was to

stack some paper and get out of the hood. However, reality had made sure that he knew better at this point.

At the moment, the feds were fed up with Redds and were pissed off that they couldn't get him to talk. Schoenberg was the kind of agent that believed everybody would talk if the pressure was applied right. He looked at Redds, and said, "You can have it your way. Trust me on this, when you're sitting on death row and all your friends have sold you out, you will wish that you had talked to me."

Redds looked up at the white agent, and said coldly, "You don't know who you are dealin' wit'. I'm not one of these jokers that folds under pressure. I'm not one of these jokers that don't have no backbone. I'm a man. My momma raised me as a man and I will be a man till the day I die. You will never laugh and tell anybody that I folded under pressure. It won't happen. You can save it. I can face my battles head up and deal wit' whatever comes my way. I'll die on my feet before I ever live on my knees. Remember that when dealing wit' me."

Redds' words sent chills through both agents' bodies. His words were strong and to the point. The agents looked at one another and could do nothing but respect the stand Redds took. They then stepped out of the room to give him a chance to think about what he was really up against.

Once he was alone, Redds sat handcuffed to the floor. His mind raced, but no matter how much he was concerned about his own situation, he kept worrying about Necci. He was dying to know if she was alright. Shaking his head, he began to blame himself for getting her caught up in his situation. The last thing he ever wanted was for her to be in harm's way.

Minutes later, both agents walked back in the room. Schoenberg looked at Redds, and said, "You still don't want to talk?"

Redds shook his head in disbelief. "Look here, cracker. We can do this shit all day. I ain't got shit to say. I've asked you to let me speak to a lawyer and you keep playin' these faggot ass games wit' me. I'm not the one. You not gon' get no information out of me. None at all. I'm not that guy."

"Look here," Schoenberg took a seat across the table from Redds and toned down his voice, "I know how things work in the streets. However, we have you by the balls and if you are as smart as I think you are, you will help yourself. If you don't, you need to know that we are going to bring down the heat on everything close to you, your mother, you girlfriend, and anybody else you can think of." The agent slid Redds a folder and nodded his head for him to look inside. As Redds used his free hand to look inside the folder, Schoenberg continued, "I've seen the hardest killers crack and save their own ass when the time was right ..."

As Schoenberg spoke, Redds looked over the papers that the Attorney General's office had signed off on for the death penalty to be official. A sick feeling shot through his gut again. After reading the paper, Redds looked up at Schoenberg, and said, "We all got a part to play ... don't we? You play your part and I'ma play mine. This death penalty shit don't change nothin' wit' me. I don't talk to the feds."

Schoenberg smiled. "You sure 'bout that?"

"I don't have shit else to say." Redds slid the folder back.

The next morning, Toya walked through the busy hallway inside the Federal Court building on her way to her son's arraignment. She was sick about what was going on. She couldn't believe the feds had caught her son and were trying to put him to death. The mere thought of Redds facing the death penalty wouldn't allow her to eat or sleep.

She was a nervous wreck. People around her could see the effects so much so that they urged her to go see a doctor. Toya didn't care about anything other than helping her son defend himself in court. She wouldn't rest until Redds was safe and out of the clutches of the federal government.

Word of Redds' arrest hit The Washington Post and spread across the city like wildfire. The headlines read: Leader of the 5th and Kennedy Street Crew Arrested ... The article that was written about Redds and his homies made them look like made men from the mafia. Things they were accused of were sinister and deadly. The media had convicted the defendants before trial even began.

Sitting in the back of the courtroom waiting for Redds to walk out and be seen by the judge, Toya silently prayed for her son. She then looked around for Redds' lawyer. She had a million and one questions for him. Her thoughts were all over the place. All she could think about was the death penalty.

A short while later, Redds and his lawyer appeared before the judge for the short arraignment. Redds looked back and saw his mother in the courtroom. He could tell that she was worried to death. He wished there was a way he could let her know that everything was going to be alright. However, he had to focus on what was at hand. He knew, without a doubt, that bond was out of the question, but his lawyer threw it out there, anyway. The old, black judge that sat on the bench actually giggled before denying bond and looking at the lawyer like he was crazy for even asking for such a thing. Assistant U.S. Attorney James Burling was very pleased to see Redds finally in court. It made his day. He could even sleep the night before. When he got the news that Redds had been arrested, he actually popped a bottle of champagne to celebrate.

The arraignment was over in minutes. The U.S. Marshal marched Redds back into the back toward the holding cell behind the courtroom. Redds was given a158-count superseding federal indictment that was waiting for him. The fully loaded indictment seemed to be a violation of every law there was. Anything that could be charged was charged. The government had done all in their power to stack the deck against Redds and his comrades.

With Redds inside the holding cell and his lawyer, T.L. Smith, on the other side, attorney and client discussed the situation at hand. Smith broke down the facts of the case to Redds and told him the truth about how things looked for him. Redds listened to what the lawyer was say-ing for a moment and didn't say a word. He looked at the smooth lawyer in his grey Armani suit and Gucci eyeglasses. T.L. Smith was not new to dealing with RICO cases. He'd defended clients that had been charged with it before. He had won the cases as well, and he let Redds know that he was very good at what he did for a living. Aside from the RICO cases that Smith had fought, he'd also beat to death penalty cases in Virginia for members of a Mexican gang called The Brothers. With the case for The Brothers, Smith really made a name for himself.

Smith could tell that Redds was a thinker by the way he took in all of the information and asked certain questions. Looking at Redds with an honest look on his face, Smith said, "Mr. Williams, I assure that you can trust me and that I have your back on this matter. I'm going to do my best for you. There won't be a stone unturned in your case. I'm going to defend you with all of my heart."

Redds looked the lawyer in the eyes, and said, "I need you, man. This is my life here. It's all or nothing for me. I don't get a second chance. My life is on the line."

"I completely understand." Smith said, maintaining eye contact with the Redds the whole time. "I'm for you all the way. Keep in mind the government has brought out their big guns for you, but, in a way, that may be a good thing in a big case like yours."

"Why is that?" Redds asked, raising his eyebrow.

"In big cases like yours, where the government is willing to do anything to get a conviction, they always do something they shouldn't do. That, in turn, gives a good lawyer a great chance of getting his client off the hook." Smith went on to explain to Redds that there was going to be a lot of foul play involved, being as though the government wanted him so bad. Redds understood what he was in store for and was prepared to deal with whatever.

Finally, Redds had a question to ask that was the most important question of all that had crossed his mind. Looking Smith in the eyes, Redds asked, "Can you beat this case? Can you get me off? Tell me the truth."

Smith took a deep breath. He looked into Redds' eyes and refused to lie to the young man that was fighting for his life. "I don't like to answer those kind of questions for real. It's very early and many things are going to arise that are going to affect your case. However, I assure you this here ... I wouldn't take your money if I didn't think I could beat the case. I'm not in the business of losing and taking peoples' money. I'm a winner. If there's a way to win, I will find it. You can rest assure on that one, Mr. Williams. Trust me. I got your back."

Redds nodded in agreement. He had to trust the lawyer because he was all he really had at the time. His life was in the hands of T.L. Smith.

"I will be over the jail to see you tomorrow and go over a few things. We have a lot of work to do and things to catch up on. Trial will be here before we know it."

"I understand. Thank you. I look forward to seeing you soon," Redds said.

After Smith left the holding area, Redds was left with his own thoughts. He played a few different things over in his mind about the case. He had to do all in his power to fight for his life. He had to learn the law himself and know what his rights were. Walking over to the back of the holding cell, Redds took a seat on the metal bench and looked over his indictment. The government had it waiting for him. As he looked over the indictment he thought about all the weak niggaz in the game. Dudes that were supposed to be gangsters, but when the heat came down they folded without a fight.

They folded and gave up information on other dudes in order to save their own asses. Redds could never see himself going like that. It wasn't in his blood. He had a backbone and lived by a code of honor that meant more to him than saving his own ass. As he looked over the different counts on the indictment, Redds shook his head. Almost every count on the indictment could send him away for life. It didn't make any sense to him. Conspiracy to Participate in a Racketeer Influenced Corrupt Organization—RICO. Continuing Criminal Enterprise—CCE. CCE murders. Tampering with Witness or Informant by killing. Use of Interstate Commerce Facilities in Commission of Murder-for-hire. Conspiracy to Distribute Ten Kilograms or More of Cocaine. The list of charges went on and on, they seemed endless. The fourteen defendants named in the indictment were alleged to have, all together, caused the death of 25 individuals. They were alleged to have committed 11 attempted murders. The murder of an undercover officer, which was the grounds for the government seeking the death penalty against Redds, Dontae, and Heavy. Shit was real. By the time Redds finished reading over the indictment, it was time for him to get on the court bus and take the ride over the D.C. Jail.

A few days later, Top, Shell, and Necci were riding down Kennedy Street in Shell's Lexus. Necci was released from custody and her charges were dropped. It was a blessing, but for some reason the feds left her alone and didn't charge her with anything. In her mind, it was part of something much bigger. Nevertheless, she headed back to D.C. where she would have to figure out what to do next, being as though Redds was locked up. Life was sure to take an uncertain turn and she had to prepare herself for that.

Sitting in the passenger seat, Top looked over his shoulder and saw a D.C. police car behind them. He cut his eyes at the blunt Shell was smoking. He told Shell not to light the weed up due to the fact they were riding through an area with high drug traffic, but Shell didn't listen. Tapping Shell on the arm, Top said, "Ay, put that smoke out. The bodeans on our back."

Necci looked over her shoulder and sighed. The police were the last people she wanted to see. She wasn't in the mood for the bullshit. She was certain they would question her for the simple fact that she was Redds' girlfriend.

Shell looked back at the exact time the siren went off. "Shit!" he said as he tossed the blunt out of the window. Half a block down the street, he pulled over and rolled down the windows. A tall, white cop approached the car on the driver's side while a young, black officer approached on the passenger's side. Both officers had their hands on their Glocks.

"License and registration, please," the white officer demanded as he glared down at Shell.

The black officer looked inside the car, trying to see if anything was out of place. He wanted a reason to search it. The strong smell of marijuana got his attention fast and that was all he needed. "Somebody has been smoking weed in the car. I'm gon' need for you all to step out of the car for me." He then opened the door on Top's side. When he got a good look at Top, he quickly pulled his gun and aimed it at Top's head. "You're under arrest, Mr. Brown!"

The young officer recognized Top as someone they had a warrant out.

"Under arrest for what?" Top said as he put his hands in the air.

The officer grabbed Top and placed handcuffs on him. "You will have to ask somebody that downtown."

Top looked at Necci and Shell, and just shook his head.

Over D.C. Jail, Redds, as well as Dontae and Heavy, were locked down 23 hours a day, being as though they were considered threats to the population. On a small jail tier in North-1, Redds was locked in a small, one-man jail cell infested with roaches. Even mice ran around at night. He was housed on the bottom-left tier. Dontae and Heavy were housed on the bottom-right tier. In order for them to see one another, the tier door had to be opened by an officer in the control bubble. However, Dontae had a job on detail that allowed him to move around the whole cellblock at certain times of the day, mostly when he was cleaning up or serving the food. Most importantly, Dontae had pull in the block. He was well respected among the other men locked up with him, and he was well respected by the staff that worked the unit. He was a boss, even in jail.

When Redds first got in the block, Dontae made sure he was well taken care of and had everything he needed. They really needed to put their heads together if they were going to have a fighting chance to win the case. Dontae put Redds on point with everything that was going on with the case while he was on the run. He let him know what was going down with different beefs they were in throughout the jail so Redds would know who was who. As they spoke about different things, some things went unsaid.

For some reason, Dontae never asked about the Apple murder, the same murder where Pinky was murdered as well. Redds knew in his heart that Dontae already knew what the deal was and charged it to the game.

Talking about all the pros and cons of their case was the most important in Redds' mind. Everything else was secondary as far as he was concerned. Looking Dontae in the eyes, Redds said, "We can't let these crackers trick us out of our lives, homes. This is the fight of our lives. You know that, right?"

Dontae nodded in agreement. "I'm on the same page as you, young." Dontae had had the same conversation with himself many nights as he lay in his cell alone.

"We gotta' pull out all stops for this. They playing for keeps, so we gotta do the same shit. We gon' make these lawyers do their job and we gon' do ours, whatever comes wit' it. You wit' me?"

"You already know it." Dontae slid his hand through the bars and shook Redds' hand. Win, lose, or draw, they were in it together. "We gon' fight these muthafuckas."

In the D.C. Jail visiting hall behind the glass with the phone to his ear, Redds spoke to Necci. It was his first time seeing her. He was so grateful that she didn't get charged with anything in connection with his case. There was no doubt in his mind that the feds were still watching her. That was a given. Redds knew that the feds knew things were about to get real ugly in regards to the case, being as though trial was on the horizon. Redds had to keep Necci on point with what was to come in the near future.

"What is the lawyer talking about?" Necci asked, knowing Redds was on top of his lawyer and all that he needed his lawyer to do for him.

"He been going over all the things I have asked him to do so far. It's a big case, things are going to be drawn out for months." Redds broke everything down for her. While he'd been on the run, countless pre-trial motions had been filed on his behalf. All of those motions were denied.

From a legal point of view, Redds was fighting against all odds on a case that was high profile. With so many code-fendants on one case, most of them had filed motions for a severance in an attempt to separate themselves from the rest of the crew. Some of them had overwhelming evidence against them that could hurt others in front of a jury. The judge wasn't trying to hear any of that. His mind was made up from the very beginning. Redds, Dontae, and Heavy would stand trial first against the death penalty, and then everyone else would be tried together in a second trial. The star-witness was going to be Mike. He was the ring-leader of the rats that were lined up to testify against the defendants that were going to stand trial. The stage was set.

Necci shook her head. The odds were stacked against Redds and his codefendants. She had no idea how shit would play out and it had her depressed. First, she lost her brother and right after that, she lost Redds to the system. Life was in a dark place for her and the future began to seem hopeless. With a deep sigh, she looked up at Redds, and said, "I can't do this without you. You know that, right?"

Redds took a deep breath. "I know how you're feeling, but you have to be strong." Redds tried to comfort her. "I know what you're thinkin'. I ain't gon' lay down at all. I'm gon' fight these crackers wit' all I got. Trust me when I tell you that."

Necci looked at the floor as she tried to block out the noise of the visiting hall. The girl beside her talking loud and cursing at her child's father that was a few spaces down from Redds. Slowly, tears formed in Necci's eyes. "I love you, baby. I'm here for you no matter what happens."

"I know, baby. I love you for that." Redds was hurt. He was hurt due to the fact that he was locked up, and there was no way for him to take care of his woman and make her feel safe. The tears that he saw in her eyes made him feel like he'd failed her. He knew he was her every-thing, just as she was his. The truth of the matter was that he didn't know how things were going to play out and he had no answers for her. All he could do was take every-thing day for day and see what was to come.

Raising up from her seat, Necci said, "I don't care what happens, I will always have your back. Always."

Her words touched Redds. He felt himself getting emotional. Looking her in the eyes, he nodded, and said,

"One way or another, it's gon' be okay. Just be strong."

"I will. I'm strong. I know you need me to be strong. It is what it is. We're in this together. I love you and that's all that matters."

Redds smiled for the first time all day.

Inside D.C. Jail, the two top tiers of North-1 housed some of the most violent juvenile offenders in D.C. Be-tween the ages of 15 and 17, they were all charged as adults for crimes ranging from armed robbery to first-degree murder. Top was no stranger to most of the juve-niles on the tier with him. He'd been locked up with them down Oak Hill, a juvenile facility a few miles outside of D.C. Top was thorough, so he carried himself like a man wher-ever he was, but it was a plus that Redds, Dontae, and Heavy were also in the block. Not only were they in the block, they had the block on lock. On the juvenile tier, Dre, Raff, Monkey D, Johann, and Lil' Ed had things sewed up; they were cool with Top, so they made sure he had every-thing he needed.

As far as Top's legal situation, he'd been waved to the adult courts by way of title 16 and charged with first-degree murder for the killing of Ivy, Apple's girlfriend. Top had no idea that he even had a warrant out for his arrest. In the blink of an eye, he was facing 36-to-life at 16-years-old. That would be frightening to most young men his age, but for Top, it was just another day at the office. He would deal with it like he dealt with everything else in life. He would face it head up and never fold.

Lying in his bed with his hands behind his head thinking about his murder case and how he would fight it, Top heard the tier door open. He got up and walked to the front of the cell. Looking through the bars, he saw Redds walking down the tier to holla at him. He laughed when he saw Redds turn his nose up at the foul smell of the tier. The tier was fucked up. The juveniles were on lock down and were bucking. They had flooded their toilets and threw food all over the tier. Most of them weren't going home anytime soon, so they made everything a big deal and went hard about it.

"What's up, young nigga?" Redds said as he stepped in front of Top's cell.

"Ain't shit, just dealin' wit' being in here. They shit wild as shit, young," Top said as he looked out onto the fucked up tier.

Looking around to make sure no one could see what he was doing, Redds passed Top an ounce of weed.

"Be cool wit' that shit. Don't make the block hot and keep these niggaz out your business."

The weed was just what Top needed. He was stressing, not knowing how he was going to fight his murder case. At least the weed would ease his stress for a minute. Top looked at Redds, and said, "You right on time wit' this shit here. I'm up this muthafucka stressin'."

"I know what you mean. I'm stressin' my damn self, but you know how this shit goes. We gotta' deal wit' it. It's a part of the game, the life we live. All we can do is fight."

"A nigga need a real lawyer to fight these people for real," Top said. He wasn't feeling the public defender he had.

"Don't worry yourself 'bout that shit. I wrote Necci and told her to take twenty Gs to the lawyer I was telling you about. She gon' get on top of that ASAP. I got you, you already know that. We family. I ain't gon' never leave you out in the cold. Whatever I can do to make sure you straight, I'm gon' do."

Top smiled. "You my muthafuckin' nigga, slim. I mean that. Ain't nothin' I won't do for you, young. Believe that."

"It's all good. We gotta hold it down. This is the time where we gotta have each other's backs. The government tryin' to fuck us around, we can't just roll over and let them do whatever they want to do. Fuck that. We ain't gon' never lay down, not as long as we breathing."

Top nodded in agreement. He was entering another stage of his life. As time passed, Redds slowly adjusted to being locked in a cage. His mind was focused on nothing but his case and what he would have to do to regain his freedom. He and his lawyer became the best of friends.

The way Redds saw it, his lawyer was the only person that could really do something that could help him avoid the death penalty. Smith seemed to really like Redds and wasn't feeling the case that the government was prosecuting him on. He felt like some of the things they charged Redds with were maybe justified, but most of them were trumped up to send another young black man away for life. Smith had seen it all many times before. After getting to know Redds, Smith seen that the young man was very bright and could have been anything he wanted to be in life had he not decided to live the life of a street nigga. Nevertheless, Smith promised Redds that he'd so all in his power to beat the RICO case.

One of the first things Smith went over with Redds was the law. He showed him how to look up case law, and find issues that applied to him and his case. Redds caught on quick and had a very good understanding of how to apply the case law to the case he was fighting. With so many RICO cases in the books, Redds had no problem finding issues that were just like his and he used those issues to help his lawyer fight for him. Being as though the law was the only thing Redds could use to fight for his life, it was the one thing that he gave all of his attention to.

In a small conference room inside the visiting area of the jail, Redds and Smith went over the case as things stood at the time. So many things had to be done to prepare for such a big case. Smith let Redds know that it was very likely that it could possibly take three or four years to get to trial on RICO cases sometimes. Redds had heard that before, but wasn't sure if it was true. Three or four years was a long time just to go to trial. Most of the dudes that Redds knew that caught cases and went to trial got it in a year or so. Smith had to make it clear that the case Redds was facing was nothing like any of the cases his friends had faced before him. The RICO case was like a heavyweight title fight between Redds, his codefendants, and the U.S. government.

After going over a few things with his lawyer, Redds leaned forward and, in a very calm voice, said, "I need the names and addresses of the witnesses against me."

Smith looked at Redds for a second and said nothing. The tone of Redds' voice sent chills through him. For the first time, he saw that Redds was not playing any games about his freedom. He knew exactly why he wanted the names and addresses of witnesses. Smith had dealt with very dangerous clients before, some of which had a lot of money and influence. Redds turned out to be one of those clients and Smith could see what was coming. In a calm voice, Smith said, "Well, Reggie, in cases like yours, where witnesses have already been murdered, the government can and mostly likely will withhold that information. That's not going to be easy to get. However, it is your right to have a full discovery, so I will try to get it. I can't promise you anything. All I can tell you is that I will try my best to get you that information."

Redds nodded. "Thanks, that's all I'm asking you to do. Try your best. I'm paying you a lot of money not because I have it to throw around, but because this is my life. You do understand that, right?"

"Yes, very much so. I fully understand what is at stake and I'm going to do everything in my power to help you. You can trust me on that one."

"Cool," Redds said.

"On another note, I know you're not going to want to hear this, but as your lawyer, I have to present it to you, so don't take it the wrong way. Okay?"

Redds raised his eyebrow, wondering what his lawyer was about to come at him with. "What's up? Talk to me."

"The government has offered you a cop."

"A cop to what!" Redds asked defensively.

"Life without parole. They'll take the death penalty off the table if you plead guilty to life without parole. I have to inform—"

Redds cut him off. "With all due respect, I don't even want to hear nothing about life without parole. I'll fight to the death of me before I lay down for life without parole. Let me make that very clear. It's not even a conversation. So, the next time them crackers bring that shit up you, tell them I said I'll never bow down to no shit like that. Never. Do we have an understanding?"

Smith nodded. He respected the stand Redds was taking. "I fully understand where you are coming from. Like I said, I had to give you the information."

"You did that and now you know that I ain't going for no shit like that. Plain and simple." Redds made his position very clear and from that point on, the line in the sand was drawn and it was time to fight fire with fire.

Lil' Moon found himself over D.C. Jail a week later. He was sent to the top left tier of North-1. Luckily for him, he knew a few young dudes on the top left tier and most of them couldn't stand Top. That was perfect for Lil' Moon because as soon as he found out that Top was on the top right tier, he knew there was going to be bloodshed. There was no other way to look at it. Top had killed people on his side and Lil' Moon had killed people on Top's side. They had a beef that would never be squashed until one of them was dead; they both understood that.

Lil' Moon was arrested and charged with a double murder for one of the many missions he'd gone on for Apple. Now that Apple and Jay were dead, he was on his own and had to fend for himself in a world of violence and madness. However, like most juveniles like himself that were sent to the adult system, he would learn that survival was the only thing that mattered.

Sitting on the bed in his one-man cell looking at the writings on the wall, Lil' Moon smoked a Newport. From his bed, he could see right into the cell across the tier from him where his man, Lil' Pete, stood at the bars to his cell. They talked about Top. Days earlier, a few juveniles from the top right tier had stabbed one of the juveniles from the left side. The C.O.s tried their best to keep the two sides separated. That was a hard job because the juveniles always seemed to find a way to get out together.

Lil' Pete was a wild little nigga that was facing three different murder charges. He didn't give a fuck about anything. He made his own rules. Talking shit, Lil' Pete said,

"That nigga Top think he built like me, he got shit fucked up if he think a nigga give a fuck that he fuck wit' them Kennedy Street niggaz. Fuck them niggaz, Moon. I got your back. You know that. It's whatever wit' me. Whatever you trying to do, young."

"It's all good. It ain't in the talk," Top said. He really wasn't into talking about what he planned to do out loud on the tier for all to hear. He knew how niggaz talked and how hearsay spread. He'd rather catch Top and handle his business instead of talking about it.

As Lil' Moon to talk to Lil' Pete, he looked around his cell and checked out the writings on the cell wall. There were a lot of RIP writings on the wall. One read: RIP Markelle, you were one of a kind my nigga. You will never be forgotten. Reading the RIP writings made Lil' Moon think about Jay. He would never rest until everybody that played a role in Jay's murder was put to sleep like rabid dogs. He put his life on that.

Lil' Pete heard niggaz banging on their windows and rushed to his window to see what was going on outside. Females made their way into the visiting hall. They all looked so good, like they were going to a club. Looking over his shoulder, Lil' Pete shouted, "Ay, Moon, these bitches lookin' good shit out here, young. We gotta hurry up and get the fuck outta' here."

"I feel you," Lil Moon said. However, he wasn't looking forward to chasing bitches when he got out, he was looking forward to killing shit. Revenge was what was on his young mind. Pussy could wait. Nevertheless, at the moment, Top was his target.

The mail had just been passed out on the bottom tier and Redds was lying on his bed reading a letter from Necci. She'd sent a few pictures and a few dollars for his account. Her letters kept him going and brightened his day every time. In her letter she assured him that she would be strong and no matter what happened, she would be down for him, forever. With everyday that went by, he missed her more and more. At times, when he looked at what the future could hold for him, he wondered if it was even fair to Necci to take her through it. After all, she had her whole life ahead of her. Redds thought deeply about how he would tell her to go on with her life if things turned out for the worse. He couldn't see himself making her suffer through the whole ordeal. However, there would be no way he could bring up such a conversation at the time. She would want no parts of it, Redds was sure of it.

After Redds finished reading Necci's letter, he opened a letter from his father.

Reggie,

As Salamu Alaikum. I pray that this letter finds you maintaining and remaining strong in the face of all that you're going through. I pray for you everyday. I hope that my letters have been a source of strength and understanding for you in your present struggle. You are my son, my flesh and blood, so I know that you are strong and can deal with all that comes your way. I wish you didn't have to go through what you are going through, but it is part of life. Somehow, it is divine decree. Allah is the best of planners and I place my trust in Him. You have been through more than most people your age. You are beyond your years, so there's no doubt in my mind that you will be just fine in the end, no matter how things go. One thing that I must commend you on is the fact that through this whole thing you have not complained about your circumstances at all. Not one bit. That is the sign of a strong man. You deal with your struggles head up. That brings honor and respect, far and wide.

I must say that I have been feeling very blamewor-
thy for not being there for you while you were growing up,
but you know that story. Yet and still, I've grown to understand that Allah tries mankind in many different ways.
Those of us that are stronger are tested harder. Allah will
never place on us more than we can handle. Always remember that, Reggie. We—as father and son—must trust
in that knowledge. No matter what you have done in life,
you can always call on your Creator. It's never too late.

Without a doubt, I know that you will stand tall
with great honor, no matter what comes your way. I don't
have to tell you that all men stand tall and never fold; you
know this. It is in your blood. Men like us always stand on
our own two feet and face danger eye-to-eye without the
option of compromise. You know this as well. You are now
in another world. A world where the rules a very different
than they are in the free world. Stay focused. Trust no one
and be prepared for the unexpected at all times. Never
give up! You have a good lawyer, stay on top of him and do
your homework. Don't leave your life in his hands. You
must do the fighting. It is your life, not your lawyer's. Never subject yourself to the will of other men.

I love you, son!

Peace
Amir
P.S. Never lay down!

Redds sat the letter down, blocked out the yells of
other men locked in their cells, and thought deeply about
the words his father had written. His father's words were
just what he needed to hear. Redds was grateful that he
had a father to give him wisdom. He trusted him and he
knew that his father knew what he was talking about.

"Never lay down," Redds said out loud. Those were words that would be etched into his mind forever.

Chapter 11

Toya visited Amir much more since Redds went on the run. She found comfort in being able to talk to him about her worries and concerns regarding their son. Amir gave her words of wisdom that strengthened her spirit to continue pushing forward. Amir took Toya's fear very seriously. In fact, he shared some of those fears with her.

However, years of struggle and faith had taught Amir that with every hardship in life came some sort of ease in due time. The Quran made that very clear to him. Many times over, Amir looked Toya in the eyes, and said,

"The Creator has this all mapped out. Have faith, Toya. Some things are out of our hands. All we can do is pray on it."

Toya nodded in agreement. "I hope so," was all she could say.

Toya's words stayed on Amir's mind all day after his last visit with her. Croc noticed that Amir was in deep thought all day, so he asked his partner what was on his mind. Standing on a long prison tier down Lorton with music blasting from a boom box somewhere on the top tier, Amir and Croc spoke about Redds. Croc loved Redds like a son, he used to watch him all the time when he was a little kid. As Amir spoke about Redds, it made Croc think about the son that he had on the streets that he didn't know. If he had one wish in the world, it would to find his son before something terrible happened to him in the streets.

Shaking his head, Amir said, "They trickin' us real good in this world. The system ain't right. This case with Reggie is clear proof. They locking our youngin's up for all kinds of different things and sending them away for life. It's like it's no way to stop their plan. By the time we wake up and fully understand how things work, our kids are already coming to prison right behind us." Amir took a deep breath as he rubbed his forehead. "It's no way we should be sitting in prison and our sons are in here with us. Somebody has to learn. Somebody has to make it. You feel me?"

Croc shook his head. "I feel you. I think about my own son. I don't have an idea where he is and what he's into out there. Every time we talk about Reggie, I think about my youngin'."

"Insha Allah, you'll find your son before it's too late. I pray you find him and catch him before he ends up like my son."

Inside the D.C. Jail, it was 12:15 a.m. when Dontae's cell popped. As the cell bars slid open, he stepped out on the dark tier. All the lights were out. He walked down the tier and through the tier door. Looking down the steps to the control bubble, he could see a sexy-ass female C.O. A smile crossed his face as he approached. Once he got to the bubble, another door slid open and he walked back into the sally port. The C.O. opened the door to the bubble and stepped out in a tight pair of dark blue uniform pants. She was thick in the hips and ass. Carefully, she led Dontae to the back.

Her name was Ms. Alston. She was short and cute with an around-the-way-girl kind of look. Her smooth, brown skin was clear and her smile was bright white. Dontae loved her smile and made it clear to her every time she was on duty. Her green eyes held his attention the most. That was a turn on. Every chance Dontae got, he put a few words in her ear and let her know that he was really feeling her. She was feeling him, too, and there was no way that she could hide it. On top of all that, Dontae knew her from the streets. She lived right down the street from his cousin in Barry Farms. Dontae was always nice to her when he saw her on the streets, but he never really took the time out to go after her. He moved too fast and couldn't sit still long enough to spark up some kind of relationship. Not to mention that he was in love with Pinky at the time. However, being as though she worked at the jail, Dontae had all the time he needed to get in her ear.

Quickly, Ms. Alston opened the mop closet for Dontae to get the mop and other cleaning supplies so he could clean the tier. Once she saw that nobody was in sight, she said, "Hurry up, boy. Get your ass in here. Hall will be back in twenty minutes."

Dontae wasted no time stepping inside the mop closet. "Shhhh, don't worry. We good. Ain't nobody coming up in here. Besides, don't worry about Hall, I got him." Dontae and C.O. Hall had an understanding. He was an undercover heroin addict and Dontae fed that addiction with good dope that Hall would pick up from the different dudes in the streets and bring inside the jail for Dontae. Of course, Dontae facilitated the whole lick.

Once inside the mop closet, Dontae shut the door behind them. There was little light inside, but through the dimness they could see what they were doing. Ms. Alston pulled down her pants and bent over. She was wearing no panties. Looking over her shoulder, she said, "Fuck the shit out of me. I ain't been to work all weekend and I need that dick. I been home alone playing with my pussy thinking about you fucking me. Ain't that crazy?"

Dontae smiled. "Hell no, that ain't crazy. That's sexy." Dontae lowered his jumper and pulled out his manhood. Instantly, he grew an erection. "I been waitin' for you all weekend, too." He grabbed her by the waist and slid inside her from the back. Her tight, wet pussy made him want to cum instantly. Even though he was fucking her almost every day she worked, he still couldn't get enough.

Bracing herself with her hands on the wall, Ms. Alston bit her bottom lip as she tried her best not to scream.

His erection felt like it was sliding in and out of her stomach. The deeper he penetrated, the more she moaned. Slamming her ass back against his thrusts, Ms. Alston exploded and came all over his dick in only minutes of having him inside of her wetness. Feeling her cum all over his dick, Dontae pulled her back to him with brute force, slamming his dick inside her pussy. Her moans grew louder and louder as he pounded her from the back. The loud slapping sound of her ass cheeks hitting his thighs was the only sound other than her deep moans. As Ms. Alston came, her body began to shake. The feeling of ecstasy was on 1000. Just by the way Dontae fucked her alone, she would do anything for him. All he had to do was say it and she would do her best to make that a reality.

Fucking her harder, she knew Dontae was about to make her cum. That turned her on even more. Just the thought of him cumming inside her made her cum again, this time, much harder than the first. "Oh, my God, I'm cummin' again, Dontae."

"Ahhhrrrgggg," Dontae grunted as he came inside of her. "Damn! Your pussy good." Breathing hard, Dontae slowed down and pulled out of her wetness.

Slowly, Ms. Alston stood up and faced Dontae as she pulled up her pants. "I'm gonna lose my job fucking with you. You know that?"

Fixing his jumper, Dontae said, "I won't let that happen." He kissed her and squeezed her ass. "Let me go clean the tier while you go to the bathroom and get yourself together."

Ms. Alston shook head and stepped out of the mop closet. Dontae had her sprung and she didn't give a fuck.

The next day, Top patiently waited for the C.O. to escort him back to his cell and take off the handcuffs after a legal visit. He was on lockdown status for getting caught with a knife during a shake-down of his cell. Standing at the control bubble, he heard a loud smack against one of the windows from the bottom tier behind him. Quickly, he turned to see what was up. Heavy had thrown a bar of Lisa soap from his cell against the window in order to get Top's attention. "Watch your back!" Heavy yelled as he pointed toward the top left tier with urgency. In a flash, Top turned around and braced himself for the worse. His heart pounded violently as he saw Lil' Moon and two other juveniles running down the steps from the top tier with knives in their hands. Top was helpless. He desperately tried to free himself from his handcuffs, causing the metal to cut into his skin. Taking off running toward the sally port, Top looked around for anything he could use for a weapon.

Lil' Moon and his comrades gave chase. An older female C.O. in the control bubble panicked and tried to shut the sally port door. Another C.O. tried to stand in the way of the attackers in an attempt to protect Top. His actions were for naught. The juveniles didn't slow down, they stabbed the shit out of C.O. for getting in their way and continued to go after Top. The C.O. in the bubble screamed when she saw the bloodshed.

Lil' Moon and the other juveniles ran into the back room and went dead at Top, swinging their blades with murderous intentions. To their surprise, Top had gotten one of his hands free and grabbed a fire extinguisher. He was much bigger than his attackers and used that to his advantage as he swung the fire extinguisher, bashing one of his attackers in the head with it. Top swung the fire extinguisher over and over as if his life depended on it. Lil' Moon and his two sidekicks didn't back off. They continued their assault like pit bills. As they attacked Top from all angles, they landed damaging blows with their blades. He began to lose a lot of blood. Things began to become a blur for him. Lil' Moon grabbed Top's jumper and tried to land a knife blow to his neck. Top yanked away and split Lil'

Moon's head open with the fire extinguisher, but Lil' Moon
kept swinging the knife. Blood was everywhere. The death
match seemed to go on forever. It didn't look good for Top.
The more he fought for his life, the more blood he lost.

The Emergency Response Team showed up seconds
later in full riot gear. As soon as the gate to the front of the
housing unit opened, they rushed inside, taking no prisoners. They attacked the juveniles and wrestled them to the
floor, fucking them up in the process. Moments later they
had them all, Top included, on the ground in the blood,
handcuffed.

One of the ERT officers looked down at Top, got a
good look at the bad shape he was in, and said, "We need
to get this one to a hospital. He's about to go out!"

With a load of paperwork in front of him, Assistant
U.S. Attorney James Burling sat at his desk talking to Agent
Bulger about the Kennedy Street case. They both had been
talking to and questioning witnesses all day. It seemed like
every joker in the city that had a case in court had some
information to offer, for a deal, about the Kennedy Street
Crew. It was amazing to the government. Burling was good
at pressing people to give up information. He had no problem making it clear that he would give a nigga life in prison
if they didn't cooperate, and if they did he might send them
away for a good five years. Under the table, he even offered some witness money and housing for their cooperation. Others, he allowed to get special visits while in prison
where they could have sex with their girls and have food
from the street. In his mind, there was nothing impossible.
Deals could be made all the way up the latter if the situation was right. Burling had put together a mean team of
government witness that was lined up to get on the witness
stand against Redds and his comrades.

"Whatever you need, just put the paperwork in,"
Burling said to Bulger. "I'm backing anything you see fit to

do. You have done a very good job on this case and I'm proud of you."

Bulger rubbed his chin, and said, "I think we can get something out of Reggie Williams' girlfriend. She knows a lot and we know that she was on the run with him. I really believe that if we put some pressure on her that she just might help us out. It could be wishful thinking, but it's worth a try."

"See what you can get out of her. If she wants to play hardball, lock her up and she can go to trial with them for all I care."

"I'll see what I can come up with," Bulger said.

"Very well." Burling stood up and shook Bulger's hand. "We have this one in the bag, Bulger."

"We sure do." Bulger smiled and left the office.

Burling paced his office for a second as he thought about the case. He'd done some things that weren't correct, but it was a dirty game that he was in, as far as he was concerned. Certain things had to be done in order to secure victory. With that in mind, Burling had made sure he destroyed the tape that his office had received that captured the killing of the undercover officer that was killed in the 500 block of Kennedy Street. Destroying evidence was nothing new to Burling. In his mind, he was doing the right thing for the cause. He knew that Mike was the cop killer and that Redds and his comrades had nothing to do with it, but it was the one crime that would be sure to get them all the death penalty and that was all he cared about.

Back over D.C. Jail, Dontae stood in front of Redds' cell in a blue jail jumper, holding a push broom. The two comrades were talking about Top and what went down with him. C.O. Alston had told Dontae that Top got stabbed pretty bad and there was no word on how he was doing. Some of the C.O.s that took him to the hospital weren't sure if he was even going to pull through. He'd lost so much blood and passed out before he made it to D.C. General. The C.O. that got stabbed was on life support; word throughout the jail was that he'd lost a lung in the attack. The vicious stabbing had the whole jail on lockdown. D.C. police came in to investigate the crime as two attempted murders. They brought in yellow tape and cameras, and treated the scene like a real crime scene from the free world. Lil' Moon and his two comrades were locked down, and were waiting to be charged. They had shut the jail down and made a serious statement. For all to see, they'd made their mark with force.

Redds shook his head. "I'm fucked up how they brought my little man that move. If I catch one of them little niggaz I'm put that knife in they ass. I'ma kill one of them muthafuckas."

"Slim, you ain't even gotta' trip," Dontae said.

"Them little niggaz that fuck wit' Top gon' roll for slim as soon as they come off of lockdown. They do it every time something goes down. Watch what I tell you."

"I hear you." Redds sighed. "I hope youngin' make it. Top like a little brother to me. You know?"

"I know, I feel the same way, slim. I think he'll pull through, though."

A few minutes later, Ms. Alston called Dontae. It was time for him to clean the sally port. She was running the block alone for a minute, so he knew what time it was.

"Redds, I gotta go. I'll be back before we lock down." Dontae smiled.

"I know that's right, slim." Redds laughed. "What we eatin' tonight?"

"Pizza Hut!" Dontae yelled as he ran down the tier.

Inside the darkness of the caseworker's office, Dontae stood with his back against the door getting some of the best head he'd ever had in his life. Ms. Alston did things with her tongue that Dontae had only seen on porno tapes.

Sliding in and out of her mouth, he did his best not to cum too fast. The way she took him all the way down her throat with no problems made his eyes roll back in his head as he coached her with his hand behind her head. Looking down at the C.O. on her knees in her uniform sucking his dick turned him on. As she went up and down on his dick, she rubbed his balls and moaned as if she loved every moment. Fast and faster, she sucked the life out of him. She wanted him to cum. She wanted to taste him, to swallow what he had inside of him. Looking up at him, she could tell he was about to cum by the look on his face. That turned her on and made her moan. "Cum in my mouth," she said, stroking his dick with speed.

"Put it back in your mouth." Dontae pulled her head forward and shoved his dick back in her mouth, making her gag. She loved it. "Ahhhh …" Seconds later, Dontae came inside her mouth. They locked eyes as he came, shooting loads of cum in her mouth. She maintained eye contact as she swallowed his load.

When she was done, she stood up and looked Dontae in the eyes. "I love you."

Dontae was blown away. He wasn't ready for that. His feelings weren't the same, at least, not at the time. Nevertheless, he played it smooth. "You really mean that?"

"I won't do what I do if I didn't."

Dontae put his arms around her, and said, "I love you, too."

She smiled. He had stolen her heart. "I can't get enough of you, you know that?"

"I feel the same way."

"Why couldn't we do this when you was on the streets?"

He smiled. "I was caught up in that life. You know how things go when a nigga is deep in the game."

"Whatever." She rubbed his manhood. "You ain't have time for me 'cause you was chasing all them other bitches."

Dontae laughed. "You trippin', it wasn't even like that. I was chasin' paper, all day, all night."

"I was reading about your case in the paper. I didn't know you were that bad."

"Bad? What you mean by bad?"

"They say you was killing people. I can see that in you."

"Don't believe everything you hear. You know that. They put a lot of shit on me and my men that we ain't even do. They trying to railroad us."

"I hope you beat your case. I would love to be with you in the free world. I would make you so happy." She meant every word that was coming out of her mouth. There were pictures of Dontae all over her bedroom. She was deeply in love with him.

Dontae kissed her, and said, "I hope I beat this case, too. One thing you can bet on is that if I do, me and you are going far away from here. I'm done with D.C."

"I would love that." She looked at her watch and saw that they had been missing for too long. "Ay, we got to get out of here before we get caught."

Ms. Alston and Dontae quietly left the office.

Days later, Necci was back in the visiting hall with Redds. She was putting him on point about a few things. Shell had dropped off $400,000 at Toya's apartment. It was Redds' share of some of the money they'd made that he'd left behind. The money was really needed at the time. Shell had also put the house that Redds had bought in Ohio up for sale and was going to give the money to Necci once everything went through. Redds was glad that Shell was on top of business and the he was able to maintain the connect with Calvin on his own. A strong Cali plug would make

Shell very wealthy if he could manage it right without the feds getting on his back. Redds knew that Shell would look out for him and make sure things were taken care of on the outside, so that took a little stress off of his shoulders.

Necci said, "Shell is on top of things. He said he gon' drop some more money off week after next. He said he used some of the money to go back."

Redds nodded. "That's cool. I ain't worried about that. He doing what he gotta do to keep shit moving. That's what I would do if I was out and he went in. I trust Shell and I understand how he thinks."

"That makes sense. Shell is really fucked up about your situation. He said to ask you if there's anything he can do to help you."

"Tell him all he can do to really help me is to keep gettin' paid, and make sure you and my mother is taken care of. I'll work this out as best as I can. As long as I can call on him when I need him means more to me than anything else."

"Okay, I'll tell him when he calls back. On another tip, you know that FBI agent Schoenberg pulled up on me."

"When?" Redds asked with concern in his voice.

"The other day. I was standing on First with Kobi and Bundy, and he pulled up on me talking about he needed to speak to me."

"What happened?"

"Kobi and Bundy was hip to him, so they stepped off. They knew I could handle myself. I ended up telling him I ain't have shit to talk to him about. Without another word, I jumped in the truck and pulled off. Later on, though, he was sitting in front of the house, like he watching me and shit."

"Don't trip off that shit. They gon' try to scare you, but if they really had something on you they would have locked you up already. What they gon' try to do now is see if they can scare you into giving them some information about us. I already know that you not gon' do no shit like that, so all you have to do is just stay firm and don't feed into the games they play. You already know the drill."

"I got you. They fuckin' wit' the wrong bitch. I hate them bitches."

"You's a rider, they can't try that bullshit wit' you. They know that, for real."

Necci nodded. She knew that the feds were going to play dirty in their attempt to get a conviction. "You don't have worry about me letting them run no bullshit on me."

"I feel you," Redds said before changing the subject. "What's up wit' Top? You talked back to shorty yet? I ain't seen him since he went to the hospital."

"Yeah, he got somebody to let him call me last night. He's okay. He's a big boy. He got hit in the chest twice. That's what really fucked him up and made him lose a lot of blood. He said most of the other wounds were cuts and scratches all over his arms and back. Shorty gotta be one of the toughest little niggaz I know. He said he already doing push-ups and shit. He trying to hurry up and get back in shape. They done made him mad now."

Redds shook his head and smiled. "Youngin' gon' fuck some shit up. He not gon' have no understanding about that shit there. I'm glad he alright, though, they was talkin' like he wasn't gon' make it at first."

"Yeah, he gon' be alright."

"Cool." Redds nodded. "Did you check on the house in Fort Washington?"

"Yeah, I checked on that and a few others. I'm gon' see what's up. Soon as Shell get shit straight with the property in Ohio, I will be able take care of everything on my end."

"That sounds like a plan. Let me know how things go."

"Will do," Necci said.

A few days later, Top was back over the jail and out for rec. by himself. Since he'd been stabbed, he was placed on involuntary P.C. Top hated being on P.C., it was not for him, but there was nothing he could do about it. The jail staff had done it. Nevertheless, he spent all of his time plotting his move to kill Lil' Moon.

On the phone with his man E Dub, Top put him on point about more important things. With all that he had going on, he was still facing life in prison if he went down for murder and he couldn't go down without a fight.

"I gave Necci some money for you, young," E Dub said, standing on his front porch talking on a cordless phone.

"Thanks, joe! I need that. But, on another note, I really need to see you tomorrow. I got some serious shit to holla at you about."

"I'll be there. Say no more!"

"Bet." Top hung up the phone and went back out onto the tier where he continued to do his push-ups.

It was just after 3:30 a.m. on Friday night and the go-go was just letting out. Rare Essence had done their thing and it seemed like the whole city had came out to see them. Go-go was a huge part of the D.C. culture and it was in the bloodline of the youth. Countless young people poured out of Coolidge High School gym on 5th Street, N.W. and flooded the street. Cars with music blasting rolled by slowed, mostly dudes checking out the girls that were flaunting sex appeal. Crews from all over town were quickly making their way to their cars to get the fuck on the road before any gunplay started. There were a few beefs in the air and nobody wanted to catch a stray.

E Dub was creeping. He bent the corner in a dark green Delta 88 on a mission. Behind the tinted windows he had on a ski mask, black leather gloves, and was strapped with a .45 automatic. He was witness hunting. In an effort to help kill Top's murder charge, E Dub was going to make the witnesses disappear. He spotted the young dude that he was looking for in a group of females. It was game time and E Dub wasted no time. In one bold move, he slammed the car in park, jumped out, and fired at close range. People ran and scattered when they saw the body fall. E Dub ran up and stood over the victim to make sure he was done. Taking one last look at the victim, E Dub pumped four more rounds into his head. In a flash, he jumped back in the car and took off flying toward Silver Spring.

A week later in a holding cell behind the courtroom, Redds, Dontae, and Heavy discussed what had just happened at their court hearing. The government was stacking the deck against them. Since they were facing RICO charges, the government got the judge to allow evidence of other crimes into the trial. That was yet another blow for the defense and the defendants didn't agree with the judge's ruling for many reasons. One of those reasons was because there was no real proof that any of them had ever committed any of the crimes that were in question. The government was only using the alleged past crimes to paint a picture of criminal of the defendants. Some of the crimes were crimes they had been found not guilty of. However, the federal court made up its own rules. The judge made his call and made it clear that he really didn't care anything about the defendants' constitutional rights. As far as he was concerned, the prior bad acts and crimes that the Kennedy Street Crew was accused of all supported the government's claim that the defendants were all criminals with a long, violent criminal history.

On top of that, every time they went to court, they learned of another one of their codefendants that had switched sides and was now working with the government. One after another, they took the trip to Orange County, VA where the government sent all the rats and cowards that turned states. Dirty was the latest one to flip the script. Redds and Dontae weren't surprised. In fact, Redds had told Dontae weeks ago that he didn't believe Dirty would hold water and in the end he was right. It was like Redds had an eye for weakness in niggaz.

Heavy was growing very fatigued as time went on. He began to second-guess his stance. Inside, he was losing faith in the fact that they may really be able to beat the case. He would never break and tell on his comrades; he'd die first. However, he started to think about pleading guilty to life in prison in order to avoid the death penalty. The thought of the government killing them all by lethal injection began to haunt him in his sleep. In his mind, they had no win. All of their homies that were weak were breaking and working with the government. In his eyes, they were going to trial for the sole purse of pride. That started to look like a dumb move to him.

"Man ..." Heavy shook his head in frustration as he sat on the iron bench thinking about his future. Or, what was left of a future. "I'm thinkin' 'bout takin' that cop," he said out loud, not really addressing it to anyone in particular.

Redds and Dontae stopped in the middle of their conversation and looked at him like he was out of his fucking mind. They couldn't believe what had just come out of his mouth.

Dontae gave him another crazy look, and said, "I know you ain't just say what I think you said. You can't be serious, joe!"

"No bullshit!" Redds raised his eyebrows. "You playin' right?"

Heavy shook his head. "Man, shit is fucked up. Y'all can't see what kind of cake they got baked for us? These crackers is goin' to kill us if we lose trial and wit' all

these hot niggaz tellin' on us, how the fuck are we supposed to win? It ain't meant for us to win. I don't know
about y'all, but I can't let them bitches kill me when I see
them loading the fucking gun. We can't even win a motion
in court. This shit is already planned out, they know what
they want to do and how it's gon' play out. It's like a damn
movie script already written out. They got all of their rats
lined up to get on the stand. After that, they gon' show a
bunch of videos and it's gon' be a rap. Ain't no jury in
America gon' believe us. I been reading all kinds of cases.
Nobody wins! Look at Newton Street, look at First Street,
and Panama and them. They all went to trial and they all
got found guilty. It ain't no beating the federal government
when they really want a nigga."

Redds shook his head. He was really disappointed
that Heavy was having second thoughts about going to trial,
yet, at the same time, he understood that facing the death
penalty affected different people in different ways. Redds
looked at life from a different standpoint than most people.
He looked at things in a way that if he was going to go out
in a blaze of glory that he was going to go out fighting, no
matter what.

Dontae was shocked and that shock instantly
turned into anger. In his mind, he, Redds, and Heavy were
the ones that would stand tall through it all. If Heavy was
having second thoughts, then Dontae was going to have to
question his honor as a man and a codefendant. "Heavy,
what's up, joe? They got you scared now that it's getting
closer to trial? You wanna' roll over like them other scared
ass niggaz?"

Offended, Heavy jumped up and got in Dontae's
face. "Ain't nobody scared! You know I ain't no scared nigga, but these bitches got us by the balls. Fuck am I supposed to do? Just let them kill me? We can all see that we
ain't got no fuckin' win. I got a son to think about, at the

end of the day. Even if I get life in prison, at least I can see him. If they kill us, that's it. It's over!"

Dontae's face grew red with anger. The two code-fendants' tempers flared and something was about to explode. Redds could see what was about to happen and didn't want it to go down like that. It was too heated. They didn't have time to be beefing with each other. Redds stepped in between them and pushed them apart. "Hold up! Hold up!" he shouted. "What the fuck is wrong wit' you two? These crackers is tryin' to kill us. We ain't got no fuckin' time to be fighting each other."

Letting out a frustrated sigh, Dontae said, "This nigga lunchin'!" He pointed his finger at Heavy. "He wanna' lay down and give up. What the fuck you think life in prison is, nigga? Life in prison is just like death. Life is over!" Dontae threw his hands up in the air and walked over to the bars to calm down. He was pissed off so bad that his head began to pound.

"You the one lunchin', nigga!" Heavy shouted. "You see how they got the deck stacked against us. You know I'm calling it like it is."

Redds couldn't be mad at Heavy. It wasn't like he was thinking about crossing over and working with the government. He was only thinking about pleading guilty to spare the possibility of lethal injection. Redds had thought about the plea deal himself, but pushed the thought out of his head. He couldn't see himself laying down and doing life in prison. It was out of the question. As Redds drifted off into deep thought, Heavy and Dontae continued to argue. The arguing began to piss Redds off, and by him being a natural leader, he stepped in and put a stop to it. "Look here!" he shouted. "We ain't gon' do this shit here. We ain't gon' let them divide and conquer. Fuck all that shit there. We gon' stand firm and we gon' fight. We all we got. If we ain't got us, we ain't got shit!"

Dontae and Heavy looked at Redds. He never raised his voice, so that alone got their attention.

Heavy piped down, and said, "This is my life here. I got a right to make my own decision. It ain't like I'm tellin' on a nigga. It's what I'm thinking about."

Redds looked at Dontae, and said, "He's right. It is his life. He's the only one that can make that call."

Dontae shook his head in disbelief.

Redds looked back at Heavy and thought about his words for a second. He knew whatever choice they made individually would affect them all collectively. "Whatever you do, make sure you think it all the way through. This is our lives we talkin' 'bout."

Dontae looked at Heavy, and said, "Slim, you my man. I fuck wit' you from the heart. I love you and will stand behind you no matter what, you know that, Fats, but whatever you do, don't give up, slim. We gotta' fight them peoples. It's no other way to look at it. It's us against the world. Don't forget that."

Heavy thought about what Redds and Dontae had to say. "You know what? Fuck that shit. I'm goin' to trial. We all we got. You niggaz right."

Chapter 12

Locked in his cell, Redds stood behind the bars talking to his man, Cook. Cook was one of his many codefendants that was scattered all throughout the jail. He'd just been sent to North-1 for getting caught with a knife upstairs in population. Redds put Cook on point with all of the games that the government was playing and how they were going to play the same game with the rest of the Kennedy Street codefendants once the first trial was over.

Cook nodded in agreement. "I know they gon' play hardball. I been preparing myself for that shit the whole time I been over this dirty motherfucker. When you went on the run and Mookie smoked all them police, shit got hot as shit. I tried to stay low and go on the run myself, but it was like the feds was hot on my ass everywhere I went. I ran from them for as long as I could. You know I was last one to get arrested, aside from you."

"Yeah, I know. I was looking at the indictment and shit. You was the only one to get caught wit' some coke," Redds said. He couldn't believe Cook had got caught with ten bricks. When Redds went on the run, Cook was only buying one brick.

"Yeah, it was just my luck, but you know how this shit goes. I got a good lawyer. I hope I can fight my way out of this shit."

"That's all you can do. We gotta' fight these people. They think we all dumb. I been in this cell reading everything I can read about our case. We got to stay in these law books. I'm not gon' let them just do whatever they want to do. I got a good ass lawyer, too, but it's my life so I'm on top of everything that concerns me. I know more about the RICO act than I know about anything I ever learned in school. That's how we gotta' be."

Cook nodded. "I feel you. I was hitting the law library hard as shit when I was in population. I got a bunch of case law on our shit."

"You ain't doing nothin' wrong. It's your life!" Redds said.

The door to Cook's cell opened and slammed shut. It was time for him to go back in his cell and the C.O. in the bubble let him know. "That's my time. I'll talk to you when I come out tomorrow."

"Bet." Redds gave Cook five. "See you tomorrow."

Redds sat down on the metal stool that was connected to the metal desk in the back of his cell and began writing his father:

Pops

What's up? I'm holding on as best as I can up here. Dealing with the madness. As you know, I have a lot on my mind, to say the least. Nevertheless, I'm remaining strong and focused as a real man should always be. At the same time, between me and you, I have been stressing over this case. The government really has the deck stacked against us. They are trying to put us to death for real. All of these weak ass niggaz are selling us out and making things worse by the hour. I feel like I can trust no one and that I have no win against the charges against me, yet, I fight on, anyway. The government was talking about offering us a cop to life without parole. I can't see it. I'd never lay down for life without parole, not even in the face of death. I'd rather fight to the death!

    Always Real
    Reggie
  P.S. I'll never lay down!

Redds finished the letter to his father and began reading over some of his legal papers that dealt with the death penalty. Researching his case was what he spent most of his cell time doing. Nothing else was more important. While others were trying to holla at the female C.O.s, or trying to regulate the phones, or selling drugs, or any of that bullshit, Redds was fighting. He was studying and getting ready for the fight of his life. He understood what he was up against and he wasn't taking it lightly at all. After all, his life depended upon it.

Ms. Alston was burning with anger on her way to work. In fact, she was so pissed off that she ran a light a got a $100 ticket. Her girlfriend had called her on her day off and told that Dontae was in the visiting hall with another woman. That bit of news had Ms. Alston so mad that she couldn't even sleep. All she could think about was getting to work so she could confront Dontae and curse his ass out. Who the fuck do he think he's playing with? She continued to ask herself that question over and over again. He had her fucked up if he thought she was going to let him play with her feelings. It wasn't going down like that and she intended to make that very clear.

When she got to work, she got her day started by doing a head count with Officer Jones. When they passed Dontae's cell, she said nothing to him, didn't even look his way. He peeped it, but had no idea what that was all about. A short while later, Officer Jones took a quick break and left Ms. Alston in the bubble alone. No sooner than Jones left, Ms. Alston popped Dontae's cell and called him up on the floor. By the time Dontae made it there, she was already in the back room waiting for him. She had a mean look on her face and her arms were folded. Dontae could tell that she had an attitude.

"What's up, baby?" Dontae asked as he tried to give her a hug.

"Don't touch me, nigga!" She gave him a hard shove in the chest with both hands. "What bitch was you all up in the visiting hall with while I was off?"

Dontae shook his head and smiled. He already fully understood where the conversation was going. "So, that's why you actin' like this? That's what this is all about? Are you serious?"

"Very serious. You need to tell me something! I ain't smiling. Who the fuck was you up in the visiting hall with while I was off?"

Dontae got dead serious and his smile disappeared.

"First off, you need to calm the fuck down." Ms. Alston saw the look in his eyes and took it down a notch. "Come here." Dontae grabbed her hands and pulled her close to him. "Listen to me, I fucks wit' you tough. I got love for you. I don't really like explaining myself to people, but since I do love you, I'm going to explain the situation to you and I hope we won't ever have to go through this again. Okay?"

"I'm listening."

Dontae explained to her who Necci was and that it was she that came to see him. Not only was Necci Redds' girl, but she was also like a sister to him and had been that way for over twenty years. Whoever told that he was in visiting hall with another woman had their facts mixed up.

"Oh," Ms. Alston said. She felt embarrassed for even being mad when she didn't have all the facts. She'd jumped to conclusions and they turned out to be all wrong. She hugged Dontae and kissed him. "I'm so sorry. Women get like this when their feelings are involved. Do you for-give me?"

Dontae smiled. "I understand. It's okay." He rubbed his hand through her silky, black hair and kissed her lips. "But, at the same time, when you fuckin' wit' a nigga like me, you gotta' look at the big picture. Things are not always what they seem to be. Before you jump out there and get mad about something, you really need to talk to me first. That way, we won't even have to go through shit like this no more."

"You're right. I'll make sure I don't jump to conclusions."

"That's what I'm talkin' 'bout."

Looking him in the eyes, she said, "Let me ask you something."

"What's up?"

"Am I your woman?"

"Huh?" Dontae gave her a confused look. He was feeling her. He even had love for her, but he was facing the death penalty. He was in no position to really have a girlfriend.

"Answer my question. I'm serious. Am I your woman or not?"

"Nikki, look, I'm facin' the death penalty. I don't even know what the future holds for me right now. Even if I beat the death penalty, I'm still facing life in prison. Shit is fucked up for me right now. You don't wanna go all the way in with me. You don't know what kind of pain you're in for. Trust me."

"I don't want to hear all of that. I love you and I need to know if you love me. Am I your woman? Yes or no?"

Dontae thought about what she was asking him for a moment. He did love her when he thought about it. "I love you. You are my woman. The situation at hand is fucked up, but I do love you."

"That's all I need to hear from you. I will always love you, no matter what they try to do to you. Don't you ever forget that."

Later on, Top was downstairs at the bottom left tier door whispering to Redds through the crack in the door. He was whispering to keep niggaz out of his business.

"E Dub took care of that business." Top said.

Redds smiled at the good news. "So, you should be out of here real soon then, huh?"

"No bullshit. I'm waitin' to hear from my lawyer right now."

"That's a good look there. I'm glad shit is workin' out for you. I need you out there for real. I really don't have a good man on the streets other than Shell, but Shell in Ohio. You can make sure things are in order for me on the home front. I need that, joe."

"Redds, you know what the deal is. You my nigga! All you gotta' do is give the word and bodies gon' drop like 64s on switches."

Redds laughed. He knew that Top meant every word of the shit he was talking.

As Redds and Top were at the tier door talking, the C.O. in the control bubble forgot that Top was at the bottom of the steps. He ended up letting one of the juveniles from the top left tier down on the floor to drop his mail in the box. It turned out to be a terrible mistake. Top heard the top tier door open. He snapped to attention instantly. He was strapped with a street knife that could cut a man from navel to neck with ease. Unnoticed, Top looked up at the top tier through the steel steps and saw the juvenile; it was one of the juveniles that was with Lil' Moon the day Top got stabbed. It was no talking to be done. Redds saw the look in Top's eyes and knew what was about to go down. Top went straight into murder mode. He pulled the knife from his jumper and took off running up the steps on a mission.

"Oh, shit!" the juvenile yelled when he saw Top coming. He tried to take off and run.

"Don't run now, bitch!" Top grabbed the young nigga by the back of his jumper and began stabbing him in the neck and back, over and over again. He swung the knife hard like he was throwing punches at a heavy bag. The victim tried to snatch away and fell to the ground. Top got on top of him and continued to punish his ass. The yells and screams that came from the victim filled the entire cell block. It sounded like Top was killing him and that was exactly what Top was trying to do. The ERT rushed the block in seconds in riot gear and pulled Top off of his bloody victim. Blood was everywhere like a cow had been slaughtered. The bloody juvenile was laying on the floor passed out; he looked lifeless.

Seeing all the commotion that was going down on the tier above him, Redds shook his head. Top had just had a murder dismissed and it looked like he was about to be charged with another one before he even got out of jail. Damn, young nigga, Redds thought.

Necci found a nice three bedroom home in Temple Hills, MD. She started getting the house together, but it made her sad and depressed that Redds wasn't around to make the house a home. It got to her so much that she didn't want to stay at home. She spent most of her time uptown around First and Kennedy, or with Redds' mother on 5th and Kennedy. Her life was so stressful that all she could do to ease her pain was smoke blunt after blunt of high-grade weed from California. Nevertheless, she was still on top of business as always. She knew she had to be there for Redds and she took pride in being there for him. He was her king and she was his Queen.

Sitting in the law office of T.L. Smith, Necci and Smith discussed Redds' case.

"As I said before," Smith said, "in big cases like this one, the government must bear the burden of proof. Don't get me wrong, I have put a great defense together, but with such a huge indictment, the government has to show the jury, beyond a reasonable doubt, that the defendants deserve the death penalty. I've been looking into a number of death penalty cases and ... huh ..." Smith fumbled with some papers on his desk. "Uh ... in this Enmund v. Florida case, it says that death is prohibited for persons who lack intent to kill or play minor roles in the crimes committed. I believe that, at the very least, we can prove that Reggie and his friends didn't intend to kill that undercover officer, nor did they know a police officer was on the scene."

Necci nodded her head. She understood what Smith was telling her. "I see. So, in so many words, if Reggie and them did shoot the undercover and didn't know he was the police, then they didn't intend to kill the police."

"Exactly, to add to that, this case is based largely on the testimony of witnesses that in one way or another played a role in the alleged conspiracy. That's something I'm going to attack. My legal team is doing their homework on that at this very moment."

They continued to discuss the case for a good forty-five minutes. Necci questioned Smith about everything she didn't understand. She had done a lot of reading herself and had researched the case like she was on her way to trial. She wanted to know everything there was about the RICO act because she wanted to know what Redds was up against. Her diligence impressed Smith. He could tell that Necci was in Redds' corner for the long haul.

Just before she was about to leave, Necci said, "You got that for me?" She raised her eyebrows, hinting at what she wanted.

Smith sighed and slid her a sealed envelope. "You didn't get that from me. Okay?"

"I understand." Necci stuffed the envelope inside her Coach bag and left the office with the names and addresses of some of the witnesses that were to testify against Redds.

Over D.C. Jail, Heavy's mother had just come to visit him. She had bad news, his baby's mother was no longer going to allow him to see his son. She stated that if he wanted to see his son, he would have to do whatever he had to do to get out of jail, and to her, that meant turning on Redds and Dontae, testifying against them. In his life, Heavy had been shot two different times, he'd been stabbed in the neck, and survived car crashes that left others dead. He had dealt with more than his share of pain. However, none of that hurt him more than having his son taken away from him. That made him hate his baby's mother.

Out of his cell for his hour of rec., Heavy stood at Dontae's cell, telling him about the move his baby's mother had pulled on him. Dontae tried his best not to say anything foul about Heavy's baby's mother, but, inside, he wished death upon the bitch.

Heavy shook his head. "When a nigga was on the streets, gettin' all that money, she ain't never come at me wit' all this bullshit. All she cared about was Gucci this, Versace that. You feel me?"

"I feel you, slim. You see how Pinky carried shit when we came in. She turned her back on me off the top. It be like that sometimes," Dontae said.

"I would have never thought shit would play out like this."

"You know what, slim, as hard as shit may seem right now, you gon' have to do what I do. You gon' have to block all that outside shit out of your mind. We in another world right now. We gotta' deal wit' this jail shit all day, every day. Sun up to sun down. This is our world right

now. Worrying about them streets ain't nothin' but a dis-
traction. I know it sounds cruel, but fuck everything you
can't control."

"You got a point right there, homes. I feel you,"
Heavy said. Dontae's words had hit home.

Days later, Necci sat in a Range Rover in the parking
lot of the D.C. Jail with the windows down, enjoying the
cool breeze. It was now the first week of May and it felt
great outside. In her slick Gucci shades, Necci nodded her
head to the sounds of Jodeci's Come and Talk to Me. As the
song pumped through the powerful speakers, it reminded
her of the time Redds had taken her to the Virgin Islands.
While in the hotel suite, they played Jodeci to death and
made love all over the room. It was during that trip when
she really fell in love with him. At that point in her young
life, she had never been outside of D.C. Redds had showed
her better times in life and she couldn't wait to have him
back in her arms.

"What's up, joe!" A voice snapped her out of her
thoughts of Redds. She turned to her right and saw Top
getting into the passenger seat of the truck. "You miss
me?"

Necci smiled. She needed something to smile
about and seeing Top in the flesh made her day. She gave
him a huge hug and held him tight as she could. She didn't
want to let him go. He was family and he was all that she
had in her life that she could really depend on. "What's up,
boy?"

"I'm good. I'm out here wit' you, I'm free. I can't
cry about shit." He smiled. His murder case had been dismissed, due to the fact that there were no witnesses
against him. The stabbing that he committed was also
dropped when the victim decided not to press charges. Top
was a very lucky man. He was once again a free man. He

was also a nightmare in the making for all of his enemies, and to Redds, he was forever loyal.

"I hope you can chill out here. I need you," Necci said as she pulled off.

"I'm here for you, sis. You know that."

Necci rubbed his head. "You my nigga."

Chapter 13

Eleven long years had passed and the parole board came to see Amir and Croc. One would think that with all of the changes Amir had made in his life that they would let him go and give him a second chance at life. However, they gave him an 18-month set off, claiming that his record and his past were filled with violence. Amir took it all in stride and accepted it as the will of Allah. He knew his time would come and he was certain of that.

Croc, on the other hand, had never followed any rules and he made parole. He would soon be on the streets and be able to go on with his life, and all the things that he wanted to do. Amir was pleased for him. It was Croc's time to shine and that was exactly what he planned to do.

Sitting in a plastic chair in front of Croc's cell, Amir spoke to him about what he planned to do when he hit the streets.

Croc shook his head. "You know me, slim. I'm tryin' to get paid. I'm gettin' straight to the money. That's all I know how to do. Everything else can wait."

Amir rubbed his thick beard and smiled. "You ain't gon' learn. You know what kind of numbers them peoples givin' out and you still wanna' play with them. Look at Reggie. The time the feds givin' out now can't even be done. You can forget about parole if you come back. It's gon' be a rap, and I ain't sayin' that to wish nothing bad on you, I'm just telling you like it is, slim."

"Amir, I respect where you comin' from and I know you always speak the truth, but my plans ain't to be in the streets workin' no punk ass job. I gotta' go for what I know. Whatever comes with that, I'm willing to take. You know me."

"I know, but I just want you think about the big picture. That's all. If you were 19 or 20 it wouldn't be a thing, but you got some age on you. You don't have any room for mistakes. The streets ain't the same no more. Whatever you do, just take your time, champ. That's all I'm sayin'. I don't want to see you get yourself trapped off. And, remember this here, if you always make the same moves, you gon' always get the same results. You're wise enough to know what the results gon' be."

In the visiting hall at the D.C. Jail, Redds listened as Necci told him what Top was up to in the streets. She wanted Redds to have a serious talk with him before he got himself killed or locked up again. Top was on a rampage and was out of control. Necci knew that Redds was the only person that could talk to him, and she wanted him to coach Top back to his senses before he crashed and burned.

In the two weeks that Top had been back on the streets, he had smacked a nigga in the face with a pistol on Georgia Avenue for some money the dude owed him from before Top had got locked up. Not only did Top smack the dude in the face with a pistol in front a bunch of people, he also took the dude's Lexus and planned to keep the car until the dude paid him the money he was owed. A few days later, Top was shot at coming out of the Black Hole; somebody let off close to thirty shots in an attempt to kill him. The attempt on his life didn't faze him one bit. In Necci's mind, Top was on some kind of death wish and it was pissing her off that she couldn't talk any sense into him.

"He's trippin', Redds," Necci said. "I don't know what's on his mind right now. I forgot to tell you that he broke his wrist racing a motorcycle down V Street."

Redds shook his head. "Tell youngin' I said come see me soon as he gets a chance."

"I think he still fucked up about Lil' Man's death, so he just running wild."

"I'm going to talk to him, don't worry yourself. Other than that, what's good wit' that other shit?"

Necci put her elbows on the counter and leaned forward. "I'm pregnant," she said. She feared that news of a baby on the way would only add to Redds' worries, but she had to tell him about the news.

For an awkward moment, neither one of them spoke a word. Necci had been having all kinds of wild thoughts since she found out that she was carrying their child. In her mind, she felt like she was in no position to bring a child into the world with all that was going on in their lives. After all, she had no idea what Redds' future was going to hold.

Raising her eyebrows, Necci said, "Well, say something."

Redds smiled. "That's great news. It would be right on time if I was out there wit' you, but being in here makes the situation."

"How?" Tears filled Necci's eyes as she got emotional. The thought of raising a child without Redds weighed heavy on her heart.

"Calm down, baby. It's going to be okay. We will figure this out, just like we do everything else. You know I'm going to do all I can to make the situation what it needs to be."

Necci wiped her tears away and nodded her head in agreement. She wanted to believe Redds. She knew that he always did his best to make situations right.

Redds said, "Have I ever let you down?"

"No."

"I won't let you down now. Whatever I have to do to make shit right is what I will do. Believe that."

Lying in the bed locked in his cell, Redds was in deep thought. He was thinking about Necci being pregnant. He always wanted a child, but the thought of having a child under his circumstances didn't sit well with him. His fate was up in the air and there was no way of knowing what was to come once trial was over. Having a child on the way only added to his stress. Thinking about his life took his thoughts back to the last letter that his father wrote him where he ended the letter with a quote from Nelson Mandela that read, 'There is no easy walk to freedom anywhere, and many of us will have to pass through the valley of the shadow of death again and again before we reach the mountaintops of our desires!' That quote stayed in Redds' mind and played over and over again like a broken record.

The more he thought about his life and the wisdom in the letters from his father, he thought about another quote that his father had sent him that was from Assata Shakur that read: ... if I know anything at all, it's that a wall is just a wall and nothing more at all, it can be broken down.' Those words from Mandela and Assata had lit a fight fire inside of Redds that would never allow him to give up, ever. He would fight to the death for all that he stood for, no matter what the outcome was.

The cell door slid open and snatched Redds out of his deep thoughts. It was time for his rec. Redds stepped out of his cell wearing a blue jumper and a pair of Timberland boots. He had a knife stuffed in his waistband nice and neat where nobody noticed. He stepped to Cook's cell for a minute, and they smoked a jay of weed as they talked about their case and a few other things. At their last court hearing, the government proved that it had more than enough information coming from different sources to be able to do whatever it wanted to do in the courtroom. With every passing the day, the case was looking more and more impossible to beat. Pressing the defendants to plead guilty, the government seemed to be winning before trial even started. Defendants were taking 30-year plea deals left and right.

"Shit ain't lookin' good," Cook said.

"Yeah, I know, but all we can do is roll wit' the punches." Redds said.

"I feel you."

"I'm 'bout to jump on this phone real quick. I'll holla at you before I step in," Redds said as he headed for the phone.

Once on the phone, he called his mother to see how she was doing.

"Hello," Toya answered. She quickly accepted the call. "How are you, baby?"

"I'm holdin' on. Dealin' wit' this madness one day at a time. You know me."

"I spoke to your lawyer today. He was telling me about the plea deal the government is offering and—"

"Ma—"

"Let me finish! I can't even imagine what you have to go through in there facing the death penalty, but I fear for you, baby. I'm scared for you. I'm having all kinds of nightmares about your situation. Nightmares about you being put to death. It's so bad that I don't even want to go to sleep at night. When I do go to sleep and have one of those nightmares, I wake up in cold sweats. What I'm trying to say is ... Necci is having your baby. She needs you. I need you. Your unborn child needs you. You have to think about us when it comes to your decision to go to trial when you know the government is trying to kill you."

"Ma, I understand where you are comin' from, but you are asking me to lay down my life without a fight and do life in prison. I can't do that. It goes against everything I'm made of."

Toya began to cry. She knew that Redds was just like his father: if he believed in something, no one could change his mind about it. "I think you should think about the plea deal."

Redds said nothing for a moment. Life without parole was out of the question. He would rather die first. "Ma, it's nothing to think about. I'm goin' to trial."

"All I'm asking you to do is think about it. Just think about it." Toya was damn near begging her son by the tone of her voice. "I don't want them to kill you. I'm looking at everything you are facing and how so many of those guys are telling, I just can't see how you can't beat it. It doesn't make sense to me. It's like you know that you are going to lose and you still want to go to trial just to fight the government. You can't win. Don't you see it?"

"Ma, I'm a man, I have to fight for my life. I don't know any other way to tell you that."

"Don't you see that they are trying to kill you? At least, if you take the plea, you are still alive. I can see you, Necci can see you, your family can see you. I don't want to bury you. I need you alive, Reggie. We need you alive. Please, think about us. The deck is stacked against you. All of your friends are turning against you to save their asses."

"Ma, I love you. I love you wit' all of my heart. I feel where you are coming from, but I can't cop out to life in prison. I can't even see it. I refuse to go like that. To me, life in prison is death, anyway. It's just a slower death."

"Reggie, don't be like that, please. Don't be dumb, they are going to kill you. You are being bullheaded just like your damn father used to be."

"Ma, I can't do that. My time is up on the phone. I have to go. I love you, but I have to do what I have to do." He hung the phone up and returned to his cell.

In handcuffs, Redds was escorted to the conference area of the visiting hall. He had no idea that the FBI was waiting for him. They had a few questions to ask him. In the past two weeks, three witnesses against the Kennedy Street Crew had been found duct taped, handcuffed, and shot in the head. The feds were highly upset about the witness killings. The U.S. Attorney's office had made sure that the names and addresses of all witnesses were to be withheld from the defendants. As far as the feds were concerned, there was no way witnesses should turn up dead. After the third murder, they decided to take a trip to the jail where they searched the cells of every Kennedy Streets defendant. They found nothing, but they were sure that Redds had something to do with the killings, they just couldn't prove it at the time.

Redds could smell the feds from a mile away. He turned to the C.O. that was escorting him to the visiting hall, and said, "I thought you told me I had a legal visit?"

"That's what they told me, Williams," the C.O. said.

Redds stopped in his tracks. "Take me back to my cell, I ain't got shit to say to the feds. I don't play that shit!"

Agent Bulger saw that Redds was refusing to speak to him, so he walked up behind him, and said, "Redds!"

Redds looked back at the agent with hate in his eyes. He was surprised that the agent had called him by his nickname; any other time Bulger would call him by his last name when they ran across each other. "I ain't got shit to say to you! Save your breath."

"I just want you to know that while you are playing tough guy, your homeboys are playing it smart. They are looking out for themselves. I thought you were the smartest one, but you aren't being so smart after all. You are going to fry if you don't get down with the program before it's too late. You can't win. It's no win in it for you. You can't beat the federal government." Bulger said.

Redds frowned. "Suck my dick." He turned his back to the agent and walked away.

"You'll be sorry, Redds. Remember that!"

"Fuck you!" Redds said.

It was a beautiful evening in late May and Lil' Moon had to be the happiest 15-year-old in D.C., as far as young killers were concerned. His double murder had been dismissed and he was now walking out of the D.C. Jail looking up at the pretty, blue sky. He was wondering how he was going to get back on his feet now that Apple and Jay were dead and gone. Lil' Moon had a team of young killers that looked up to him, and he planned to hook up with them and take things to another level in the streets.

Walking up to a black, tinted window, 92 Nissan 300 ZX twin turbo, Lil' Moon jumped into the passenger seat still wearing his jail jumper. The strong smell of weed smoke welcomed him along with the sounds of Tupac. "What's up, young?" Lil' Moon gave his man, Boogie, five and shut the door.

"Ain't shit." Boogie smiled and passed Lil' Moon the blunt he was smoking. "Good to see you on this side, nigga." Boogie pulled off and headed uptown. As he drove, they smoked and Boogie told Lil' Moon how a homie of theirs had been shot by Prince George's County police the night before. As the young dude ran from the police, he tried to jump a fence and was shot in the back nine times, dying instantly. Aside from that, Top had killed one of their other homies. Top was a problem that was going to have to be dealt with as soon as possible. Since Top had been home, he and his crew had been dogging Lil' Moon's crew. Gunplay seemed to be an every night thing. "I caught the nigga Top comin' out the Black Hole 'bout three weeks ago and tried to take his head off. The nigga looked like Flash Gordon tryin' to get out of there. No bullshit."

Lil' Moon laughed. Passing the blunt back to Boogie, he said, "We gon' get at his bitch-ass in due time. I put that on everything. I tried to kill that nigga while we were over the jail. We put the knife in his ass about thirty times, almost killed the nigga."

Pulling up behind an old, blue van, Boogie stopped at a light on 21st Street as he Lil' Moon continued to talk and smoke. A bad ass broad in a money-green BMW 735i pulled up beside them and caught Lil' Moon's eye. He hit the button for the window and lowered it so he could holla. "Hey, baby. How you doin'?"

"I'm good." She smiled.

"Can I get your number and call you sometime?"

"Sure." She called out her number over the loud roar of an oncoming motorcycle.

A roaring green motorcycle pulled up behind the car Lil' Moon was in. The person on the bike was dressed in a black leather jacket and a green helmet. He impatiently revved the powerful engine of the Ninja as he waited for the light to change. Slowly, the biker pulled between Lil' Moon and the girl in the BMW, and came to an abrupt stop. In one swift motion, the biker whipped out a small Uzi that was on a strap around his neck and sprayed bullets right into Lil' Moon's face in seconds. The loud sound of fully automatic gunfire ripped through the air as countless shells spit high in his face and fell to the ground. Lil' Moon never had a chance. His brains flew all over Boogie. All the other cars at the intersection took off flying like they were in a drag race. Boogie jumped out of the car, he was hit in his chest with bullets. He tried to make a run for it. The biker/gunman revved the bike and rode around the car, over the median, and sprayed Boogie again. He collapsed in the middle of the street. The gunman rode up on him and let another burst of bullets rip through his body with a quick wave of his hand. The fully automatic Uzi finished Boogie off in seconds. The biker roared away like an F-15 fighter jet with blue/orange flames coming out the pipes.

Necci sat on a cream-colored leather sofa in her living room talking to her mother on the phone. She wasn't trying to hear what her mother was talking about.

"... you are throwing your life away dealing with Reggie. You see what's about to happen to him and you still want to bring a child into this world under those circumstances? That makes no sense, Necci."

"Ma, I'm not killing my baby. I will deal with whatever comes with it."

"You are being foolish, Necci. Reggie's life is over. Why would you bring a child into this world with no father?"

Dressed in all black, Top let himself into the house. Necci gave him a look that asked a million questions.

Turning her attention back to her mother, Necci said, "Ma, I gotta' go. I'll call you back later. I have company." Necci hung the phone up and looked at Top with raised eyebrows. "Well, what's the word?"

Top smiled as he sat on the sofa beside Necci. "I took care of that shit, dogged that nigga and his man, Boogie."

Necci rubbed Top on the head as if to say, job well done. She had kept up with Lil' Moon's case and when his case was dismissed, Necci had Top waiting on him. She had heard how Lil' Moon was over the jail bragging about how he had killed Lil' Man, so she felt that he got what he deserved. "That will hold his little ass, fuck 'em," she said.

"Now all I gotta' do is crush the rest of them witnesses and we can get Redds home." Top said.

Chapter 14

Croc was back on the streets once again. He'd been in Hope Village halfway house for just over a month. The halfway house was in a deadly section of Southeast, D.C. Just two days after Croc was placed in the halfway house he saw a young dude murdered at the front door. The killer was outside waiting for the young dude early in the morning when people left out for breakfast. That opened Croc's eyes to how things were going down in the streets. It was not a game. He was back in the mean streets of the Murder Capital. After seeing the young dude murdered, Croc had his girl, Jayde, bring a pistol with her every time she picked him up in the morning.

Jayde was a beautiful woman about 5' 6", 125 pounds, with a wonderful shape. She looked like something out of a girly magazine. Her skin was golden brown with a sexy glow. She had long, black hair that she let hang to her shoulders. She had just turned 26 and met Croc when she was 21 while visiting her cousin down Lorton. After weeks of letters, phone calls, and visits, Croc and Jayde hit it off. She was his type of woman, a real soldier. For five years, Jayde did all that she could for Croc and was there for him like no other woman had ever been. For that, he loved her with all of his heart and would do anything for her.

Sitting in the passenger seat of Jayde's red '94 Ford Escort, Croc took in the sights of the city as she drove him around town, taking care of his business. She took him through all of his old hangouts so he could holla at dudes that he needed to see in order for him to get back into position. 5th and O, 7th and T, and 14th Streets were at the top of the list for Croc, being as though all of his old comrades had things going in those areas.

"Ay, baby, I need you to take me up John-John's shop real quick before we shoot on the other side of town," Croc said. John-John was an old comrade of Croc's and also Necci's uncle. He owned a sporting goods shop on Georgia Avenue. Since Croc had been home, he had a "fake" job at the shop in order to get out of the halfway house for more hours in a day.

"Okay, but we need to get something to eat, baby. We been on the move all day. We gotta' eat something."

Croc smiled. "You right. I'm hungry as shit myself. Let's get something to eat soon as I take care of this real quick."

Jayde pulled up in front of the shop on Georgia Avenue and parked. Croc hopped out and ran inside. A few minutes later, he came back out and got back in the car. "Cool, let's go get something to eat."

"That was fast."

"All I had to do was get a few dollars. I told you I wasn't gon' be long."

Jayde smiled.

They headed uptown and grabbed something to eat real quick, and then it was back to making rounds for Croc. "Take me over Toya's house real quick. I need to drop off this money for Big Redds." Croc separated $2,500 from the $5,000 that John-John had given him. For the time being, being as though Croc was just coming home, a few good men made sure he was straight, but he knew that would get old fast. He knew he needed to put his plan into effect before he got out of the halfway house.

With a smile on her face, Jayde said, "Why does everybody keep given you money?"

"Niggaz owe me, at least that's how I feel." Croc rubbed his girl's thick thighs. "In a minute, shit gon' be exactly how I want it and we won't need to ask nobody for anything. I'll be out of the halfway house soon. You won't want for shit."

"Whatever you do, please, just take your time. Don't rush it. You just came home. Things ain't like they used to be." Jayde knew exactly where Croc's mind was and she didn't want him to get caught up by moving too fast. "I need you out here with me. You know that."

"I got you. Don't worry yourself." Croc kissed her. "I love you, baby. I got your back."

A short while later, they pulled up in front of Toya's apartment. A crew of young dudes was leaning against the fence hustling. Croc shook his head thinking about how he used to be the same way when he was their age. He got out of the car and made his way through the group, catching mean glares, and knocked on Toya's door.

Croc and Toya were real close, like brother and sister. It had been that way since back in the day when Toya and Amir first fell in love.

Toya answered the door. "What's up, stranger?" she said excitedly, giving Croc a big hug.

Croc flashed a huge smile. It felt good to see Toya out in the free world. It had been a long time coming. "I'm good. I see you still lookin' good."

"You too, boy. I was wondering when you were going to stop by."

"You know how it is. I'm just getting things together. I'm rippin' and runnin'. I'm only working with a little bit of time. You know how it is in the halfway house. I'm not all the way free yet."

"I know that's right. Whatever you do, just take your time."

"Well, look here, I can't stay long. I have a thousand things to do in a little bit of time. I just stopped by to give you this money for Big Reggie." Croc handed Toya the thick wad of cash."

"Croc, you just brought some money over here the other day. What you out here doing? You not back in the mix that fast, are you?"

Croc laughed. "No, not yet. Dudes been looking out for me, so I gotta' look out for my man."

"Thank you, you know he appreciates it. I do as well."

"We family. You know that. You okay?"

"Yeah, I'm as good as I'm going to be right now. This case that Reggie is fighting is driving me crazy, but other than that, I'm holding on."

"Yeah, I know how you feel. All you can do is pray on it and take it one day at a time. Things will work themselves out."

Toya sighed and shook her head. "I sure hope so."

Croc gave Toya a hug. "Trust me, things will work themselves out one way or another."

"Okay. I'm gon' let you go. You be good, and don't be a stranger. Stop by anytime."

"I will. Love you." Croc left and jumped back in the car with Jayde. As they pulled off, he glanced back at the young dudes in front of Toya's building. He wondered about his son. For all he knew, his son was standing on a corner somewhere selling drugs. He hoped he could find him somewhere now that he was free.

Seeing that something was on Croc's mind, Jayde asked, "What's on your mind, baby?"

Snapping out of his train of thought, Croc said, "I was wondering about my son. Sometimes, I wonder if he's still alive or if he even lives in D.C. I don't know anything about him. Never got to know him, you know?"

"Don't worry yourself. D.C. is so small. You'll find out something soon, trust me." Jayde knew that one of the things Croc really wanted to do once he made parole was to find his son. She planned to help him do that.

"Shorty should be damn near grown by now. He ain't gon' want to hear shit I got to say to him. I ain't been around all this time. If I was him, I would feel the same way."

"Don't think like that. You don't know how he's going to feel once you run into him. He just might understand. You never know. The only way for you to know is to find him."

She had a good point. Croc thought about what she said and it made him feel a little bit better. Croc had a lot of women when he went to prison. One woman, Karmen, swore that her son was Croc's child. Croc brushed it off and didn't take it serious. After all, she had been with a lot of different men and Croc knew it. However, Croc's thoughts changed some time later after he'd been in prison for some years.

Top walked into Necci's house wearing a black Hugo Boss sweat suit carrying a brown paper bag containing Chinese food that he went to get for her. Top took good care of Necci for Redds. He waited on her like she was a queen. She was the only family that Top had and he made sure that she wanted for nothing.

Looking up at Top, Necci said, "What's up, boy? You was gone long as shit. Where you go? Uptown?"

Top laughed. "I wasn't even gone that long. Stop fakin'."

Necci's friend, Karrine, walked in the living and saw Top. "What's up, handsome?"

"Ain't shit. What's good wit' you?" Top said, taking a seat on the leather chair across from Necci.

"I'm okay." Karrine took a seat beside Necci.

Karrine was a bad-ass stripper that had a Spanish look, but she was black. She and Necci had been friends since grade school, but Karrine moved away for a second and recently moved back to the D.C. area. Necci considered Karrine real peoples and that was the only reason she allowed her into her circle. On top of that, Top was somewhat feeling her.

Looking at Karrine's thick thighs in her skin-tight body suit, Top said, "You lookin' real good in that body suit."

Karrine smiled. "I look even better with nothing on."

Top smiled.

Necci shook her head. "Oh, Lord. You two need to get a room somewhere and stop all the flirting."

Top agreed. "That's what I'm talkin' 'bout. Bullshit ain't nuthin'."

With a smirk on her face, Karrine said, "Top wouldn't know how to act if he get some of this. He'd be all in his feelings and shit. I can see him now runnin' niggaz away."

Top folded his arms. "You for real?"

"Yeah, I'm for real." Karrine said.

Necci laughed. "You better stop playin' wit' him."

"Don't tell her nothing. She'll learn soon enough." Top then looked at Karrine. "All you gotta' do is give me some of that pussy and we'll see what the deal is."

"You know what, I'm gon' see what you talkin' 'bout when the time is right." Karrine sat beside Top and rubbed his dick.

Top put his arm around her, and said, "You keep playin' wit' that pussy, I'm gon' take it."

Laughing, Necci said, "You crazy, boy."

Karrine said, "I'm gon' give you some of this pussy as soon as I get a chance. I wanna' see what you can do wit' it."

"Fair enough." He got up and went to get a bottle of water from the fridge. Coming back sipping the water, he looked at Karrine, and said, "You trying to make some money?"

"Yeah, how?"

"I need you to take a trip wit' me."

"What's in it for me?"

"Five Gs."

"Shiiiid, hell yeah, I'm wit' it. When?"

"This weekend. I already got it laid out. Ain't nothin' to it."

"Let's make it happen."

Top pulled a knot of cash out of his pocket and tossed it Karrine. "That's a G. It'll hold you until we make the move."

Necci got up. "Top, let me holla at you real quick." She headed for her bedroom and he followed.

"What's up, Necci?"

"I don't know if I want you putting her in your business like that. She's cool, but I don't know if she can hold water."

"I feel you, but I already thought the shit out. I got it. Don't trip. It's gon' be smooth. I promise."

"You sure?"

Top nodded. "Trust me. Me and Shell already talked about it. It's all good."

"Okay," Necci said. "Just be careful."

"I got it, Necci," Top assured her.

A week later, Top and Shell were sitting in Top's brand new black convertible Corvette on Georgia Avenue. Shell had come to town to check on Top and Necci, and to make sure all was well with them. He made it his business to do so every so often.

"So, everything went well with the chick Karrine, I see," Shell said as he lit blunt.

"Yeah, she ain't have no issues at all. I can fuck wit' her." Top said. Karrine had made the trip to Ohio for him and made it back with two bricks of powder coke.

"That's right on time. You gon' need a good soldier like her on the team. But, once you get your money all the way up, you gon' have to step your game up."

"Say no more. I'm on point," Top agreed.

"So, what's up with Redds' case?"

"Shit movin' along. I been taggin' the witnesses. If I got anything to do wit' it, won't no witnesses be alive to get on the stand against my man."

"I know that's right," Shell said. "I wanna' go see cuz for real."

"Why don't you?"

"Necci said he don't want me coming over the jail to see him cause he don't want the feds on my back."

Top nodded. "That makes sense. After all, you are the one that still has the connect."

"Yeah, I'm sure that's what he's thinking. I just hope he can beat the case and get back out here so we can get this money. It's so much money to be made, you know? I ain't never seen so much cash until he came to Ohio and we got the Cali plug."

"Yeah, I miss my nigga. They don't make 'em like him no more."

"Tell me about it."

"Trust and believe, I'm gon' do all I can to make sure he beats that case. That's on my mother."

For Redds, being in jail was hardening his heart and making him a cold motherfucker inside. So many people were crossing him, and selling him and his comrades out. Every time he looked up, somebody else was turning states. It was crazy. The government was stacking the deck and they were finding all kinds of ways to get people to say whatever they needed them say. It was sickening to Redds.

All the stress that he was dealing with had his fuse short and he seemed to be snapping about any little thing. He ended up getting into an argument with a dude two cells down the tier from him about an extra food tray. When Redds came out for rec. with the dude, he ended up beating the shit out of him. After thinking about what he'd done, Redds really had to check himself. He wasn't the kind of guy to get into dumb shit. He knew that it was the stress from the RICO case that was getting to him.

With a thousand things on his mind, Redds sat in the visiting hall with his lawyer going over a few things about the case. Everything seemed to be dragging along at a very slow pace. It seemed like it would end up being years before trial even got started. The thought of being in jail for years before trial started was stressful in itself as far as Redds was concerned. His lawyer had told him about another group of dudes that had stayed in jail for five years before trial even started. Redds had never heard of such a thing.

As far as his lawyer, Redds was pleased with the job Smith was doing. He really seemed to be worth the money that Redds was paying him, and Redds was paying him top dollar. Smith was attacking every aspect of the government's case like a hungry wolf. Smith and Burling, the lead prosecutor, were locked into a fight to the death. Neither one of them was known for losing in trial. Smith seemed to be getting the edge on Burling in some ways, he'd gotten a lot of the electric surveillance thrown out of the upcoming trial because the feds had violated the constitution and other criminal procedures when obtaining it. A few bullshit charges were taken off of the indictment as a result. Nevertheless, there were still over one hundred counts on the indictment, and that was more than enough to get Redds the death penalty. Smith was trying his best to get some of the murder counts taken off of the indictment. A number of murders had been beaten in D.C.'s Superior Court, but were now back to haunt Redds and his codefendants in federal court, being as though they were now facing RICO charges.

In Redds' mind the federal government could do whatever they wanted to do. It made no sense to him that he could beat a murder in one court and them have to stand trial for the same murder in another court. After all, America claimed to protect all from double jeopardy in its courtrooms.

Redds shook his head, and said, "I really don't understand how the hell they gon' charge us wit' murders that we were found not guilty of. We beat that shit. Ain't that double jeopardy?" Redds had a frustrated look on his face as he looked over his indictment.

Smith sighed. "We are going to attack that from every angle, but between me and you ... those murders now have new witnesses, witnesses that took part in the alleged killings, plus, those murders are now being called murders in the furtherance of a C.C.E. It sounds like it's the same thing, and, in reality, they are, but the government is saying they violate different statutes. It's not fair, but it's the way the system works."

Redds shook his head. "That's crazy, man. A jury of our peers said that we were not guilty. That shit ain't right."

"You have a point. I made that same point in the collateral estoppels motion I filed. I'm standing on grounds that a jury acquitted on these charges in question. The government is playing a legal game of semantics. They are saying that the prior acquittals don't bar them from bringing the new prosecution because they weren't required to prove that the murders took place to further a criminal enterprise. That's the way it is. It's no way around it at the moment. It's going to be in the hands of the jury."

Redds was a very bright young man. He understood what his lawyer was telling him, and the shit was depressing as he thought about it. The only word he could
come up with when thinking about the matter was injus-
tice. He also understood that the only way to defend himself to the fullest was to get into the laws that were being
used against him.

Smith could see the concern on Redds' face. "I will
fight for you like it's my life on the line. Trust me on that
one!"

Redds nodded. "I trust you. You give off a good
vibe."

Croc was riding up 7th Street, passing the O Street
Market. Freedom was priceless. He was out of the halfway
house on a work pass. Instead of being at work, he was
riding around the city taking care of his business. Finding
his son was at the top of his list of things that he needed to
be done. He'd just left Sursum Corda checking on a lead
about a young girl that his son was supposed to be messing
with. He came up with nothing so far, but he planned to
keep searching. He'd also checked on a few leads around
Clifton Terrace where he tried to locate the woman that
claimed to have had his child. He had no luck finding her,
but learned that she was in prison. In due time, he was
sure he'd find his son. He was getting too close to the
source not to.

After riding around looking for his son, Croc returned to Jayde's house. Amir called almost as soon as he
walked in the door. Croc told Amir what he'd been doing
all morning. "If I can find the young girl that shorty was
messing with, then I know I can find him. D.C. is so small,
you know?"

"Insha Allah, you'll find him. Just stay on top of it.
What's meant for you will never pass you by. Before you

know it, the information will come your way. You only been on the streets for a second. Everything takes time."

"I know. It's all good. My nephew say they know the young girl, so it shouldn't be too hard to run her down."

"That's a good thing. Like I said, just stay on top of it."

"You know I will," Croc said. "On another tip, I spoke to a lawyer about your parole situation. He said that he can file an appeal for you, so I gave him some money and asked him to get on top of it. I need you out here with me. It's your time to shine."

"Thanks, partner. You have always been nothing but a brother to me. That means the world to me. I pray that something comes of it. I'm sure tired of being in here. I'm somewhere else in my life now. I need to put this pris-on stuff behind me."

"Big homie, I'm on it. Trust me." He and Amir spoke for a few more minutes, and then the called ended.

After talking to Amir, Croc needed to go holla at John-John, so he shot uptown and went to the shop. On his way inside the shop, Croc bumped into an old timer by the name of Big Wolf. They spoke for a second. Big Wolf was getting a lot of money in the streets. He and Croc knew each other from back in the day. They exchanged numbers and went their separate ways. Croc planned to get with him later and see what he really had going on.

Inside the plush back office of the shop, Croc sat on the brown leather sofa with John-John. Croc hand been taking hand-outs long enough, but it was time to talk busi-ness. Croc got straight to the point. "John-John, I been thinkin', and I feel like it's time for me to start gettin' some real money. I'm 'bout to be out of the halfway house in a minute. It's about that time. I been checkin' a few things out. I see what's what. I know everybody gettin' paid wit' this crack shit, but I'm gon' stick to what I know. That's the only way I'm gon' be able to get some money. You know?"

John-John understood what Croc was getting at. He knew that sooner or later Croc was going to come at him in such a way. "I see your vision, Croc. I wanna' see a good man like you get some money. You deserve it. You have always stuck to the code and that means something these days. I respect it. So, how can I help you? What can I really do for you?"

"You got all the connections. You are the man. The way I see it, if you can throw me something to get me on my feet, I can get my money up and start doing my own thing. You know how it works. Once I get my groove back, I can take care of myself."

John-John nodded. "Let's say I throw you half a brick of boy. Can you get started with that?"

"For sure."

"Cool, come back through here later on tonight and I'll have that for you."

"Bet," Croc said. He was ready to put his plans in motion.

It was a beautiful Saturday afternoon and the Kennedy Playground was packed like an NBA finals game was being played. Fast Lane Entertainment was sponsoring an outdoor basketball tournament. It was finals time and a best of five series was under way. A team put together by Gunplay Records was playing a team put together by the Madness Connection. The Madness team was up two games to one, thanks to the outstanding shooting from their point guard. The Gunplay team was fighting hard to win the current game, their point guard was pulling tricks out of his hat like Allen Iverson and hitting almost every shot that he threw up. The crowd was loving the show.

Across the street in front of the O Street Market, Top was getting out of his Corvette in a grey Hugo Boss sweat suit. He looked around and took in all of the sights. People from all sides of town were out and about. Crossing 7th Street, he looked down at his sweatshirt to see if he was showing. His Glock was poking out just a little bit on the side, but not enough for him to be worried about it. He was sure that damn near everybody was strapped that was at the game.

Walking through the crowd, Top saw his men, Boone and Stone, he stopped to holla at them for a second. As they spoke, they passed a Backwood back and forth. They were all young niggaz that were getting money and had names for themselves. Within minutes, the basketball game got heated. Top looked around, and said, "Niggaz gon' be shootin' out this bitch in a minute."

Boone shook his head. "Nah, shit gon' be cool. Ain't nobody got no real beefs out here right now."

On the other side of the playground, dressed in a tan linen outfit by Armani, was a smooth old timer. He was focused on Top. The old timer made his way to the other side of the playground and stepped to Top. "Can I holla at you for a second?" he asked Top.

Top gave the stranger a quick glance. "Who are you?"

"My name Croc." Croc extended his hand. Slowly, Top shook his hand. "I know you don't know me, but I think we need to talk. Your mother's name is Karmen, right?"

Top gave Croc a confused look. He hadn't seen his mother in a long time. Top decided to step off with Croc to see what he was talking about. "Yeah, my mother's name is Karmen. Why you wanna' know that?" Top wondered if something had happened to his mother.

Croc explained to Top who he was and what his connection to Karmen was. Top listened and took in everything. He felt mixed emotions. Croc went on to explain how he'd just done eleven years in prison, and that for

years he'd been searching for his son. Top seemed interested and couldn't believe where he thought the conversation was going.

Top suddenly cut Croc off, and said, "You tryin' to
tell me that you my father?"

"Yeah, that's exactly what I'm tellin' you," Croc said
as they approached Top car.

"No bullshit?" Top was blown away. He couldn't
believe that he would one day meet his father under such
circumstances.

"No bullshit, young nigga. I been looking for you
for years."

Top smiled. "So, where this leave us?"

"It leaves us with a lot of catching up to do, for
starters." Croc smiled.

Father and son stood on the sidewalk and went
back in time, feeling each other out and filling each other in
on different aspects of their lives. Top's mother had always
told him that his father had disowned him and due to those
lies, Top had always felt hatred for whoever his father was.
Making no excuses, Croc let Top know that he never disowned him, although, he wasn't there for him, but he explained to him that his reason for not being a part of his life
was not because he didn't want anything to do with his son.
It was because he was caught up in the streets and after
that, he was in prison. Everything Croc said to Top made
sense to him. For some reason, he understood what his
father was saying and where he was coming from. Croc
couldn't fix the past, but he could try his best to get to
know his son and have some kind of future with him. Top
was all for it.

Top smiled, and said, "You know what? I thought I
would hate you, but on some real shit, I have always wanted to know who you were. I always wanted to understand
what kind of nigga my real father was, you know?"

"I feel you." Croc smiled. "I would feel the same way. I know you still gotta' have mixed feelings right now. That's understandable. All I really want from you is a chance to get to know my son. I can't make up for lost time, but it's like having a second chance just to meet you and get to know you. I dreamed about this moment when I was locked up. I feared that I may never find you, or that I would run into you in prison somewhere, or, even worse, that you would be dead by the time I found you. Anyway, I'm glad that I was able to find you. I'm glad that you are alive and well. I hear that you can take care of yourself."

Top laughed. "Where'd you hear that?"

"The streets talk. I hear you are real close with the Kennedy Street dudes that got that RICO case."

"Yeah, Redds, that's my nigga right there." Top said.

"Small world," Croc said. He then went on to explain to Top his relationship with Amir, Redds, and Toya. Top was amazed. All along, his father was connected to him in spirit through Redds and his father.

"Damn! It's a small world. We been connected in one way or another all along."

Croc smiled. "Couldn't ask for a better storyline in a movie."

Top laughed. "We got a lot of catching up to do."

Chapter 15

Surrounded by her mother, Toya, Top, Karrine, and her cousin, Tamia, Necci held her newborn baby girl. She gave birth to Tawana Juatiah Williams on January 15, 1995. It was a great moment in a way, being as though the baby brought new life into the family, but, on the other hand, Necci was seriously depressed due to the fact that Redds was over D.C. Jail fighting for his life.

Trying her best not to bring everybody down, Necci enjoyed the birth of her first child. She gave Tawana to her mother, and watched her and Toya marvel over the beautiful baby girl with the smooth brown skin and light-brown eyes that seemed to open like the sea when she looked into the eyes of the person that had her attention.

As Top took pictures for Redds and Amir, Necci's cousin, Tamia, was checking him out. She could tell he was getting money. He had that kind of swagger with him. Karrine peeped the whole thing and wasn't feeling the way Tamia kept eyeing Top.

At the time, Karrine was a full-time mule for Top. She was hitting the highway several times a month transporting coke and seemed to be good at it. She never drew attention from law enforcement. Top loved that and made sure she was well taken care of. With her on the time, he was able to keep the coke coming without interruption.

Top's beeper vibrated, and he went in Necci's bedroom to call the number back. Tamia's eyes followed. She was going to crack on him in due time, it was written all over her face.

Turning her attention back to Necci, Tamia said, "Necci, girl, I never thought you would have a baby before me."

Necci rolled her eyes. Who the fuck cares what you think? She didn't care too much for her cousin for real. She knew Tamia well and ever since they were kids, Tamia wasn't to be trusted. When they were young, Tamia had fucked a dude that Necci was messing with at the time. She never forgave her for real, although, she claimed to have forgiven, her being as though they were young girls back then. Secretly, Necci was pissed off that her mother even brought Tamia to her house to see the baby. However, Necci was trying to be nice and, on the other hand, she had too much on her mind to deal with any drama. "Tamia, I always wanted a baby by Redds."

"You better than me. I don't see how you had that nigga's baby and he locked up and shit." Tamia said.

Necci gave Tamia a look that could kill. "Nobody really gives a fuck what you think. You can keep your feelings to yourself. I ain't tryin' to hear none of that shit that you talkin'! If you ain't got nothin' good to say, you need to keep your fuckin' mouth closed or get the fuck out my house."

"Excuse me?" Tamia looked shocked.

"Bitch, you excused! You can excuse your muthafuckin' ass right on out the door. Fuck is wrong wit' you? I don't know who the fuck you think I am." Necci was beyond pissed off at this point.

"Ladies, ladies," Top tried to calm things down. "Let's chill."

"Chill my ass," Necci said. "I want that bitch out of my house." She got up and went to her room.

It seemed like trial was never going to come for Redds. Months dragged along at a snail's pace and it had Redds frustrated. He was ready to get the shit over with and out of the way, however it was going to go. The birth of his child while he was in jail had him stressed out. His attitude and temper were off the chain. He found himself having run-ins with the C.O.s that ran the block about the smallest things. Aside from that, he seemed to keep running into niggaz that he had beefs with from the streets. Almost every time he, Dontae, and Heavy went to court, they were in the holding cell fighting some niggaz. A cousin of a dude that Dontae had shot, stepped to them with a few other niggaz in the bull pen and all hell broke loose. They stomped one of the dudes out so bad that the government was thinking about bringing attempted murder charges.

With that and much more on his mind, Redds walked down the tier on his way back from a visit with Necci. All he could think about was not being around to raise his daughter. That burned him up inside. Stepping inside his cell, the bars slammed shut behind him. He noticed that his cell had been searched by the C.O.s while he was on his visit. The cell was a mess. Shit was thrown all over the place in a disrespectful manner. Pictures of Necci, among other things, were all over the floor like somebody did it on purpose to fuck with him. A blanket of rage fell upon Redds. He turned around and banged on the outside of the cell to get the attention of the C.O. on the floor. His cell was popped to see what he wanted. Redds made his way straight to the control bubble and questioned the C.O. inside about the way his cell had been trashed in name of a shake down. "What the fuck is that all about?" Redds questioned.

"Write it up." The C.O. waved Redds off like he wasn't trying to hear anything that he was talking about. "I didn't do it and I don't have shit to do with it. You need to step back in your cell. I thought you had a real issue."

"Fuck you think you talkin' to? You think I'm one of these weak niggaz that you can say anything you want to out of your mouth?"

"Step in your cell, Williams. If you don't, I'm going to have to call a code."

"Fuck you and your code. Do what the fuck you wanna' do," Redds said. He was steaming mad by this time. He didn't give a fuck what was to come his way. He wanted to address somebody about the way his picture had been thrown all over the floor.

"Step in you damn cell!"

"Fuck you! Make me step in my cell!"

"Don't make me come out of this bubble, Williams. I'm warning you."

"You can come out of that bubble if you want to and I'm gon' knock your sucka ass out. I promise you that. You better call them turtles, if you know what's good for your dumb ass."

The C.O. came out of the bubble. Without another word of shit talking, Redds blasted the C.O. in the face with a bone crushing right over hand punch. The C.O. was a big man, but he staggered when Redds caught him. They clutched. The C.O. could fight, he was holding his own.

They mixed it up like they were in the ring under the lights in Atlantic City. Trading heavy blows, Redds began to get the best of the fight. The C.O. tried to grab Redds, but got caught with a mean uppercut that had him out on his feet. The next punch that Redds threw, a left hook, sent the C.O. to the floor with a busted nose and a split over his left eye. Once the C.O. hit the floor, Redds stomped him out with his Timberlands. C.O.s rushed Redds from all directions seconds later, followed by the ERT looking ninja turtles. They latched on to Redds and beat him down to the ground like he'd stolen something. It had to be a good twenty C.O.s stomping him and punching him while he was down on the ground. Redds continued to fight back as long as he could. After a while, they got him into handcuffs and continued to beat him. He had no win after that. They made an example of him after that.

Amir was still behind the Wall, but he was now in a 7 Block, which was a population block, so he was able to move around a little bit more. It gave him the ability to spend more time in the law library where he could research his son's case. Amir was good with the law and knew how to research a case better than most lawyers that were getting paid top dollar. In prison, he'd secured new trials for a number of other convicts that had received unfair trials. Digging into the law books, Amir studied every case that he could find that had anything to do with the RICO act. He wanted to help his son in any way that he could.
Sitting in the back of the law library reading a huge law book, Amir found something that caught his eye. This could be just what I'm looking for, he thought.

Croc was back at it. To him, time was money and he wasn't wasting any time getting back to business. He knew he was moving too fast, but that didn't make him slow down. He was on a mission to get his paper up. Riding down 14th Street in his black Benz with Top in the passenger seat, Croc was on his car phone talking to his nephew, Juan. Top was counting a handful of money as he glanced out of the window here and there. Life was looking up for them both.

Croc and Top clicked like they'd known each other for years. They were exactly the same, the only difference was that Croc was older. Instantly, they formed a bond like Suge and Pac in the early Death Row days. They began spending more and more time together. Top made sure he put his father on point with all that was going down in the streets. He let Croc know who was who, and who was not to be fucked with. Croc listened; he knew that that his son was on point about what was really happening in the streets. Together, they were a team that wasn't to be fucked with. Aside from business, Croc and Top made sure they had some fun together. They hit Vegas, Atlantic City, and a few other spots. Living life was what they did, by all means.

In no time, Croc had stacked a little bit of money and bought an old car repair shop that he turned into a car detail shop. He knew he had to have something legit to clean his money and a car detail shop was just right for him. He had dope on 5th and O Street; it was some of the best dope in town. Being from the old school, Croc named the dope Blackout. Everybody was looking for Blackout from uptown to the south side. The dope he had was at an un- believable rate for the sole fact that for every one gram that a person got they could cut it and make it two or three grams with no problems at all. They way Croc did his thing, he left room for everybody to get some money, all the way down to the users. Most heroin users could buy a gram, get their fix, and then sell a little bit so they would have just enough money to get high again, but with Blackout they could get high and put a couple hundred dollars in their pockets, if that's what they wanted to do. The streets were loving him just like back in the day.

Top didn't know too much about the dope game, but he was a fast learner. When he saw that Croc was bringing in close to $15,000 every few days between 5th and O and his nephews on the south side, Top started thinking about jumping in the dope game as well. After all, he had enough money coming from the crack game to get a nice piece of weight to start off with. What better partner was there than his own father, so he thought.

Croc pulled up on the corner of 5th and O Street, and parked. His nephews, Juan and Rob, walked up to the car. After speaking to Top, they focused their attention on Croc and gave him the run down on how things were going. They were flying through the blow they getting from him and felt they needed to step their game up. No one in the area could fuck with the blow they had, so it was gone as soon as they put it in the hands of the workers. Croc was pleased that things were going so well. In no time, they would all be rich, as far as Croc was concerned.

Juan, the oldest of his nephews, was 17-years-old and was somewhat of a ladies' man, but, at the same, he was not to be played with at all. His brother, Rob, was 16 and was a cold-blooded shooter. He wasn't with any kind of talking. Together, they made a great team and Croc knew they would go far as long as they had the right plug. That was where he came in at.

"Well," Croc said, "it looks like ya'll got this shit under control. I'll be back through later on."
Juan smiled. "Later on might be too late. I might need to meet you at the house so I can re-up."

"No bullshit," Rob added.

"If that's what you need to do, then just beep me and I'll be on it. It ain't no thing, family."

"Bet." Juan gave his uncle five and stepped off.

A few nights later, Croc pulled up in the driveway of his Rockville, MD home in a brand new red Benz 500 with chrome rims. The car stood out, even in the upscale suburbs of D.C. He got out of the car and took a good look at it. It was a sight to see. Money changed a lot of things in life for a man like him. He was able to do whatever he wanted to do when he was sitting on some real paper. Heading to the trunk of the car, he pulled out a big, red ribbon and wrapped it around the car. Jayde is going to love this here, he thought.

Knocking on the front door, he waited for his baby girl to lay eyes on her new car. All he wanted to see was the smile on her face. Her smile was worth more to him than the money he spent on the car.

"Hey you." Jayde opened the door with a smile.

"Look what I got for you." Croc waved his hand at the Benz.

Jayde covered her mouth. "Oh, my God! For real?" She jumped in his arms and kissed all over his face. He had made her day, again. "I love you so much. You are always thinking about me and trying to make me smile. I want to test drive it right now." She ran to the car and jumped inside. Croc followed behind her and got in the car as well.

Pulling off, she looked at Croc, and said, "You the muthafuckin' man."

Croc smiled and laid his seat back. "We just getting started, baby."

Time began to fly and by the end of 1995, Redds and his codefendants still didn't have a trial date. It wasn't even on the horizon. Redds couldn't believe it could take up to four years to go to trial. He knew he was in the fight of his life and he had to keep that at the fore front at all times.

In the visiting hall with Necci and Tawana, Redds tried his best to enjoy his short time with them, but he knew he needed to be in the free world with his family. He planned to do everything he could to make sure he beat the case.

"Show your father that you can walk," Necci said, holding Tawana by her hand, helping her take a few steps. Tawana stumbled and smiled at her father, melting his heart. Redds knew his baby girl was going to need him. His eyes watered when he looked into her eyes. "Baby, she's getting so big."

"I see her. She fly, too." Redds checked out his little girl in a gray Hugo Boss sweat suit and a pair of black Jordans."

"Top be spoiling her, gets her anything that he sees that looks cute. He thinks she's his daughter." Necci laughed.

Redds smiled. He respected how Top looked out for his daughter. "Top a real nigga. I fucks wit' shorty from the heart."

"He really is. He's always there for me and the baby," Necci said.

"That's real shit there. What's up wit' Croc? Him and Top gettin' close?"

"Hell yeah. They are just alike. If you see how they get along, you would think they have been around each other for years."

"Like father, like son." Redds was surprised when he learned that Croc was Top's father.

"Croc on top of his business. He just opened a salon. I'm thinking about going back to doing hair. He wants me to run it."

"That sounds like a good move there. I think you should do it."

"I will think about it after I get things together with the baby. I need some time being mommy."

"For sure. That makes sense."

"So, what's up with trial? How much longer you gon' have to wait?" Necci asked.

"For real, I don't have an answer. It might be another year."

"Another year? What the fuck!"

"I feel the same way, that's how this shit works. "Our case is so big, it's no way around it."

"As much as the shit be on the news, they need to hurry up and get the shit over with."

"They call they self stackin' the deck. But, I will have my day soon."

Chapter 16

     Fifteen months later, trial was finally on the horizon. In fact, it was less than a week away. The stage was set. March 8th was the date. Winner take all. Redds and his codefendants were as ready as they would ever be. Nevertheless, the stakes were at an all time high.

     Mike's grandmother had been kidnapped a week prior. Police had no idea who was behind it, even though they were convinced that the Kennedy Street defendants had something to do with it. In other attacks, homes of witnesses had been shot into. The FBI took swift action.

     They went right after Redds, Dontae, and Heavy. They tried their best to cut off all communication with the outside world. The codefendants were separated, locked down, and had their phone calls and visits taken. Dontae was moved from D.C. Jail to another jail in Upper Marlboro, MD. Heavy was sent to Alexandria City Jail in Virginia. Redds was kept in D.C., but he was moved to C.T.F., which was a building next to the jail. The government released a statement saying that they took such actions because of witness intimidation. The government also put a little extra pressure to Redds by having agents watch the homes of Toya and Necci. A car was outside at all times.

     Sitting in his cell doing push-ups, Redds focused all of his mental energy on what was ahead for him. "I'm ready," Redds said out loud.

     The courtroom of the Honorable Judge Joseph Pinch was packed. The case of the United States v. Reggie Williams Jr. et al. was about to get underway. Judge Pinch was a hardnosed judge that used to be a federal prosecutor; he ran his courtroom with an iron fist and never allowed his authority to be questioned. Looking over the rim of his glasses at the courtroom from the bench, Judge Pinch took in anything. He wanted to make sure that everything was in order. The defendants were all seated behind the thick, oak wood table with their attorneys. The prosecution was in place, going over their opening arguments. The jury was behind a bulletproof glass looking at the defendants like they were all highly dangerous. The prosecution had asked for a bulletproof glass, claiming that the defendants had power and influence, and could get them murdered in an attempt to kill the case. In the back of the courtroom, family members took their seats waiting for the trial to start.

Moments later, Assistant U.S. Attorney James Burling slowly walked toward the jury box. Giving each and every juror a moment of eye contact, he said, "Ladies and gentleman of the jury ... the case I am about to present to you is one of grave concern. It affects the core of what we are made of and stand for as citizens of the District of Columbia. This case is one of a group of people thinking they are above the law. It is a case about drugs, money, and murder, the murder of young and old people alike."

A Korean lady in the jury box cringed when Burling said the murder of young and old people alike. The bulletproof glass started to make sense to her.

Burling continued. Lowering his head as if he ,was thinking about the victims, he said, "You will see pictures of victims that have seemingly been shot dead in the streets like animals. You will see that the defendants have earned the reputations that they have. You will see the weapons they used to terrorize the streets with." Burling went on and on about the evidence that he planned to present to the jury. When he was done he turned around and walked back to his table.

Smith addressed the jury with a tone of ease when it was his turn. He knew the trial was going to be a very long. He planned to slow walk every stage of it. With his hands behind his back, Smith said, "Many times, the truth is under layers of perception. With the law, however, the truth is clear, either the evidence states that a crime happened or it didn't. There is no in between. There is no room for lies or make believe. The defendants in this case are not monsters. They are not who they have been painted to be. I will prove this to you beyond a reasonable doubt. Once again, please, remember and take note of all the evidence. The evidence alone is all that matters when it comes to your verdict in this case." Smith went on to explain to the jury that it was important for them to keep an open mind and an understanding of justice as the trial moved forward. After all, the trial would mean life or death for the Kennedy Street defendants.

Getting down to business, Burling called his first witness to the stand. U.S. Marshalls escorted Mike Barns from the back. His head hung low as he got on the stand in an old, faded, orange jail jumper. He looked like a defeated man with no direction. His eyes were cold with no trace of emotion. He gazed around the courtroom. He looked at the jury, and then to the back of the courtroom where some reporters were, and then he laid eyes on Dontae.

Dontae gave Mike a look that was so cold and full of hate that the judge picked up on it. Heavy shook his head. He couldn't believe that Mike was really going to testify against them. Redds gave up no sign of what he was thinking. It was chess, not checkers, and he felt as though he was a move ahead of the prosecution. He waited patiently to see what move Mike would make on the stand.

Taking a deep breath, Mike looked over that the prosecutor. Burling greeted Mike with a sinister smile. He knew he had him by the balls and that Mike had to do exactly what he wanted him to do.

Aside from all the other things that were on Mike's mind, he had to deal with the fact that his grandmother had been kidnapped and her life was in his hands. Burling knew that Mike's grandmother had been kidnapped; he didn't give a fuck.

Burling began, "Mr. Barns, would you tell the court how you know the defendants?"

"Yeah." Mike lowered his gaze out of shame. He knew what he was doing was dead wrong, but he didn't give a fuck. Looking up, he caught Redds glaring at him. He could read Redds' mind. His grandmother's life was in the balance. "What do you want to know about them?"

"They are all members of the Kennedy Street Crew and that is a well known drug organization. Correct?" Burling walked toward the witness stand.

For an awkward second, Mike stared at the floor. All kinds of thoughts raced through his mind. His grandmother was at the top of the list. Slowly, he looked over at Redds, Dontae, and Heavy. He then looked at the crowd in the courtroom. Everyone knew what he was about to do. Then, he spoke. "I don't know anything about a drug organization."

"What!" Burling shouted as he spun around to face Redds. Turning back to face Mike, Burling lowered his voice, and said, "Must I remind you that you are under oath? This is a court of law. It is a very serious thing to lie under oath, Mr. Barns."

Redds smiled within. He looked at his codefendants and could tell that they were relieved that Mike was playing dumb. If he knew what was good for him he would surely say nothing about things he knew.

Mike spoke again, "I don't know anything about a drug organization." There were all kinds of gasps in the back of the courtroom.

Burling's face turned red with anger. "Have you been threatened?!" he shouted.

"Objection, Your Honor!" Smith protested. "The witness said he knows nothing about a drug organization. That is his answer."

"Sustained!" He took a strong stance and called the lawyers to the bench. He glared at Burling, and hissed,

"What the hell is going on in my courtroom?"

Burling accused the defendants on trial of having Mike's grandmother kidnapped. Smith quickly came to the defense of the defendants by stating that there was no proof of any of them having anything to do with a kidnapping. Smith also asked for a dismissal of all charges since Mike was the star witness for the prosecution. Burling couldn't believe his ears when he heard Smith ask for a dismissal. Burling and Smith argued at the bench. After a few seconds of that, the judge cut it short and made a decision to go forward with trial, even through Mike had created a circus of the government's entire case with his little stunt.

Mike was dismissed as a witness for the government. His prior deal was off the table for sure. When trial was over, he was sure to feel the wrath of Burling. Burling made a mental note to try his best to get Mike the death penalty.

After things were back in order, the defendants were sent back to jail until trial was to resume the next day. Part of Redds' planning was beginning to work. Outside of Richmond, VA, Top and E Dub were held up in a two-bedroom apartment that Croc had set up for them to use for the kidnapping of Mike's grandmother. They had the old lady locked in one of the bedrooms. She was terrified and spent her every waking moment in prayer. She knew that her grandson was the reason for what she was going through.

With a huge .45 on his lap, Top sat on the sofa in the living room beating E Dub's ass in John Madden. "We can start this one over, my nigga," Top said as he scored another touchdown with the Washington Redskins.

"You got it. Let's run it back."

When Top got up to reset the game, he looked at his watch. It was a little after 4p.m. "We should be hearing something soon."

E Dub nodded in agreement. "When you think we gon' hear something?" He was ready to get back to D.C. Holding an old lady hostage wasn't one of his favorite things to do. He had a heart, and his conscience was killing him. When they first kidnapped the old lady, he couldn't even look her in the eyes.

Returning to his seat on the sofa, Top said, "All this shit will be over within a minute. I feel your vibe. I know you ain't feeling this shit. I ain't feelin' this shit, either, but it is what it is."

"No doubt, my nigga," E Dub said.

Halfway through the next game, Top's beeper went off. It was Croc's code. Holding the beeper to the side, Top looked at E Dub, and said, "It's that time. Let's get this shit over wit'."

"What's the next move?" E Dub said as he stood up.

"We gon' let her go. Everything must have went well at court." Top shrugged.

At 2:00 a.m., they blindfolded the old lady and put her in the back of an old van with a sliding door. They then drove for a short time and dropped her off at a gas station with $100 in her pocket. Hurrying away from the scene, Top and E Dub headed toward North Carolina where they ditched the van and hooked up with Karrine.

The Kennedy Street trial continued to move on. Burling put a few FBI agents on the stand for the next few days. After that, he called a childhood friend of the de-

fendants to the stand. His name was Dirty and he'd been
involved with all kinds of crimes with all three defendants.
He knew dark secrets about them all. Dirty took the stand,
and painted vivid pictures of murders and kidnappings that
he knew about. He went into detail about how Redds sold
weight in the coke game, how Dontae was the one who did
most of the killing when there was a real problem that
needed to be addressed, and how Heavy had most of the
connections with out of town drug suppliers. Burling questioned Dirty for hours and got him to go all the way back to
the late 80s and early 90s when the crew first started getting some real money in the streets. Dirty testified that
when he was in the eighth grade, it Redds that gave him his
first 62 of coke and put him on his feet.

Redds couldn't believe his ears. He'd never given
Dirty any drugs. Every word that was coming out of the
nigga's mouth was a lie. Redds wanted to get up and choke
the life out of Dirty. He wondered what kind of deal the
government gave him for him to get up on the stand tell so
many lies. He sold his soul to the devil for all to see.

Days went by with Dirty still on the stand. On his
fourth day of testimony, Dirty talked about the murder of a
dude they all grew up with by the name of Kenney. "Me
and Kenney was real cool at one time," Dirty said as he
glanced at Dontae. "Anyway, we found out that he was
workin' wit' the feds ... he was telling on a body—"

"You mean a murder, correct?" Burling clarified.

"Yeah, a murder. We found out that he was telling
on a murder."

"So, what happened? What was done about that?"

Dirty took the jury back in time like a news report-
er. March 16, 1992 was the date in question. Dontae had
learned that Kenney was talking to the police about a murder that Heavy was a suspect in. As far as Dontae was concerned, there was nothing to talk about. Kenney had to go.

Dontae and Dirty tricked Kenney into going on a robbery with them on the south side of town. Dontae rode in the back of the car and sat right behind Kenney, who was sitting in the front passenger seat. Riding down Chesapeake Street, Dirty pulled over into a dark alley where they were supposed to enter an apartment building. Instead, Dontae wasted no time blowing Kenney's brains all over the windshield with .44 magnum. Without a second thought, Dirty reached over the body, opened the door, and kicked the body out of the car. Without another word, they pulled off.

Sitting behind the defense table as Dirty testified, Dontae looked at his old friend in disbelief. In Dontae's mind, Dirty would one day pay for breaking the code. He would make sure of it, even if it was the last thing that he did. Thinking back about their friendship as kids, Dontae could remember when they used to sleep in the same bed.

Dirty called Dontae's mother Ma. They were close like brothers at one time. Yet and still, Dirty was on the stand trying to help the government kill Dontae and his codefendants. Loyalty was out of the window and it was every man for himself.

Burling folded his arms in the middle of the courtroom and addressed Dirty, "So, is it safe to say that Mr. Davis is a murderer, a drug dealing murderer?"

Dirty looked at the jury, and said, "Yes. Dontae is the kind of dude that's all about his money and if you play with his money, he will not think twice about killing you. If you work with the police, he will not think twice about killing, either. That's the code. That's how it goes in the streets with dudes like him. It's not a game."

Burling nodded in agreement. Dirty was giving the kind of testimony that he really needed in order to recover from what Mike did on the stand. "Well, birds of a feather flock together. So, would it be safe to say that all the defendants are into drug dealing and murder, to your knowledge?"

Smith objected, but the judge batted it down and let Dirty continue his testimony. Dirty smiled. "Look here, it's like this here. Where we come from, we all get our hands dirty. Either we moving drugs or we robbing. It's not a lot to it. We made a name for ourselves in the streets, and we did it by getting money and killing anybody in the way of what we were doing. Cut and dry." Dirty went on for another hour or so with tales of all kinds of things. When he was done, he had went into three more murders that he knew about, and pointed the finger at Dontae for two of them and Heavy for one. He also painted vivid pictures of a number of unsolved shootings the crew had been involved in. Dirty did plenty of damage before he stopped running his mouth.

"No further questions, Your Honor," Burling said. Smith slowly stood up and smoothed out his Armani suit with a swipe of his hand. He cleared his throat, and said,

"Mr. Henry, you said that you and Mr. Williams grew up together and that at one point, he even stopped you from being put out of your apartment. Is that correct?"

"Yeah. That's true," Dirty said coldly.

"The defendants, these men, they are your friends. Correct?"

"Yeah, I mean ... we used to be cool."

Smith gave Dirty a smirk and dug his hands into his pockets as he paced the courtroom floor. "I don't know about you, but I view friends in a very different light. However, since you claim to be cool with the defendants I'd like to go back to something the D.A. said a few days ago. If I remember correctly, Mr. Burling said that birds of a feather flock together. Do you remember that?"

Dirty shook his head. "Nah, I don't remember that." He cut his eyes from Smith to Burling.

Smith smiled. "You remember murders from five years ago, but you don't remember a few words from a few days ago? I find that hard to believe," Smith stated sarcastically. Moving right along, he rubbed his hands together, and said,

"Anyway, if birds of a feather flock together, then murderers would do the same. That's how that term goes. It means the same thing. So, I ask you, are you a murderer? Are you a murderer that's trying to get out of trouble so you have made a deal with the government to testify against these defendants here?" Smith waved his hand at the defense table.

"Objection!" Burling shouted. He had to try his best to protect his witness' credibility. However, the judge overruled the objection. Burling sat back down, pissed off. Smith continued. Folding his arms, he said, "You, yourself, played a role in the murders that you are testifying about, correct?"

"In a way, but I ain't kill nobody," Dirty said, losing his cool.

Smith cut his eyes at the jury to see how they were reacting to Dirty. They all seemed to be intensely focused on what he was saying, but, at the same time, they didn't seemed moved. Smith continued. "Is it true that you have a double murder of your own pending right now?"
Dirty was stuck. He didn't know what to say. He looked over at Burling, hoping to get some kind of lifeline. There was nothing Burling could do. Shaking his head, Dirty said,

"Yeah, that's true."

"And, did this have anything to do with your willingness to testify against your so-called friends?"

"No. Not at all. That has nothing to do with it."

"Then, may I ask why you have waited for more than five years to bring all of this new information to light?"

"You don't understand—"

"Help me understand. Help this court understand."

"If I was to tell what I knew about those murders back then, while they were still on the streets, I wouldn't last a day. I would have been found in an alley shot in the back of the head somewhere." Smith said, "With that being said, you still withheld all of this information until you found yourself facing murder charges yourself."
Dirty shrugged.

Smith continued to attack Dirty's credibility for close to another hour. He pointed out a number of contradictory statements that Dirty had made on the witness stand, to FBI agents, and at the grand jury. When Smith was finished punching holes in the testimony of Dirty, it started to look like the government's case wasn't so strong after all.

Chapter 17

Lying in his bed looking out of the tiny window in the back of his cell, Redds gazed out at the recreation yard. His cell was on the ground floor, therefore, other inmates could walk right up to his windows. At the moment, the females were out for rec. Most of them were ex-crackheads, but after a few months of being in jail, they looked like strippers. Redds hadn't had a visit or a phone call in over six months. As he watched the females walk around the rec yard, he wondered what Necci was doing and how she was holding up at the time. He knew she missed him and needed him around. In her letters to him, she was always missing him and letting him know that she would always be by his side.

Among other things he had on his mind, Redds had to deal with the fact that trial wasn't going well just a few days later. Codefendant after codefendant, friend after friend, all took the witness stand against him. The thing that got under Redds' skin the most was the fact that most of the witnesses had crimes just as bad. Nothing surprised Redds anymore. For months, he and Cook had been on the same tier at the jail. Everything was cool. As soon as Redds was removed from the jail, Cook switched sides and join forces with the government. He took the stand and swore that Redds had admitted to countless crimes while they shared the same tier at the jail. Some of the crimes went back to 1989. Cook detailed how he used to buy weight from Redds when he was a kid. As time went on, he began to buy weight from Redds and made that very clear to the jury be detailing a number of transactions. Burling made sure that he used Cook's testimony to tie Redds and the other defendants to actual drugs sells of cocaine.

Cook's testimony put the government in position to prove their RICO case. They needed a witness to testify that he actually got drugs out of the defendants' hands.

A C.O. approached Redds' cell and popped the food slot on his steel door. Redds walked over to the door and grabbed his mail from the C.O. Mail call was really the only thing Redds had going for him. It was his only contact with the outside world. Every time the mail was passed out, Redds was looking for a letter from Necci. Looking at his mail, he walked over to his bed and sat down. Going through the mail, Redds saw that Croc had sent him a few hundred dollars and some pictures. It was good to have a good man on his team like Croc. Seeing Croc and Top together in pictures was amazing. When they stood next to one another, they looked like twins. Opening another letter from his man, Moose, Redds learned that Mike had been stabbed in the face over the jail. A dude that Redds didn't even know had stabbed Mike for the sole reason that he was a known government informant. The next letter he opened was from his father. Amir's letter was full of wisdom and direction. He wanted Redds to remain strong no matter what he faced. Nothing was going to be easy. Amir was sure that Redds was well aware of that fact. His letters always gave Redds strength. It made him look at things clearly.

Opening Necci's letter, he could smell her. Her letters always smelled good. After opening one of her letters, it made his cell smell like she was in it. Before reading it, he looked through the pictures that she sent. Pictures of Necci and Tawana always touched him. He wanted so badly to hold his baby girl, to kiss her, to play with her, and tell her how much he loved her.

Unfolding Necci's letter, Redds began reading:

Redds   8-15-97

What's up, boo? As always, I miss you very much. I
pray that you are holding you head up and being strong.
I'm trying hard to stay strong myself. I know that you will
be okay. I have been praying for you. You are my everything and I need you very much. You are my life. I can't tell
you that enough.

I have your baby girl lying here right next to me.
She is so pretty. Every time I look at her, all I can see is you.
I swear to God. With her running around here, I can't help
but to think about you all day long. Nobody knows it, but I
cry in here alone with you not here and it's just me and the
baby. I think I cry because I really don't know what the future holds for us all. To tell you the truth, I'm scared. At
the same time, I love you so much that all I can do is be
strong and hope for the best because no matter what goes
down I will be right by your side, forever.

I love you and will always love you. I'm down for
you forever!

Love
Necci
P.S. There's nobody like you.

Rubbing his chin, Redds sat Necci's letter down and
walked over to the sink. He took a long look in the mirror.
Something had to give. Turning on the water, Redds
washed his face and tried to clear his mind. Thinking about
the things that Necci said in her letter made him want to go
to sleep early. He did just that.

Days later, Redds, Dontae, and Heavy were in a
holding cell behind the courtroom while court was in recess
for lunch. The codefendants weren't thinking about lunch,
they were busy going over the things that had happened in
court. The government had just begun to present evidence

for the murder of the undercover officer. The jury seemed to be very interested in the details.

Addressing his codefendants, Redds said, "Slim, look, without them surveillance tapes they ain't got shit as far as who was doing the shooting. You can bet that. They need somebody to point the finger and say that it was so and so."

Heavy shook his head, and said, "The jury gon' believe the police before they believe us. Anything the police say is the truth to them muthafuckas."

Redds folded his arms and thought about what Heavy was talking about. "Man, on the some real shit, the police that was just on the stand tried to say he seen us all shootin', but my lawyer gon' put him in a trick bag 'cause he got his first police report where he said it was too dark to see who was really doing the shootin'. By the time he got to Kennedy Street, shit was already done wit' for real."

Dontae nodded his head. Redds was on point. "Well, one thing for sure and two things for certain, we gon' see what the deal is when we go back in this bitch."

A short time later, they were back in court with trial in motion. Smith was cross-examining a police officer that was a government witness. "Mr. Peterson," Smith said, "you said in one of your earlier reports that when you arrived on the scene that you saw the defendants engaged in a shoot out. Correct?"

"Yes, sir," the officer stated.

Walking back toward the defense table, Smith spoke as he flipped through some papers, "Well ... isn't true that the undercover officer was shot before other officers arrived, yourself included?" Smith turned around and folded his arms as he made eye contact with the officer. In his hand, he held the documents he was looking for.

The officer looked over at the jury, and said, "Uh, I ... well ... yes, but—"

"But, you can't say you saw the defendants shoot the officer. Correct?"

"Well, we all know who shot Officer Bishop!" the officer snapped, clearly angered. "Bishop was a good cop. He was my friend. And, he was killed in the line of duty. His killers must feel justice."

Smith raised his eyebrows. "Oh, I see." He looked over at the judge, and then to the jury. "You don't care about the facts and what you wrote in your report. You want somebody to pay for Officer Bishop's death, and I respect that. I feel for Officer Bishop, I would love to have his killers pay for what happened to him. However, the facts and the evidence are the only things the jury must take into account. If I could, let me read your report back to you so you can remember what you wrote." Smith flipped to the page he was looking for. "... when I arrived, I could hear the shooting before I could see who was shooting. When I tried to get a good look at what was going on, it was too dark to make anyone out."

The officer's face turned red with anger. He'd really forgotten about the old report. He looked over at Burling and could tell that the D.A. was pissed off. Redds' lawyer was punching another hole into the case. No one could be more pissed off than Burling, the FBI had never informed him about the report and it came back to make him look like a fool in open court.

"Sir," Smith continued, "you can't change your statement in the middle of trial. What you are trying to say is very close to impeachment. You seem to have the facts mixed."

Smith crossed the officer up in so many ways that it seemed like there was no reason for Burling to have ever put him on the stand.

For Amir, freedom was still on hold. The parole board seemed like they didn't want to let him go. He'd done everything that they'd asked him to do. He took more anger management classes, stayed out of trouble, and took college courses. Yet and still, the parole board gave him another 18-month set off. The reason for the set off, according to them, was the fact that no matter how much progress he'd made, he was still a far greater risk than his paper work indicated. Amir was used to hard times. He continued to maintain his faith in Allah and trusted that things would be alright in the long run.

Even with all of the hardships in his life, Amir still found joy in the visits with Necci and his granddaughter. It was a blessing from above to be able to hold his grand baby in his arms. Necci also found a great deal of joy and comfort in being able to visit Amir and taking Tawana down to see him. Being as though she couldn't visit Redds or talk to him on the phone, it really helped her out a lot to be able to talk to Amir. They had gotten very close over time. She had a lot of respect for Amir and looked up to him. When he spoke to her, he always made sense.

Necci was amazed that Amir had taught Tawana, at and a half years old, how to recite the first surah—Al_Fatihah—of the Holy Quran. Tawana not only remembered the Arabic version, but the English version as well. Amir had gone over the surah with her for the last few visits and called her every night on the phone to see if she remembered what he'd taught her. Tawana was so proud to recite to her grandfather what she'd learned. The little girl was highly intelligent.

Amir smiled. "Who's the smartest little girl in the world?"

"Me!" Tawana jumped up and down with a bright smile on her face.

Necci smiled. She loved the way Tawana and Amir dealt with one another.

After playing with Tawana for a moment, Amir turned his attention to Necci. "So, how are you holding up? You keeping your head up?"

"I'm doing the best that I can do. It gets hard, I ain't gon' lie. I miss Reggie and I need him around to help me, but, like I said, I'm doing the best that I can do right now."

"I know what you mean. You are a very strong, young lady. Reggie is blessed to have someone like you in his corner. You are doing everything right. Trust that. All you can do now is keep doing what you are doing. You have what it takes. I can see it in you."

"I hope so. I really do," Necci said.

Top walked into Necci's house with countless shopping bags. He sat them on the floor and shut the door behind him. As soon as he turned around Tawana came running his way and jumped into his arms. Top caught her and smiled. "Hey, pretty girl. How are you?"

"Fine. Just watching TV," Tawana said.

"I got a present for you," Top said, putting her down.

"Where? Where?" she asked.

Top opened one of the shopping bags and went inside. "I got you a few things," Top said as he pulled out a toy camera.

"I love to take pictures." Tawana smiled as she grabbed the camera. "Thank you."

Top smiled. "Anything for you, baby girl." He then took the other shopping bags to the sofa ,and said, "Your daddy sent you all this other stuff. Check it out."

"For real?" Tawana ran to the sofa and went through the gifts. When Top told her that her father had sent the rest of the gifts to her, it made her day. The first thing she grabbed was a white box that had a nice little gold chain in it. It had her name as a charm, covered with diamonds. The smile on Tawana's face made it clear that she felt very special. Top got a great deal of joy out of buying gifts for her and giving them to her as if they came from Redds. It made her feel loved by her father.

Top's cell phone went off. It was Shell. "What's good, Shell?" Top answered.

"Shit fucked up on my end, cuz."

"What's up?" Top's eyebrows went up. "You okay?"

"Yeah, I'm good, but shit fucked up right now. The feds raided a bunch of spots up here and locked up some of my folks. They ain't even find nothing, no drugs, no money, none of that shit."

Top sighed. "If it ain't one thing, it's another."

It looked like things were getting worse with every passing. Shell was already dealing with a situation where he wasn't getting any product from his connect for the last three weeks. He began to feel like something had happened to Calvin. There was never a time when Calvin wouldn't return his calls, however, he was nowhere to be found at the time.

"We may need to look into some other options, homie," Shell said.

"I feel you on that. I already started doing that. We need to talk in person so I can run some things by you. You wanna' hook up in Atlantic City so we can talk?"

"Sounds good. How about this weekend?"

"I can do that," Top said.

"Cool, that's the plan." Changing the subject, Shell said, "So, what's good with Redds? How is his shit looking?"

"Man, I don't know for sure. Shit be up and down. One minute it look like shit is going his way, then it look like the government is winning. That shit crazy."

"I know how that shit goes. I'm praying for cuz. I hope he make it out okay. We need him out here wit' us."

"For sure. Hopefully, all works out. I'll keep you on point."

"Cool. Talk to you later." Shell ended the call.

Toya walked in the room just as Top got off the phone. She gave Top a look like something was wrong.

"What's on your mind, Toya?" Top asked.

"Your mother left the program."

Top's mother was released from prison, but was ordered to check into a drug program. After only a few days in the program, she'd left and didn't return. Wanting to get high, she returned to her old neighborhood and began searching for a way to get some crack.

Top sighed out of frustration. He loved his mother, but her actions always let him down. Standing up, he pulled out his car keys, and said, "I'll be back."

Days later, Redds and his codefendants were back in court. Burling was in rare form, presenting evidence of a double murder that Redds and Dontae were accused of. Burling had the U.S. Marshal to show the jury exactly what an AR-15 looked like. He also showed them a short video of what kind of damage the weapon could do. Once he was sure that the jury really understood what the weapon could do, Burling put a young lady on the stand that was the girlfriend of one the victims of the murder in question.

The young lady told her story: She was waiting for her boyfriend to pick her up from her mother's apartment on 14th and Newton Street. Her boyfriend pulled up in a black BMW 735i with his right-hand man. Hearing the horn blow outside, the young lady ran down the steps from the third floor. Just as she got to the first floor, she heard what she called machine guns firing. Her heart dropped as she stepped outside where she saw two masked gunmen spraying the BMW with bullets. The young lady screamed as she fell to her knees. She sobbed as she watched the shooters murder the love of her life. She swore she knew Dontae was one of the killers because, as she put it, he took off his mask as he jumped into a blue Z28. She claimed that she knew that Dontae had a beef with her boyfriend because her boyfriend owed him $21,000 for drugs that Dontae had given him on consignment. Her boyfriend couldn't pay the bill because he had been arrested with the drugs.

The young lady's testimony was so powerful that it caused one lady in the jury box to cry.

Dontae listened to the young lady's testimony and felt her pain, although, he showed no emotion. He and Redds had murdered her boyfriend and his man, but it wasn't over money. In fact, the dude did owe Dontae and when he questioned him about the money, the dude had pulled on Dontae and said some disrespectful things to him. Dontae made up his mind to kill the nigga as soon as he caught up with him again. A few days later, Dontae and Redds caught up with the nigga and murder his ass. When the young lady was done testifying, the government rested its case for the day.

In his cell doing push-ups, all Redds could think about was the end of trial. Things weren't looking good. He mentally prepared himself for the worst outcome. At one point, he really thought that they could beat the case, but as witness after witness got on the stand, things began to lean toward the government's side. All Redds could do was face the situation head on.

After knocking out a thousand push-ups, Redds jumped in the shower in his cell and got ready to write Necci a letter. Just as he was about to write, the C.O. came to his cell and told him that he had a legal visit.

Redds wondered what was so important that Smith would come to see him in the evening. He'd just seen Redds the day before.

Redds was handcuffed and escorted to the conference room. His mind raced with all kinds of wild thoughts. Nothing surprised him anymore.

Seeing his lawyer, Redds said, "What's up, man?" He sat down across the table from Smith.

Waiting for the C.O. to leave the room, Smith said, "I have some bad news, Reggie."

Shaking his head, Redds sighed. "What's up, just spit it out. I'm ready for whatever it is."

"Do you know a Calvin Jones?" Smith asked as he flipped through some papers.

"Calvin who?" Redds asked. The name didn't ring a bell off the top.

"Calvin Jones. He's a big drug supplier from the west coast. You know him?"

It hit Redds like a sack of bricks. He never knew Calvin's last name, but when Smith said that he was a big drug supplier from the west coast, Redds knew exactly who he was talking about. "Yeah, I know the dude. What's up with him?"

"He's talking ... he's talking about a number of guys that he used to supply, you included, Reggie."

Redds shook his head. "These niggaz ain't got no honor at all. Damn!"

"He caught a case and he's searching for a way out. You know how it goes, he's now cooperating."

"He can't jump on my case this late, right?" Redds asked.

"Burling is playing a dirty game, but I'm going to fight it. The judge doesn't want a mistrial after damn near six months. He knows we haven't had time to prepare for this bullshit here. However, Burling is going to try to say

that this guy is the missing link to the drug conspiracy."
Redds shook his head.

Chapter 18

Burling pulled it off and got the judge to allow Calvin to testify in the Kennedy Street case, knowing full well that the defense didn't have enough time to properly prepare. Smith took a firm stand against the move, but it did no good. The judge claimed that the witness was in the best interest of justice. Simple as that.

Calvin got on the stand and told everything he knew for five days. He told how he first met Redds and his cousin in Atlantic City, and how they both bought large amounts of cocaine from him when he was in Ohio. Redds knew he was done when the judge allowed Calvin to get on the stand.

The sounds of Hypnotize by Biggie was pumping through the speakers of Top's metallic-blue '97 BMW 740il as he drove down 14th Street. He had a lot on his mind and he wasn't in the best mood. He was on his way down Clifton Terrace to look for his mother. She'd told him that she was going to go back to the drug program the last time he saw her, but she never did it. He was focused on finding her and taking her back to the drug program.

Top pulled up on Clifton Street. It was a whole different world, it was as hood as it gets. The apartments towered above the crowds of people that were moving about up and down the street. The scene was like something out of New Jack City.

Top parked his car and got out into the chilly, September evening air. Being around Clifton Terrace brought back a lot of memories for Top. He grew up in the neighborhood, right in building 1350. Making his way across the street, Top spoke to a few dudes that he knew and kept it moving. Once inside the building, walking down the dark hallway, he pulled out his Beretta and flicked his lighter to navigate his way to the third floor. The strong smell of piss reminded him of how far he was away from living in the hood at the time. Once on the third floor, he headed for the apartment at the end of the hall where his mother was known to hang out. Just as he was about to knock on the door, his mother and another drug user came out of the apartment.

"Top!" Karmen said. She was shocked to see her son. "What are you doing up here?"

Top slid his pistol in his waistband as the female that was with his mother made her way down the hall, leaving them to take care of their business. "I'm lookin' for you." Top tried to hide his anger, but it was clear that he was pissed off. His mother was high as a kite and that didn't sit well with him. "Ma, what are you doin'? I thought you told me that you wanted to clean yourself up."

"I'm just having a little fun. I've been gone for a long time. I needed a break. I got a lot on my mind."

Top shook his head in disgust. "We all got a lot on our minds out here. That don't mean you gotta' be hangin' out down this dirty-ass joint smokin' coke and shit!" Top grabbed his mother by the hand. "Come on, let's go."

"Where are you taking me?!"

"Away from here. You deserve better!"

The loud sound of power tools and men at work filled The Auto Shop—Croc's detail shop in Takoma Park, Maryland. The staff at the shop were the best in the business. All the young dudes and dudes that were getting money in the area took their cars to the shop to get them tight. From rims, to tints, to systems and more.

Upstairs in the office, Croc sat on a white leather sofa drinking Remy with Juan and Rob. Life was treating them good, they were winning by all means.

The phone rang, grabbing Croc's attention. It was Amir calling. "What's up, champ?"

"All is well, holding on. You know me. What's up with you?"

"Taking care of a little business, but other than that, I'm chillin'."

"I hear that. Ay, when the last time you been down the court building to check on that trial?"

"I was down there yesterday," Croc said.

"What things look like?"

"Man, you know it goes up in them court rooms. It ain't no tellin'. The government got so many rats, it makes the defense look like they ain't got no win, but the defense lawyers are putting up a good fight. They know what they are doing. I give 'em that much."

"How much longer do you think the trial is going to last?"

"The way things look, it could be a week or two."

"Keep me posted."

"You know I'm going to do that. It ain't even in the talk. You need anything?"

"Nah, not right now. I'm good. I'll let you know. Anyway, they 'bout to count in this joint. I'll talk to you later. Love you. Be safe."

"You too," Croc said.

"This shit is almost over, y'all," Redds said as he got dressed for court in the holding cell behind the courtroom. He was surrounded by Dontae and Heavy, who were getting dressed as well. They were all mentally and emotionally exhausted after being in trial for close to seven months. "It's all or nothing now."

Dontae nodded. "I'll be glad when this shit is over wit'. They been doin' whatever they want to do. Everybody they puttin' on the stand ain't doing nothin' but lying and shit."

"No bullshit," Heavy said. "All the government witnesses are rats and pipeheads."

"And police," Redds said.

"Yeah, especially the police," Heavy said. "Without
all the bullshit they done put in the game, we supposed to
beat this shit for real."

A short while later, court was in session. Smith was
on his job. He had an old lady on the stand by the name of
Ms. Rosedale. She was a defense witness, and a member of
the neighborhood watch that saw the entire police shooting
from her bedroom window.

"Ms. Rosedale," Smith said, "Can you please tell the
jury what you saw on the night in question?"

"Yes, sir," Ms. Rosedale said in her soft voice. She
told her story slow and carefully. She heard a lot of young
guys making too much noise in front of her apartment. She
looked out the window and was about to call the police, but
before she could, she saw all the young guys duck behind
the car they were hanging around.

"So, someone was shooting at them?" Smith asked,
making a point that the defendants weren't the ones doing
the shooting as far as the police murder was concerned.

"Yes, those boys started shooting after someone
shot at them first. The first gunshots came from somewhere else."

"Ms. Rosedale, how long have you known the defendants?"

"About twenty years. They all grew up in the
neighborhood."

"So, you are saying that you know the defendants
well and you know that they didn't start shooting first. Another gunman was in the dark alley where the undercover
was killed, correct?" She nodded. "Thank you." He turned
around and walked back to the defense table.

A week later, Burling was just finishing his closing arguments. He made sure the jury remembered all the things he wanted them to remember. He made sure that he painted a picture of the defendants as cold-blooded killers that had found a way to side step the law for many years. He stressed to the jury that it was their duty to make sure that the defendants never again made a fool of justice. When Burling was done making all of his points, he closed by saying, "Overall, in the last eight months, you have seen with your own eyes and heard with your own ears what kind of people the defendants are. The evidence against them is strong and clear."

Redds looked at the faces of the jurors, they all had blank looks on their faces. He didn't know if that was a good sign or not. Whatever it was it would be known very soon.

Days later, there was still no word as far as the verdict. Redds, Dontae, and Heavy were in the holding cell behind the courtroom, waiting and hoping that a verdict would come that would be favorable to their cause. For Redds, the feeling of someone else holding his fate in their hands was not a feeling he liked. As he thought about what the verdict could be, he tapped his foot and zoned out in thought.

"Will you stop tappin' your damn foot?" Dontae said with a smile on his face. He tried to ease the tension in the air. They were all nervous, although, no one would admit it.

Heavy looked at Redds, and said, "I feel you, my nigga. My stomach feel queasy as shit."

They all laughed.

"Don't get scared now, nigga," Dontae joked.

"Fuck you, nigga," Heavy said. "This shit serious. It's life or death."

"I ain't gon' lie," Redds confessed, "I'm 'noid for real. These crackers got us by the balls. Our lives are in their hands. It ain't no fun when the rabbit got the gun."

Dontae nodded. "I'm glad the shit is over. It's all or nothin' now."

Heavy looked at Redds, pointed at Dontae, and said, "This nigga trippin'. He don't think shit stink. He act like these crackers won't kill us."

"It ain't that," Dontae said, "I just know that it's nothing we can do at this point. We went to war wit' they ass. We gave it all we had. It's out of our hands now. All we can do is take it in stride now. I done already came to grips wit' this shit."

"So, what you think they gon' do?" Redds asked Dontae.

"You wanna know what I really think?" Dontae asked.

"Yeah," Redds said.

"They gon' railroad us. We all know it. We may not want to accept it, but that's how these crackers play. They tryin' to make an example out of us. We can't beat the case when the case all in the newspaper and shit, all on the news every day we go to court. They gon' play us just like First Street and Newton Street. All we can hope for is an appeal. That's how I see it."

Heavy was hoping for the best, but he knew Dontae was making sense.

Redds, on the other hand, was prepared to deal with the situation however it went.

Time passed quickly and by the end of the day there was still no verdict.

The next day, things went pretty much the same way until a huge, redneck marshal came back to the holding cell and said, "It's time for the moment of truth, fellas."

The defendants were then escorted inside the courtroom. The tension was thick and it seemed like everybody was on edge. Redds, Dontae, and Heavy stood behind the defense table awaiting the verdict with their attorneys. Seconds seemed like hours.

"How does the jury find the defendant Reggie Williams Jr. on count one: Conspiracy to Distribute and Possess with Intent to Distribute Ten Kilograms or More of Cocaine?" they asked the foreman, who was a white lady in her thirties.

Redds took a deep breath and looked at Heavy, who had his head bowed in prayer. Redds looked back at the foreman and braced himself for what was to come.

From behind the bulletproof glass, speaking into a microphone, the foreman began. "We find the defendant, Reggie Williams Jr. guilty of count one."

Dontae shook his head in frustration. He already knew how shit was going to go down.

The foreman went on. Count two, Conspiracy to Participate in a Racketeer Influenced Corrupt Organization. Guilty. Continuing Criminal Enterprise Murder of Jimmy Bluestone. Guilty. The foreman read off a guilty verdict for every count up to nine. Then, she got to the count which carried the death penalty, the charge of the murder of Officer J.R. Bishop. The whole courtroom seemed to hold their breath. "We, the jury, find the defendant Reggie Williams Jr., not guilty."

Redds let out a small sigh of relief.

The foreman continued to answer guilty to almost every other count on the indictment. Dontae and Heavy were also found guilty on almost every count, except for the police murder. It was clear to everybody in the courtroom that the three defendants were done. No matter what happened, they were going away for life.

On their way home from the grocery store in Top's Benz, Necci and Karrine listened to the radio. Tupac's Dear Mama was on WPGC 95.5. As they rode down the street, the song went off and the DJ came on the air, and said, "That was Tupac's Dear Mama. Much love to all mothers out there. I got some Biggie and some Mary J. coming your way in the hour. In other news, there has been a verdict in that big case the whole city has been talking about."

Necci's heart dropped as she focused on what the DJ had to say. Redds had asked Necci to stay at home and not come to the court building. He didn't want her in the courtroom when the verdict came down, no matter what it turned out to be.

The DJ continued, "Today, less than an hour ago, Reggie Williams Jr., Dontae Davis, and Henry Jones—all members of the Kennedy Street Crew—were found guilty of multiple charges stemming from a federal racketeering indictment. Let that be a lesson to all of you knuckle heads. Do the crime, you do the time. The system got a place for ya!"

Necci smacked the radio off violently and began to cry uncontrollably. Life as she knew it would never be the same.

Having dinner at Ruth's Chris, Croc and Top went over a few things. With the coke connect fucked up, Top decided to partner up with his father and get some dope money. Croc had recently made contact with some Mexicans that had some heroin that was like nothing he'd ever seen before. Top was looking forward to making a killing with the new connect.

Sipping a glass of water, Croc said, "So, how you gon' play shit. You need to stay under the radar if you want to get some real money."

"I'm gon' open up shop down Clifton. Everybody down that joint already know me, so it's no better way to get shit crankin'."

"Why don't you fuck wit' Juan and Rob? They got shit moving real smooth down 5th Street. If you go down Clifton, you gon' have some issues wit' New York Cee, he got a strong hold on the dope game down there."

Top smiled. "That ain't 'bout shit. If anything get out of hand, then body bags gon' be moving in and out of that joint. I grew up down there. Ain't no way in the world I'm gon' let a New York nigga stop me from gettin' money in my own city. It ain't goin' down like that there."

Croc laughed. "You just like me, young nigga. I love that about you."

"It is what it is. You know how shit go out here. Only the strong survive. Simple as that."

"I feel you." Croc cut into his huge steak and put a forkful of the meat in his mouth. Thinking about Redds, he changed the subject. "The whole city talkin' about Lil' Reggie and them losing trial. That's fucked up."

"Yeah, I know. I'm fucked up 'bout that bullshit. That's my nigga, too."

"Shit ain't over, though. He got all kinds of appeals and shit to file. That's how that court shit works," Croc said.

"That shit ain't a for sure thing, though. They still gon' give them niggaz life. Shit ain't gon' be the same without them out here. I was doing all I could to make sure that all them hot muthafuckas that was telling on them turned up dead. I guess it wasn't enough."

"You did the best you can do. Fate will work it out. All we can do is make sure we stand by them and support them. Lil' Reggie's trial was like a movie, that shit was out of this world. It may take some time, but they will get back in court. I'm sure of it."

"You ever seen a nigga get back on a RICO joint?" Top asked. He couldn't believe they had found Redds guilty and were set to give him life without parole.

Croc rubbed his chin. "I don't know a lot of niggaz that done went down on that RICO shit. When I first went to prison, they wasn't using that shit on D.C. dudes like they are now. That shit was only for mob niggaz and shit. Anyway, one thing I know for sure is that as long as a nigga don't lay down and give up, there is always hope. Bet that."

Chapter 19

Down Lorton, behind the Wall, the 3-Block visiting hall was full of life. Little kids ran back and forth as if on a playground while convicts—in handcuffs and shackles—enjoyed a brief hour with their loved ones. Redds enjoyed spending time with Toya, Necci, and Tawana. It was the only joy he had in his life at the time. After not being able to get visits or use the phone for over a year, it was a blessing to see his family and be able to touch them, hold them, and look into their eyes. It was a painful time for them all and being to be close to them helped out a little bit.

Redds, Dontae, and Heavy were sentenced to multiple life sentences on February 21st 1998. At the time, Dontae and Heavy were in federal prison in El Reno, Oklahoma waiting to be shipped to their deferral destinations. Heavy was on his way to Lewisburg, in Pennsylvania. Dontae was on his way to Leavenworth, in Kansas. Redds had been sent down Lorton until his Superior Court matters were resolved—he had taken the charge for the money and pistol that was found in his mother's apartment when the feds raided it. Once his legal matters were over and done with, he would be on his way to the feds as well. There was a long, dark road ahead of him, and he knew that he had to man up and face it no matter how he felt about it.

Due to his high-profile case and his federal life sentence, Redds was housed in 3-Block with the most violent convicts behind the Wall. He was placed in cell 20, all the way in the back. His father's comrade, Gator, was on detail and made sure that Redds had everything he needed once he was in the block. It was no secret who Redds was. His name was in the newspapers all the time. Aside from that, everyone seemed to know that he was Amir's son, and that carried a lot of weight down Lorton. At the same time, Redds had killed a Bluestone and that name carried a lot of weight as well. Redds knew he would have to deal with that sooner or later. He was ready for whatever.

"Daddy!" Tawana pulled at Redds' arm with bright smile on her face. "I don't like those handcuffs on you. Who put that on you? I want them to take them off."

Toya and Necci looked at Redds, and wondered how he was going to address Tawana.

"Come here, baby girl." Redds picked her up and sat her on his lap. "You see the dude over there behind those bars?" He pointed at the C.O. that was in charge of the cell block. Tawana looked at the C.O. and nodded her head. "He put these handcuffs on me."

"Why?" she asked.

"Because some people said I did some bad things."

"Did you?"

"No. I didn't."

"Well, why you gotta' wear those handcuffs?"

"Because until I can prove that I didn't do the bad things, I have to wear these handcuffs." Redds tried to explain the situation as best as he could to his little girl.

"I don't care what they say you did, I don't want you wearing those handcuffs. I want them to take them off."

Redds smiled. "What you gon' do if he don't?"

"I'm gon' tell my Uncle Top," she said with authority.

Everybody laughed.

A short time later, Tawana fell asleep in Redds' lap. He spent the last part of his visit talking to his mother and his woman about his plans to fight his case on appeal. He made it clear to them that such things could take years. However, he planned to fight the case every step of the way. His lawyer was already on top of everything to get the ball rolling.

"What are your chances?" Toya asked.

"It's no telling right now. All I can do is hope for the best and give it my all. That's how I'm looking at it."

"I'm praying for you, baby," Necci said as the visit came to an end.

Two weeks later, a young convict by the name of Dominic walked down the tier heading toward Redds' cell. He and Redds had gotten tight while Redds was at the D.C. Jail. Stopping at his cell, Dominic told Redds that two new dudes had just moved into the block and were placed on the top tier. One of the dudes was a convict by the name of Flood—he was a cousin of the Bluestone brothers.

Flood was a well-respected convict with a serious reputation from the streets. He was a known killer and made it very clear that if he ever caught up with Redds, Dontae, or Heavy, that it would be work call on sight. Knowing what time it was, Redds was ready to address the situation.

Rubbing his chin, Redds looked at Dominic, and said, "I'm gon' see the nigga off the top. It ain't in the talk."

"I got your back, slim. It's whatever."

Redds and Dominic began to plot their move.

Frankie Beverly and Maze were doing their thing at Constitution Hall in downtown D.C. The crowd was a mature, well-dressed one. Everybody that was somebody was in the building for a night out. Croc and his woman were chilling and sipping Remy in their seats. They were dressed to impress by all means. Every chance Croc got, he took Jayde out to show her a good time. The time they spent together was priceless, as far as he was concerned.

A little while into the show, Croc got up to use the restroom. Along the way, he ran into a few dudes that he knew. They chopped it up and he kept it moving. On his way back to his seat, he ran into a good man that he knew from Clifton Terrace by the name of Big Nation.

"Damn, it's funny that I ran into you," Big Nation said. "I was going to give you a call."

"Oh yeah, what's on your mind, big homie?" Croc asked.

"I just heard some wild shit." Big Nation went on to tell Croc that he'd just ran into a partner of his by the name of Shaka, and Shaka had told him that he'd ran across some information about New York Cee not being too happy about Top setting up shop around Clifton. As far as New York Cee was concerned, Top was taking food out of his mouth and he wasn't feeling that. He'd put $25,000 out for a nigga to kill Top to get him out of the way. A young killer by the name of Youngblood was supposed to take the hit, but he ran the situation by Shaka, who put a stop to it when he learned that it was Top that was supposed to get hit. "I tried to call Top a few times, but he's not answering his cell phone."

"Yeah, youngin' outta' town right now," Croc said, showing no emotion. However, he was pissed off. There was no way he was going to let some bullshit go down about his son. He had a feeling that New York Cee was going to be a problem as soon as Top opened up shop down Clifton. "Anyway, I need to holla at your man so I can get to the bottom of that right there. Anybody that got an issue with Top got an issue with me. You know how that goes."

"Get wit' me when you leave and we can take care of that. You got my word on it."

"Thanks, big homie."

On his way back to his seat, he was already plotting Cee's murder.

Early in the morning behind the Wall, a group of convicts, chained and shackled, was being escorted by a C.O. to their medical appointments. The short walk to the infirmary was a nice breath of fresh air after being caged up in 3-Block. Redds was in the middle of the line kicking it with his man, Zulu. Zulu was putting Redds on point about a few things that were going on; he also let Redds know that he was with him all the way with anything that was going to go down with the beef Redds had with Flood, and whoever else with him. "I don't do no playin' wit' these jokers. I'm playin' for keeps!" Zulu said.

Redds nodded in agreement. "Same here, it's not a game."

Once inside the infirmary, the convicts were locked inside big cages. All the convicts from 3-Block were placed inside the same cage. Coming out of the back of the infirmary, Amir spotted Redds in the cage. He made it his business to always holla at his son when Redds made his way to the infirmary. "What's good with you?" Amir asked as he walked up on the cage.

"I'm holdin', you know me. I'm taking everything one step at a time. Waiting to get back on the phone wit' my lawyer." It really tripped him out to be locked up with his father.

"What your lawyer talking about right now?" Amir said, grabbing a broom to sweep the floor as he spoke to Redds.

"Well, you know how it goes. He said he's putting everything in motion for me to fight on appeal, but as of right now I'm hold on dealing with all these other little charges. My lawyer said Maryland might try to mess with me for the double homicide out there." Redds had recently received news that the murders of Apple and Pinky may be brought up against him.

Amir shook his head in disbelief. "They bluffin', they not going to mess with you about nothing like that. They think they got you where you at. All of that is a waste of time."

"I'm not really too worried about that. Like you said last time, if they really had something on me they would have already came at me with it. Aside from that, I know it's no eye-witness to the crime."

"I feel you on that. All you need to focus on now is getting to the feds and getting in the law library so you can work on your case. Don't get caught up in all that other foolishness."

"I know. You don't have to worry about me. I'm on it. I'm not trying to lay down and give them peoples my life like that."

Amir nodded. That was exactly what he wanted to hear from his son. "Stay sharp. You know what has to be done."

"Trust me on that one there." Redds nodded.

"What's up with the situation with the dude Flood?" Amir was well aware of the beef between Redds and Flood.

"I'm on top of it, just can't get close to him when I need to, but I will. We never seem to be out on the tier together."

"Be careful. Don't take that situation lightly. Where there is the least presence of evil, there is the great-est danger of the unseen. Remember that at all times."

"I got you, say no more. I'm on point."

"Think first with these guys. Let them play them-selves out of pocket, you stay on your toes. A man that at-tacks first is just eager, the one that attacks when necessary is justified. That's the law of the land."

Redds nodded. What his father was talking about was law, and he understood what had to be done.

In a hotel suite in Aspen, Colorado, Top laid in the bed with Karrine. For the past week, they'd been far away from D.C. Top wasn't taking any calls, so he didn't really know what was up back home. All of his attention was on

Karrine and having a good time. However, when the phone in his suite rang, he knew that it had to be important. His father was the only person that knew exactly where he was. "Hello," Top answered.

"How you doing, champ?" Croc said.

"I'm good, what's up on your end? I see you calling me on the hotline."

"Had to. When you think you will be back in town?"

"In a few days, why, what going on?"

"Some wild shit. I gotta tell you about it when I see you, but do me a favor and stay out there a few extra days. I got some things going on and I don't want us in town, feel me?"

Top's mind raced, but he knew Croc was on top of whatever was going on. "Okay, cool. I'll see you next week some time."

"Cool, love you, see you then." Croc hung up the phone.

Hours later, Croc was sitting in Shaka's silver Jaguar as they road down Bladensburg Road. Croc was putting his move together for New York Cee. The way Croc wanted things done, New York Cee would be dead in less than twenty-four hours. Croc had $25,000 on deck to see the move through. "I need this shit done real quick and clean. I don't want it coming back to us at all."

"Say no more. I understand what needs to be done. My young nigga knows what to do," Shaka said.

Croc and Shaka shook hands.

Hard Knock Life by Jay-Z was pumping through the speakers inside Silky's barbershop on Minnesota Avenue, Southeast. The spot was packed. All five chairs were filled and four other dudes sat against the wall waiting their turn. The overall vibe was cool. The conversation of the day was sports. Redskins fans and Cowboy fans were going back and forth.

A barber by the name of Darren spun his patron around in the chair so he could get a better look while he faded the back of his head. When he was done, Darren spun the patron back toward the mirror so he could tighten up his shape-up. Finishing off the haircut, Darren looked through the huge window out onto Minnesota Avenue at the busy traffic going up and down the street. The night was still young and he had things to do. Handing the patron a hand-held mirror, Darren said, "You good to go, slim. Check it out."

Behind Darren, the front door opened, but he paid it no attention until a dark feeling came over the shop. All talking stopped and the only thing that could be heard was Jay-Z. Darren turned around and death walked into the barbershop. He felt helpless as his heart raced. For some reason, he couldn't move, it was like his feet were locked in place. Everyone else in the barbershop must've felt the same way because none of them moved, either. A masked gunman dressed in black with a Mac-10 walked toward Darren with his weapon pointed at his head. Darren took a deep breath and closed his eyes. Gunfire exploded inside the small barbershop. Darren jumped out of the way just in time to see the flames spit from the weapon. All of a sudden, everybody that had legs took off running. The gunman sprayed the patron in the chair with everything he had in the weapon. When the shooting stopped, the body fell to the floor lifelessly. The gunman looked down at New York Cee's body and was sure the job was done. Without a care in the world, he turned around and walked out of the barbershop.

Early the next morning, Redds, Dominic, and two other convicts stood in the visiting area of the block with chains and shackles from their hands to their feet. They waited for the C.O. to escort them to the infirmary. As Redds and Dominic waited, they spoke about a letter that Redds had just received from Dontae. In the letter, Dontae put Redds on point about how things were in Leavenworth. The homies from D.C. were strong.

Dominic had heard that the homies were standing firm in the feds. "I heard Dontae and Antone is cellies out there."

"Yeah, they cellies. That's a good thing for Dontae to be around Tone. I know they both ain't going for nothing, and they both gon' be in that law library together," Redds said.

As Redds and Dominic spoke, they kept their eyes on the door. A C.O. brought Flood off tier. They knew what time it was and they were ready. Redds and Flood locked eyes and exchanged murderous glares. The tension in the air was thick. Nevertheless, timing was everything. The moment had to be right to make a move.

Moments later, the C.O. escorted all of the convicts out of the cellblock and onto the walk. Fenced in all sides, the walk was somewhat of a death trap. There was nowhere to run or hide. Well aware of their surroundings, Redds and Dominic made their way to the front of the line. They wanted to be well ahead of the group so they could get the jump. Flood wasn't far behind. He knew what was up and had a plan of his own. Spitting a handcuff key out his mouth, Redds discreetly undid his handcuffs without the C.O. seeing what was going on. When he was done, he passed the key to Dominic, who wasted no time undoing his cuffs as well. Flood saw what they were up to and knew that they were about to make their move. He undid his cuffs as well.

"I'm gon' make my move at the end of the walk," Redds whispered to Dominic as he eased his knife out of his boxers.

"Let's go," Dominic said as he looked over his shoulder to see what Flood was doing. Flood gave him a look like, What the fuck y'all waiting for?

At the end of the walk, the C.O. unlocked the gate. He had no idea what was about to go down. Redds made his move and went straight for Flood with his knife out. The C.O. spun around and saw Dominic going after Flood as well. Before the C.O. could get on the radio, Redds and Dominic were already stabbing Flood in the face and neck. Flood was holding his own, trying his best to fend off the attackers, but it did no good. Every time he swung his knife, he got stuck again. As the attack continued, Redds and Dominic got Flood to the ground and continued to stab him. C.O.s came from everywhere. Redds and Dominic were pulled off of Flood, and roughed up on their way to the control cells where they were thrown into solitary confinement.

Chapter 20

The June sky was clear and blue. Traffic on the highway was moving along well. Top was behind the wheel of a rented Grand Marquis heading south. Necci was asleep in the passenger seat while Tawana was in the back playing a hand-held Sega Nomad. They had been on the road for hours. As they crossed the state line into Georgia, Top felt a sense of relief. Their journey was almost over. They would be able to see and talk to Redds in person at U.S.P. Atlanta.

After Redds and Dominic stabbed Flood, almost killing him, they spent the rest of their time in Lorton in the control cells. Redds ended up pleading guilty in the state of Virginia to assault charges for the stabbing; 60 months was added to the life sentences that he already had. Dominic was cleared of all charges, being as though Redds took the charge. Once all of that was out of the way, Redds was sent to the feds. His first stop was at U.S.P. Atlanta.

"Necci, wake up, sis. We here," Top said as he pulled up in the front of the Four Seasons.

"Okay, give me a second," Necci said as she stretched. The only thing that was going to wake her up was a good, hot shower.

Getting out of the car, Top looked back, and said, "I'm going to get somebody to come take our stuff to the room."

"Okay. I'm ready to see my baby. I'm going to be ready as soon as I take my shower," Necci said, stepping out of the car.

"Take your time, sis," Top said as he stepped through the revolving door.

Once in the hotel room, Necci laid Tawana down on the bed, and then got in the shower. Top got on the phone and called his father.

"What's up, young nigga?" Croc answered.

"I'm in the A. We 'bout to go see Redds."

"Good. Make sure you get on top of that situation. See what you can work out."

"No doubt. I'll let you know what's up after the visit."

"Bet." Croc ended the call.

Hours later, Top, Necci, and Tawana were in the visiting hall with Redds. The visits were much different than they were down Lorton. For one, Redds didn't have to wear chains on the visit so that was a good thing. His daughter didn't have to see him chained up like an animal. The visit was much longer as well. Even though Redds was locked up with life sentences, it was a joy for him to be able to sit and hold his baby girl close to him for a few hours. It made his day.

"I miss you, Daddy," Tawana said, sitting in Redds' lap.

"I miss you, too." Redds smiled. "You been good?"

"Yes, ask Mommy. I been good." Tawana smiled.

Redds and Tawana had a bond like he was always around. She loved him and showed it all the time.

Necci smiled. "She couldn't wait to get in here to see you. She acted like we took too long to get here."

"Oh yeah?" Redds laughed.

Top cut in. "Every hour on the hour, she kept asking how long it was going to be before we got here."

Redds kissed his daughter, and said, "You couldn't wait to see me, huh?"

"I just wanted to get here. It was taking too long. I just wanted to hurry up and get here, so I could give you a hug and kiss."

Redds hugged his daughter tight and gave her kiss. "I love you so much. Don't you ever forget that."

"I love you, too."

Redds talked to Tawana for a while and before he knew it, she was asleep in his arms. He looked at her, and then to Necci, and said, "I guess she stayed up too long on the ride down, huh?"

Necci smiled. "Yeah, that's what it is. She's always so excited that we are coming to see you that she can't sleep during the ride, and then she's gets in here and falls to sleep in your lap. She is funny."

"I know." Redds laughed. "So, how are you?"

"I'm okay," Necci said. "I'm missing you. Other than that, I'm holding on as best as I can. Working and taking care of Tawana."

"I love that about you, Necci. I really do. You are one of a kind. I don't know what I would do without you. Thinking about you and our baby keeps me going in here. I can't give up. I know I have to find a way to get out of here so that I can be there and take care of you both."

Necci rubbed Redds' hand. "I know. I have been praying a lot lately and I really believe things will get better in time. We just have to go through this for a reason. No matter what, I'm here for you. Forever. I love you."

"I love you, too."

"So, how is my father doing out there?" Redds asked.

"He's okay. He just got that job he was looking into."

Amir finally made parole and was in a halfway house in Southeast.

"That's a good thing. I'm glad he finally made it home," Redds said, rubbing Tawana's head.

"She loves her grandfather, can't get enough of him. I don't know who she loves more, you or him."

Redds smirked. "You know she loves me more."

Necci laughed. "I'm just playing." She stood up and looked around. "I'll be back, I have to use the bathroom."

"Okay, baby."

Once Necci was on her way, Top looked at Redds, and said, "So, how you holdin' up, my nigga?"

"I'm doing this shit one step at a time. You know how it is. I got these life sentences and I'm trying to find a way to give this shit back."

Top nodded. "Is it anything we can do to get you back in court faster?"

Redds shook his head. "I wish it was. All I can do is go through the motions now. It ain't no overnight way for me to fix this shit. Right now, I'm focused on going through my case as best as I can, and finding everything that's wrong and pointing it out to my lawyer. Aside from that, I need to find a way to get some money while I'm in here so I can take care of my family and keep paying these high-priced lawyers. Trust me, I got a plan and I ain't gon' let this time do me."

"I know that's right." Top knew Redds was far from dumb.

"Speaking of gettin' some money, I got some shit I need to run by you before the visit is over, but what's good with you? How did things turn out with that New York Cee situation?"

Top shrugged. "It was light work, for real. My father had that shit taken care of before I even got back in town, but, trust and believe, I took it upon myself to run the rest of them niggaz out of town. You know me, I ain't gon' play no games with them niggaz. I'm playing for keeps."

"I hear you on that. I know you can take care of yourself out there. I just don't want you to let them niggaz get you off track. You done already been through a world of shit. It's time for you to get your money all the way right and lay back. You done seen more than most niggaz your ages. Feel me?"

"I feel you on that one there. I'm on point."

"I was thinking about a lot of mistakes I made before I caught this case, and, on the real, it was the bodies and the gunplay that really got the heat on us. When we was just getting money and shit, it was all good."

"I feel you on that, but when the money started coming niggaz started coming with all the bullshit, so it was time for gunplay. That's the law of the land right there. You taught me that."

Redds nodded in agreement. Top had a good point. "You are right, that is the law of the land, but we now understand that the feds really bring the heat when the bodies drop, so you need to try your best to stay clear of the gunplay. It's the only way you are going to stay out there. I need you out there, my family needs you out there."

"I know, I understand."

"Okay, I ain't gon' talk you to death about it. You grown, you know how shit goes, I just want to keep you on point."

"I respect that."

"Anyway, on another tip, like I was telling your earlier, I got a plug with some Mexicans in this joint. That got it for the low."

Top smiled. "That's what I'm talking 'bout."

"I'm working everything out in here, but knowing that you and Croc need something sweet, I'm gon' to give you the hook up with his peoples on the streets. From there, you gon' be plugged in like never before. These boys will get you rich in months. Trust me."

"Say no more." Top knew Redds would see the move through.

Necci returned from the bathroom, and said, "The picture man just came in. Let's take some pictures."

They went to take a few pictures. After that, they got some food from the machine, and sat back down to eat and kick it.

Eating some wings, Redds looked at Necci, and said, "What was you saying before the phone hung up last night?"

Necci smiled. "I don't think your father likes John."

"My mother's boyfriend, John?" Redds asked.

"Yeah. Some kind of a way, John said something to Toya about Amir coming over there to get Tawana. Amir ended up having some words with him and I ain't heard nothing else about it."

Redds and Top laughed.

Top said, "John don't want no problems with Big Redds."

"No bullshit, I hope they don't get into nothing. I hate for my father to end up smacking John out."

"I don't think it's going to get out of hand," Necci said.

Top snapped his finger. "Damn, I hate to change the subject, but it was something I meant to ask you about, slim."

Redds raised his eyebrows. "What's up?"

"They had some shit in the paper 'bout the second Kennedy Street trial, they was saying the joint could end in a mistrial. What's up with that shit?"

Redds shrugged. "It was some accusations against the D.A.'s office about the cracker Burling playing with evidence. I don't know much about it yet, but my lawyer was like it could be big in regards to our case overall."

"So, that can help you in some way?" Necci asked.

"If the accusations turn out to be true, then, yes, it can help us all."

Hundreds of miles away, Heavy sat in his cell reading a novel by the author Dutch as he waited for dinner to be served. Drama had been coming his way left and right. Two months earlier in Lewisburg, Heavy, his man Titus, and a few other homies from D.C. were in the gym watching the D.C. basketball team play against some dudes from Philly. The game was high-flying and had more action than some NBA games. However, while the game was going on, back in the cellblocks, murder was being plotted. Two Nazis stood at the end of the tier with their knives concealed. They were waiting for one of their Nazi brothers distract the C.O. so they could sneak in the cell of their victim while most blacks were in the gym. The orders for the hit had came from a high-ranking Nazi in another federal prison. At just the right moment, the Nazis saw their opportunity and rushed into the cell of a D.C. dude by the name of Roc. Roc was asleep when the Nazis entered. They went to work instantly, stabbing him in the face and chest over forty times in seconds. Roc was dead before they left the cell.

About an hour later, Roc's body was discovered. The prison went on lockdown for close to three weeks after the murder. The two Nazis that had committed the murder ended up going to the hole and being charged with murder in federal court.

The first day the prison came off of lockdown, the convicts came out of their cells and went to war. D.C. dudes stabbed Nazis, Skinheads, and Abs in every block they were in. Two Nazis died in the attacks. Once again, the prison was put on lockdown. Heavy, Titus, and a few other D.C. dudes were taken to the hole and placed under investigation.

Heavy's introduction to the feds was in full swing.

Top pulled up in his BMW by the basketball court in Barry Farms. He had a good man by the name of Lil' Ed that he would meet on the south side every now and then. Lil' Ed was moving a lot of dope and Top was giving him the best prices, so it was a perfect fit.

Seeing Top's BMW pull up, Lil' Ed smoothly got out of his Lexus and got in the car with Top. "What's up, slim?"

"Same ole shit out here. You know how it goes." Top gave Lil' Ed five.

"I feel you on that. Same on my end."

"So, what did you want to holla at me about?" Top said, looking in his rear view mirror, watching his back like a wanted man.

"What kind of numbers you working with on the coke?" Lil' Ed asked.

"Well, right now, I ain't really fuckin' wit' the coke, only the boy. But, at the same time, I think I'm about to get back into the coke real soon. We got these Mexicans we 'bout to start dealing with and I know they got it. So, give me a week or two and I can let you know something. Cool?"

"No doubt. That sounds good. I think I'm gon' go 'head and get some of this coke money."

"I don't see why not," Top said. "We can make something happen. On another note, I just got some more blow. You trying to go?"

"Yeah. Same number?"

"For you, it is."

Lil' Ed reached out to shake Top's hand. "Get at me. You know my money right."

"You got it. That'll be coming your way tonight."

"Cool." Lil' Ed got out of the car and headed up the street.

Top's car phone rang as soon as Lil' Ed got out of the car. "Hello."

"What's up, boo?" Karrine said.

"I'm good, just taking care of a little business. What's up wit' you, baby girl?"

"Your father just got locked up. I don't know exactly what happened, but from what I'm hearing, Croc, Juan, and Rob were down 7th and T Street taking care of some business with the old timer, Freddie. The police popped up and stepped right to Croc like they'd been tipped off. They supposed to have found eighty-thousand in the trunk of the car along with a gun."

"Damn." Top shook his head. His father was on parole. The last thing he needed was a new case. "I'll be uptown in a minute. In the meantime, I need you contact Redds' lawyer and get him on top of my father's situation. Cool?"

"No problem, boo. I got it."

"If it ain't one thing, it's another." Top sighed.

"It's more."

"What?"

"Shell called. He done got locked up. The feds raided some spots up there where he at and took down his whole crew."

Top scratched his head. The heat was coming down from all sides. Everybody that he was dealing with was getting arrested so it seemed. "Shit fucked up."

"Whatever you do, please, be careful out there. I don't want to get no calls about you, okay?"

"I'm good. I'm all the way out of the way. Don't worry about me. I'll see you in a little while."

"Okay." Karrine hung up the phone.

Top put the phone down and headed uptown. He had some unfinished business around Clifton Terrace, so he stopped there first. Top had a few runners in the 1350 building and, went to holla at them. After taking care of his business he learned that his mother was upstairs getting high. He went to see about that off the top.

Walking into the apartment where his mother was supposed to be, Top was greeted by the smell of crack smoke. Two pipeheads were sitting on the sofa sharing a Kool. When they laid eyes on Top, they looked like they had seen a ghost. "Where the fuck is my mother?" Top hissed. One of the pipeheads nodded toward the back. Top wasted no time heading for the back. He kicked open the bedroom door with a loud, crashing sound. Rage took over him. Humiliation came next. Then, a strong desire to kill followed. His eyes watered as he pulled out his Glock. His mother was bent over with her pants around her ankles while some dirty ass pipehead fucked her from the back. The two were so caught up in what they were doing that they didn't even stop fucking.

Top charged and smacked the pipehead in the head with his pistol, knocking him on the floor. Karmen screamed, pulling her pants up as Top stomped the dude's head into the floor. Blood was everywhere. It looked as if Top was going to kill the man. After a few more stomps on the man's head, he was out cold and motionless. Top pointed the Glock at the man's head and put his finger on the trigger. His chest heaved heavily. He was openly crying and filled with mixed emotions.

"George," his mother whispered as she began to cry. "Please, please, don't kill him. I'm sorry, I'm so sorry."

Top glared at his mother with cold eyes as tears streamed down his face, and shouted, "Shut up! Shut the fuck up! I don't want to hear that shit!"

"George," Karmen whispered. "I'm sorry. I have a problem. I can't help it. You don't understand what I go through."

"I don't want to hear that shit!" Top wiped tears from his face with a quick swipe of his arm. "You don't wanna' live no more? Huh?" He approached his mother slowly. "You don't care about your life no more? Huh? This is how you wanna' live your life? Like this?"

Karmen never thought that she could be afraid of her son, but, without a doubt, she was scared to death as she looked into his eyes. "Baby, please. Put the gun down. You are scaring me. Just put the gun down.

"If you don't wanna' live no more, you don't have to do it like this here. Just tell me. Say it! Say you don't wanna' live no more! I swear to God I'll put you out of your fuckin' misery before I let you do this shit to yourself like this. I swear to God!"

Karmen fell to her knees and sobbed heavily. She didn't know what to say or do. She felt like shit. She was at her lowest point ever. Her life was out of control and she had no way of fixing it. "I don't know what to do! I don't know what the fuck to do! There ... I said it. I don't know what the fuck to do!"

Watching his mother cry about being a victim of addiction crushed Top. It broke his heart into a thousand pieces. He helped his mother up and hugged her like it would be the last time. "We gotta' get you some help."

The next day, Amir was sitting in the passenger seat of Top's BMW. They were on Suitland Parkway headed back to the city. With Amir's help, Top checked his mother into a drug program. He hoped with all of his heart that she would get herself together. Ever since he was a child, all he ever wanted was to be able to take care of his mother and see her clean and happy. Drugs always seemed to destroy their relationship in one way or another.

"Your mother will be okay," Amir said. "Allah has a plan for her. All you can do is try your best to support her. She suffers from addiction. That's not a small thing. It affects a lot of people out here. A person has to want to change their ways."

"I know. I just hate to see her out here carrying herself like she be doing. That shit don't sit well with me, you know?"

"I understand exactly what you saying. That's from the heart. I respect how you speak from the heart." Amir nodded. He had a lot of love for Top. The young nigga was ahead of his time.

"All I know is what's really going down around me and I call it how I see it." Top looked in the rear view. There was a cop car behind them.

Amir saw the cop car as well. He cut his eyes at Top and said, "We ain't dirty, right?"

Top smiled. "Nah, we ain't dirty, I wouldn't even let you ride wit' me if I was dirty. I'd hate to see you in a situation like my father."

"You right about that." Amir shook his head. He was hurt about Croc being locked back up. It seemed like he'd just came home the other day. "Croc should've known not to be hanging out in that part of town dirty."

"That's the first thing I said when I heard that he got locked up."

"That shit gotta be killing him, sitting over that jail with a fresh case." Amir shook his head.

"Now I gotta' do what I gotta' do to try to get him out. The lawyer talking 'bout he may be able to get the gun charge thrown out, but the parole board still might play funky."

"That's how that thing works." Amir rubbed his thick beard.

Thinking about his father's situation only added to the number of things Top had on his mind. He and his father had formed a partnership in the game and with his father in jail, Top had to make sure the operation in the streets continued to run smoothly. That alone was a full-time job. He had a lot on his shoulders.

"What don't kill us only makes us stronger," Amir said. "Life always finds a way to test us. From Croc to Redds, we have a lot to deal with out here. They are family and we have to back them, no matter what."

"I feel you on that one there. As long as I'm free and alive, I'm gon' hold it down for them. I put that on my life."

Amir smiled. "You are one of a kind, I like your style."

Inside her living room, Necci sat on the sofa reading over the transcripts from Redds' trial. She looked for any mistakes that she could find from the trial. If there was anything she could do to help her man get out of prison, that was what she was all about. Her love for Redds was the only thing that kept her going when times were hard, and she sat in the house lonely and crying. All she wanted was for Redds to walk out of prison so they could go on with their life. That seemed life times away at the time. Necci tried hard to be strong. She focused all of her attention on her daughter so she wouldn't get down and depressed about life without Redds.

The phone rang and snapped her out of her thoughts. She answered and heard the recording stating that it was a call from a federal prison. She accepted the call. "Hey, baby," she said, sounding kind of down.

"Hey, baby," Redds said with a bunch of jailhouse noise in the background. He could tell that she was down by the sound of her voice. "You holdin' on out there, boo?"

"I'm trying. This shit gets real hard out here without you. You just don't know."

Redds sighed. "I know, I understand, baby. Things will get better in time, trust me on that. It ain't over for me. I will be back on the streets before it's all over. I will be back out there with you and my baby girl. If it's the last thing I do, I will be back out there. I'm in here working hard on my case. Everyday I'm in the law library trying to find a way out of here. I will never give up."

"I know," Necci said. "I'm in here right now reading over your transcripts. It's got to be more we can do to get you a new trial."

"I ran across a few different issues I'm looking into. I was on the phone with my lawyer and he said that as soon as he's done looking over the transcripts thoroughly that he's going to file everything to get us back in court in one way or another. I'm banking on that, but, at the same time, I'm doing my own homework as well."

"Something gotta' give, I'm dying without you out here with me and our daughter. Shit just ain't the same."

Redds thought about her words for a second before he spoke again. He could feel her pain. When he was on the streets, they were together all of the time. For him to be locked up and not be able to be there for her and his child in the physical was weighing heavy on his heart. "Baby, I know things are fucked up right now, but they will get better. Trust me on that."

"I want to trust you. I really do. You are my everything. You are my world. My life is all about you and our child. That will never change." As Necci spoke, her eyes watered. The absence of Redds was getting to her more and more. It seemed like she was crying herself to sleep every night, missing him, and wanting him by her side. When the feds snatched him, it was like they had snatched a part of her at the same time. "I love you more than I have ever loved anybody, Reggie. You just don't know." She wiped tears from her eyes. "I love you so much that it hurts."

"I love you, too, and I will always love you. I will fight until I can't fight no more. You know that about me. I just need you to be as strong as you can. The road ahead ain't gon' be easy, baby. I won't lie to you about it. You know how this shit goes. There is no way to know how this shit will turn out, but no matter how it turns out I will always love and do all that I can to be there for you, no matter where they put me or what they do to me. You are my everything."

"I know. That's what keeps me going."

Before Redds could say another word, the recording came on and warned them that the phone was about to hang up. "Listen, this phone is about to hang up. I'm going to call you back after count, okay?"

"Okay."

"I love you."

"I love you, too."

Toya was doing her best to stay strong and support Redds by any means. The life sentences that her son had received had crushed her, but, at the same time, she was very pleased that the government didn't give him the death penalty. With life in prison, she firmly believed that he would one day get another day in court.

Sitting at the dining room table writing Redds a letter as she did once a week, Toya put him on point about everything was going on out in the free world. The talk of the town at the time was the second Kennedy Street trial. It was over and all of the defendants had been found guilty of RICO conspiracy charges. No one was surprised. The stage had been set a long time ago. Aside from that, Toya had just received a letter from Heavy, who was still in the hole in Lewisburg under investigation for murder. Things weren't looking good. He told Toya that he really didn't know how things were going to play out, but that he was going to fight the charges to the bitter end. He also informed her that he had just fired his appeal lawyer for the RICO case. Top was supposed to help him get another lawyer. Dontae had called her and given her a few messages to pass on to Redds; she made sure to put that in the letter as well. Dontae had got someone to send her some flowers and a card. He always did little things like that for her. Inside the card was $1,000 and a few words thanking her for being a mother to him. When Toya was done with her letter, she put it in an envelope and headed to the mailbox.

Chapter 21

By the summer of 2001, Redds found himself on the west coast in Lompoc U.S. Penitentiary. Time was flying. In the past three years, he had been moved twice. While in Atlanta, he had gotten caught up in a geographical beef between D.C. dudes and Miami dudes because a young dude from D.C. had disrespected a Miami dude on the basketball court. One thing had led to another, and blood was spilled. The entire prison was placed on lockdown and dudes had to be shipped out. In the mix of dudes that were shipped out was Redds and a comrade of his by the name of Chico. After months in the hole, Redds ended up in Terre Haute, Indiana. Once there, he found himself in the mix of a beef that was already going on between dudes from D.C. and the Vice Lords. There was nothing Redds could do to get away from the beef. He was from D.C. and that automatically put him with the beef. One thing led to another, and Redds found himself in the hole again, along with his homies Antone, Smooth, and Mike Lucas.

At first, Redds couldn't stand Lompoc. He was too far away from home and that put a stain on his relationship with his family. They couldn't make it to see him as much, but he knew he had to deal with it. In time, he got adjusted and focused all of his attention on his case.

Facing the harsh reality of having life in prison made Redds focus all of his time on finding a way to get a new trial or a sentence vacation. It was a must that he focus all of his attention on his case. His first appeal had been denied. He really didn't think he would win the first appeal anyway, but Necci did. When the appeal was shot down it crushed her. Redds knew it would. He tried to school her to how things went in the federal courts, but she still had her hopes up on Redds winning the appeal and getting a new trial. Their relationship was becoming very strained to say the least. Seven long years had flown by and Redds was now 27-years-old. He knew that in a blink on an eye, he would be 37, then 47 and so on if something didn't give in his favor. All of his energy was now being put into another motion to try to find a way to get him out of prison; it was a 2255 motion that he and his lawyer were working on. The 2255 motion in federal court was an attempt to vacate, set aside or correct the life sentences Redds' had. The motion was also to challenge the legality of his confinement. It was getting to the point where he was putting all of his eggs in one basket, so to speak. The 2255 was an all-or-nothing kind of thing.

As for Dontae, he was fighting hard for his freedom as well. He made sure to follow Redds' lead on the case, being as though he was the one that stayed up on what new cases would help them in court. Dontae was in U.S.P. Marion, Illinois. He'd stabbed a dude at his last spot and was shipped out.

Heavy had a new lawyer that Top had paid for that was supposed to be one of the best in the area for appeals. The lawyer had already gotten two life sentences over-turned for other federal inmates. Heavy hoped and prayed that the lawyer could work some of the same magic for him. It would truly be a blessing. Being locked up started to get to him. He had no contact with his son at all and that alone weighed heavy on his heart. Aside from that, he was confined to a cell for 23 hours a day in the mountains of Colorado in a federal super max called ADX. Heavy had been in ADX for a little over three years at the time. It was all behind the murder at Lewisburg. Heavy was never charged with murder, but due to his alleged involvement with the beef, he was sent to ADX—the Alcatraz of the Rockies. ADX was a very serious prison and it pushed most men to their breaking points. It was the final stop for men like Wayne Perry, Timothy McVeigh, Ramzi Yousef, John Gotti, and many others.

Thinking about all that was going on in his life, Redds walked into his cell and sat on the bed. He had mail on the bed that his cellie had to have placed there. It was a letter from Necci. Her letters always made his day a little bit easier. He opened it and saw that there were also pictures. He glanced at the picture real quick, and then read the letter. Necci planned to visit him at the end of the month. That was good news. It gave him something to look forward to. It had been close to five months since he last saw her and his baby girl. From reading the letter, he knew she missed him very much. Nevertheless, Necci wouldn't give up on Redds. Turning her back on him was out of the question. In her eyes, there was no one in the world that could compare to him in any way.

Necci's whole life was built around Redds. He stayed on her mind all the time, everyday. When his first appeal was denied, Necci began to doubt that he could ever make it home. She thought that maybe it was true that he would be in prison for the rest of his life. That made her wonder what life would be like to forever be without the one man that she loved with all of her heart. Even with all of that playing on her mind, she found a way to deal with the stress and frustration by focusing all of her time on raising her daughter and staying on top of Redds' case from the outside would. She made it her business to travel all across the country to visit Redds no matter where the feds sent him. In many ways, Necci was locked up and doing time as well. She and Redds were codefendants, in a sense. Her prison was not federal, it was emotional. She had no way out unless Redds was freed, and until he was free she was entangled in the razor wire of loving a man that was doing life in prison. Most people didn't understand her reasons for standing by Redds, but, to Necci, nothing anyone else had to say matter when it came to her love for him

After reading Necci's letter, Redds laid back on the bed and drifted into deep thought about his queen. He was blessed to have a strong woman by his side. He wouldn't trade her for anything in the world. He looked at her pictures. Some of them had been taken on one of their trips to Florida some years back where they'd gone to Disney World, Universal Studios, Miami Beach, and few other places just to chill and get away from D.C. for a minute. Memories of the good times with the love of his life kept him going and energized to fight his case to the best of his ability.

In the streets, Croc was at the top of his game. He didn't let any setbacks get in his way. After doing two years for a parole violation, he was back in the swing of things and getting money. He was the heroin king in town. He had the best product and the lowest numbers for the work. It seemed as if he was untouchable. Aside from the illegal things he had going on, he also had a firm grip on the legal businesses as well. His hair salons and his auto shop were doing great.

Top was on his A-game as well. He was well established in the dope game. While Croc was away doing his violation time, Top controlled things and maintained the heroin connect. Things worked perfectly. Heroin was all Top was dealing with. He'd left the coke game alone after Shell went down on RICO charges.

Standing in the business office of the Auto Shop, Top looked down through the huge office window at the spacious indoor garage. All top-flight cars lined the garage in rows with different things being done to them. Top's new silver Porsche Boxter with the black drop top was up on the hydraulic lift. Two dudes in black Auto Shop jumpsuits put chrome Baccarat rims on the car. Top looked over his shoulder at Croc, and said, "On another tip, you really need to look into the shit that's going on with Juan and Rob before bullets start flying, and we find ourselves right back in some gunplay."

Word on the streets was that Juan and Rob had killed a dude from Edgewood by the name of Rick. Rick had been robbed and killed a few weeks ago, and his crew was looking for the killers. The truth of the matter was that Juan and Rob had nothing to do with the murder, and Top knew that for a fact. Nevertheless, being as though Juan and Rob's name came up, something had to be done before Rick's people made a bad move.

Croc rubbed his chin. "I was hoping this shit ain't play out this way. We got too much money to make to be going to war right now."

"I know, but we need to address it before it gets to that point," Top said.

"Who's pointing the finger at Juan and Rob?"

"Well, from what I'm hearing in the streets, it's Rick's brother, Nick. We already know Nick ain't got the muscle to bring us no move, but his father got some pull and we would have to address him real quick."

Croc thought about Rick and Nick's father. He was an old timer and a street legend in the D.C. streets by the name of Big Wolf. "I'm going to have a talk with Wolf and see where his mind is."

"Let me know what comes of it 'cause Juan and Rob feel like they need to make a move before somebody makes a move on them. I can understand where they're coming from with that one."

"I'll talk to Wolf. You talk to Juan and Rob. Tell them to lay back for a second until I see what's what. Cool?"

"Say no more," Top said.

The sound of the phone ringing filled the living room as Amir offered his salah. Nothing was more important to him than worshipping his Lord. The phone would have to wait. As he prayed, Amir thanked the Creator for granting him his freedom. He prayed for guidance. By all means, he planned to stay on the right track no matter what came his way. He'd done all he wanted to do on the other side of the law. At this point in his life, all he wanted to do was enjoy his freedom and continue to be a devout Muslim. He prayed for his son. Redds needed all the help he could get from above. Amir truly believed that one day Allah would answer his prayers and free Redds. Until that day was to come, Amir planned to be by his son's side as best as he could.

Life in the free world wasn't bad for Amir. He'd been released from prison and never looked back. He focused all of his attention on changing his life. He got married to a Muslim sister by the name of Salima. Together, they had a son by the name of Ali. Family life was good. He and his wife didn't have a lot, but they were good. Amir had a nice little job, a two-bedroom apartment in Northwest, D.C., he drove a used BMW 740.

As soon as Amir finished praying, the phone rang again. He answered it this time. It was Redds. After accepting the call, Amir said, "What's up, baby boy?"

"I'm holding on, dealing with this madness in here. You know how it is."

"That I do. I feel you all the way on that one there. All a man can do when they are in there is hold on and stay focused on the big picture, and the big picture is always trying to get your freedom back. You know what I mean?"

"I feel you. That's all I ever have on my mind. I don't want to die in prison. Every day I think about getting out of here one day. I don't know what God has in store for me, but I'm fighting to get out there with my family."

"I know that's right." Amir felt very confident that Redds was smart enough to stay on top of his case and never lose sight of his ultimate goal, his freedom. "When you fighting the government, the main thing you want to do is stay on top of it. Read everything and double-check the facts with the law books. You know how the game is played."

"Trust me, Pops, I'm all over it."

"Okay, so how's things otherwise?"

"Up and down, I'm taking things one day at a time in here. Necci told me that she was coming to see me, so that gives me something to look forward to. Anytime I get to see her and my baby girl, I'm excited."

"I know that's right. I used to be the same way. When I knew your mother was coming to see me and she was bringing you with her, it always made my day."

"When can I get you to come out here? I'd love to see you."

"Soon as my parole officer clears me, I'm coming that way. You sure they gon' let me in that joint, being as though I got a record?"

"I told you I got it. Don't worry about that. I got that on my end. Soon as you ready to make the trip, just let me know. I'ma get Top to get you a plane ticket and you gon' be on your way. Simple as that."

Amir laughed. His son was too much like him. "Okay, Reggie. That's what it is then. I'm going to make it my business to stay on top of that, insha Allah."

"Well, other than that, what else is going on out there?" Redds asked.

"I stopped by your lawyer's office earlier today. Heavy's lawyer was there. They were working on some legal papers for your case. They said they had just finished a twenty-seven-page motion outlining a rack of occasions where the government witnesses were paid with money from another case in Superior Court. The D.A. on your case is accused of a lot of dirty work. I think it will be grounds to get you back in court and maybe even get your case over-turned all together. I've prayed on it."

"Yeah, I've said a few prayers about that myself. I spoke to my lawyer a little while ago, he was telling me about that. I hope we can get some play. The appeals court know that them peoples did us dirty. The prosecutor on the case is the same joker that was on the Newton Street case."

"Yeah, I heard. He was on Panama's case, too, right?"

"Exactly. That's him. That joker right there, he's gon' be the reason we get back in court if all else fails. I can see it. The Washington Post had a big article about his mis-conduct. We gon' get some play, I'm telling you, Pops."

"I'm praying for it. I'll stay on top of it out here and you do the same from your end, and let's see what hap-pens."

"Cool. I'll talk to you a little later. They're about to count in here. Love you."

"Love you, too," Amir said.

Redds returned to his cell after spending the after-noon at the law library with his homie, Jason Poole. Jason was real good with the law and helped Redds with his case. They'd been going over RICO case law all day. Jason had read Redds' trial transcript and ran across a few things that would be strong issues to attack for a new trial. Redds took in all that Jason pointed out. With every passing day, Redds became more knowledgeable with the federal laws. To him, the laws of the land were all word games. When he found a strong issue to get back in court and get a new trial, the government always found a way to shoot him down. That always frustrated him, but he knew that he had to still push forward. Nothing was going to be easy and he was prepared to fight to his last breath for his freedom.

Redds and Jason had spent most of their time researching the Newton Street RICO convictions while they were in the library. Jason explained to Redds that he should have never had separate sentences imposed on him for 21 U.S.C. 846 (conspiracy to distribute cocaine) and 21 U.S.C 848 (continuing criminal enterprise) because that was called cumulative and it violated the Fifth Amendment's Double Jeopardy Clause. A recent Supreme Court holding in Rulledge v. United States made that very clear. With that being said, Redds' 846 conviction had to be vacated by the Court of Appeals. It was good news for him. He had a number of things in his favor at the time. All he had to do was get back in front of a judge. That was the hard part, but he was down for the fight. At the same time, with multiple life sentences, even if the Court of Appeals took the life sentence back for the 846, Redds would still have life in prison. He desperately needed to find a way to give all of his time back. Nevertheless, he understood that when fighting a case as big as his, he was going to have to attack every little error in the government's case one at a time.

Sitting on his bed, Redds pulled out a copy of the Newton Street case and read it again. As he flipped through the case, his cellie, Black, walked in the cell.

"Ay, slim, you heard about the nigga Mike?" Black asked.

"The hot nigga on my case?" Redds asked.

"Yeah, he got killed out ADX a few days ago."

"How you know?"

"My man just told me. He be writing Wayne out there. They say the nigga got punished out there."

Redds shrugged. He had no love for Mike. "That's what he deserve, with his hot ass."

Black shook his head. "These hot niggaz is out of control. They need to get that knife in they ass soon as they get off the bus."

"I feel you on that one there. It is what it is. Right now, I'm focused on getting back in court. Fuck them niggaz."

"I know that's right. You gon' get back. You be on your shit like you supposed to be. That's how niggaz give that time back."

Redds sighed. "Something gon' have to give."

In the visiting hall with Redds, Necci and Tawana enjoyed their time with him. He was so far away from home that it wasn't everyday they got to see him, but when they did, it was a great time. Tawana was so big and smart.

Holding his daughter in his arms, Redds looked at Necci, and said, "I may have some good news with the case."

She smiled. "What?"

"Well, I was looking over a few things and some of my convictions are illegal. I'm looking more into that as we speak for real. My lawyer is looking over it as well."

"So, you are going to get a new trial or what?"

"Not sure how things are going to work out as of right now. You know how this stuff works out, but it looks real good. Aside from that, I have all that other stuff that my lawyer was working on in my favor as well. We'll pray on it and see what comes of it."

"That's great. I needed to hear that. It's so hard out here without you. I hope they give you some play on that stuff there. It would really be a blessing, by all means."

Redds rubbed her hand softly, and said, "It will all work itself out, one way or another."

"How soon will you know something about it?" Necci was excited about the news.

"Not sure, we got to give it some time. None of this stuff happens overnight. I'm on it, though."

"That's all I need to hear."

Changing the subject, Redds said, "What's up wit' Shell? How's he doing?"

"He good, trying to get some time taken off of his sentence. He just sent a letter to the house. He told me to give you his love."

Redds shook his head as he thought about how they were living when they were on the streets. Now, they were both serving life in federal prison. Shit didn't seem to add up, the risks weren't worth the rewards. "I hope Shell get some play. I wouldn't wish prison on my worst enemy."

"I know what you mean. It seems like everybody from back in the day is locked up or dead." Necci shook her head.

"One day, this will all be behind us."

Back in D.C., around 5th and O, Juan, Rob, and a few of their homies were shooting dice in the parking lot. Juan was doing pretty good on the dice, he'd won a few hundred dollars in only a few rolls. It was looking like it was going to be a good day for him.

After winning a few more times, Juan stepped off to put his money up. There was no sense in standing around with a pocket full of money so the police could jump out and take it from him. As he was walking down the street, Top rolled up on him and pulled over.

"What's up, slim?" Top said as he got out of the car.

"Same ole shit, just another day. I'm good though. What's up wit' you, cuz?" Juan said as he gave Top five.

"Riding around checkin' my traps. You know me."

"I'm gon' need some more blow before the night is over. You got me?"

"Yeah, just hit me. I got you."

Out of the blue ,automatic gunfire exploded in their direction. Top and Juan dove behind a park car and pulled out their pistols. They really couldn't see where the bullets were coming from, but they knew somebody was shooting at them by the way the bullets were hitting the car and crashing through the windows. People screamed and ran in all directions. Two masked gunmen with assault rifles emerged out of the cut, spraying at the car Juan and Top were behind.

From down the street, Rob heard the shots and grabbed his Tec-9. He ran down the street firing at the gunmen. That gave Juan and Top a chance to get their shit together. They popped up and fired at the gunmen as well. One of the gunmen caught slugs in the chest, but from the way he staggered it was clear that he was wearing some kind of vest. Nonstop gunfire roared for close to forty seconds in the downtown neighborhood. Top slid from behind the parked car and fired a few more shots at the gunmen, as Juan and Rob blasted from the other side of the car. The gunmen ran back through the cut, taking heavy fire.

Chapter 22

The 5th and O Street shooting was all over the news for more than a week. Sadly, a seven-year old girl was killed in the cross fire as she tried to run into the house during the shooting. The community was in an uproar, demanding justice for the murder of the poor little girl. FBI agents and homicide detectives were all over the place. The heat was on and nobody in the area could make any money in the street.

Word in the streets was that Nick had sent the shooters to hit Juan and Rob in retaliation for the murder of his brother. Now that Nick had made his move, there was no turning back. War was on the horizon.

Croc knew exactly how serious shit was about to get. He didn't want things to get bloody, but there was nothing he could do. It was not like he didn't try to keep things under control. He'd had a man-to-man talk with Big Wolf, who assured him that things wouldn't get out of hand and that he could control his son. It was now clear that Big Wolf couldn't control his son nor the situation at hand. Croc had no choice in the matter. Big Wolf's son had sealed the fate of everybody in his circle.

Prices were put on the heads of Nick and the jokers that played a role in the 5th and O shootings. Croc learned that Nick had paid a young killer by the name of Snap to hit Juan and Rob. Snap and his crew were from Edgewood; they were known to take hits. For some reason, Nick thought that if Snap and his crew took the hit, it wouldn't come back to him. He was clearly wrong.

Juan and Rob were on a mission, and planned to take no prisoners. They did their homework and were hot on the trail of everybody that was against them. Within days, they located two gunmen that were down with Snap. Catching the gunmen in a Firebird at the corner of North Capitol and Kennedy Street, they sprayed the car, leaving no one alive. They made it a point to spray the car with everything they had in order to let the other side know that there would be no playing when they came.

Almost overnight, things were out of control and there was nothing anyone could do to stop it. Nick had no proof that Juan and Rob had killed his brother, but he still started a war that spread across the entire city. Nobody was off limits.

Top was tired of the bullshit and was ready to make a move of his own. "This shit is out of control, joe. I'm not going to sit back and wait for them bitch niggaz to make a move on me," Top said to Croc as he started his Boxster. Croc was sitting in the passenger seat. "I got money to make and I can't focus on getting money with this bullshit in the air." Top pulled out of the Auto Shop as he spoke.

Croc nodded in agreement. "I tried to warn Big Wolf that this shit was going to go down like this. I guess he didn't take it serious. It is what it is now."

"Fuck Big Wolf! If he really wanted to dead this, he could have done so before it got to this. He better hope I don't run into him first. I ain't playin' no games."

Croc sighed as he ran his hand through his greying hair. The stress of the streets was aging him faster than normal. He looked at his son and could see himself in the fearless, young man. "Top, I know you don't give a fuck about none of these niggaz and I respect that, but you can't just walk up on a nigga like Big Wolf and gun him down. It don't work like—"

"That's what niggaz think. I don't buy that. Most of these old niggaz think they can't be got because of who they are. That's what makes them vulnerable. Big Wolf don't think a nigga will walk up on him and blow his brains out, but that's where he's wrong." Top turned down New Hampshire Avenue.

"I'm with you, Top. It's time to put an end to this shit."

Pop! Pop! Pppppppp … ppppppppop! Pop! Pop! Gunshots came crashing through the driver's side door, blowing glass into Top's face and all over Croc.

Top slammed on the gas, making the tires scream, and covered his face as shots continued coming his way. The car rocketed into traffic and smashed into a pickup truck with a loud collision. Bullets continued to fly. Top jumped out of the car as horns blared and cars swerved. He opened fire fearlessly with his 50-shot Uzi. His attackers seemed shocked that he was firing back at them. They were certain that he was hit too bad to put up a fight. They were wrong. They traded shots in the middle of the street like cowboys. The Uzi Top was spitting chased the attackers off; they fled across the street and into the woods as police sirens hit the air.

Workers from the Auto Shop ran outside to help Top and Croc once the gunfire died down. Breathing hard with his smoking weapon in hand, Top ran to help his father, who was stuck in the passenger seat bleeding. "Watch out, y'all!" Top shouted as he checked on his father. "I got to get him to the hospital!"

Disoriented, Croc looked up at Top, and saw blood all over his face and shirt. "Where you hit at?"

"I'm good, don't worry about me. We need to get you outta' here."

Wasting no time, Top got his father away from the scene before the cops showed up.

The hole of U.S. Penitentiary Lompoc was loud and packed with convicts that had broken some kind of rule in population. For the past month, Redds had been in the hole. He and a few other D.C. dudes had been locked down for a beef that kicked off in the unit between D.C. dudes and Mexicans. Redds was now waiting to see what the administration was going to do with him. However it went, he would be just fine. Nothing that came his way in prison got him down.

In the small cell that he shared with one of his homies by the name of Kobi, Redds laid back in his bunk reading over a case that had just been ruled on in federal court. Kobi was down on the floor doing push-ups and crunches like a machine. Redds normally worked out with Kobi after lunch, but when legal mail was passed out and Redds got the case he was looking for, he decided to give all of his attention to the information in the case. Anything that could help him get out of prison always got Redds' full attention.

Legally, Redds' options were getting slim. His 2255 motion had been denied and that took a lot out of him. Even though he wouldn't admit it to anyone, he was really banking on that motion to at least get him back in front of a judge so he could attack all other issues that he'd found in his case. Redds was pissed off that the courts kept denying everything that he filed. He was starting to wonder if there was even a reason for him to keep fighting. If it wasn't for letter from his father, Redds would have snapped by this time. Amir made sure that he wrote his son to keep him focused. He didn't want Redds to ever give up hope on his freedom.

Kobi could tell what was on Redds' mind by the way he had zoned out while reading the case. "Ay, slim," Kobi said in between sets. "Don't let that shit get you down. You know how this shit goes. You gon' get some play. All you got to do is keep fighting."

Redds nodded. "I'm hip. I'm gon' always fight, I'ma fight till the last day. I just be gettin' mad as shit when they know what I'm filing is right and they just be saying fuck their own laws. You feel me?"

"I know exactly what you sayin'. That's how them peoples play." Kobi stood up and paced the cell. "You got strong issues, though, slim. They gon' have to give you some play. Trust me."

Redds sat up and laid the papers down on the bed. "Yeah, I want to look at it like that. But, if that's the case, they still want to get twenty or thirty years out of a nigga."

"You right about that, but, at other times, you see niggaz give that time back in ten or fifteen. You never know how shit gon' play out. What you gotta' do is focus on getting out so when that time comes, you don't have another life sentence waiting for you somewhere. That's the key."

"I know, slim." Redds shook his head in frustration. "I'm gon' fight till the end and pray that something goes my way in time. My young nigga, Top, be on top of my lawyer for me out there, but lately shit been fucked up. You know all that beefin' they got goin' on be affecting everything. I think if I can get some more money up to hire another investigator, I can really crack this shit open."

"Slim, Top gon' get it together for you. I'm hip to youngin', he know what he doing. Trust me." Kobi said.

Redds sighed. "I just hope youngin' can stay alive. He been out of the hospital for a minute now. I know he about to start plottin' his next moves."

"Whatever he do, you better believe he gon' be playing for keeps." Kobi said.

Redds nodded in agreement.

On the other side of the country, Biggie's Missing You was pumping out of the speakers that lined the walls of Necci basement as she ran frustration off on the treadmill. Her sweat suit was soaking wet. Sweat was rolling down her face. She was trying her best not to think about the pain of being separated from Redds. With every year that went, by she grew more and more bitter with the way the system played with Redds' life by not giving him a new trial on strong legal issues. When Redds' 2255 motion was shot down, Necci was crushed. She began to question if Redds was ever coming home. The feelings that came along with that reality seemed to control Necci's life in one way or another. Nevertheless, she could never give up on Redds; if she was to ever turn her back on him, she was sure she'd never be able to look at herself in the mirror.

Aside from the pain she was dealing with concerning Redds, Necci also had to deal with the drama that came with Top and what he was into in the streets. Her stress level was at an all-time high. After being shot and getting out of the hospital, Top had been staying at Necci's house. She was taking care of him. Her sisterly love for Top ran deep and she would never allow anything to happen to him if she could help it. Knowing there wasn't much she could say to him about the way he lived his life, she still tried her best to encourage him to think his way through what he was caught up in.

Top was blessed to be alive. He was shot nine times. Five bullets slammed into his bulletproof vest. Two bullets hit him in the arm and broke it. He had a cast on that arm. Two more bullets tore through his thigh and had him walking on a cane for the moment. Every minute that he spent getting himself back together, he was plotting the deaths of all those that were against him and his circle. As for Croc, he took two slugs in his vest, was grazed across the top of the head, and hit in the shoulder. There was going to be hell to pay.

Karrine walked in the room where Top was resting and saw him lying across the bed in deep thought. She knew what was on his mind. It was no secret that he was plotting his next move. Hearing the door open, he looked up and saw her standing by the nightstand with a gym bag in her hand.

"What's that, baby?" Top asked.

"I picked that money up from C." She sat the bag down next to the bed. "I counted it. It's all there."

Top nodded. He really appreciated having Karrine on the team. She was a team player and showed it every time. "Who told you to count my money?" he joked.

She smiled. "You don't need to worry about counting no money right now. All you need to worry about is getting better so you can get back on your feet. Nothing more, nothing less."

Top smiled. "You right. Did you holla at my pops?"

"Yeah, I did. He said that everything is in motion and that all you gotta do is lay back."

"Cool. Did you get that change to Redds' lawyer for me?"

"You know it. Took care of that."

"What would I do without you?"

"Act right and we don't even have to worry about nothing like that. I love you. I got your back."

"Real shit. I love you, too."

Karrine walked over and gave Top a long kiss.

The Federal Bureau of Prisons had dubbed Dontae a "predatory inmate" a few years into his sentence. There was no getting around it. The type of things that he was involved with were always serious and worthy of more time if he was prosecuted for them. For the last 18-months of his bid, Dontae had been locked down in U.S. Penitentiary Marion. He'd already been involved in a stabbing at Marion where he and a homie of his stabbed a supporter of the Aryan Brotherhood. His mind-state was fuck whoever stood against him. With a number of life sentences, he felt that there was nothing for him to lose.

In his one-man cell on C range, Dontae sat on his bunk reading George Jackson's Blood In My Eyes. The tier was loud and noisy, but Dontae didn't let that bother him. He'd learned to deal with life in solitary confinement after spending months in the hole in Leavenworth. Reading the writings of George Jackson made him look at life in prison as well as life in America as a black man in a totally different way. Life without parole was a reality that Dontae had to come to terms with. Although, he would never give up the fight, he had to be ready to deal with whatever came his way in the future. Revolutionary words from brothers like George Jackson made it clear to Dontae that the U.S. government would always set out to make an example of the strong men. Like George, Dontae had waged war against his oppressors and anyone else that stood in his way. He wasn't exactly on the same page with Brother George, but he was very much in constant rebellion against the system.

He now understood the system was set up to keep brothers like himself caged forever. Once in prison, no man was ever guaranteed freedom, not even the men that had small sentences. Anything could happen in prison, and Dontae knew that he had to be prepared for the unexpected at all times. George Jackson was a very clear reminder that the system could eat a man alive. George went to prison with a sentence of 1-to-life; he ended up doing eleven years in the California prison system before prison guards murdered him. Seven years of his bid he did in solitary confinement. Nevertheless, he was never counted among the broken men. Dontae admired that.

Sitting Blood In My Eyes down, Dontae contemplated the words of Comrade George: "Try to remember how you felt at the most depressing moment of your life, the moment of your deepest dejection. That's how I feel all the time. No matter what level my consciousness may be, asleep, awake, in between. The thing is there and it keeps me moving, pins my eye to the ball, uptight, twenty-four hours a day. ..."

Shaking his head as he thought about his life, Don-tae pushed all his thoughts to the side and began doing push-ups. He began to formulate another plan.

Rob's white Cadillac Deville with black tints cruised down South Dakota Avenue, Northeast. Snap and his man, Soup, spotted the car and followed it in the Grand Prix they were in. It was all-out war in the air. Gunplay was on-sight.

"This dumb-ass nigga don't even know we on his back," Snap said from the passenger seat. He had a smoke-gray MAC-10 in his hand with thirty shots in the clip. "Get up beside that joint. I'm gon' smoke this nigga right here in traffic."

"I got it." Soup eased up beside the Cadillac as it made a left on Rhode Island Avenue. "This nigga ain't even paying us no attention. This shit gon' be too easy."

The Cadillac stopped at the light on 20th and Rhode Island Avenue. Soup pulled up right beside it at the light. Snap hopped out of the car and sprayed the driver side of the Cadillac. The MAC-10 roared. Shells flew all over the place as bullets crashed through the driver side window. In seconds, the gunfire stopped and Snap jumped back in the car with Soup. The Grand Prix took off, running the light, and turned onto 20th Street where it disappeared.

The driver of the Cadillac lay slumped across the passenger seat as the car slowly drifted out into the inter-section. Rob's girlfriend had been murdered, unknowingly, for something she had nothing to do with. He'd told her not to drive the car because everybody in town knew it be-longed to him. Her life was now over all because she didn't listen.

The beef that was raging out of control had been in full swing for more than a month at this point. The casual-ties were up to eight people. Eight lives lost all over some false claims.

Meanwhile, on the south side of town, Juan and Rob were riding down Mississippi Avenue in a gray Chevy Astro van strapped with fully automatic weapons headed for Condon Terrace. Juan had some girls all over the city that were his eyes and ears. One of his girls had spotted Nick's Lexus GS 430 parked outside of one of his hoe's apartment. That was all Juan and Rob needed to hear. They dropped what they were doing and got right on the mission.

A short while after Juan and Rob arrived on the scene, Nick stepped out of the building drunk and staggering. There was no one outside. Ghost town was an understatement. After taking a few short steps down the walkway, Nick looked up and saw two masked gunmen in his face.

"Bye, bitch!" Juan hissed from behind his mask. He then unloaded his pistol in Nick's face. "Dumb mutha-fucka'!"

As soon as the body hit the ground, Rob stood over Nick pumping slugs into his head and chest.

After the shooting, Juan and Rob walked back to the car nice and smooth as if they were just getting off work or something.

The body count wasn't slowing down at all. The city was extremely dangerous and the feds were being pressured to do something about the spike in violent crime. The FBI was going to have to be called in to help.

Lying in her plush bed talking to Redds on the phone, Necci wished that he was lying next to her. The years were dragging on. She felt so far away from him. Her every day and night was spent thinking of Redds and doing all that she could to help him one day regain his freedom. No one really knew what was next for him. Necci prayed that something good would happen to lessen the struggle, but she wasn't too confident about what the future would hold. She was sick and tired of what the lawyers were telling her about the appeal. Everything that could be filed had been filed and nothing had worked, not even a time cut. Nevertheless, Necci was there every step of the way. Death before dishonor was a code she lived by as well.

"I really wish they would move you closer to home. If I could see you more, it would help out a lot."

"I know. That would be right on time. Maybe I can work on that when I get where I'm going." Redds was still in the hole waiting to be transferred to U.S. Penitentiary Beaumont, down in Texas. The transfer would take a few months.

"Try not to get caught up in all that bullshit down there. I know how you are. I want you to stay focused on coming home."

"You don't have to worry, baby. Trust me, I'm fighting every step of the way, but you got to understand where I am. Sometimes, shit is out of my control."

"I know, all I'm saying is that I need you to think about us, your family. We need you out here. We don't need you in there. If we can get you out, that's what we want to do. I got your back as long as I have life in my body. I need for you to know that."

"I feel you, baby." Redds thought about her words for a second. Necci was more than any man could ask for. She was down to ride for the long haul. "Right now, I got my mind on this move with Heavy's lawyer. I think he's on to something about the prosecutor being dirty. I been reading up on it and it's a few good men that got back on an issue like that. The Newton Street dudes and Panama worked a move like that. It's in the law books."

"How long is something like that going to take?" Necci asked.

"Not exactly sure, it could take a few weeks or it could take a few years. I'm not sure, but what I do know is that if Heavy's lawyer can get the issue back in front of the judge, we got action."

"Well, let's just pray on it."

"For sure, we need to pray on it and work on it at the same time."

Necci laughed. "You right."

"I gotta' get off this phone. I love you."

"I love you, too."

Rob was crushed when he found out about his girl's murder. He swore that her funeral wouldn't be the only one; a few more funeral were in the making. The day after Rob buried his girl, he caught Snap's baby's mother coming out of the go-go on the late night and shot her in the face five times, leaving her body in the middle of Georgia Avenue. He knew what he did was low, he wasn't into killing family members, but Snap put shit in the game first.

Croc didn't approve of killing family members. He had a sit down with Rob about the way things were playing out in the streets. Croc made it clear that he supported Rob all the way and would always have his back, but, at the same, time there had to be limits. Rob agreed. Croc was on top of his game and Rob knew it, so he had no problem listening to the old timer. Croc had found out who shot Top and quickly got on top of it. He gave Shaka and Young Blood $50,000 to put heads to bed. Days later, both gunmen were found dead duct tapped and handcuffed with .45 slugs in the back of the head. The killings were all over the news and were the talk of the streets. Those who really knew what was good would never say, and those that didn't know made all kinds of assumptions. Big Wolf had sent the gunmen in the first place, so Croc put a price on his head as well. For $100,000, Top's man, E Dub, took the job without second thoughts. Time was quickly ticking away for Big Wolf.

"I'm going to make sure we are on the winning team, slim." Croc looked Rob in the eyes. "Trust me on this."

Rob nodded.

Inside a hotel room in Silver Spring, MD, Snap was deep inside some of the best pussy he'd ever had in his life. He was loving it and couldn't get enough. With her bent over the bed hitting her from the back, she moaned as if he was really killing her.

"Yeah, daddy, just like that," she moaned. "Sssss ... ahhh ... ummmhhmmmm ..."

While Snap enjoyed the sex, he paid no attention to his cell phone that kept ringing every few minutes. As far as he was concerned, whoever was calling could wait until he was done. After several minutes of pounding in and out of the tightness of the pussy he was in, Snap finally came.

With a smile on her face, the girl said, "Damn, that was good. I want some more."

Snap, breathing hard and sweating, said, "That ain't no thing. Give me a second to catch my breath and we back at it."

"That's what I'm talking about."

Snap got up, grabbed his cell phone, and headed to the bathroom. Once in the bathroom, he returned a few missed calls. His man, Soup, answered the phone with B.G.'s Cash Money is an Army playing in the background. "What's up, moe?" Snap asked almost in a whisper. He didn't want the broad in the other room to hear what he was talking about.

In the other room, still ass-naked, Karrine tiptoed to the bathroom door to hear what Snap was talking about. He had no idea who he was dealing with. Karrine had him thinking that she was from out of town. She'd been throwing the pussy on him for close to three weeks. In that time, she'd discovered that Snap talked very loosely whenever he had a few drinks. With that being said, she was able to take information back to Top. Hearing the toilet flush, Karrine dashed back to the bed quietly.

Snap walked out of the bathroom in a different mood. He had a look of urgency on his face. It made Karrine nervous. She wondered if he'd learned who she really was. He grabbed his pants and cut his eyes at her. "We gon' finish this later. Okay, boo?"

"Nah, I don't think so," Karrine hissed.

"Huh?" Snap looked back at her and saw that she was pointing his 9mm Ruger at him. He slowly smiled. "Girl, stop playing. Put that down." He approached her.

She stood up and gripped the pistol tightly. "Stay right where you are. Don't try me. I'm warning you."

"You can't be serious, baby." Snap looked her up and down. She actually looked sexy standing in front of him naked and wet holding a pistol. "Stop playing."

She cocked the hammer on the pistol. "I'm not playing. Put your hands up in the air!"

"What the fuck is this all about?!"

"Who the fuck was you on the phone with in the bathroom?"

"You know you playing with your life right now, right?"

Karrine smiled. "I'm the one holding the gun right now. It looks like you the one playing with your life. Now, I'm going to ask you one more time. Who the fuck was you talking to on the phone in the bathroom?"

"Bitch, you must be out your fuckin' mind."

Karrine laughed. "You turn me on when you talk like that." She then aimed the pistol at his dick. "I'm gon' ask you one more time, and then I'm gon' shoot you in your dick. Don't try me."

Snap covered his dick with both hands as if that would really help the situation. "Soup! I was talkin' to my man Soup!"

Inching closer to Snap, Karrine said, "Get on your knees, nigga."

Slowly, Snap got on his knees, not knowing what to expect next.

Karrine grabbed her cell phone off the nightstand and called Top, all the while still aiming the pistol at Snap.

Top answered, "What's up, boo?"

"Got this nigga on his knees, daddy."

Sitting behind the wheel of his Benz on Georgia Avenue, Top smiled, and said, "Good girl. I got it from here. Hold fast right there for a second."

"Okay, I got you." Karrine ended the call.

Snap looked up at her in surprise. It was at that moment that he knew he'd been played. "You fuck wit' Top?"

Karrine shook her head. "Nigga, you must be slow."

Minutes later, Juan and Rob and saw Karrine fully dressed sitting on the bed with the pistol still pointed at Snap.

Juan smiled and rubbed his hands together. Looking at Karrine, he said, "Go 'head and dip. We got this shit from here." He then pulled out his Glock.

"Say no more," Karrine said. She slipped the pistol in her Gucci bag and left the room.

Rob then proceeded to kick Snap in the face. "Where Big Wolf at?"

"Ahhhh, shit!" Snap yelled. "I'll tell you, I'll tell you what you want to know."

Juan and Rob got all the information they needed from Snap, and then put an end to him. He was found in Rock Creek Park duct taped, handcuffed, and shot in the back of the head. Another clear message was sent to all that opposed Croc and Top.

A heavy rain beat down on the highway, making nighttime driving a dangerous tasks for most people that were headed south on I-95. For E Dub, the rain was not an issue. He was on a mission, headed to Springfield, VA in a metal-blue Mitsubishi Eclipse. Top had given E Dub information on where Big Wolf laid his head.

After a little more than an hour on the highway, E Dub pulled up on a quiet street lined with tall trees that made it appear much darker than it really was. Huge homes and top of the line cars made up the scenery. Dressed in all black, E Dub stepped out of the car into the heavy rain and looked around. There was no one in sight. He approached the bushes of a fenced in front yard and laid in the wet grass on his stomach. E Dub knew for a fact that Big Wolf came home around 11:30 p.m. every night.

Soaking wet, E dub wiped the rain from his watch and made it light up so he could see the time in the dark. It was 11:36p.m. Moments later, a big black Benz pulled into the driveway on the other side of the bushes. The hit was supposed to be nice and clean. E Dub had a 9mm Berretta with a silencer on it. However, there was a problem. Big Wolf got out of the car with a white dude that was carrying a black gym bag. E Dub had to change the game plan; he refused to leave any witnesses. Ready to get the job over with, he popped up from the bushes in a flash and let five shots go. Two shots hit Big Wolf in the back of the head. He fell lifelessly to the ground. The white dude spun around and caught slugs in the head. He fell on his back with the gym bag right beside him. E Dub turned around and crept off into the night.

Chapter 23

The sounds of a man in chains echoed off the walls of the super max prison as Dontae was escorted to an interrogation room where the FBI awaited him. The FBI had made the trip from D.C. to ADX in Florence, CO where Dontae had been sent along with his comrade, Titus.

Shortly after Dontae stabbed the white dude in Marion, two A.B.s killed a black dude from D.C. Things got out of control all over the federal system. Marion was placed on locked down for more than a month. Nothing was moving. As soon as things went back to normal, blacks attacked whites. Most of the blacks were from D.C., Philly, and Baltimore. A number of dudes were stabbed in the process. When it was all said and done, a bloody body laid lifeless on the ground. After a thorough investigation, Dontae and a few others got the beef for putting the violence in motion. Dontae was accused of being a leader and that got him sent to ADX. Now, he was the focus of the murder investigation.

"Mr. Davis," a tall, white FBI agent said, sitting behind an old metal desk. "Have a seat. We have a lot to talk about."

Dontae looked at the agent like he was out of his mind. He had nothing to say to the FBI and as far as he was concerned, there was nothing they could do to him. He already had multiple life sentences. Looking the agent in the eyes, Dontae said, "I don't have shit to talk to you about. If you need to talk to me, you need to talk to my lawyer. You know how this shit goes."

The agent smiled. "Okay, tough guy, but know this here, you already got life. If we prosecute you for murder, you will face death this time around."

Dontae gave the agent a vicious glare, and looked him up and down. "That ain't nothin' new to me. I faced the death penalty on the case I'm in on and I stood firm." Turning his attention back to the C.O. that escorted him, Dontae said, "Take me back to my cell. I ain't got shit to say to these jokers."

"Have it your way, tough guy," the agent said as Dontae was led back to his cell.

The murder of Big Wolf allowed a lot of the violence in the streets to die down. It was clear to all concerned that Croc and Top were the victors of the street war. They sat tall at the top of their game. With Big Wolf out of the picture, there was really no one to stand in the way. The pull they had in the D.C. streets was legendary, and it had all happened so fast. No one man could say that he ran the whole city, but, at the same time, Croc, along with his son, called a lot of shots.

In his basement, shooting pool and having a drink with his son, Croc was talking business. The heroin market had opened up in a way that he never foresaw after the beef with Big Wolf and his crew. Even though a lot of lives had been lost, in the end, all the riches were up for grabs and Croc intended to grab them. From one hood to the next, he was laying his claim. If he didn't know who was who, Top did. Together, they took things to another level.

Sitting on the leather sofa sipping Remy, Top said, "All the young niggaz in that Brentwood area jammin' blow. I been hittin' them for a second. I don't know if they know it, but it got to be damn near twenty to thirty thousand dollars coming through there a day."

Croc nodded. "Might be more than that. When my man Sean was around there, they was doing numbers that were double that. The only thing about that joint is that it's always so damn hot. Shootings and shit be getting in the way of making money at times."

"Yeah, I'm hip. It's like that in most of these hoods now. A real hustler gotta' find a way to get around all that shit there."

Croc laughed as he shot the eight ball into the corner pocket. "That's easier said than done, youngster. You see how much heat came with the shit we just went through. All money ain't good money."

"I feel you on that one." Top nodded in agreement.

While Croc and Top were talking, the intercom buzzed. It was Jayde, she needed to speak to Croc and she made it clear that it was urgent.

Top gave Croc and look of concern, and said, "What's up wit' that?"

"I'm 'bout to find out," Croc said as he headed for the door.

Once upstairs in his plush den, Croc listened as Jayde gave him the details of what was so urgent. At in the D.A.'s office, she'd came across a very important email that she was never supposed to see. The email was in regard to a memo that was sent from one prosecutor to another warning him about an ongoing investigation by the Justice Department into a FBI agent by the name of Herbert Schoenberg, who was murdered while off duty in Springfield, VA along with a known drug dealer by the name Wilfred Wilcox, a.k.a. Big Wolf. The FBI had been trying to keep the whole thing under wraps, but someone leaked it and they were now trying to cover it up, being as though agent Schoenberg was carrying five keys of heroin in a gym bag when he was gunned down.

Croc was shocked by the news. He knew most of the dirty law enforcement agents in the area, but Schoenberg's name never came across his desk. As soon as he heard the news, he knew that it was big. It was some of the best news he'd heard in a long time. Schoenberg was one of the agents that helped get Redds and his crew life in prison.

"This is big news, baby," Croc said to Jayde.

"I know, that's why I rushed home to put you on point. The DA's office don't know what to do about it."

Croc smiled. "Them crackers know they gon' have to let a bunch of niggaz go when this shit hits the fans. Redds and them gon' be able to work the shit out of this shit here."

Croc wasted no time getting Amir on the phone.

"So, this gotta help get my son out of prison, right? I don't have to be a lawyer to see that," Amir said to Redd's lawyer, Smith. Amir made it his business to pay the lawyer a visit first thing in the morning after Croc gave him the information about Schoenberg.

Sitting behind his desk, Smith rubbed his chin, and said, "It is the best news I've heard in a very long time. For me, it screams new trial all day long."

Amir felt a sense of relief come over him and he thanked Allah inside. However, he knew that there was more work ahead. "So, what's next?"

"Well, as you know, with anything concerning the law, it will take time, but I will have the paperwork ready to go in no time. It looks very promising."

Amir reached out and shook the lawyer's hand. "That's what I need to hear."

In his cell alone, Redds tried his best to clear his mind by doing push-ups. He knocked them out by the hundreds. When he was done, he washed up in the sink and sat on his bed and began to read the Qur'an. He was searching for answers that had to come from something greater than himself.

"Williams," a C.O. called out. Redds looked up and saw a C.O. at his cell door with mail in his hand. "You got legal mail."

Redds walked over to the door and signed for his legal mail. "Thanks," he said to the officer. Wasting no time, Redds returned to the bed and read the mail. It was a letter from Smith explaining to Redds that some very important things were in motion that would reduce his life sentences and those of his codefendants. The D.A.'s office had already contacted Smith with a deal. Smith was doing all he could to make sure that he got the best deal there was for Redds. Within months, Redds was to be returned to D.C. Jail.

Redds couldn't believe what he was reading. He read it over two more times. A huge smile crossed face. "Thank God." He understood what the letter meant and needed no one to explain it to him. He was giving his life sentences back and could very likely be a free man in the near future. His prayers were being answered.

Hundreds of miles away, Dontae had other things on his mind. The FBI decided to pay him another visit about the Marion murder. With the new developments in the Kennedy Street case, they felt that he may have a different outlook on things. They were wrong.

As soon as he saw the agents, Dontae's temper boiled. "Why the fuck you crackers keep comin' at me sideways! If you got somethin' on me, charge me. If not, leave me the fuck alone."

The agent sitting in front of Dontae said, "Well, it would be sad for all of your codefendants to go home once their sentences are overturned and you are the only one still sitting in federal prison because you want to stick to the code. We now have information pointing to you as the one that committed the murder back at Marion."

Dontae laughed. "You got me mixed up with one of these jokers that just started dealin' you bastards. If you had something on me, you wouldn't be here talkin'. You would be charging me with somethin'."

"Have it your way," the agent said.

"Fuck you!" Dontae said as he was taken back to his cell.

Back in his cell, Dontae sat on his bunk and thought about what was to come next. He knew that he was about to give his life sentences back and maybe even get a new trial. However, if the FBI really wanted to sweat him about the Marion murder that could be another life sentence in the making. Dontae wasn't the one that did the killing. He knew who did, but he would never speak a word of it to the feds. Never would he break the code.

National Airport was busy with people coming in and going out of the Washington, D.C. area. Top and Karrine were coming back from Puerto Rico. They'd just spent a week on vacation. He had shown his baby a good time and now it was time to get back on top of business.

Top and Karrine walked out of the terminal with a small crowd of people. For some reason, Top had a bad feeling in his gut when he looked around at the crowd of people. His instincts told him that something wasn't right. Without warning, he took off running back toward the plane with the speed of an NFL running back. Karrine was shocked. She didn't understand what was going on; all she could do was watch in amazement as Top shoved people out of his way.

Out of the crowd came five FBI agents with their guns drawn. They ran after Top yelling for him to freeze. Paying the agents no attention, Top ran down the long and narrow aisle of the plane. Running into a small, white stewardess that he knocked to the ground, Top tried his best to make it to the back on the plane. He could see that the back of the plane was being lowered to the ground. It was his only hope of escape. He gave it his all as he looked over his shoulder to see how far behind the agents were. They were right on his ass, no more than fifteen feet away.

One yelled at the top of his lungs that he was going to shoot if Top didn't stop running.

Running down the steps of the back of the plane as it lowered, Top jumped about ten feet and hit the ground running across the runway. Airline workers cleared the way, not understanding was going on. He ran under the plane and headed for the first door that he saw. The door led to some kind of boiler room. In the darkness, Top ran down some metal steps and then through another door. As far as he could see or hear, the agents weren't right on his back. He felt that he could shake them and maybe even get out of the airport. Bursting through another door, Top found himself in a long hallway. A few airline workers jumped out of his way. Frantically, Top looked around for another exit. He saw a set of double doors and kicked them open. After a few kicks, the doors flew open and Top dashed out into the parking lot.

All of a sudden the heat was on from all angles. The FBI raided a number of locations all over the D.C. area. Croc's Auto Shop was hit hard and more than twenty arrests were made, including Croc himself. When the agent put the cuffs on Croc, he smirked, and said, "You had a real good run. You can't be mad. You had to know this was coming." Croc had nothing to say as he was placed in the back of a government van to be hauled off for questioning.

On the evening news, Croc was accused of being the leader of the 5th and O Street Crew. All the violence of the summer that had just past was being blamed on him and orders that he gave. RICO charges were being filed.

The next day, Top was laying low in Annapolis, MD over a girl's house by the name of Lee-Lee. By this time, he knew exactly what was going on. He'd seen the news and knew the heat was coming down from every direction.

Lee-Lee walked into the living wearing nothing but her bra and panties. "Your man just called," she said.

"Cool." Top nodded, smoking a Backwood. "Get dressed so we can handle business."

Lee-Lee got dressed, and she and Top left the house. A short while later, they pulled into a Safeway parking lot. Slowly, Lee-Lee drove to the back of the parking lot as Top scanned the area from the passenger seat with a .45 automatic on his lap. Everything looked normal as they parked. Top used Lee-Lee's cell phone to call his man, Boone.

Boone answered the phone. "I'm here."

"Me too."

"Cool, it's a blue Avalon at the other end of the parking lot. Everything you need in the trunk."

"Thanks, homie," Top said.

"You know it. You my nigga. Be safe. See you when the smoke clears."

Top hung up the phone and told Lee-Lee to drive over to the Avalon. She pulled up beside the car and looked at Top. "Be careful and call me if you need me," she said.

"I will." Top gave her a kiss and got out of the car. He jumped in the Avalon and looked around. The keys were in the ignition. There was a gym bag on the floor in the back. Top grabbed the bag and looked inside. There was $50,000 inside and a Glock 19. Top grabbed a $10,000 stack, rolled down the window, and tossed the money to Lee-Lee. The cash fell right in her lap. "Stay on point."

"Okay, thanks. Now, get out of here."

Top started the car and headed for the highway.

Chapter 24

Redds walked into the D.C. Jail visiting hall and saw his father on the other side of the glass. A smile crossed his face as he picked up the phone and took a seat. "How you doin', Pops?" Redds asked.

"I'm good, I'm on the outside. You know how it is," Amir said as he glanced around the visiting hall.

Redds, Dontae, and Heavy had been sent back to D.C. Jail in order to address the new legal issues in their case. They thought things would be in their favor all the way around the board, but the government was playing hardball. The D.A.'s office was only willing to reduce their life sentences to thirty years flat. Redds couldn't believe it. It was clear that the investigation that led to his arrest and the trial that led to his conviction was all corrupted by the action of a dirty federal agent and a host of lies told by government witnesses that were facing life in prison themselves. When Redds looked at the situation for what it was worth, he had to focus on the fact that he had only done eight years in prison. If he took the thirty-year deal the D.A. was offering, he would still have twenty more years in prison. That wasn't the way Redds wanted things to turn out.

"I have been thinking about what we spoke about," Redds said to his father.

Amir raised his eyebrows. "What'd you come up with?"

"I'm not taking the deal they tryin' to throw us," Redds said firmly.

Amir nodded in agreement. He knew that Redds was man enough to make his own decisions. "So, I take it that you have thought this one all the way out. You know that it's a gamble to take those people all the way back to trial. Thirty years isn't what we were hoping for, but it's much better than life in prison. I just want to make sure you get out of prison one way or another. That's all."

"I feel you on that one, Pops. I've thought this one all the way through. I see it like this here, we got them by the balls. If we have to go to trial again, they don't have a leg to stand on. All their rats have messed up the case and the agent on the case is dirty. What can they really do with us in court if we force a new trial?"

Amir gave his son's words a moment of thought. He put himself in his son's shoes. If he were Redds, he wouldn't be willing to lay down for twenty more years. He'd put it in Allah's hand and fight it out to the end. He couldn't expect his son to do anything different. "Well," Amir spoke slowly and selectively. "Everything is in your favor if we only look at the facts. The government has their backs against the wall. Nevertheless, anytime you go up against the government you are gambling with your life. It's no getting around that. It's a critical roll of the dice. If you crap out, you could be back at square one with those life sentences."

"I know. I thought about that."

"I'm sure you have. So, with that being said, it's all about faith at this point. I support you all the way." Amir trusted that all would work out. "We'll just stay firm and fight the fight. Nothing comes easy."

Redds nodded. It felt good to have his father on his side. They went over a few different issues concerning the case and then the subject changed.

"What you think they gon' do with Croc and them?" Redds asked his father.

Amir shook his head and sighed. He felt that Croc was too old to be getting caught up in the system again. However, he knew that Croc was his own man and that he was going to do whatever he wanted to do. He'd always been that way. "All I can say is that he is going to fight them. He's not going to lay down."

"I know that for a fact." Redds raised his eyebrows. "Top still ain't been seen or heard from."

"I know what he's going through out there." Redds shook his head thinking about how things were for him when he first went on the run. "Knowing Top, he gon' run as long as he can."

"That's how it goes. It's crazy how things repeat themselves over and over again in time. It's seems like yesterday you was just going through the same thing they going through right now."

"Tell me about it. I saw Croc in the law library the other day and he was saying the same thing. The game don't change, the people do." Redds rubbed his chin as he thought about his own words.

"That's one thing that will always be true. Never forget that." Amir nodded his head as he spoke.

As things began to move forward for the Kennedy Street defendants, their lawyers pulled out all of the stops trying every legal maneuver that could think of to get the best outcome. Heavy's lawyer was going hard; he knew for sure that the government had no win and was in no position to play hardball. He threatened the D.A.'s office with the idea of them having to re-try or let hundreds of convicted felons go free due to the fact that Burling, as their prosecutor, or Agent Schoenbuerg, had done illegal things concerning their case.

Smith had huge claims already filed in court that made claims of Burling not handing over important evidence that could have vindicated the Kennedy Street defendants from the very beginning of the case. Everything was falling apart for the government and falling right in place for Redds and his comrades. Within weeks, the D.A.'s office began to break—the government offered the defendants ten-year sentences. The government claimed that they were offering such a deal because it was in the best interest of judicial-economy. Everyone with eyes could see that was bullshit, but no one said a word about it. The lawyers and the Kennedy Street defendants knew they had to take the deal before the government tried to put some more bullshit in the game.

Redds was content with the ten-year sentence. That was damn near letting him out of the door, giving him new life and a second chance at freedom. He couldn't ask for more out of the situation. There was no way to get the time back that he'd lost, but it still felt good to be able to go on with his life in the free world. He felt blessed for that alone.

As soon as Redds got the news of the ten-year deal he called Necci and let her know what was good.

"Ahhhhhhh!" she yelled, going crazy as she drove along the beltway in her Benz C 280. "I can't believe it!" She couldn't contain her excitement. It felt like the best day of her life. After all she'd been through with Redds, she felt like she was being released from prison. She banged on the wheel and blew the horn like a crazy woman. She didn't care what other people thought, all she was concerned with was the news that Redds had just told her about. "Oh, my God! Boy, stop playing with me like that. For real?"

On the jail phone, Redds smiled. "It's real, baby. They gon' have to let us go. I don't know how long it's going to take, but it's in motion right now. It's only a matter of time."

"So, you coming straight home?" Necci asked, feeling like she was dreaming.

"Well, not exactly, I will still be in for a while until all the paper work goes through, but I've been in for eight already. All I have to give them on ten is eight for real, so

I'll be home sometime in the next few weeks or months. It's for sure."

"I can't believe it. This is the best news I've heard in years, boo."

"Look, baby. I gotta' get off this phone right now. I love you. Talk to you in a little while."

"Love you, too." Necci said.

Two days later, Redds faked chest pains so he could meet Dontae in the infirmary. It was the only way he could get to see his comrade since the jail had Dontae locked down due to the fact that he was sent to the jail from ADX and was being charged with the Marion murder. As soon as he was done with his legal issues in D.C., he was to be sent back to Illinois. Dontae's situation was rough. The reality was that he was going to have his life sentences reduced to ten years, but he could very well get another life sentence or the death penalty for the jailhouse murder.

Locked in a cage in the infirmary, Dontae was able to talk to Redds, who was on the other side sitting against the wall. The C.O. that was in charge gave Redds a few minutes to speak to Dontae.

"We really gon' come off on this case, huh, man?" Dontae said, standing at the cage door.

Redds nodded. "We got 'em this go 'round, for sure. I told you all we had to do was keep fightin', slim."

"You was right about that, slim. To keep it real wit' you, I wasn't too sure about all this shit. I was carrying it like I was doing life. You know me."

"I feel you. I know how this shit go. It was times when I was like fuck it, but Necci and my little one stayed on my mind," Redds said, looking down the hall at a group of prisoners that were on their way back to the cellblocks.

Dontae shook his head in disappointment as he thought about Redds' words. "It's just my luck that these people gon' let us get some play and I gotta go fight this muthafuckin' body."

"I feel you, but you know what you got to do. You gotta fight them peoples. We done looked death in the eyes together before, so I know you got what it takes." Redds knew Dontae was in a terrible situation and that he had a serious fight ahead of him. Nevertheless, Redds knew from firsthand experience that the only way to address the situation was head-up, so to speak. Dontae had one of the best lawyers money could buy. All they could do at this point was have some faith.

"Ay, Redds, I'm a fighter, slim. I'm gon' do what a real nigga supposed to do. I'm gon' stand tall and fight the case. I didn't do the shit and, on the real, it's no way for them to really put it on me. All they gon' have is some cracker lying and shit, saying they saw me do it. I got witnesses saying I didn't. It's death before dishonor with me, Leez up, feds down, slim."

Redds nodded in agreement. "That's right, slim."

"I'm built to last. Don't worry about me. Right now, let's focus on the most important thing at hand and that's gettin' this case RICO case behind us." Dontae stuck his hand out of the slot of the door to shake Redds' hand.

"I love you, homes," Redds said as he gave his comrade a firm handshake. "I'm always here for you. We're always brothers! It's always death before dishonor."

"Always," Dontae added.

Within the next few days, the news hit the streets and spread all across the prison system. The Kennedy Street Crew was headline news. The Washington Post's headline read, The Kennedy Street Crew will soon be free. Their life sentences have been vacated ...

Walking down the top tier of Southwest-3 of the D.C. Jail as he glanced at the newspaper, Redds headed into Croc's cell. He found the old timer sitting on the bunk in his laid-out cell smoking a Black and Mild. On the old metal desk sat a small radio, which he wasn't supposed to have, that was tuned into WHUR.

"What's up, slim?" Croc said.

"Slow motion. Just waiting for all my paperwork to go through."

"I always knew y'all was gon' get back on that case. It was all a matter of time. Y'all came off on that joint. I know the government fucked up 'bout that." Croc shook his head and smiled.

"They tried to wash us up for real."

Croc sighed. "They did for a second. Y'all just ain't lay down. I respect that, slim. No bullshit. I always knew you was a man, but after seeing what you went through and how you stood tall and stuck to the code, I respect you on a whole 'nother level."

"Real talk." Redds was honored.

"I know I got a long fight ahead of me, but you know I'm gon' fight all the way to the end."

"That's the only way you can approach it. You know that. I don't have to tell you that. At the same time, you know I'm in your corner all the way. Whatever I can do for you when I touch down, all you gotta' do is holla at me."

Croc nodded in admiration. "I respect that. We family, that's how it's supposed to be."

"Always will be," Redds said.

With Top being on the run, Karrine was dying inside. She was missing him as if he was dead or in prison. He had seemed to disappear for real. However, she was sure that he would resurface one day. At least, that was what she hoped for. Top was on her mind everyday and in her prayers every night. With Top on her mind, Karrine took a trip to Atlanta to visit his mother, who was clean and sober at the time. When Karrine got to Atlanta and hooked up with Karmen, she was proud of her. After getting off of drugs, she got herself together and was living a normal life in Atlanta working a job and living her life as best as she could. Karmen and Karrine spent most of the day shopping and talking about Top. They were both worried about him. Their main concern was that he wouldn't get killed by the police while on the run.

"One thing I know about my son is that he can take care of himself. I know that for sure," Karmen said, riding in the passenger seat of Karrine's Benz.

"Yeah, I know that's right. I just miss him so much. I don't know how this is going to end."

"Only time will tell, but trust and believe that he has a plan. I can promise you that."

After spending the day with Top's mother, Karrine decided to go out and hit Club Frequency. The club was packed. The DJ had crowd turned up off the new Young Jeezy. She knew a few people that she'd met when she used to hit the A on business with Top. A few dudes stepped to her and asked about Top. She told them that she hadn't heard from him since he went on the run. Keeping it moving, Karrine made her way to the bar and had a few drinks. A little while later, she'd had enough and headed for the door. Little did she know, she was being followed.

Hours later, Karrine was in a deep sleep the guest room of Karmen's house. It was close to three in the morning. A screech of the floor made Karrine jump from her sleep and pull her Glock from under pillow. In the darkness, she aimed it at the figure that was approaching her.

"Put the gun down, baby," a familiar voice said.

Karrine knew the voice well. She tossed the pistol on the bed and jumped to her feet. "Oh, my God!" she shouted as she ran to Top and jumped in his arms, giving him a big hug.

Top smiled. "Be quiet."

"My bad. I can't believe it's you!"

"It's me, baby. Listen, I can't be here long. Them peoples be watching my mother's house. I only snuck over here because I knew you were here. I had to come get you. I need you by my side."

"I'm here for you, baby. Ain't nothin' changed wit' me. I been waitin' for you to get me."

"I got to tell you this, it ain't no turning back wit' me. If you choose to go wit' me, it's no turning back for you, either. I'm not goin' to jail alive."

"I'm with you, baby. Death before dishonor."

Top kissed Karrine. "Love you, girl!"

Over the D.C. Jail, Redds was sitting in Croc's cell talking to the old timer while they ate Pizza Hut. Redds noticed that Croc had something on his mind that he wasn't talking to Redds about.

"What's on your mind, slim? I mean, other than the case and shit?" Redds asked.

Croc sighed. "That's all that's on my mind for real. These peoples tryin' to wash my ass up and I can't let it go down like that."

Redds raised his eyebrows. "What you mean by that?"

"You know what—" Croc stopped in mid-sentence and shook his head. "The less you know, the better, Lil' Reggie. Just stay in your cell when we come out tomorrow."

Redds didn't ask another question.

The next day, gunshots rang out inside the D.C. Jail. Pop! Pop! Pop! Prisoners scattered in all directions. The C.O.s that were working the block took off running. Minutes later, a sea of C.O.s in riot gear flooded the block, yelling, "Lockdown! Lockdown!"

Laying in the bed in his cell with his heart thumping, Redds wondered what the fuck was going on. Whatever it was, it had nothing to do with him. He was sure of that. Croc had warned him to stay in his cell and that was exactly what he did.

In less than thirty minutes, the news of a shooting inside the D.C. Jail was all over the TV. D.C. police and FBI agent had converged on the jail like it was a war zone. On the other side of the parking lot from the jail was D.C. General Hospital, the hospital where victims from the D.C. Jail were sent in case of emergencies. In the ER were two black males suffering from gunshot wounds. Suffering from a gunshot wound to the shoulder, Croc was handcuffed to the bed as a doctor worked on him. The pain that Croc was in was something he could deal with. He seemed more concerned with the time on the clock on the wall above. It was 10:30 a.m. The day was starting off with a bang.

Just outside of the room Croc was in stood two C.O.s with .38 revolvers. They kept their eyes on everything moving in the hallway. With the exception of a few nurses hurrying back and forth, the hallway was pretty much empty.

"What the hell is goin' on?" one C.O. asked the next

"One of them damn fools done got a gun in somehow. A lot of muthafuckas gon' lose they jobs about this one here. You can bet your last dollar on that one," the other C.O. replied.

While the C.O.s were talking two masked gunmen rushed around the corner with assault weapons. Before the C.O.s even knew what was going on, the gunmen were right up on them. Point-blank range.

With his gun to the face of one of the C.O.s, the gunman that looked to be in control said, "Don't lose your life about this shit here." The gunmen took the pistols and radios the C.O. s had, and forced them into the room with Croc.

"Uncuff him!" The gunman pointed his weapon at the other C.O.

The doctor and the nurse stepped back, scared speechless.

"Get on the ground!" barked the other gunman, waving his weapon at the doctor. As quickly as they could, the doctor and the nurse jumped on the floor.

As soon as Croc was out of his handcuffs, he grabbed one of the .38s. "Let's get movin'," he said as he looked out the door and into the hallway. Everything was cool. Croc and the two gunmen took off down the hallway.

Moments later, they came out the side door and jumped into a waiting Nissan Pathfinder. Calmly, they pulled off. As they exited the parking lot of the hospital, they could see a sea of police cars all around the jail. The driver turned down 19th Street and headed for I-295 South. Croc kept his eyes in the side mirror until they made it to the highway.

As the Pathfinder mixed in with traffic, the driver took off her mask. Croc looked to his left and was surprised that she was a female, a beautiful one at that. "Damn," he said. "For real?"

Karrine smiled.

Top leaned up from the back seat, snatching off his mask, and looked at Croc's wound. "I got a broad at the spot that can take care of that as soon as we get where we going."

Croc looked at the bullet wound and nodded. "Yeah, it looks worse than it is. I wasn't trying to kill my-self," he joked.

Croc had been mapping out an escape plan for months. He knew that if he could get to the hospital while the D.C. Jail was in total confusion, he could get Top to come get him. His plan worked perfectly.

Looking in the rearview mirror, Karrine said, "Looks like we're clear."

Croc and Top looked back and saw no cops on the highway behind them.

"They gon' have to catch me when they can," Croc said as they continued south.

Aftermath

Three Years Later

The huge Carrera cruise liner gracefully sailed through the beautiful waters of the Caribbean Sea as the sun lit up the clear, blue sky for miles and miles. Redds sat on the deck in a pool chair looking out across the water. He was in deep thought about his life—his past, present, and future. Freedom was something that still felt unreal. Even though he was a free man and he knew it, it still felt unreal at times. He had to take a little time out every day to really take it all in. Nights spent in prison cells, and years away from his family were memories that he couldn't push out of his mind. Wanting to get away from D.C., Redds took Necci on a cruise to Venezuela. He planned to use the time to relax. It was a blessing to be free, but things still weren't perfect. A lot of lives had been changed forever over the years. He'd learned to deal with that reality.

By this time Redds was getting legit money in the free world, he had his own barbershop on Georgia Avenue. He was cutting hair and had a few other barbers renting booths while Necci and two other girls did hair in the back. Things were working out well. It was nothing like things were when he was flipping bricks, but it beat being in a federal prison any day of the week. Unlike a lot of dudes that did time, Redds made sure that he looked out for his comrades that he left behind in prison by doing whatever he could do to support them and hold them down. He'd gotten a few of his men good lawyers to help them with their cases. He got Shell a lawyer that got his sentence down to twenty years. That was, indeed, a blessing.

Redds' codefendants were doing pretty good as well. Heavy was co-owner of a nightclub with his man, Cuz C, from Southwest. He also reconnected with his son. That was a good thing, but it was also a challenge. His son had become one of the biggest drug dealers in the Montana Terrace projects. Heavy could see life repeating itself and he was doing all he could to warn his son of what was going to come of the game. His son wouldn't listen though, the youngster felt like he knew what he was doing. Only time would tell how it would turn out.

As for Dontae, he became Muslim when he went back to Marion to fight the murder case. He beat the case and that opened his eyes up to a higher power. It had to be a Creator looking out for him, as far as he was concerned. He'd ducked life sentences and death penalties back to back. When Dontae came home, he and Amir got very close, being as though they both practiced Islam. That helped Dontae out a lot. It kept him out of the streets and away from the game.

The other Kennedy Street defendants came home also. For the time being, they were able to stay under the radar. Most of them were back in the drug game getting plenty of money. Connects they'd met while in the feds turned out to be the best thing that ever happened to them, as far as drug connects were concerned.

The 5th and O Street Four, as they were called, had been on America's Most Wanted several times. Croc, Top, Juan, and Rob had the FBI looking for them around the globe. It was said that Juan and Rob were in the slums of Kingston, Jamaica, but no one knew for sure. They cut off all contact with everyone they knew. According to the FBI, Croc and Jayde had been seen in Amsterdam. As for Top and Karrine, they both disappeared after getting Croc out of the hospital. Top's mother had received a Mother's Day card a year after they disappeared, inside was a check for

$500,000. Only time would tell if they would ever be heard from again.

"Redds?" a voice called out.

Redds looked up and saw Necci. He smiled. She looked beautiful in her Gucci bathing suit. "Hey, baby."

With her hands on her hips, Necci said, "What you out here doing, day dreaming?"

Redds laughed a little. "Not really day dreaming, more like reflecting. Thinking about all I've been through."

Necci leaned in and kissed him on the forehead.

"You stood tall through it all and now you can put it all behind you. The future belongs to us."

Redds nodded. "You couldn't have said it any better. The future belongs to us."

Never Lay Down

DC Bookdiva Publications
#245 4401-A Connecticut Avenue, NW
Washington DC 20008
dcbookdiva.com

Order Form

Name_____

Inmate ID_____

Address:_____

City/State_____

Quantity	Titles	Price	Total
	The Secrets Never Die, Eyone Williams	15.00	
	Lorton Legends, Eyone Williams	15.00	
	Money Ain't Everything, Eyone Williams	15.00	
	Hellrazor Honeys, Eyone Williams	15.00	
	Hellrazor Honeys 2, Eyone Williams	15.00	
	Que, Dutch	15.00	
	A Beautiful Satan, RJ Champ	15.00	
	The Hustle, Frazier Boy	15.00	
	Tina, Darrell Debrew	15.00	

Sub-Total $_____

Shipping/Handling (Via US Media Mail) $3.95 1-2 Books, $7.95 1-3 Books, 4 or more titles-Free Shipping

Shipping $ _____
Total Enclosed $ _____

Certified or government issued checks and money orders, all mail in orders take 5-7 Business days to be delivered. Books can also be purchased on our website at eyonewilliams.com. Incarcerated readers receive 25% discount. Please pay $11.25 per book and apply the same shipping terms as stated above